WICKED
SCORN
HAVOC WILDE

Contact: authorhavocwilde@gmail.com

www.havocwilde.com

Cover Designer: Shay @ Disturbed Valkyrie Designs

Photographer: xramragde

Editor: Amanda Leach

Proofreading: Kristen Seeson

For all the girls that had the biggest crush on their brothers best friend in high school and wanted nothing more than for him to teach you and please you

Jeremiah "Pretty Boy" Blackwood

PLAYLIST

- Young And Beautiful -Lana Del Rey
- Graveyard - Halsey
- 11 Minutes - YUNGBLUD ft. Halsey & Travis Barker
- Moments Passed - Dermot Kennedy
- Comedown - Bush
- The Offering - Sleep Token
- Another Life - Motionless in White
- Dangerous Woman - Ariana Grande
- Dusk Till Dawn - ZAYN ft. Sia
- Obsessive - Chase Atlantic
- All I Wanted - Paramore
- Flawless - The Neighborhood
- idfc - blackberry
- Take Me to Church - Hozier
- love me - Ex Habit
- Love Lies - Khalid with Normani
- War Of Hearts - Ruelle
- Nightmares - Ellise

PLAYLIST

- Friends - Chase Atlantic
- on your knees - Ex Habit

PLAYLIST

- Young And Beautiful -Lana Del Rey
- Graveyard - Halsey
- 11 Minutes - YUNGBLUD ft. Halsey & Travis Barker
- Moments Passed - Dermot Kennedy
- Comedown - Bush
- The Offering - Sleep Token
- Another Life - Motionless in White
- Dangerous Woman - Ariana Grande
- Dusk Till Dawn - ZAYN ft. Sia
- Obsessive - Chase Atlantic
- All I Wanted - Paramore
- Flawless - The Neighborhood
- idfc - blackberry
- Take Me to Church - Hozier
- love me - Ex Habit
- Love Lies - Khalid with Normani
- War Of Hearts - Ruelle
- Nightmares - Ellise

- Friends - Chase Atlantic
- on your knees - Ex Habit

AUTHOR'S NOTE

This is a dark romance and will have many common tropes that you would expect to see in dark romance. If you have any possible things that could affect your reading experience please check out the list of content included in the back of this book or on my website.

This is a sports romance but I did take liberties with this story.

Don't hold it too much against me!

Thank you for reading!

x Havoc

PROLOGUE

JEREMIAH

I'm sprawled on the couch, my fingers swiping through the screen's endless scroll with the kind of numb dedication you reserve for three a.m. The phone casts a glow that no doubt shows the creases under my eyes—tired, yeah, that's me.

I need this year to be over. I need to start my freshman year at St. Charles and get my brothers and me the fuck out of here. I know Dad has a house on campus for us, he's held it over our heads for so damn long. The caveat is that we all have to be in school and since Graham and I are a year behind grade wise because of some dumb shit called birthday cut-off from kindergarten, that means Linc and Penn have been unable to move out even though they are well into their freshman year.

Robert Blackwood was hell-bent on creating his own little army of sons and made sure we arrived months apart. The thought process behind that still baffles me. Each of us with different mothers, absent, whether by force or choice. My own mother is a free love, go where the music takes her type of person and had no fucking problem leaving me with the Devil of Whispering Ridge.

Bzzzt. I squint at the name lighting up my phone. Bunny. What's she doing up?

BUNNY

Can't sleep

Her message reads. Concern licks at my insides, chases away the exhaustion clinging to my bones. The truth is, she's the reason I can't fall asleep. If I'm being honest, she's the reason for everything.

"Shit," I mutter, thumbing back a reply.

I'm coming to get you. Motorcycle ride might clear your head. Be ready

The air is brisk when I get outside and kick the bike to life; its growl eats up the silence and sends a shiver down my spine. I race through the streets under the night sky, the hum of my bike's engine vibrating through me.

Oakley's place comes into view, all picket fence perfection and quietness. She's just there, wisps of blonde hair and pale skin, bathed in the moonlight. My heart does this stupid little stutter-step when I see her, standing alone, vulnerable out here. I want to protect her. Fuck. I want to possess her.

You can't have her. She'll never belong to you.

"Hey," I call out, pulling up beside her. She jumps, startled, but relief blooms across her face when she sees it's me.

"Rem." Her voice skims over the nickname she gave me, sending ripples down my neck. No one else calls me that, just my bunny.

"How many times am I going to have to tell you to dress warmer?" I tease, killing the engine and swinging off my bike.

I don't mind the view, but something inside me is feral at the thought another man might see her like this.

She shrugs, the action small and defeated. "My mind was somewhere else, I guess."

I peel off my hoodie without a second thought, tugging it over her head and watching as it swallows her up. It's an excuse to touch her, and we both know it. My fingers graze her skin, and something forbidden passes between us—we've been like this for the last year, since her sweet sixteen birthday. Oakley's only a year and a couple of months younger than me but it always felt like the age difference between us was vast. She's my best friend's little sister, but everything about her is woven into my very being. She's supposed to be mine, but it'll ruin everything for everyone if I cross that line.

"Thank you," she whispers, slipping her arms into the sleeves. The fabric hangs loose on her frame, no doubt my scent is enveloping her.

"Helmet on, let's go." I help guide it over her head, our faces inches apart. I can smell her shampoo, strawberries, and it twists my insides in knots.

"Where are we going?" she asks, her breath ghosting against my cheek as I fasten the strap under her chin.

"Anywhere but here," I say, climbing back onto the bike and then holding my hand out and helping Oakley get on the back. Her hands settle around my waist, her touch is tentative at first but grows bolder as if she's grounding herself to something solid in the midst of her restless thoughts tonight.

"Ready?" I ask, looking back at her.

"Always," she breathes out the word, and it's all the cue I need.

We take off into the night and it swallows us whole, the city pulsing under us as we cut through the streets. Oakley's arms tighten, her grip fierce, unyielding—like she could anchor me to her in this moment forever. I lean into the bike, and she follows, seamless, a part of me. She's been riding with me for so long, I don't worry about having to coach her on what to do.

"Too fast?" I shout over the engine.

Her laughter is light, almost like a fucking fairy. "Never with you!"

The cool air nips at my skin, but her warmth bleeds through my shirt, stirring something reckless in my blood.

"Tell me something good," I yell back to her, craving the sound of her voice.

"When I'm with you, nothing else matters," she calls out, and the simplicity of it kicks me in the ass.

"You're going soft on me, bunny."

"No, I'm just me but pretty boy, your pocket's having a seizure or something," Oakley teases, her breath hot on my neck.

"Damn technology," I mutter, the spell breaking, reality creeping in with its sharp claws and jagged teeth.

"Trouble?" There's an edge to her voice, concern lacing it. My sweet little bunny who cares about far too much. This world will eat her up and spit her out.

"Probably nothing," I lie. Who the hell bombards someone with messages at this hour? My gut twists, intuition screaming that something is wrong.

"Let's head back." I hate the words as they leave my mouth, but curiosity is a hungry beast.

"Back? But we just..." Disappointment colors her tone, yet she clings tighter.

"Trust me." Two words, heavy with meaning.

I downshift, the motorcycle growling beneath us, almost

like a living thing that echoes my frustration. As we turn around, the tension coils between us, thick and suffocating.

We roll up to her house, the bike's hum dying into silence. I can't shake the feeling that we're stepping right into the middle of a shit storm. I dismount, pulling off my helmet, and run a hand over my head—anxious, already gearing up for whatever comes next.

The world shrinks to the beat of my heart, a dull thud against my ribcage as Oakley's brother and my best friend, Royce, materializes from the shadows of the house. His stance, rigid and unyielding, cuts through the night.

"Jeremiah fucking Blackwood," he spits out my name like its poison on his tongue, "I should've known you'd stab me in the back—you and Penny?"

"Royce, man—" My words choke in my throat, disbelief has to be painting my features. "What the fuck are you talking about?"

He moves closer, eyes narrowed to dangerous slits. His scorn is almost palpable, mingling with the tang of impending rain.

"Stop." Oakley's voice slices through the tension, small but mighty. Her hand lands on my arm, something to anchor me while my best fucking friend stands there accusing me of fucking with his girl. "He hasn't done anything."

"Like hell he hasn't!" Royce roars, muscles coiled, ready to strike.

"Royce," I say, steadying my voice, "I swear on my brothers, there's nothing between me and Penny." If he only knew that his little sister has had me wrapped around her pretty little finger for some time now.

"Your word ain't worth shit right now." His accusation hangs heavy in the air, a razor blade slicing into me. I may be a fucking Blackwood, but to me, my word fucking means something.

"Your trust issues are your own damn problem, not mine," I shoot back, anger lacing my words. My hands ball into fists at my sides, itching for an outlet.

Oakley steps closer, her crystal blue eyes fierce with conviction. "Ro, listen to me. Jeremiah's been with me, okay? Just me—no one else."

"Always jumping to defend him, huh?" He sneers, a wild glint in his eye that says this is far from over.

Royce doesn't bother to mask the disdain in his voice, throwing accusations like punches I couldn't dodge. And somehow, Oakley is caught in the crossfire between us, her delicate frame trembling with a mixture of fear and defiance as she stands her ground. "You think this is some kind of game?" he advances, the night seeming to curl around him.

"No," Oakley's voice quivers but doesn't break. "But I won't let you bully me into believing lies about Jeremiah."

The air grows thick with unsaid words, laden with distrust and betrayal, a storm ready to burst. Royce's nostrils flare, his voice is a low growl now, "You're his alibi? How convenient. How many times has he pulled the wool over your eyes, little sister? You're a joke to him."

"Don't talk to her like that," I warn him. My blood boils; it's one thing to come at me—I can take it. But Oakley? That's crossing a line.

Royce's laughter dies in his throat, transforming into a low growl. "You've got some nerve, Blackwood."

He turns on me then, his every sinew alive with fury and something else—something wounded lurking beneath the surface of his rage. We stare each other down. "Stay away from my sister."

"Like hell I will," I retort without missing a beat, fueled by anger and adrenaline. The fragile thread holding back my own aggression snaps. "She's just as much as part of my family as you are, you're just being a fucking dick right now."

He steps forward until we're practically breathing the same hostile air. "Everything's connected when you screw with my life." His fist clenches at his side like he's fighting every instinct to throw a punch.

I take a step forward, opening my mouth to speak, when suddenly that same fist flies toward me with the force of every accusation he's hurled. The punch lands square on my jaw, a sharp jolt that radiates through my skull.

"Royce!" Oakley cries out, but her voice is distant, drowned out by the ringing in my ears.

I taste copper on my tongue as I stagger back. Pain and anger mix together like venom in my veins. For a second—just one—I consider letting loose the fury building inside me.

In that heartbeat before chaos erupts, Oakley slips between us—her softness a stark contrast to our hard edges. "Stop it!" Tears streak down her cheeks as she pushes against Royce's chest. "This isn't you!"

Royce's gaze flickers from Oakley to me—the fire in his eyes giving way to confusion before he blinks it away.

He grabs Oakley by the arm, none too gently. "Get in the house," he orders gruffly.

"No," she defies him again, her spirit unyielding even while her voice cracks.

"Now!" Royce yells, dragging her behind him.

I lunge forward instinctively but stop dead as Royce pins me with a glare that could cut steel. "Leave it be, Blackwood." His words are a final warning—a line drawn deep in the sand between us.

"Look, Ashford," I try again, desperation creeping into my tone. "Whatever you think happened, didn't. We can figure out what the fuck is going on together, though."

"Together?" His laugh is sharp and cold. "You think some pretty words will fix this?"

"I think you're seeing red and not fucking thinking clearly," I counter, every muscle tensed, ready for whatever comes next.

Oakley wriggles free from his grasp and whirls on me; her blue eyes pools of turmoil as she mouths 'sorry.'

"Rem?" Oakley's voice trembles slightly, pulling me back from the edge of rage. Her tears are silent as they carve tracks down her cheeks.

"I'm okay, bunny," I assure her, but my voice is thick with my own anger and hurt. She doesn't need to see how close I am to unraveling. How one fucking moment in time has just ended a friendship that was supposed to be thicker than blood.

I watch as my best fucking friend and the only girl a Blackwood gives a fuck about turn and walk up their wraparound porch and the blue front door closes behind them. A picturesque setting of the quintessential American home.

Heading back to my bike, I pull my phone out to check what the fuck is going on and why it's been ringing nonstop. Countless missed calls and unread messages show up in my notifications.

Exhaling harshly, I pick one to open. It's Lincoln—my brother who has never met a party he didn't love or a rule he didn't break—with dozens of frantic texts asking where I am and why I'm not answering him.

LINC

Jere, shit has gone sideways. It's Penn and Dad. Come home now.

The words send a shiver straight to my core, different from the sting still radiating off my jaw. I take one more look at the Ashford house and vow to myself to fucking tackle that issue tomorrow.

My brothers can't wait.

There is nothing more important in my world than a Blackwood brother and duty calls, even when all I want to do is check up on Oakley.

CHAPTER 1
JEREMIAH

The bass vibrates through the floor like a goddamn earthquake, and the air's so thick with sweat and sweet-smelling smoke that you could slice it with a knife, and it would barely move. The underground scene is a breeding ground for all things raw and untamed—and here we are, the kings of campus, wading through a sea of writhing bodies. It's fucking exhausting sometimes having to do this, be this, but I can't deny this is one of the best outlets outside of football for me.

"Jeremiah." Lincoln's voice cuts through the music, his tattooed arm nudging me in the ribs. His eyes are locked on someone dancing in the center of it all.

I follow his gaze, and there she is—Oakley. Fucking Oakley Ashford. My heart goes rogue, thumping against my chest like it wants to break free. She's a vision in pastel, her golden hair a halo in the strobe lights, body swaying with a grace that belongs in a dream, not this hedonistic nightmare. My brain goes dumb for just a split second as I see *the girl*, the one good thing I had in my life show up in front of me.

"Jere?" Penn's voice is barely audible over the chaos, but I'm already gone, pushing past him and Graham, who's trying to say something about not doing anything fucking dumb. It goes in one ear and out the other. I already know I'm going to do some dumb ass shit, even though I'm supposed to be the most put together. Not when it comes to her.

"Shit," I mutter, brushing off his concern. My strides are deliberate, each step narrowing the gap between me and the girl who has been haunting my dreams for two damn years since Royce ripped us apart, and I let him.

"Oakley..." Her name's a whisper on my lips, drowned out by the chaos of this party, but she doesn't hear me, lost in her own little world amidst the madness. I need her attention, need those crystal blue eyes on me.

"Oakley!" Louder this time. And just like that, I'm close enough to reach out, to pull her away from all this noise and into the quiet battle building within myself. Because I can't fucking stand it anymore—the distance, the silence. It's been too long, and right now, I'm nothing but raw need wrapped in human skin. I need her to be part of my life, and this is my second shot at it.

"Jeremiah?" She turns, and there's a flicker of recognition, a spark that ignites something dangerous within me. Her gaze locks onto mine, and it's like we're the only two people in this godforsaken place.

"Hey, bunny." My voice conveys every emotion I've been harboring, rough around the edges but sincere as hell. "It's been a while."

Her eyes widen, those deep royal pools drowning in a storm of emotions. She stumbles a step closer, the scent of her perfume wrapping around me—something light and slightly floral. Something that reminds me of her virtue in this fucked up world.

"Oakley, what the hell are you doing here?" my voice cuts through the noise. She's the only person that could cause the kind of volcanic explosion that is threatening to spill out of me.

"Jeremiah Blackwood," she slurs, her eyes wide with a drunken innocence that doesn't fool anyone. "Fancy seeing you here."

She lets out a scream, loud enough to slice through the bass. And then the words I never wanted to hear spill from her pouty little mouth. "Ugh, I fucking hate you!"

It's a slap to the face, a punch to the gut. The crowd's noise fades into a dull roar, her voice the only clear sound in my head.

"Hey man, what the fuck? Get your own bitch!" A frat boy, all smug grin and cheap cologne, steps up, his glare stabbing at me.

"Back off," I growl, low and menacing. He's just another obstacle between me and Oakley, and I don't have time for this shit.

"Make me." That's his mistake.

The frat boy's eyes widen as I step in, my voice a dangerous purr. "Shut the fuck up and get out of my face unless you want to end up buried in a canyon." My words are laced with venom, a clear threat that chills the air between us.

He hesitates, his bravado crumbling under the weight of my gaze. I see it in the way his shoulders tense, the way his gaze darts around, looking for an escape. And like the coward he is, he backs away, slinking back into the circle jerk of frat bros that are standing behind him. Like little cookie cutters of each other with their Greek letters displayed proudly across their chests. I make eye contact with each of them, daring someone to step to me. The need for a little bloodshed is thrumming underneath my skin, but they all avert their own gazes, one by one.

I turn my attention back to Oakley, her eyes glazed with something more than alcohol—a vulnerability that fucking rips at my insides. She giggles, a sound that's both sweet and sad, directed at the retreating figure of the frat boy. "I wasn't even going to fuck you," she says, and there's a defiance there, a spark of the girl I knew before everything went to hell. The girl that was all sunshine unless you made her mad and then you got a little demon.

Her words hang heavy, tinted with amusement that doesn't quite reach her eyes. I'm caught in the moment, watching her lips curve into a mischievous smile, the sound of her laughter mixing with the thumping sounds around us. It's intoxicating, and for a second, I forget the chaos, the heat of bodies pressing close, and the sticky floor. I forget the fuck boy still glaring at me from his circle of 'protection'.

"Christ, Oakley," I mutter under my breath, the need to protect her gnawing at me. Her innocence is a red fucking flag, and I'm drawn to it, the darkness in me craving the light she exudes, even now.

"Jeremiah," she slurs again, reaching out to me with a fidgety hand, her movements clumsy yet somehow still graceful. "You're here."

"Always," I reply, the irony not lost on me. Always, except when it mattered most. She went from I hate you to you're here and I know if she was sober, I wouldn't be getting the back and forth. I catch her hand, steadying her, feeling the softness of her skin against mine, the contrast sending a jolt through me that I have never felt with another person.

"Let's get you out of this mess, bunny," I say, but the pet name feels like a betrayal on my tongue right now. My guilt gnawing at me and warring with my need to get Oakley out of here and to myself. I have questions.

She leans into me, her body warm and pliant, her head tilting back to look at me, her expression a complicated tangle of emotions I can't begin to decipher. "Why do you care, Jeremiah?" she asks, her voice a whisper that cuts through the noise.

"Because I never stopped," I confess, the words slipping out before I can stop them. Because it's the truth, no matter how fucked up this whole situation is.

"Fuck off, pretty boy," she snaps, using the old nickname, and my patience has fucking run out as well. Before she can protest further, I bend down and hoist her up and toss her over my shoulder. Her legs kick, her hands smack against my back, but it's no use. I place one hand at the bottom of her ass where it meets her leg to keep her fucking flirty dress down. She won't be fucking flashing anyone at this goddamn party.

"Put me down, you neanderthal!" Oakley screeches, but I just tighten my grip, my jaw set in determination.

And as I guide her through the throng of bodies with her weight leaning on my shoulder, I know I'm fucked. Now that I have eyes on her again, hell, now that I have hands on her again and I can feel her fucking heartbeat through her damn thighs...I'm not letting her out of my sight again. But right now, none of that matters. All that matters is getting Oakley safe, away from prying eyes and hands that aren't mine.

Tomorrow I'll decide who's getting their ass beat for thinking they could look at her tonight.

"Fuck," I curse softly as I navigate the maze of intoxicated college kids. This isn't love or lust—it's obsession, a feeling I haven't been able to shake in the last three years. And as much as I hate myself for it, I relish the feel of her against me.

I look down at her legs and I know there's nothing pure about what I'm feeling. It's desire, raw and unyielding, and it scares the shit out of me because Oakley is the only one I've ever felt this way with.

"Jesus, Jere, you sure know how to pick 'em," my brother says, unable to hide his amusement.

"Shut up, Lincoln," I grunt without turning back. "And help me get her out of here before she pukes on my shoes."

"Fuck you too, Lincoln Blackwood," she hisses, her words muffled by my hoodie.

"Not my type, sweetheart," he shoots back, as I realize he won't be any fucking help and walk past him. Thank fuck we drove the Escalade tonight because I have zero patience on waiting on a fucking ride share and she's sure as shit not sober enough to ride on the back of my bike.

I set her down, leaning against the black exterior of the truck as I dig into my jeans trying to find my goddamn keys while she mumbles about how much of an asshole I am. Yeah, tell me something I don't already know, bunny.

"Too fucking bad. You're fucking coming home with me," I growl, the words fierce and unyielding. "You're sloppy fucking drunk and can't be trusted on your own clearly."

Her eyes, usually so vibrant but are dulled by whatever liquor she drank, narrow as she tries to focus on me. She looks like a pixie caught in a hurricane, just wild hair and stumbling grace. "I only had a couple of sips. Why the fuck do you care now?" Her voice is liquid, spilling over with hurt and accusation before it's cut off, her body going limp mid-taunt.

"Shit," I mutter under my breath, realization hitting me like a freight train. She's been drugged. The signs are all there

—the unsteady movements, the sudden pass-out. Rage bubbles up within me, but I tamp it down. Focus. Get her out of here first.

And tomorrow *everyone* is getting their ass beat.

I lift her with ease, her weight barely registering against my chest. Her scent—uniquely Oakley—fills my nostrils, stirring memories and emotions I've tried to bury. But right now, it's not about that. She's light as a goddamn feather, too light, her head lolling against my chest, golden hair cascading over my arm like spilled sunlight as I put her into the front seat of the truck, buckling her in tightly.

"Hang on, bunny," I whisper, more to myself than her.

Jeremiah Blackwood playing the hero? Something a Blackwood would never be called. The question hangs in the air mockingly, turning my blood to tar. I don't answer it. Can't. Because right now, I'm anything but a hero. I'm an addict, and Oakley's my fix. And as much as I tell myself I'm doing this for her, part of me knows that's a lie. I'm doing this for me—for the hit of feeling her skin against mine, for the power rush of having her life in my hands.

"God, what the fuck is wrong with me?" I mutter to the sleeping form before me and then shut the truck door. My steps are quick as I round the front and climb in behind the steering wheel.

"You're mine," I murmur. "You can hate me all you want, bunny. I'll love you enough for the both of us," I tell her softly.

Her breathing is steady, her body turning toward me, seeking me out as if she belongs there. And maybe she does. For now, that's enough. But later? Later, I'll find the motherfucker who did this. And they'll wish they were never born.

Because whether she hates me or not, Oakley Ashford is mine to save.

Mine to protect.

Just fucking mine.

I shoulder the front door open and step inside, the familiar scent of polished wood and leather filling my senses. The house is quiet, everyone else still gone. Good. No interruptions. I take the stairs two at a time, my grip on Oakley firm but gentle. Her soft breaths tickle my neck, and it's both a comfort and a torment.

Reaching my room, I nudge the door open with my foot and step inside. The room is dimly lit, shadows dancing on the walls. I lay Oakley gently on the bed, her delicate frame sinking into the mattress. Her dress is askew, and I notice for the first time just how vulnerable she looks.

"Goddammit, bunny," I mutter, frustration and something else—something darker is twisting in my gut. I kneel beside the bed, carefully slipping off her dainty heels. They fall to the floor with a soft thud. My hands move to the zipper of her dress, and I pause, my breath catching.

"Fuck," I curse softly as I glide her zipper down, watching it yield under my fingers with a sound that is far too loud in the stark quietness of the room.

I hate the way my hands shake as I watch the fabric split, revealing too much and yet not enough. I don't fucking act like this...not with anyone. But this girl, who was once someone I viewed as a little sister, is now grown up and so much has happened between us.

"Sleep now, okay?" I brush a strand of hair from her face, my touch gentler than I knew it could be. I'm the monster that my family name has made me to be, but for Oakley, I'd walk through fire just to see her safe. All I get from her is a sigh of mhm.

"Tomorrow, we deal with this shit between us," I tell her sleeping form, but I might as well be speaking to the ghosts that linger in the corners of my room, watching, waiting. Tomorrow, the war with Oakley begins because I have no doubt that the last two years have changed her, and I'll have at least some sort of battle ahead of me when it comes to her. But tonight, I'll stand guard over this girl who's carved herself into the darkest parts of my soul.

I slide the dress off her shoulders, letting it pool around her waist before lifting her slightly to remove it completely. She's left in nothing but her cheeky little underwear, and I reach back and pull my hoodie and shirt off in one pull. This is the first time I've seen her partially nude, and it's taking everything in me not to touch her, kiss her, claim her in ways she could never imagine. She's out of it, and I want her fully aware the first time I feel her delicate skin. The air is a cool slap against my skin as I pull the shirt out of the crumpled hoodie, tossing it on the floor before slipping the sweatshirt over Oakley's still form, letting the cotton swallow her small frame. It serves a dual purpose, erasing her curves from my eyesight and putting my mark on her anyway I can.

My hands are steady as they tuck the covers around her, every move like a pledge to myself to keep her safe. Safe from the world. Definitely safe from me.

"Christ, bunny." The nickname slips out, a reminder of innocence that feels like a knife twist.

I step back, feeling the pull of her even now. My body throbs with need, demanding release.

Fuck, what am I doing? She's Royce's sister, and he'd kill me if he knew what I was thinking right now, I'd like to see him try and fucking blackmail me now. But the sight of her lying there, so innocent and yet so goddamn intoxicating, makes it impossible to focus on anything else. Where the fuck was he tonight, anyway? How did she end up at a random frat party unattended to the point someone spiked her drink? I gave him the courtesy of backing off when our friendship went up in flames, but if he's not going to do his job and protect her, I will.

Pacing the room, my mind races with images of Oakley. Her body pressed against mine, her soft lips against my skin, her back arching as I wring pleasure from her. The thought of those delicate hands wrapped around me, not even able to fully close, is too much to bear.

I can't deny myself any longer. Retreating to the privacy of my bathroom, I stand in front of the mirror, the harsh fluorescent light casting shadows across my face. My eyes look blown out and I'm struggling between anger at Oakley for going to that stupid party, anger at whoever slipped her the GHB, and the intense fucking need to claim ownership of her.

"Fuck it," I growl under my breath, unbuttoning my jeans and sliding them down my legs, taking my underwear with them until they catch at my knees. I can't be bothered to take them all the way off. I'm too desperate to fucking come.

Gripping myself tightly, I let the images my mind conjures up consume me, her soft moans filling the air as I bring her to the edge again and again. The thought of her surrendering to me, giving herself over to me, pushes me closer to the brink.

Fuck, I'm so goddamn hard as I stroke myself over and over. If I go any harder, I'm liable to cut off the blood flow or chafe my shaft. Chasing the images of making her come and watching my cum drip out of her spurns me on. I don't fuck raw, but the thought of it being her, of finally indulging myself in the one kink I've never felt comfortable doing with anyone else has my cock leaking. I lean back against the cool wall, my legs barely able to hold me up as my pleasure heightens. I always knew she made me fucking weak. The proof is here, smacking me in the face. But fuck if being weak for her isn't one of the greatest things in this life.

My breathing becomes ragged, my heart pounding in my chest as I imagine burying myself deep inside her, claiming her as my own. I feel a guttural groan working its way up and out just as I reach my climax, releasing spurts of cum across my hand and watching as they drop to the bathroom floor.

Closing my eyes and leaving my head back, I can almost picture her on her knees before me, licking the sticky evidence of how much I want her from the tip of my dick.

"Fuck." It's a curse and a prayer, and I don't know which one is more blasphemous. Pushing back off the wall, I brace myself against the sink, gripping the granite wondering how the fuck I got to this point, looking into the mirror but not recognizing the man staring back. He's got my face, my green eyes, but there's a wildness that wasn't there before Oakley walked back into my life.

"Get it together, Jere," the whisper is harsh, a command I'm not sure I can obey. But I have to.

Tomorrow, I'll deal with this shit.

But tonight, I'm just Jeremiah. And she's just Oakley. And for a few hours more, that's enough.

Tucking myself back into my jeans, I wash my hands and splash water on my face, trying to center myself before walking back into my room.

"God damn," I mutter, raking a hand through my hair as I take a seat beside her, kicking my boots off. My pulse still races, and I can feel it against my ribs. I've been in fights, stared down linebackers twice my size, but nothing gets my blood pumping like the challenge I see in her even when she's unconscious.

I lean back, propping an arm behind my head, and just fucking watch her for a moment. Her chest rises and falls with soft, even breaths.

"Never been simple with us, has it, bunny?" I whisper, allowing the nickname to slip out. A reminder of a past that's both a balm and a blade to my heart. My fingers itch to trace the curve of her cheek, to tangle in the golden waves of her hair, but I hold back. Can't touch her—not now.

I'm acutely aware of the weight of my decision to bring her here. She's here, in my space, breathing the same air, and that's got to count for something—even if it's just the prelude to the shit storm that's coming this way.

"Tomorrow's going to be a bitch," I say to the silence, my voice a raspy confession in the night. There are questions that need answers, and despite everything, a small part of me can't help but feel...content.

CHAPTER 2
JEREMIAH

I've tossed and turned for the last two hours, desperate for sleep to claim me, but my mind won't turn off. I'm not going to sugarcoat it; I can't stay here right now and do nothing. I planned on handling it tomorrow, but fuck that. Because when you fuck with what's mine, patience leaves the fucking building. My money is on the fucking frat boy, considering he was circling and sniffing around my girl like a dog.

I scroll the frat social pages on the campus website until I come across the same letters that were sprawled across that dude's chest. Zooming in on the dumb little fucking portraits they take, I find him.

Brock Matthewson. Senior and a 'business major'. No need to tell me that daddy Matthewson coddles you and probably is worse than you in his behavior.

Switching apps, I jab at the screen, my thumb hammering down hard enough I keep fucking missing the right letters. The phone lights up with my tech wizard little cousin Ramsey's contact, and I curse loudly.

The phone rings, once, twice, mocking me, "Come on, come on..."

"Jeremiah?" His tone is groggy. Probably just woke him up. Why the fuck is he asleep so early on a weekend, anyway?

"Rams, listen up," I cut in, no time for pleasantries. "I need you at the house. Now. And I need you to track where Brock Matthewson is. He was at the party tonight, but if he left, I want to know."

"What's going on?" He's alert now, his tone sharpening. Having a hacker in the family comes in handy sometimes.

"Just get your ass over here and get me his location," I snap. "It's urgent. Oakley's involved, and I need you to do this for me." I hang up before he can ask any more questions. No point wasting time explaining the mess right now. He can get the cliff notes version from me later.

My cousin bursts through the front door just as I reach the bottom of the stairs. He looks half-awake, but his bag is slung over one shoulder, no doubt filled with a variety of tech shit. "What the hell is going on?"

"I've gotta go handle something and I need you to stay here and just keep an ear out for Oak," I grit out. "But you're not to go near her unless you hear her retching or fucking screaming."

"Alright," Ramsey nods, throwing his hands up. "I like my balls right where they are and so do the puck bunnies, so I won't go near your little librarian. I sent that fuckhead's location to your phone. You're welcome, by the way."

Rolling my eyes, I leave the house and head straight for my bike. The engine roars to life under my hands. The scent of gasoline fills the air, sharp and acrid, mixing with the faint smell of pine from the woods nearby.

Arriving at the old, unmanned gas station right outside of

town, I spot Brock leaning against a rusty old pickup truck, watching the dial click as he fills his tank. That cocky smirk on his face sends my anger into overdrive. I park my bike hard, gravel crunching beneath the tires, and step off, fists clenched tightly at my sides. The place smells like stale cigarettes and cheap beer, a fitting backdrop for the showdown that's about to go down.

"Jeremiah Blackwood," Brock greets me, his tone oozing with fake friendliness. "What brings you here?"

"Looks like you know who the fuck I am now, Brock," I snap, my words dripping venom. "You drugged Oakley."

"Drugged? I don't know what you're talking about, man." He raises his hands in mock innocence, but I can see the lie in his eyes.

"You fucked with the wrong damn one." My rage is unrelenting. I close the distance between us in a few quick strides and grab him by the collar of his douchebag frat polo, lifting him slightly off the ground. "Just what the fuck were you planning to do and spare me the excuses. We both know this wasn't your first time. You're a piece of shit."

"Hey, hey, calm down!" he sputters, trying to wriggle free from my grip. "I didn't do anything!"

"Shut up!" My grip tightens with each passing second. The world around us seems to fade, leaving only the sound of our heavy breathing and the distant hum of the gas station lights.

"You're gonna pay for this, Brock," I hiss through gritted teeth, bringing my face closer to his, feeling my anger mingling with the cool night air. His eyes dart around, searching for an escape, but there isn't one. Not now.

Out of the corner of my eye, I spot it—a baseball bat lying in the back of his pickup. Perfect. I can feel my eyes crinkle just a bit at the corners as I release my hold on

Brock. He stumbles back, gasping for air, but I'm already moving.

"Think you can throw me around?" he sputters, trying to regain his cocky composure. "You don't scare me, Blackwood."

"Good," I say, tone cold and even. "Because I'm not here to scare you."

I grab the bat, feeling the rough wood under my fingers. My knuckles turn white as I tighten my grip. Brock's eyes widen, finally realizing the gravity of the situation.

"Whoa, man, let's talk about this," he pleads, backing up against the truck. "We can work something out!"

"Talk time's over," I snarl. "Actions have consequences, Brock. And I'm the fucking consequence you never saw coming."

I lift the bat over my shoulder. The world narrows down to the sound of my heartbeat and the adrenaline surging through my veins.

"Jeremiah, please—" His words break off as I bring the bat crashing down. The sickening sound of bone meeting wood echoes through the night, sending a shiver down my spine. Brock crumples to the ground, but I don't stop. Swing after swing, the bat connects with flesh and bone, each impact urging me to go further.

"You disgust me. She could've died!" I roar, punctuating each word with a strike. Blood splatters across my clothes, the metallic scent mingling with the smell of gasoline and sweat. Brock's pleas turn to gurgles, then silence.

I finally stop, chest heaving, staring down at what I've done. Brock lies motionless, blood pooling around him, staining the gravel dark red. For a moment, everything is still. The only sound is my ragged breathing and the distant hum of the lights.

"Fuck," I whisper to myself, the reality of now needing to clean this shit up hitting me.

"I told you that you fucked with the wrong one, Brock," I murmur, more to myself than to him. I drop the bat, letting it clatter to the ground, and wipe a smear of blood from my brow.

"Shit," I whisper, pulling out my phone. My fingers fumble as I navigate to Penn's contact. We always knew days like this would happen from a young age. My brothers and I have a code word prepared for just about everything. I type quickly, the prearranged word glaring up at me.

Hotwheel

"Come on, Penn," I hiss, hitting send. The seconds stretch into agonizing minutes. I keep glancing at Brock's lifeless form, half-expecting him to jerk awake like some horror movie villain.

The phone finally vibrates in my hand. Penn taking his sweet ass time to answer while I'm having a damn crisis.

PENNYWISE

I love it when you talk cars to me

Relief floods through me, but it's short-lived. I need to get back to Oakley. She needs me, no matter what she says in her intoxicated state.

I take another look around, ensuring no prying eyes are watching. The hum of the cicadas buzzes in my ears, the night eerily silent otherwise.

Before I can even process it, headlights pierce the darkness. Penn's jumping out of a truck that rumbles into view.

"Jere, my man," Penn calls out as he hops down from the

passenger seat, his grin wide and almost too casual for the situation. "Looks like you had a bit of fun without me."

"Shut up and help me," I snap, my tone harsher than intended. But there's no time for Penn's comedic bullshit.

"Alright, alright," Penn chuckles, but there's an edge to it —a hint of excitement that's unsettling. He flips his hat backward, ready to help me clean this shit up. He steps around the truck, and for a moment, I catch a glimpse of the tattoos snaking up his arms. The truck drives away and if I thought for one minute it was someone who would say something I'd question it, but whoever dropped my brother off has clearly been vetted by him.

"Let's get this over with," I say, bending down to grab Brock by the ankles. His body is heavier than I anticipated, dead weight that pulls at my muscles.

"On three," Penn says, taking hold of Brock's shoulders. "One...two...three."

We heave him up; the effort drawing a grunt from both of us. The sound of Brock's lifeless body hitting the bed of the truck is sickening, a dull thud that seems to echo in the stillness of the night.

"Good riddance, fucker," Penn mutters, brushing his hands off on his jeans. He turns to me, that sly grin back in place. "You gonna be okay, pretty boy?"

"Just get it done," I reply, my voice tight. "I need to get back to the house."

"Don't worry," Penn says, giving me a mock salute before climbing into the driver's seat of Brock's truck. "I'll take care of everything. You go play knight in shining armor."

"Fuck off, Penn," I shoot back, but there's no real anger in it. Just exhaustion.

He laughs, the sound carefree and almost jarring given the circumstances. "I gotta go see a man about a junkyard."

With a final sarcastic salute, he drives off into the night, the taillights fading into the distance. I stand there for a moment, the silence pressing in once again.

The urgency to get back to my bunny gnaws at me, driving me forward. I swing my leg over the bike seat, the engine roaring to life beneath me.

I throttle the bike, as blood still pumps hot in my veins, and I can't shake the image of Brock crumpling under the bat's brutal swing. The rush was intoxicating.

The whips at my face, seeping into my helmet and making my eyes water a bit. I need to get back to her. To make sure she's safe.

I kill the engine and glide to a halt as I pull up to the house. Silence envelops me, broken only by the distant hoot of an owl. Every creak of the wood as I push open the door sounds so loud.

I walk across the foyer and up the stairs before I walk into my bathroom.

I strip off my clothes, the scent of sweat and blood clinging to them. They hit the floor with a thud.

"Fuck," I hiss, stepping into the shower. Hot water pelts my skin, washing away the tension in my body. Steam swirls around me, thick and suffocating, but also cleansing. I lean my forehead against the cool tile, washing away the grime.

The water mingles with the remnants of blood on my hands, turning pink before swirling down the drain. I scrub harder, nails digging into my skin, trying to erase any evidence. The scent of iron fades, replaced by the sterile aroma of soap.

I turn off the water, the sudden silence almost deafening.

Wrapping a towel around my waist, I step out of the shower, droplets still clinging to my skin.

I push open the door to my bedroom, feeling the weight of the night pressing down on me. The room is dimly lit, the soft glow from the bedside lamp casting a warm halo around Oakley's sleeping form. She lies curled up under the covers, her golden hair splayed out on the pillow.

"Fuck," I mutter under my breath, rubbing a hand over my face. The adrenaline has left me, replaced by bone-deep exhaustion. Each step feels like I'm trudging through quicksand.

"Rem?" The word is a whisper, barely cutting through the thick silence of the room. My heart skips a beat, and I freeze. Did she wake up? No, she's probably just murmuring in her sleep.

"Shh, bunny, it's okay," I murmur softly, slipping into bed beside her. The mattress dips under my weight, and she instinctively shifts closer, her warmth seeping into me. I feel a flicker of something—peace, maybe—as I watch her breath steadily.

"You're safe now," I whisper, more to myself than to her. Her steady breaths are a balm to my nerves, each exhale grounding me.

"Why'd you have to get mixed up in this shit, Oak?" I ask quietly, not expecting an answer. The memory of Brock's bloodied face flashes before my eyes, but I force it away, focusing instead on the gentle rise and fall of Oakley's chest.

"I missed you, Rem, but you're always gone in the morning. I wish my dreams could last forever." Her tone is tinged with a sleepy confusion.

CHAPTER 3
OAKLEY

My head throbs with a dull, relentless ache as I slowly open my eyes. My vision is blurred, and everything around me is a hazy swirl of shadows and light. Panic washes over me in waves as I realize I don't recognize this room. The unfamiliarity tightens like a vise around my chest, and my heart races, pounding against my ribcage like a trapped bird.

"This can't be good. Gosh, Oakley how did you get yourself into this mess?" I whisper to myself, my tone shaky and foreign in this strange space. My mind races, desperately trying to piece together how I ended up here, but the memories are hazy, fragmented, slipping through my fingers like sand.

I feel trapped—like a mouse caught in a maze with no way out.

Sitting up, I notice something that sends a fresh jolt of panic through me. I'm not wearing the same outfit I had on at the party last night. Instead, a hoodie that isn't mine hangs loosely from my frame. My breath catches in my throat, clawing its way out in ragged gasps. Tears well up in my eyes, blurring my already foggy vision. I can feel panic creeping in, and now my vision blurs for an entirely different reason.

"I only had a couple sips of my drink," I mutter, but the words do nothing to soothe the rising tide of fear. The sensation of not being in control of myself or my actions is overwhelming. I feel exposed, vulnerable, like a raw nerve. How could I have been so dang careless?

The room spins around me, the walls closing in. I struggle to find something familiar, something to anchor myself. There's nothing. Just unfamiliar furniture and dim, suffocating silence.

I try to grasp at the fragments of memory from last night. The party, the laughter, the music—all disjointed images that refuse to form a coherent picture. My pulse hammers in my ears, drowning out any semblance of rational thought. The fear claws at me, relentless and unyielding.

My thoughts are a chaotic jumble of panic and confusion. Just as I feel the panic tightening its grip, the creak of the door sends a jolt through me. My eyes dart to the entrance, where Jeremiah Blackwood stands, his green eyes widening with concern.

"Bunny, it's me," he says, his words a mixture of warmth and firmness that cuts through the fog in my mind. He steps closer, extending a hand toward me. His touch is grounding, something tangible that I've missed since the last time we saw each other, and it's everything I need right now.

My words tremble, barely above a whisper. "What happened last night? How did I end up here? Why are you looking at me like that?"

His expression softens, but there's an intensity in his gaze that makes my heart race for reasons beyond fear. Memories of our past. I had such a silly crush on him back then, back before my life was flipped upside down. He left me. He protected me all along and then he left me to fend for myself because he wasn't friends with my brother any longer. My anger, the resentment I have toward him comes crashing back, making it hard to breathe. I'm torn between wanting answers and wanting to bolt from the room, from him. I don't want him to know what happened to me those years he was out of my life.

"Bunny, you need to calm down for me," he murmurs, his hand steady on my shoulder. "You're safe now."

"Safe?" I echo, my tone tinged with sarcasm and disbelief. I'm mad at him and it has nothing to do with waking up in his room. I'm trying my hardest not to show it, and I'm failing miserably. "How can I feel safe when I don't even remember how I got here?"

"*I* brought you here," Jeremiah begins, choosing his words carefully, and I know him well enough to understand that he's trying to restrain his anger, too. "You were at the party, and things got out of control."

"Out of control?" My laugh is hollow, devoid of humor. "That's the understatement of the year."

"Look, bunny, you weren't in any state to get back to your dorm, especially not by yourself." His tone is measured, almost too calm, like he's trying to soothe a wild animal. "So, I brought you here so I could keep an eye on you."

"Here," I repeat, the word tasting bitter on my tongue. "Your room."

"Yes, my room in my house," he confirms, his tone unwavering. "I couldn't leave you alone like that."

"Why not? You've done it before." The question bursts out

before I can stop it. The old wounds, the shattered friendship—they're all there, just beneath the surface.

Jeremiah's jaw flexes and I know I've hit a nerve. "Because I care about you," he says simply, his eyes locking onto mine. There's something raw and unguarded in his gaze, something that makes my breath hitch.

"Care about me?" I scoff, though my tone lacks conviction. "Since when?"

"Since always," he replies, the barest hint of frustration creeping into his words. "Despite everything that's happened between me and your brother."

"Everything that's happened," I mutter, shaking my head. Cutting me out of his life is more accurate, but I'm choosing to pick my battles because something else is really bothering me. "Who took my clothes off?"

His eyes flash with anger and hurt that I would all but accuse him. "Oakley. I didn't touch you. Not like that."

"Not like that?" My voice cracks, a tear slipping down my cheek. "Then why am I wearing...this?" I gesture to the pretty boy sized hoodie hanging loosely from my frame.

"Your clothes were all rumpled up from the tantrum you threw when I dragged you out of the party, and I hardly think sleeping in that dress would have been comfortable," he explains, his tone softening again.

The conflicting emotions swirl within me, and I can't get them to agree on which one I should feel first so they all refuse to settle.

Jeremiah must notice because he says, "Trust me or not," he says quietly, "I'm here. And you're not leaving until I know you're okay."

"I'm fine." I want the words to sound harsh, but they come

out in a whisper, and end up feeling foreign on my tongue. Can I ever be fine in his presence?

"I know when you're lying. Something's up," he snaps, stepping closer. The scent of his musky cologne fills the air between us. "Why did you transfer to St. Charles? What are you hiding?"

Defiance ignites within me. My heart pounds against my ribcage, each beat echoing to me to resist him. "It's none of your business."

"None of my business?" he repeats, incredulous. His eyes bore into mine, searching for answers I'm not ready to give. "Everything about you is my business. I've always looked out for you."

"Really, Jeremiah?" I snort in disgust, shaking my head. "You're sadly misguided."

"Yes," he growls, stepping even closer. I can feel the heat radiating off him. "I need to understand why you're here."

My words are steady despite the turmoil inside me. "I was forced to transfer. That's all you need to know."

"Forced by who?" he presses, frustration clear in his words.

"That's none of your concern," I snap, suddenly feeling exposed, vulnerable. "Where are my things? I need to leave."

"You're not going anywhere until you tell me the truth," he says, blocking my path. The tension is suffocating, an insufferable force between us.

"Move," I say, pushing past my fear. I'm no match for Jeremiah Blackwood's massive frame when my head doesn't even reach his shoulders, but I'll pretend like I don't notice that fact. "I won't stay here another second."

"Oakley," he starts, but I cut him off.

"Where are my clothes, Jeremiah?" I demand, my tone rising. "I'm leaving."

"Tell me what happened," Jeremiah says, barely moving his body to block me from moving. "Oakley," he starts, but I cut him off the same way he did to me.

"Don't Oakley me, while I'm here in your room half-naked and with no memory of how I got here."

He snaps, his words sharp and accusatory. "Do you really think I'd do something to you while you were passed out?"

"I don't know you anymore, Jeremiah," I spit out, turning back to face him. "I trusted you once, and you completely let me down. How do I know what you're capable of?" I gesture toward his hoodie that I'm currently swimming in.

"Oakley, I already told you that I didn't touch you—" he snarls, his green orbs flashing with anger.

"How comforting," I retort, rolling my eyes. "What a gentleman you are, Jeremiah. Just let me leave."

"Don't tempt me, bunny. I can be the monster you want me so badly to be," he growls, frustration simmering beneath his calm facade. I've seen a protective side of Jeremiah before, but there's an edge to him now that makes my stomach flip.

Shaking my head, I implore him, "Just tell me where my things are."

"When did you become so stubborn?" he asks, exasperation creeping into his tone.

"When I learned the hard way that I'm on my own and that trusting people doesn't get you anywhere," I reply, my tone softening despite myself. I fidget with the hem of the hoodie, trying to keep my hands steady. My movements feel small and delicate, as if I am trying to subconsciously not entice the monster that could be in the room.

"You're impossible," he mutters, running a hand through his shorn hair.

"Maybe I am," I admit, my eyes searching his face for any sign of understanding. "But can you blame me?"

"Oakley..." he begins, his tone gentler now, almost pleading.

"You can't just run away because you're mad at me." Jeremiah sounds calm, measured, but there's an edge to it that makes my heart race.

"Run away? You think I'm running away?" I scoff, turning to face him fully. "You're the *king* of the disappearing act. I guess I always did look up to you, so maybe I learned it from you."

"Bunny, you know I had shit going on with my family and then..." He takes a step closer, and I can feel the tension crackling between us like static electricity. "Things were blurring and then the fight with Royce blew up out of nowhere. The only one who was going to get hurt was you."

"Don't call me bunny, I've let it slide, but it makes me sick to hear that from you now," I gesture around the room, my hand shaking slightly. "Whatever twisted game you're playing isn't going to make up for the fact that you told me you'd always be here, and you weren't. You left me just like Royce did. I chose you always."

"Twisted game?" he repeats, a bitter smile tugging at the corners of his lips. "You think I enjoy this, seeing you like this? You think I wanted to see you hanging all over some prick like he was the best fucking thing you've ever seen in your life?"

"Don't act all high and mighty now," I snap, my anger flaring up again. If it was anyone else, I wouldn't feel so dang comfortable speaking up. "You should have done what you did two years ago and left me alone. I don't need your pity."

His voice rises, frustration seeping into his words. "You were a mess last night, Oakley. You could barely stand."

"That doesn't give you the right to—" I stop myself, breathing heavily, my mind racing with fragmented memories of the previous night.

"To what?" he challenges, stepping even closer. "To take care of you? To make sure you were safe?"

"Safe?" I laugh bitterly, the sound harsh and grating. "Is that what you call this? You played the hero and then waltz in here, calling me bunny like I'm supposed to fall at your feet and worship you like I used to. Those days were over last year, Jeremiah, and they'll never be back. Especially not because you randomly found me at a party. I'm doing fine on my own."

"You're not going to talk around it," he says, a hint of ironic humor in his words. "What happened last year? The last I checked you were thriving at your college doing fine without me or anyone else hovering over you."

"You were checking up on me? You cut me off, but you were watching everything I was doing? That's supposed to make me feel better? If it's even true." I spit out, my anger bubbling over. "You're such a—"

"Careful, bunny," he interrupts, his tone low and dangerous. "I don't have the patience I had two years ago. We've been apart a long time." The way his eyes darken sends shivers up my spine. Jeremiah Blackwood used to look at me with a softness that he did not hold for anyone else. Now, though, he looks like he wants to devour me piece by piece until I only exist for him.

"Don't call me that," I snap at him again, my cheeks flushing with anger and embarrassment. When I hear the nickname that only he used to call me, it brings back so many feelings I'd much rather forget. "You lost the right to use that name a long time ago."

"Did I?" he asks, tilting his head slightly, his dimples showing as he pulls his mouth up into a tight smile. I always saw Jeremiah Blackwood as being different from his brothers. He was the kind one, the gentle one. Well, at least he was all of those things to me, but this morning I finally see what everyone else always said about him. He's cocky, arrogant, an always-gets-what-he-wants son of Robert Blackwood.

"I won't do this with you. You're bigger than me. Congratulations. You're bigger and badder than ninety-nine percent of the people at St. Charles," I say, my words trembling with rage and desperation and it doesn't help that I see his chest puff out like my try at sounding dismissive or condescending has only given him an ego boost. "That does not mean you can force me to stay here, and it certainly does not mean you can control everything I do."

"Control?" he laughs, a hollow sound. "If I wanted control, Oakley, you'd know it."

"Then what is it?" I demand, stepping closer until we're mere inches apart. "What do you want from me, Jeremiah?"

"Everything," he whispers, his eyes darkening with intensity. "I want everything, Oakley."

"You're just taunting me at this point," I say, my tone firm despite the fear gnawing at my insides. "If I was so damn important to you, we wouldn't be meeting at a party randomly that you were no doubt going to pick up a jersey chaser from."

Jeremiah speaks softly, his gaze piercing through me, "You're more important than you realize."

"Stop it," I plead, feeling the walls closing in. "Stop trying to twist this. Just let me go."

"Not until you tell me why you transferred to St. Charles," he demands, his words tinged with desperation.

"That's none of your business," I retort, my heart pounding against my ribcage.

"Make it my business," he urges, his eyes searching mine. "Tell me the truth, Oakley."

"Why should I?" I challenge, my tone wavering. "So, you can use it against me?"

"Because I can't fix it if I don't know what it is," he says, his words filled with raw emotion. "And I need to understand."

"Understand what?" I ask, tears welling up in my eyes. "That I'm broken? That I've been through hell and back?"

"Yes," he admits, his tone barely above a whisper. "I need to know, Oakley. Please." Jeremiah finally takes a step toward me, and I can feel the heat radiating off his large frame. I'm not a tall girl, but next to him I feel miniature.

"Shut up," I whisper, hating the way my body reacts to him, the way my pulse quickens, the way my skin tingles. I have not had this reaction to another man since he left me two years ago. I tried to be happy, I really did, but then my world got flipped upside down and I've been in survival mode ever since. With Royce and Jeremiah gone, that left my parents who can only be bothered to participate in a distracted, dismissive phone call once a month. On one hand, I'm livid with Jeremiah, but having him this close and not feeling like I'm going to be swallowed whole by my anxiety is something I didn't anticipate but am grateful for. "I can't do this right now. I need you to let it go."

"Not until you tell me why," he insists, his hand reaching out to touch my arm. His fingers are warm, firm, a stark contrast to the cold fear gripping my heart.

"Why does it matter?" I ask, my voice breaking. "Why do you care?"

"Because I've never stopped giving a shit about you," he confesses, his eyes locking onto mine. "And because I need to protect you. I need to know why you're so scared. I need to know why you were at that party. That's not something the Oakley I knew would have done. Like it or not, you're mine to look after."

"That's bullshit," I spit, pulling away from his touch. "You don't own me, Jeremiah. You never did."

"That's open to opinion, I suppose," he concedes, his voice dropping to a whisper. "But I won't let you walk away without knowing the truth."

"Then maybe it's better if we don't see each other again," I say, my voice trembling. "Maybe it's better if we just forget everything."

"Is that what you really want?" he asks, his eyes searching mine. "To forget?"

"Yes," I lie, my heart aching with the weight of the unspoken words between us. "It's exactly what I want." I sit back on the bed, pulling at the sheets as if they were some sort of security blanket. They smell like him, and I don't know if I want to sigh or cringe. I hate feeling this way.

CHAPTER 4
JEREMIAH

The moment hangs heavy in the air, like a suffocating weight pressing down on both of us. Oakley's bright eyes meet mine in an unforgiving stare, her golden blonde hair framing her face, and my fingers itch to reach out and move the strands that are trying to hide her from me.

She looks fucking beautiful as she sits tangled in the sheets of my bed. All soft curves and pale skin, begging to be touched, to be marked, to be made mine.

"No, I don't think it is what you actually want. You're irritating me by avoiding the damn question. What the hell were you doing at that party, Oakley?" The question rips from my lips, jagged and raw. The anger pulsing inside me isn't just about her being there; it's about the two years that have stretched between us, vast and silent.

She doesn't flinch under my glare. "I go to school here now, Jeremiah. It's not a crime to attend a party."

"Cut the bullshit," I snap, the frustration boiling over.

"Since when do you care what I do?" There's a challenging lift to her chin, that same stubborn tilt I remember too well.

She would use it against me and her brother all the damn time.

"Since always, bunny and if you think we can just *forget* everything then you're delulu." The nickname slips out, laced with a possessiveness I've no right to feel. It also makes me smirk when I see the annoyance wash over her face when she hears it. But damn it, she's always been mine, even if she's never really been mine at all.

"Stop calling me that," she hisses, but there's a hitch in her voice. She's as affected by this as I am.

"Answer the question, Oakley. Why now? Why here?"

"Maybe I missed your charming personality," she retorts, the snark dripping from each word like honey, thick and sweet.

"Is that so?" My laugh is humorless, edged with the bitterness of our shared history. "Last time I checked, which was mmm five seconds ago, you couldn't stand the sight of me."

"Things change." She shrugs, but there's something in her gaze, a flicker of something deeper, darker, that makes my chest tighten.

"Change," I echo, feeling the weight of the word between us. It's loaded, full of unspoken truths and the ghost of whatever may have been between us years ago.

"Everything about you pulls me in, Oakley. It's always been like that. Even when I know it's fucking madness." The words spill out, reckless and raw. This girl, this infuriatingly beautiful fucking girl, has me tied up in knots, her name etched into my bones.

"Stop it, Jeremiah. Just...stop." Her breath catches, betraying the cool exterior she's trying to maintain.

"Can't do that, sweetheart. You walk into a room, and it's

like everything else fades away. It's always been you." I'm standing now, the space between us just fucking electric.

"Jeremiah..." Her voice is a warning, but her body betrays her, leaning toward the heat radiating off of mine.

"Tell me to stop, Oakley. Tell me, and I finally will." It's a lie, and we both know it. I can't stay away from her any more than I can stop breathing.

But she doesn't say it. She doesn't say anything at all. And that silence is all the permission I need. I don't care how much I have to chase this girl. She's going to be mine. One way or another. I'll use every underhanded trick I can.

"It's none of your damn business why I was there," she snaps, her voice low but sharp enough to cut as she gets up from the bed. "You're not my father, Jeremiah."

"Clearly," I retort, "not your brother either but since you're here someone's gotta fucking look out for you."

"Fuck you," she hisses, her cheeks flushing with anger. Before I can react, Oakley rips off my hoodie, exposing her delicate skin. The sight sends a jolt straight to my groin, and I have to bite back a groan as she pushes past me to grab her dress folded up on the armoire and hurriedly pulls it on.

"Oakley," I say, my voice rougher than I intend, "you can't just walk away from me. You're going to tell me what I need to know."

"Watch me," she tosses back, a challenge in every syllable.

My hand shoots out, grasping her arm tightly. Her skin is warm under my fingers, but she flinches as if my touch burns her.

"Don't touch me without permission!" she snaps, her voice filled with anger and something more fragile.

I release her immediately, my own frustration boiling

over. "Oakley, this conversation isn't over," I say, my tone hardening. "You think you can just leave me?"

She scoffs, but doesn't say anything as she gathers up the rest of her stuff.

"Do you really want to make me involve your brother?" I threaten, leaning closer to her. The mention of Royce brings a flicker of pain to her expression, quickly masked by another layer of stubbornness.

"Royce isn't part of this," she says through clenched teeth, though I can see the vulnerability in her eyes.

"Maybe he should be," I counter, my voice low and dangerous. "Seems like someone needs to look out for you."

"Get over yourself, Jeremiah," she spits back, grabbing her bag. "You don't get to play the hero and it's not exactly like you can call my brother up right this second, is it?"

"Haven't I always been that for you?" I ask, stepping into her path, blocking her exit. She can deny with her words all she wants, but we both know it's true.

"Move," she demands, her eyes narrowing at me, filled with a mixture of emotions I can't quite decipher, fear, anger, maybe even a sliver of longing.

"Not until you tell me why you were there," I insist, my voice unwavering.

"Don't hold your breath," she repeats, her chin lifting defiantly.

"Then we'll stay here all damn day," I challenge, crossing my arms over my chest.

"Fine," she hisses, her eyes blazing. "But don't think for a second that you can intimidate me, Jeremiah Robert Blackwood."

"Wouldn't dream of it."

"Rem," she whispers, an edge of desperation in her voice. "Just let me go."

"Not until I get some answers," I respond, my voice softening slightly, though the determination remains.

"Fine," she says, voice trembling but eyes fierce. "You want answers? My brother's been absent from my life since you ruined it. You think you can just threaten me with him?"

Her words hit me like a punch to the gut.

"Ruined it?" I ask, my anger flaring up again. "What are you talking about?"

"Don't act clueless, Jeremiah," she spits out, her eyes flashing with pain and fury. "After that night, after Royce—" She stops herself, shaking her head as if to clear the memory. "He disappeared. Because of you."

"That's not fair, Oakley," I say, my voice low but intense. "You know there was more to it than that."

"Fair?" she laughs bitterly, picking up her phone. Her fingers fly across the screen, each tap like a punch to the gut. "I'm done with this conversation."

"Who are you texting?" I demand, stepping closer. I have no problem beating the piss out of whoever it is, especially if it's part of that little frat pack from the party last night.

"I'm getting a ride back to my dorm," she snaps, glaring at me, her dress clinging to her body in a way that makes my throat dry. But there's no beauty in this moment, only the ugly truth of our past, the craving and the hurt that festers beneath the surface.

"I'll drive you back," I tell her, because how the fuck does it look if I let a stranger take her back to her dorm? I shake my head. I still can't believe she's here on my campus.

Oakley's fingers pause over her phone, a slender brow

arching in disbelief. "You think I'd get in a car with you?" Her laugh is sharp and haunting.

I lean against the door frame, arms crossed, trying to mask how damn much I want her to say yes. "We used to cruise around all the time, remember? My bike between your thighs, your hands gripping me like you'd never let go."

Her eyes flash. But she's not having it, not today. "That was then, Jeremiah. This is now. And right now, I'd rather hitch a ride with a serial killer than share a seat with you."

"Christ, Oakley." I rake a hand through my hair, frustration gnawing at the edges of my composure. "Fine, play it that way. But don't act like there wasn't something real between us."

"Something real?" she scoffs, stepping closer, her floral scent hitting me like an uppercut. "What's real is the mess you made. What's real is me wanting to forget every second I spent fooled by your pretty boy demeanor."

"Is that what this is about?" I shoot back, my voice laced with sarcasm. "Forgetting? Because from where I'm standing, it looks like you can't stop remembering."

"Fuck you, Jeremiah." The words slice through the air, her voice low and lethal.

Her cheeks flush, a rosy hue that betrays her true feelings. She grabs her purse, slinging it over her shoulder with a huff. "Just pretend you never saw me last night. Let's be strangers. It's better that way. I mean you haven't noticed me on campus for weeks, so it shouldn't be too hard."

"Oak," I call after her, but she's already turning away, her golden hair tangled and flowing behind her as she moves down the stairs.

"Just stop," she bites out, her tone icy. "Those days are dead and buried. Just like whatever friendship we had."

"Dead and buried?" I scoff, trailing down the stairs after her. "Funny, because it doesn't feel that way right now."

"That's because you can't let go." She shoves her phone into her bag, her movements jerky with frustration. "But I have. And I suggest you do the same."

I follow her to the front of the house, where the car idles impatiently. I mentally note that it's some dark-haired girl, so I don't need to bloody another bat right this second. She opens the door, glancing back at me one last time. Her eyes are full of emotion: anger, pain, maybe even regret.

"Goodbye, Jeremiah." Her voice is softer now, almost a whisper.

"I'll be seeing you around, Oakley," I tell her, knowing I didn't keep the cockiness out of my voice.

She slips into the car, slamming the door shut and blocking me out. The engine revs, tires crunching against the pavement as the car pulls away. I watch until the taillights disappear.

I stand there, rooted to the spot, before heading back into the house. I've been stuck in the monotony of my life and had packed her away in my head. But now she's back and I'm going to figure out just what the fuck is going on and what the fuck really happened years ago.

CHAPTER 5
OAKLEY

The room feels like it's closing in on me. I sit cross-legged on my bed, my single dorm room suffocatingly small as I rant about Jeremiah Blackwood to nothing but air.

Seriously. I was not on his mind for two years and then just because he saw me talking to another guy; he wants to go apeshit. He says that he checked in on me, but that has to be a lie. You can't care about someone and walk away the way he did over my brother accusing him of sleeping with his girlfriend. I slam my fist against the mattress; the sound echoing off the cold walls. "His bunny, my ass."

Jeremiah's face flashes in my mind—those piercing green eyes and that infuriating smirk. He can analyze a play in seconds, but when it comes to our friendship, he's clueless.

I glance at the clock. Time's slipping away. With a groan, I leap off the bed, urgency hurrying my movements. I don't really want to do this right now, but my therapist thought it would be a good idea. My coworker, Willa, told me about Starlet Streams, but she uses it more as a side hustle. Then again, she thought going to the party would be a good idea and look how that turned out. My cam show waits for no one, I guess. I shove the desk aside, making space for my backdrop. My fingers work quickly, hanging the black curtain and draping fairy lights across it. Their soft glow casts a whimsical, albeit semi-eerie ambiance in the dimly lit room.

I adjust the lights until they create just the right amount of shadow. My heart pounds with frustration and anticipation, the weight of Jeremiah's insistence still heavy on my mind.

"Showtime. I guess." I roll my eyes, because deep down I don't think this is going to work or make me feel any better.

My fingers trace the lace edges of the masquerade bunny mask, feeling its delicate intricacy against my skin. The mask is more than just a prop; it's my shield and sword, an invitation to step into another world where I can be anyone but myself. Sliding it on, I feel a rush of empowerment, a tingling sensation that travels down my spine. The weight of anonymity settles over me like a cloak, allowing me to shed my insecurities.

"Here we go," I whisper, the words barely audible even in the quiet of my room.

I sit in front of the camera, adjusting the angle with care. Everything needs to be perfect—the lighting, the backdrop, the way the shadows play across my face. It's the little bit of control I can count on. One last check and I take a deep breath, that familiar nervousness and anticipation bubbling up inside me.

"Hey, everyone," I say, hitting the button to start the live stream on Starlet Streams cam site. The screen lights up instantly, a flurry of messages flooding in from eager viewers, most of which refer to themselves as fanboys. I feel safe here in a way I don't feel in real life. I can control how much of me they have access to and how much I can keep to myself. Usernames flash in bright, gaudy colors against the dark background. Some of them I recognize and some of them I don't.

Missed you, BunnyGirl!

Looking gorgeous as always!

How was your day?

The chat box explodes with greetings and compliments, a surge of virtual affection that's both intoxicating and overwhelming. My heart races as I scan through the messages, trying to keep up with the torrent of attention.

"Hey there, lovelies," I respond, my voice dripping with playful charm. "You've got no idea how much I've missed you all."

Tell us something naughty, VelvetVix

One message reads, accompanied by a barrage of emojis.

"Patience, patience," I reply, a smirk tugging at my lips. "Good things come to those who wait."

I lean back slightly, letting the fairy lights cast a soft glow around me, enhancing the atmosphere. As the minutes tick by, I lose myself in the rhythm of the interaction, the ebb and flow of desire and fantasy intertwining seamlessly.

Show us a little more. PLEASE

Another message pops up, and I can almost hear the collective holding of breath on the other side of the screen.

He's a regular chatter in my room, and he knows I don't take my clothes off, but without fail he asks every time. My therapist says this is a good way to find my voice without feeling unsafe without going back to the night my voice and my choices were taken away from me.

"You know I don't do that," I say, winking at the camera. "But thank you for asking nicely this time."

> Lose the mask, sweetie. Let us see that beautiful face.

Another message fires off and I can't help but smile. They're relentless and I don't have to bend to any of their wills. None of them can grab me. None of them can force me to do anything I don't want to do. None of them can take anything I'm not willing to give them.

With practiced ease, I let the lace strap of my mask slip down just a bit; the fabric caressing my skin as it moves. I'm careful not to show too much of my face, but it gets the reaction I wanted, and that makes me feel like I really *am* in control. The chat box goes wild, their excitement palpable even through the screen. I revel in the power, the control, the way they hang onto my every move.

"More?" I ask, my tone laced with seductive promise. "Or is this enough for tonight?"

> Never enough!

Comes the unanimous response, their desperation almost tangible.

"Greedy boys," I chide gently, my smile widening. "But I suppose I can indulge you...just a little longer." My stomach sinks. None of this feels right, but I keep pushing through like my therapist told me to.

Tell us about your day

One user types, their excitement palpable even through the screen.

"Ah, today was quite an adventure," I say, leaning closer to the camera as if sharing a delicious secret. "I stumbled upon a hidden garden on campus. You wouldn't believe the beauty—roses as big as my head, and the scent... intoxicating. I felt like Alice in Wonderland."

Did you fall down any rabbit holes?

Another fanboy asks, his username flashing in bright green.

"Not this time," I reply with a sly smile. "But who knows what tomorrow will bring?"

Any tips for surviving this semester?

A different user chimes in, shifting the conversation.

"Ah, the eternal struggle," I laugh softly. "Balance is key, my loves. Study hard, but don't forget to take breaks. And caffeine—lots of it."

The chat box fills with a mix of laughter, heart emojis, and more questions. I make sure to respond to each one, weaving in bits of humor and advice, keeping the energy lively and engaging.

Can we have a 1-on-1 chat?

One message stands out, repeated persistently by a user named Knight99. I ignore it, focusing on the collective experience rather than indulging one individual.

What's your favorite book?

Another user asks, pulling me back into the flow.

"Hard to choose just one," I say thoughtfully. "But 'Wuthering Heights' always has a special place in my heart. The passion, the torment...it's beautifully dark."

Just like you

Someone comments, and I can't help but chuckle.

"Flattery will get you everywhere," I tease, but it's not a genuine warmth spread through me. Despite the mask and the distance, I truly feel fine, and I haven't felt that way in a long time.

Please, just 1-on-1

Knight99 insists, his messages now tinged with desperation. I glance at them briefly before dismissing them once more. It's crucial to maintain control, not just for my sake, but for the entire audience. They deserve my full attention.

"Alright, loves," I announce, sensing the hour slipping away. "One last question before we wrap up. Make it good."

Are you happy

Comes a sudden, simple query. It hangs in the air, heavier than the rest.

"Am I happy?" I repeat, caught off guard. "Happiness is...complicated. But in this moment, with all of you, I find joy. And sometimes, that's enough."

As the hour draws to a close, I feel a twinge of reluctance. Despite the thrill, a part of me longs for something real, something beyond the virtual veil that I've created. I want to feel this comfortable when I'm walking across campus, while I'm at work in the library, when a random man looks at me. I don't want to question if he'll be another man to hurt me. But tonight, this will have to suffice.

"Time's up, loves," I say, my voice dropping to a sultry whisper. "Until next time."

With a final wave, I log out; the screen going dark. The room feels different now—emptier, quieter. I remove the mask, placing it back on the desk with a sense of finality.

"Another night, another show," I murmur, reaching for my journal. The pen feels heavy in my hand as I begin to write, the words flowing out in a torrent of conflicting emotions. Empowerment, doubt, fear—they all blend together, forming a tangled web that mirrors my state of mind.

Is this really what I want?

I write down, but the answer remains elusive, hidden beneath layers of uncertainty and longing. For now, all I can do is keep searching, hoping to find clarity in the chaos. My mind drifts back to Jeremiah Blackwood. I might have felt in control during my cam show tonight, but the only place I've ever felt safe is with him. That's for another day and another therapy session to figure out, I guess.

The pen scratches against the paper, each stroke a release

of pent-up frustration. The black ink bleeds into the fibers, creating words that feel heavy with meaning and doubt.

Why does this feel so wrong?

I write, biting my lip as the question hangs in the air. The room is silent except for the soft hum of the mini-fridge and the distant murmur of campus life filtering through the walls.

Growth is uncomfortable, Oakley. My therapist's voice rings in my ear, her tone calm and measured. *You owe it to yourself to embrace uncertainty.* The problem is that I'm uncertain about almost everything at this point and nothing I do seems to swing things back to the way they were before. I always had trouble sleeping, but Jeremiah was there to soothe that ache. Since he's been gone, nothing has felt right and now, he's back in my life and I want nothing more for him to leave me alone.

Bitterly, I realize how contradictory that sounds. I'm so twisted up in my head over the night he left me and never looked back even more than the night I was attacked.

This isn't even about him and yet he invades every aspect of my life just like he has been doing for years. I wish I could erase him from my mind, my life, my everything.

I'm doing this for me, right?

Or am I just chasing validation? I can't ignore the nagging thought that maybe, just maybe, I'm seeking approval from faceless strangers. Each comment, each tip—it fills a void, but it's temporary. Fleeting.

I toss my journal to the side because I'm not getting anywhere with this whole exercise and pick up my phone. There are seventeen messages from Jeremiah Blackwood, and I hate the fact that his number is still stored in my phone as **Pretty Boy** instead of just his name.

PRETTY BOY

You can't ignore me forever bunny.

I know every move you make. I know everywhere you go. Everyone you talk to. Every thought you think is mine. You're back in my crosshairs now, Oakley.

I roll my eyes and refrain from texting him back that if he knew I was chatting with strangers online tonight, he'd already be over here kicking my door in. Well, the old Jeremiah would. I don't know what this version of him would do, and I choose to keep ignoring him. After two years of silence, I'd say he deserves it.

PRETTY BOY

Answer me.

You can't keep your secrets forever.

Oh, but I can, pretty boy.

CHAPTER 6
JEREMIAH

"Move your ass, JB!" Coach's voice cuts through the evening air, and I know he's talking to me. I still remember Coach bitching about how the fuck was he going to deal with four Blackwoods on his team. And why the fuck was my name such a damn mouthful?

"Yeah, yeah," I mutter under my breath, pushing through another drill. My muscles burn, but it's nothing compared to everything building up inside me right now. Oakley's name keeps bouncing around in my head like a fucking pinball, and every time it hits, it urges me on.

Sweat drips into my eyes, stinging like hell as I shove past another padded shoulder. The sun's beating down on the St. Charles College football field, like a goddamn torture chamber of turf and grit. I'm out here busting my ass while Oakley's tucked away in some quiet corner of the library. It pisses me off how much she's under my skin. I can't think of anything else. She consumes every fleeting thought even when I'm sleeping.

"Still brooding over Oakley, huh, pretty boy?" Penn's voice

cuts through the grunts of our practice session. We both know the nickname is meant to jab at the raw nerve that is my obsession with Oakley Ashford. I shoot him a glare. The kind that's had lesser men back down, but Penn? He thrives on this shit.

"Keep her name out of your filthy mouth, Penn," I snap, shoving my helmet off and wiping sweat from my brow. The smell of fresh cut grass assaults my nose just causing my annoyance at my current situation to rise.

Penn just chuckles, that damn smug ass look on his face as he tosses the ball from hand to hand. "C'mon, little bro. You just need to bang it out and get it over with. Might help you get her out of your system."

"You're an asshole, you know that?" I spit back, feeling the heat rise in my chest. I don't give a fuck how he talks about anyone except for her. He knows she's the one person I won't stand for his shit on. Oakley Ashford is not the type of girl you just bang out.

"What's going on over here?" Graham strides over, his hair disheveled from practice. He looks between us, sensing the tension immediately.

"Your brother thinks I should screw Oakley to forget about her," I say, voice dripping with sarcasm.

"That's your solution for everything, isn't it, Penn?" Graham crosses his arms, staring down Penn with those piercing brown eyes. "That kind of shit won't solve anything, Jere. It'll just make things worse."

"Stay out of this, Graham. Both of you need to worry more about Linc," I warn, but he's right. He always is.

"Jere, listen to yourself. You're obsessed, and Penn's bullshit isn't helping." Graham's tone is firm, his words heavy with something that sounds a lot like disappointment.

"Fuck you," I spit back, the words slicing the tension between us. There's nothing brotherly in our exchange now, just a dark cloud of anger and frustration that seems to bleed from my pores right now.

"No thank you, you aren't my type or G's either, for that matter." Penn retorts, rolling his eyes.

"Both of you, shut the hell up," I growl, throwing my helmet onto the ground.

"Obsessed. Obsessed. Obsessed," Penn sing-songs with a sly grin that doesn't quite reach his eyes. They're always watching, calculating.

"From the tip of my dick, Penn, shut the fuck up. It's not like letting go is exactly my strong suit," I admit through clenched teeth, vision clouded by images of Oakley's eyes and the way they used to light up for me.

"Damn right it isn't, and that's the fucking problem," Graham mutters under his breath, shaking his head. The whistle blows, signaling the end of practice as Coach starts yelling, and we start peeling off our gear, each lost in our own thoughts, the air still thick with tension as we make our way into the locker room. I stop to pick up my lid from the ground on my way into the tunnel.

"It's about why she's here. Why now?" I growl, tossing my helmet into my locker.

"Ask her and if she won't tell you, then either fucking make her or figure it out another way. Instead of fucking fighting with us about it. I didn't piss in your cereal, but can't say the same for Deadpool 2.0 over there." He tosses his head in the direction of Penn's locker where he's joking with some of the other guys on the team.

"Yeah, 'cause that's gonna be a lovely conversation," I

scoff. But deep down, I know he's right. The curiosity, the obsession I try to deny—it's eating me alive. I need answers.

"Seriously, man, you need to get your head straight," my brother Lincoln says, as he rounds the lockers. "This thing with Ashford is gonna fuck with your head, just like it always did. I don't know why you have such a hard-on for the fucking Ashford family, anyway."

"Yeah, thanks for the therapy session. Last I checked you have your own clusterfuck to deal with. How is your new step-sister, by the way?" I mutter. But he's right, damn him. Every thought circles back to her. Every goddamn one.

"I've got my shit handled," Lincoln shrugs, heading toward the showers. "You might want to figure your shit out before it eats you whole."

"Whatever," I say, more to myself than to him.

I smell and my mind wages war on whether I should just leave now and go find my bunny or if I should wash my damn ass first.

Showering wins, but barely as I walk into the showers and fucking clean off quickly. I need to confront her, figure out what game she's playing at. I rush to change into my jeans and t-shirt when I hear my brother behind me.

"Hey, you coming to grab food with us?" Lincoln slaps my shoulder, his dark eyes glinting with a mischief I'm not in the mood for. "Or are you too busy brooding?"

"Fuck off, Lincoln." The words snap out sharper than I intend, but he just smirks, unfazed.

"Chill, man. I have plans tonight unlike you it seems like. You should see someone, get that stick out of your ass," He chuckles, enjoying the rise he gets out of me.

"Good for you," I mutter, tossing my towel in the bin and grabbing my wallet and keys out of my locker. I'm just out here, losing my shit over a girl who can't stand the sight of me.

But damn it, I need answers. I'm not playing this game with her. The only games I play are the ones I can control.

"Good luck, man," Lincoln says, a hint of real support breaking through his usual sarcasm.

"Thanks," I reply, the words dry as dust in my mouth. I don't wait for another word from any of my brothers. I stride out of the room and into the hallway leading to the middle of campus. These damn cobblestones echo as my sneakers beat against them. Old world charm or whatever bullshit SCU spews about why we still look like we belong in an old period movie.

"Jeremiah!" someone calls, but I ignore it. My pace quickens until I reach the looming stairs that will take me up to the library. The last few days of following little Ashford around have shown me that she frequents the library more than any other place on campus except for her dorm room. I know she'll be here.

I push open the library doors, the cool air rushing to meet me. The scent of old books and worn leather greets me. Bookshelves tower around me, hiding secrets and knowledge. There's something oddly comforting about history. Doomed to repeat it, so it's like you already have a vague idea of what happens.

I find her tucked into a corner, the girl who's been running circles in my head, turning every thought to an obsession. Oakley's perched at a table like some kind of fairy, her golden hair spilling over the pages. She doesn't look up, doesn't even twitch; doesn't even realize she's like prey caught by a predator.

I position myself behind a nearby shelf, pretending to

browse books while stealing glances at her. Her fingers trace the lines of text, her eyes narrowing in concentration. God, she's beautiful. And infuriating. And everything in between.

I can't take my eyes off her. Her lips part slightly as she reads, a small crease forming between her brows.

My fingers trail over book spines, feigning interest in titles I couldn't give a damn about.

There's something so damn intoxicating about watching her when she's not watching back. Lurking.

The way she tucks a stray lock behind her ear, the concentration, the fucking pleated sundress and cardigan she has on. The goddamn Esperanza wedges that I still remember the fucking name of because she nagged on and on about how they were her favorite type of shoe to wear. It's a fucking scrapbook of innocent gestures that have no right to turn me on. But they do. They really fucking do.

My gaze slides over her form again, taking in the rise and fall of her chest, the curve of her breast where it meets the edge of the table. She shifts in her seat, and the movement sends a surge of heat straight through me. She looks so small, how easy it would be to cocoon her and swallow her whole.

I need to chill the fuck out. A low chuckle escapes me, scratching at my throat. There's humor there, dark and twisted. She's fucking driving me insane, and insanity is reserved for my unhinged brother. Maybe I'm more like Penn than I care to admit.

For now, I'm content to watch, to wait, to let the tension build until it's ripe and ready to burst. Because when it does, when I finally get my hands on her...God, the things I'll do to make her mine.

Fuck. That's not the plan. Find out why she's here and then lock her up in a damn ivory tower. I need to keep my dick in my pants and my hands off her. Tongue also because I just know the first taste of her I get will be my ruin.

As if sensing my thoughts, she shifts in her seat, a subtle change in her demeanor. Her fingers tap the table lightly, a sign of unease. Something's bothering her. Something big. Just let me in bunny and whatever is bothering you, I'll slay. No bigger monster than me when it comes to you.

I lean back against the bookshelf, feeling the hard spines press into my back, grounding me and keeping me from doing something stupid like Penn or Lincoln.

"Excuse me, do you know where I can find the history section?" someone asks, disrupting my thoughts. I snap my head in their direction, trying not to let my irritation show.

"Uh, sure," I reply, forcing a smile. I don't want to be memorable right now. I point off in a random direction. I don't care where they go as long as it's away from me. "It's just down that way." As they walk off, I return my focus to Oakley, but she's gotten up and disappeared from her table. Shit. I need to find her, to see her up close without her knowing I'm there.

It doesn't take long for me to relocate her—she's moved deeper into the library, running her fingers along the rows of books as if they hold the secrets to the universe. I can't help but imagine those fingers on me, tracing patterns across my skin, as we ride.

She sighs, her breath fogging up the glass of the display case in front of her. **"The tragedy of love that can never be."**

She doesn't hear me just behind her. She's too wrapped up in her own thoughts, lost in the story that unfolds within the pages of the book she looks at so fondly. What fucking book has her so enamored?

And that's how I want her—completely unaware of my

presence, allowing me to watch her without interruption. It's a dangerous game, but one I can't seem to resist. I refuse to admit it to my brothers, but they are right. I'm fucking obsessed with her. How could I not be? She's the one good and pure thing I had in my life.

My mother is non-existent. Vanished as soon as she gave me up to dear old dad. When I was old enough, I looked for her, thinking my dad had her killed. I was ready to kill him until I found her in some hole in the wall town, living a normal life with a truck driver husband and two kids. She was alive and well, just didn't give a single fuck about me.

My father is a devil incarnate and my brothers and I are made wholly in his image just as he intended. We'll never escape that. It's been burned into our skin, leeched into our bones, and invaded every molecule of our DNA. We're the monsters he wanted us to be, all of us born and bred just how he designed.

I lean in just a bit further, putting my nose right into her hair and inhaling as quietly as possible. Pure fucking sunshine greets me and soothes the ache welling in my chest at the thought of my fucked-up life.

"Hey Oakley! Did you decide if you could take my shift on Thursday? I have a session I just can't miss." I hear someone ask and I have just enough time to back away and disappear back into the stack of books as my dream girl spins around and heads to the other girl suddenly appearing.

Fuck, that was a close call, and I really don't need to get caught stalking someone in the library and then clean up the fucking mess that creates.

CHAPTER 7
OAKLEY

The bass reverberates through the floor, the scent of spilled beer and sweat heavy in the air. I stand awkwardly amidst the throng of bodies moving to the rhythm, feeling out of place. My eyes dart around, searching for an escape route, when suddenly, a familiar figure looms into view.

Great. I don't need to be hassled on top of everything. I thought I was ready to come back out to a party, make it through a few hours of not panicking, and the number one person who can get my heart rate up is heading toward me. I refuse to let anyone see how much I'm bothered right now.

"What the fuck, Oakley?" Jeremiah's voice cuts through the noise, filled with intensity and something darker. His green eyes narrow, pinning me with a gaze that almost feels like a physical touch. "What are you doing here? After what happened last time?"

"I thought you know everything I do and everywhere I go?" I snap right back at him, trying to keep my cool despite the knot forming in my stomach. I hate the fact that even when I'm trying to be assertive or show that I'm angry, I still sound so small. It doesn't help that I wasn't graced with height, so looking up at him is like looking at a giant. "Isn't that what you told me?" The words come out sharper than intended, laced with ironic amusement. Our eyes lock, his filled with anger and concern, mine with defiance and confusion.

"Don't push me, bunny. You won't like how this ends."

"Why don't you just leave me alone?" I snap, frustration bubbling over. His presence is suffocating, yet there's an undeniable magnetic pull between us.

"Not until you give me a damn good reason why you're here," he retorts, stepping closer. The heat radiates off him, mingling with the surrounding chaos. His proximity sends a shiver down my spine. It's fear and...something else.

Unfortunately for me, I think I'll always have a physical reaction to Jeremiah Blackwood. Even with the anger I feel toward him, my body wants to sway closer to him. I want to seek comfort in his warmth. I want to be wrapped in his hoodie and trapped in his big, dumb football arms. I want to use him as an anchor.

I can't afford to let him get in my head again. It's a slippery slope and I'm already on the edge of sliding. I did that once before, trusting him without question, and look where that got me.

"I'm here to prove to myself that I can handle it." I say, my voice barely above a whisper. "It's therapy," I blurt out before I can stop myself and then instantly regret it, but unfortunately for me, I can't shove the words back into my mouth.

"Therapy," he repeats, almost mockingly. I can feel his breath on my skin, each word he speaks vibrating in the air between us. "Does this therapy of yours involve getting drunk and reckless again?"

"Fuck you, Jeremiah," I spit out, though my voice wavers. The intensity in his eyes is unbearable, and yet, I can't look away. "Go away, Jeremiah Blackwood. I don't need you to save me anymore and I've more than proved that to you and anyone else who cares. You're embarrassing both of us."

"You want to see embarrassing?" he says, his voice dropping lower, almost a growl. The raw emotion in his words makes my heart skip a beat. "I can make a real spectacle right now and you'll be the star of the show. You must not remember the way I fucking threw you over my shoulder and carried you out of the last party. Your entire ass was almost on display as you beat your tiny little fists into me. Thanks for the lower back massage, by the way, bunny."

"Why are you doing this?" I challenge, taking a step closer, our faces inches apart as he bends down to get in my face. The tension is heady, the air thick with unspoken words and unfulfilled desires.

"Because you're mine to protect," he whispers, his hand brushing against my arm, sending jolts of electricity through me. The possessiveness in his claim should infuriate me, but instead, it ignites a fire deep within. I know he doesn't mean it the way it sounds. I know that he feels some kind of duty to protect me because I'm Royce's baby sister, but the way he says I'm his makes me wish he meant it a different way. On a deeper level. He was all I wanted back then.

I'm a stupid, stupid girl for that.

"You're free, Jeremiah. I don't expect anything from you. Let me be," I manage to say, though my voice betrays me. The line between anger and desire blurs dangerously as we stand there, locked in a battle of wills.

"That's not happening," he concedes, leaning in closer. The world around us fades. The only thing that matters is the space between our lips, shrinking by the second. I almost think he's going to kiss me until he grins at me and says, "If you're staying, I'm staying. It's as simple as that. Unless you want me to throw you over my shoulder and carry you out like I did last time? Your choice, but I'll never say no to getting to be a caveman when it comes to you, Oak."

"Oh, how gallant of you to give little old me options." My voice conveys my annoyance, but my body betrays my mind as it leans into his touch as his fingers find the back of my neck. The smell of his cologne mixed with the possessive way he's holding me, his fingers flexing into my skin is intoxicating.

"Yeah," he murmurs, his lips ghosting over mine, teasing, taunting, but not touching. The anticipation is maddening, the forbidden feeling of this connection crackling in the air.

"I'm not the same girl you left behind, Jeremiah," I challenge, my breath hitching as his hands leave my neck and find their way to my waist, pulling me even closer.

His jaw tightens, but he doesn't back off. Instead, he steps even closer, so close that I can feel the heat radiating from his body. Like a starfish clinging to a rock, he attaches himself to me, his presence a protective barrier against the partygoers who glance our way. Any closer and we might as well crawl into each other's clothes.

"You're not staying," he insists, his gaze darting around the room as if daring anyone to come near me. His rigid posture and brooding demeanor make it clear he's not going to let this go easily.

"Watch me," I challenge, crossing my arms defiantly.

"Oakley," he warns, his voice softer yet filled with a

tension that sends shivers down my spine. "This isn't a game. Any one of these assholes could slip you something again."

"You're insane," I manage to choke out, my mind reeling from the intensity of his claim. The air around us crackles because for once I'm not following Jeremiah like a little lost puppy.

"Maybe," he admits, his lips curving into a dark smile. "Everyone in this building will see how insane I really am if something happens to you, bunny. So do them a favor and let me take you back to your dorm."

"Just forget about me. It's easy to do," I snap, trying to regain control as I step back putting some distance between us. But the truth is, his words stir something deep inside me—a mixture of fear and reluctant longing. I hate how he makes me feel, how he breaks down my walls with just a few words.

"Never," he murmurs, his eyes burning into mine as his fingers move around to the front of my throat, squeezing tentatively as if he's testing out both of our strengths. Fingertips gently tap on either side of my neck, and I'm caught in his trap. He's not hurting me, not even trying to, but the fact remains he could. Maybe I want him to, maybe I want what so many others have talked about.

The whispers about what he likes, what his brothers like have never been quiet. Not even in high school.

"You're sick," I say, though my voice lacks conviction. His presence is overpowering, and despite my anger, a twisted part of me finds solace in it.

"Only for you." His confession hangs heavy in the air, shrouded in the shadows that surround us. The night is far from over, and as much as I hate to admit it, I'm drawn into the darkness he offers.

"You're not ruining this for me," I repeat, my resolve

faltering. But he just smiles, knowing he's already won this round.

"We'll see about that," he says, his voice a low rumble that sends chills down my spine. The game between us continues, each move more perilous than the last. And though I hate myself for it, I can't help but be intrigued by his newfound obsession with pestering me. It's everything I ever wanted before he ruined everything.

"Back off, Jere," I hiss, trying to put some metaphorical distance between us, but he doesn't budge. His eyes lock onto mine, pupils dilated, and it's like a magnetic pull drags us closer.

"Make me, and don't call me fucking Jere. My brothers call me Jere. To you, bunny, you can call me anything but that," he taunts, stepping forward, invading my space again, his breath warm against my cheek. I don't feel threatened like I do with other men. Instead, my heart pounds in my chest, echoing the heavy bass of the music around us. It's like he takes over all of my senses. He's all I see, and his scent invades my nostrils, reminding me of a time when all I wanted was to breathe him in. Have him settle in my lungs since he already took up residence in my heart. The music and sounds of laughter mingled with murmured conversations fade into the background.

"Why do you always have to—" My words cut off as his hand snakes around my waist, fingers pressing into my lower back possessively. The heat of his touch seeps through the thin fabric of my frilly dress that makes me stick out like a sore thumb, igniting a fire in my veins. Jeremiah always liked my style back when we were friends, or whatever it was we were. The more lace, bows, and soft fabrics I wore, the more he complimented me. I can tell by the way his fingers are soothing down my side that not much has changed in that department.

"Stop asking questions you're not ready for me to answer," he whispers, leaning in so close that our lips are mere inches apart. His other hand cups my face, and the metal of his Blackwood ring is cool against my skin. His thumb brushes over my cheekbone with a gentleness that contradicts the intensity in his eyes. "I protect what's mine, and that's all you need to know."

"Jeremiah..." I breathe his name, feeling the electric tension crackle between us. My anger melts away, replaced by a confusing blend of desire and fear. I should push him away, but it feels impossible because I'm leaning into his touch instead.

"That's not what you want to call me," he says, his voice a seductive murmur. "Say it."

"Never," I manage to choke out, even as my pulse races and my skin tingles under his touch. But the defiance in my voice wavers, and he knows it.

"I think you will. I think in your head you still call me pretty boy when your lips speak my full name. If you're so infuriated and want me to leave you alone, why aren't you pushing me away right now?" he challenges, his lips ghosting over mine, sending shivers down my spine. His hands tighten their grip, pulling me flush against his body. The sensation is overwhelming. It's such a dangerous combination of comfort and excitement that I have not been lucky enough to experience for two years. I've fucking missed it and I hate that I'm admitting to myself that really, it's Jeremiah Blackwood that I've missed more than anything. Even more than my brother. What kind of sister does that make me?

"Because..." I start, but the words die on my lips. I don't

have an answer, and he knows it. His presence is intoxicating, drowning out my doubts and fears. In his arms, the chaos of the years fades away, and my mind goes quiet for the first time in just as long.

"Relax," he presses, his breath hot against my skin. "I'm here now."

Now.

But not when I needed him and that slaps me back to the present.

"Stop acting like you have me, that you own me," I hiss, my voice sounds barely audible over the whooshing sound of my blood in my ears. People whirl around us in a dizzying blur, but it's like we're in our own bubble. Jeremiah's grip tightens on my arm—an unspoken promise, or perhaps a threat, knowing him. He was always kind to me before, but I was agreeable back then. I was so star-struck with my big brother's best friend that I would have done anything he wanted.

"You're Blackwood property, bunny," he counters, his eyes smoldering with that infuriating arrogance and something darker, something more primal. "The sooner you realize that the easier it'll be for both of us."

"You're impossible," I snap, yanking my arm free. But even as I pull away, a part of me aches for his touch. His possessiveness is suffocating, yet there's an undeniable magnetism to it. My heart pounds, caught between wanting to flee and wanting to stay wrapped up in him. I don't want to admit the thrill that ran through me hearing him call me Blackwood property. I shouldn't want that, shouldn't be turned on by it. Women aren't property, but in his world being marked by them means something. They're a bunch of neanderthals, but gosh the way they have each other's backs is something I've never seen with anyone else.

"Am I?" He steps closer, closing the distance between us once more. His breath is hot against my ear, sending shivers down my spine. "Tell me you don't feel this connection, this... inevitability. Just submit."

"You're so full of yourself," I manage, though my voice wavers. Of course he is. He's a Blackwood. They're all insufferable unless you're unlucky enough to fall in love with one of them. Damn him. He knows exactly how to get under my skin, to make me question everything.

We just stare at each other, no more words being said as we silently battle with just our eyes, and our touch as the world goes on around us. Bodies press in from all sides, but it's Jeremiah's presence that feels most suffocating. Some random frat guy bumps into me roughly and I swear I hear him growl as he swiftly shoves the guy out of the way and knocks him down to the ground in one sweeping motion. "I'll fucking kill you if you bump into her again. Watch where you're walking," Jeremiah's voice is tinged with a darkness that I've never heard from him. His hand grips mine, leading us through the throng like he owns me, and I follow. Just like the way I used to. So maybe he actually does.

"That was an accident. You didn't have to throw him on the floor like a rag doll. Where are we going?" I ask, trying to keep the edge out of my voice. It's difficult when every fiber of my being is screaming for clarity, for understanding.

"Somewhere quieter," he responds, his tone leaving no room for argument. His grip tightens, as if sensing my hesitation. "And for the record, he's lucky I didn't take his head off for touching you." Jeremiah's smoldering gazes locks me in place as he looks over his shoulder at me. He looks absolutely murderous and something inside me unfurls. I press my thighs together, needing the friction that I really want from Jeremiah. He's the only man I've ever fantasized about, and I still wake up dreaming about him despite how scared I am of touch.

We push through a side door, emerging into a dimly lit hallway. The scent of alcohol and sweat fades, replaced by a musty, almost forgotten smell of old wood and aged wallpaper. I'm not sure why there's a secret hallway in this house. My head spins with the sudden change.

"You have two choices. I can either follow you around, stuck to you like a fucking shadow tonight," he whispers, his mouth brushing against my ear. "Or I take you home right now."

"I..." My words falter, lost in the haze of desire and fear. I can't deny the pull between us, the magnetic force that keeps drawing me back to him. "Fine. You can *accompany* me, but no more punching people," I finally agree, the truth burning on my tongue.

"Good girl," he purrs, his lips turning up into what can only be described as a Blackwood grin. "And I didn't punch him. But keep giving me ideas. I'll fuck him up."

CHAPTER 8

JEREMIAH

I crack my neck and roll my shoulders, trying to relieve some of the tiredness and stress from my body after being out late babysitting Oakley at that damn party. It's been two weeks since she's been back in my life, and she's all I see now. Awake, asleep, it doesn't matter. Everything is Oakley Ashford.

The smell of sweat and anticipation fills the visitor locker room, and I can almost taste the energy crackling in the air as my teammates buzz around me. We're getting ready to face our archrivals, St. Vincent's, and tonight's game promises to be a brutal one. The noise is deafening. Guys are hyped up, yelling and smacking pads.

"Yo, check out this chick!" Zeke, one of the receivers, holds up his phone. "Been watching her cam shows all week. Took these screenshots last night."

A few of the guys crowd around for a look. I ignore them, focusing on taping my fingers. Don't need the distraction.

"She's some cam girl, but she's got this mysterious vibe,

always wearing masks and shit. Drives me wild because she doesn't actually show anything."

"Let me see that." Jameson snatches the phone. He whistles low. "Definitely has that fairy princess vibe going on. You tap that yet?"

"Nah man, building the anticipation, you know? She keeps things anonymous, no names. Makes it hotter, but I'm gonna get her under me soon. I just need to convince her to let me fly her out to St. Charles." Zeke grins like the cocky bastard he is.

The surrounding circle grows tighter as they crane their necks for a glimpse.

"Ease up, you'll drool on my phone," he jokes, tilting the screen just enough to tease them. "She's like a drug, ya know? The less you see, the more you want."

"Sounds like a pain in the ass," I mutter, my focus drifting from the knotted tape on my wrists to my teammates salivating over some internet girl.

"Ah, come on, Jere," a lineman chides, clapping me on the back hard enough to make me stagger. "You telling me you wouldn't wanna unwrap that present?"

"Didn't say that," I shoot back, my tone clipped. "Just not into chasing ghosts."

"Suit yourself, bro," Zeke chuckles. "More for the rest of us, then."

I roll my eyes and slam my locker shut. I just lied through my damn teeth. All I do is chase ghosts. Well ghost, singular because it's only the one that's got me all twisted up. The last thing I need is Zeke's sexcapades invading my headspace before a big rivalry game. I need to be focused, ready to shut down their offense.

"Hey eighty-seven, c'mon just check her out for yourself!" he calls out as he strides closer to me.

"Fuck off," I mutter, not even bothering to look up from my cleats. He ignores my dismissal and shoves his phone in my face, eager to share his latest interest. Apparently, fuck off and I ain't interested, don't comprehend in his thick ass skull. We have a fucking game, but I can help him weed through the cobwebs occupying his fucking brain afterward.

"Look at her, man." He grins, swiping through the photos of a girl wearing a bunny mask, her eyes hidden behind dark shadows. Her lips are painted a deep red, and she oozes sensuality in a way that would make any man weak at the knees. She's dressed simply, in a blue skirt and white top.

"Where'd you find her?" I ask, feeling a strange mix of curiosity and unease that I can't quite put my finger on. Something about her draws me in, and I can't help but stare at the screen, captivated by her allure.

"Found her on the Starlet Streams site," Zeke says, still grinning like a cat that caught the canary. "Makes you wonder what she's hiding under that mask, doesn't it?"

My chest tightens as I scrutinize the photos, searching for any clue that could reveal her identity. There's something about her. The curve of her neck, the arch of her brow—that feels achingly familiar. But it can't be her. It just can't.

"Get that shit out of my face," I snap, shoving my teammates' phone away as I force myself to refocus on the game. Tonight is about one thing and one thing only, kicking St. Vincent's asses all the way back to their campus. And I won't let anything stand in the way of that goal.

I try to block out the noise and chatter, the image of that girl in the mask. But something about it niggles at my mind.

Zeke is still talking shit, walking around showing everyone those pics.

Against my better judgment, I let myself look them over

again. I'm unable to shake the feeling churning in my stomach. The moment I zero in the photos, really looking at them, it feels like I've been punched in the gut. I fucking know that beauty mark on the left side of her collarbone. Oakley, wearing a bunny mask that barely conceals her bright blue eyes, staring back at the screen.

"Fuck!" I roar, snatching the phone and smashing it against the cold concrete floor. The shattered pieces scatter across the ground. I grab Zeke by the collar, slamming him into a row of lockers with a crash. "The girl, what's her fucking name?!"

"Hey! What the hell is your problem, Jeremiah?" he gasps, clutching at my iron grip on his shirt. His eyes are wide with fear, but I don't care. All I can think about is Oakley, my sweet, innocent Oakley, parading around like a piece of meat for men to ogle at.

"Answer me, you piece of shit! What. Is. Her. Name?" My voice is deadly, and I see everyone except my brothers take a step back. They're all staring at me now, but I barely register their presence. My rage is blotting out everything else.

"Christ, man! It's fucking VelvetVix! She's just some chick with a cam and an account. Everyone's talking about her," Zeke stammers, his earlier bravado evaporating under the glare of my wrath.

My heart hammers in my chest, pounding harder than the anger coursing through my veins. Oakley, my Oakley, reduced to this? The thought makes me want to tear someone apart. I push him away from me with a violent shove that sends him sprawling across the floor.

"Stay away from her," I growl, my voice a low, dangerous rumble that echoes through the locker room like a warning shot. "If I ever see you or anyone else looking at those pictures again, I'll fucking end you. Do you understand?"

Zeke nods frantically, his face pale beneath the overhead lights. Good. Let him be afraid. Let them all be afraid. Because I'll be damned if I let anyone touch Oakley. Not while there's still breath in my body and rage burning in my soul. He's not bucking back, but I feel the need to add, "Oakley belongs to me. If I hear you talk about her, or even fucking look at her for too long and I'll break your kneecaps. This is your one and only warning."

I move to walk away from everyone in the locker room when a shoulder slams into mine, sending me stumbling sideways. Heat flares in my chest, ready to unleash on whoever was stupid enough to do that, but it's Graham's familiar scowl that greets me.

"Jesus fuck, Jeremiah! You trying to get kicked out of the game before we even play?" he snaps, muscles tense judging but the grinding of his teeth I hear.

"Back off, Graham," I growl, clenching and unclenching my fists, trying to leash the anger boiling in my veins. But all of it is in vain because it doesn't abate, only shifts targets.

"Talk to me," he insists, stepping in front of me to block my path. "You're not usually like this. What's going on?"

"It's Oakley," I admit, the words tasting like poison on my tongue.

"Oakley?" His brow furrows, confusion etched across his face. "What about her?"

"Photos," I spit out, "The chick on Zeke's phone. It's Oakley on a damn website in a bunny mask. Dammit, Graham, what the fuck is going on?"

"Shit." He runs a hand through his hair, piecing it

together. "Alright, let's deal with this rationally. Going all Hulk on everyone isn't going to help her."

"No." The word is a sharp blade.

"Okay, okay." Graham holds up his hands. "Let's think this through. You go full Hulk, and what? Coach benches you, maybe worse. Then what good are you to anyone else?"

"Fuck." I scrub a hand down my face. It's annoying as fuck when someone else is the logical one in this family. "I know, I know."

"Listen," he says, his tone shifting, "we'll sort this out. But right now, you need to get yourself together. We've got a game to win."

"Did not have me being irrational on today's bingo card," I snort, but the sarcasm fades as I meet his steady gaze.

"Thanks," I mutter, the gratitude genuine despite everything churning inside of me.

"Anytime," he replies, clapping me on the shoulder roughly. "Now let's show St. Vincent's who they're messing with."

We turn back toward the sounds of the locker room, the feel of anticipation thick in the air.

A sudden burst of laughter cuts through the tension in the locker room, and my head snaps up to see Penn grinning as he leans against a row of lockers. "Well, well," he drawls, his eyes flicking between Graham and me. "This is fucking great. Looks like Linc's fucking his sister and your little bunny is a stripper. I really need to start carrying popcorn around with me everywhere. There's always a fucking show."

"Shut the fuck up, Penn," I snarl, my fists clenching at my sides. His answering laugh is a jagged thing, cutting into me deeply. He's fucking unhinged, psychotic more than any of us, just how Dad wanted it. I don't know what he saw in my brother that he didn't in the rest of us, but when Penn fixates on something, there's no drawing his attention elsewhere.

I can taste the anger, bitter and metallic on my tongue.

"No need to get all worked up." Penn smirks, raising his hands defensively. "Just stating the obvious. I mean or do and take that shit out on St. Vincent's so we can shut them out."

"Enough!"

"Aw, come on, Jere. Can't take a joke?" He chuckles, and the sound grates against my skull.

"Joke?" I spit back, sarcasm dripping from every syllable. "You think this is funny?"

"Lighten up, brother," he says, his eyes glinting with mischief that only serves to fuel my scorn. "Just some locker room talk, right?"

"Locker room talk," I echo hollowly, my heartbeat pounding in my ears like it's trying to escape. "Stay the hell away from Oakley."

"Or what?" he challenges, eyebrows raised in mock surprise. "You'll break another phone? Damn, baby bro, you've got it bad."

"Enough, Penn," Graham interjects, but his words are distant, drowned out by the roaring in my head.

"She's off-limits," I mutter under my breath, forcing my hands to uncurl from fists.

"Off-limits, huh?" Penn says, smirking. "That's not really our style, is it?"

"Fuck off," I say, my voice low and lethal. The locker room is a pressure cooker, and I'm the steam screaming for release. I can smell the sweat and testosterone, the sharp tang of determination, and beneath it all, that dark, musky scent of rivalry that makes me want to claim what's mine.

"Watch yourself, brother," Penn says lightly, but there's a warning there, one I'm too pissed to heed.

"Keep pushing me," I warn, my tone promising retribution. "See what happens."

"E-fucking-nough. Penn, stop instigating shit for once in your goddamn life," Graham cuts in, his voice hard and annoyed. "We have a game to win."

"Right," I say, though it comes out more like a snarl.

"Jeremiah, you need to calm down before you do something you'll regret," Graham cautions, stepping in front of me to block my view of Penn's infuriating smirk. My chest heaves with ragged breaths, and I try to force my racing thoughts into submission.

"Fuck, this is hard," I mutter under my breath, my hands shaking with the effort it takes to restrain myself. I hate feeling this powerless, this out of control. But I can't let my emotions dictate my actions.

I force myself to take a deep breath. Graham's right. I can't let this situation spiral out of control. But damn, if it doesn't feel like everything is slipping through my fingers.

"Since when did you become so damn possessive over little Ashford?" Penn sneers from across the bench, his eyes narrowed.

"Fuck you," I snap, my teeth gritted. "You don't know anything about what happened between us."

"Neither do you, apparently," he shoots back, a smug grin playing on his lips.

"Enough," Linc cuts in, his voice cold and commanding. "This isn't helping anyone."

"Let's go do this shit," Graham says, clapping me on the shoulder, pulling me back from the edge and nudging me toward the door that leads to the field tunnel.

"Let's fucking do this," I echo, channeling all the chaos into something fierce, something that will help us crush St. Vincent's under our cleats.

The game's about to start, and I'm supposed to focus, but how can I when my mind is a battle zone?

"JB! Your head in the game?" Coach barks, snapping me back to the present.

"Always," I lie through gritted teeth. The whistle blows, and with it, I'm thrust into the tunnel, ready to kill someone on the field.

CHAPTER 9
OAKLEY

My room is a sanctuary of dim, comforting light. The hallway outside is quiet, as everyone is at the game tonight. This campus breathes sports and right now football is center stage. At least I know Jeremiah is there and I don't have to glance over my shoulder, wondering when he's going to come in and ruin my day.

A soft breeze flutters the sheer curtains, casting playful shadows on the walls. My heart beats in sync with the ticking clock as I prepare for tonight's cam session. The bunny mask rests in my hands, its smooth surface cool against my skin. Like a shield, a barrier between me and the world that allows me to become someone else—someone free.

I slip it on, feeling the familiar weight settle over my face, and take a deep breath. Tonight's outfit is a blend of innocence and allure: a pastel pink dress that barely reaches my thighs, paired with white knee-high socks. Cute, yet tantalizing. Perfect. I feel sexy. I feel powerful.

And the best part is that Jeremiah would drool over my outfit.

"Now or never," I murmur to myself, adjusting the camera. "Let's give them a show."

The screen lights up with notifications as I go live. Familiar names pop up in the chat, mingling with new ones. I smile, letting the thrill of anonymity wash over me. Here, I am in control.

Hey, Bunny! Looking cute tonight

One user types.

"Thank you, darling," I reply, hoping my voice sounds sweet and inviting. The banter begins, light and playful, just as I like it.

Hey Vix, what's your favorite guilty pleasure movie?

Another viewer asks, his username appearing brightly in the chat box.

"Definitely Twilight," I reply, grinning. "I feel like that shouldn't surprise anyone. It's all of ours and you all know it." I leave out the part about how Jeremiah used to make a big deal about how he didn't want to be roped into watching a chick movie, but would hum the songs in my ear while we cuddled.

Vix, what do you love most about college life?

Someone inquires, and judging by all the emojis, I think he's eager for my response.

"Probably the campus," I muse, my mind wandering back to the gothic architecture that envelops St. Charles. "It's beautiful, especially at sunset, when the light hits the buildings just right. It feels like stepping into a different world."

Tell us a secret

A daring fan prompts, and I can't help but chuckle at the request. I pause for a moment, considering my options before deciding to play along.

"Alright, here's a little secret," I say, leaning closer to the camera, my voice hushed and conspiratorial. "I've had a crush on my brother's best friend since I was a teenager. He's always been forbidden to me. But let's keep that between us, shall we?"

If you could have dinner with anyone dead or alive, who would it be?

Another chatter asks, clearly intrigued by my responses thus far.

"Easy," I reply, grinning mischievously. "Harry Styles. He's my number one childhood crush."

The chat box comes alive with a flurry of activity, usernames and messages flashing across the screen in rapid succession talking about their favorite movies and their dream dinner dates. It's like watching a field of fireflies light up the night, each one vying for my attention. I can't help but feel a thrill at their eagerness—it's intoxicating.

Pretty bunny girl, what's your favorite ice cream flavor?

One particularly enthusiastic fan asks, his username standing out among the rest because it's bunnygirllover09. I can't help but snicker at that choice.

"Ah," I say, feigning deep thought as I narrow my eyes playfully. "That would be a tie between dark chocolate raspberry truffle and salted caramel bourbon." I lick my lips, imagining the taste, and laugh softly. "Clearly, I have a sweet tooth."

A new message pops up, this time from a different fan, ClarkKent1968.

> If you were a superhero, what would your superpower be?

"Interesting question!" I exclaim, tapping my chin thoughtfully. "I think I'd want the power to manipulate time. Just imagine all the books I could read, the places I could visit, and the moments I could savor without ever running out of time." I pause for effect, then add with a smirk, "Not to mention, I could make some people's lives very...interesting."

My words seem to ignite something within the chat, the fans responding with laughter and playful teasing amongst themselves.

As the questions continue to roll in, I find myself becoming more and more immersed in the world I've created, this digital stage where I am both the star and the puppet master. It's a heady combination of power and vulnerability that leaves me feeling alive, electric even.

A new message catches my eye.

> What's the most daring thing you've ever done?

An impish grin spreads across my face as a memory resurfaces. "Well," I begin, leaning in conspiratorially toward the camera, "it involves a senior prank and a stolen motorcycle."

The chat erupts into a frenzy of speculation and excitement; the fans clamoring for more details, but like any good performer, I know when to leave them wanting more.

A question catches my eye, and a mischievousness zips through me. I'm genuinely having fun tonight because they're keeping it fun instead of asking me what color underwear I have on.

> If you could travel to any era in history, where would you go?

I lean back in my chair, twirling a strand of golden hair around my finger as I ponder the possibilities. "Hmm, I think I'd have to say...the Roaring Twenties. A time of jazz, flappers, and breaking free from societal constraints. Plus, who wouldn't want to dance the Charleston in a fabulous beaded dress?"

I savor the thrill of controlling the narrative. In this digital realm, I am no longer Oakley Ashford, the soft-spoken girl with a haunted past. I am a seductive enchantress, wielding her power with grace and wit, leaving all who cross her path helpless to resist her charms.

Is this my villain origin story?

One fan writes, his username pulsing at the edge of the screen.

> What's your idea of the perfect date in the Roaring Twenties?

"Hmm, the perfect date," I murmur, tapping my chin and letting my eyes flutter closed for a moment as I envision the scene. "It would begin at a hidden speakeasy tucked away behind a secret door, where we would sip illicit cocktails and listen to the sultry sounds of a live band." My voice grows husky as I continue, my words painting a vivid picture for my captivated audience. "As the night wore on, we'd find ourselves on a deserted rooftop garden, lit only by the glow of a thousand candles, where we'd share our deepest secrets and desires beneath the watchful gaze of the moon."

The guys must like that one because their comments are racing by in a blur of longing and envy. I can feel their desire to be part of my world, to experience the intoxicating blend of passion and danger that permeates every moment of my life.

Then, a new message catches my eye.

> Do you always wear that same perfume?

My fingers hesitate over the keyboard. The question feels off. Intimate. I glance at the username—a string of random letters and numbers, unfamiliar yet unsettlingly so. Before I can spin out of control, the viewer adds.

> Most women have a signature scent. What is yours? I'd love to send you some.

Relief floods me and I reply in what I hope is a breezy manner, "I switch it up." I try to keep the shakiness out of my voice. I need to maintain control and not let a small misunderstanding send me over the edge into a spiral.

> Is your bedroom always tidy?

Another message from the same user. My pulse quickens. How do they know that? My chat is going fast, but this person's messages are the only ones I'm hyper-focusing on.

Ever thought about streaming without the mask? Your face is stunning. Why hide it from me?

The words feel like a punch to the gut. I've blocked this person before. I'm almost certain that this is the guy who was pushy during my last show, asking for a private chat room.

"Who are you, 3u//y1ovr?" I ask, keeping my tone casual despite the unease gnawing at me. The chat continues to scroll, other users oblivious to my rising discomfort.

Just an admirer. Do you feel close to me? Like you know me well?

The response sends a chill down my spine.

"That's enough," I say aloud, moving the cursor to block the user. But in that moment, an ear-splitting bang reverberates through the room. A crash shatters the silence. My heart jumps into my throat as the door flies open.

"Jeremiah?" I barely whisper his name. My eyes widen as he storms in, and I'm gripping my laptop like it's a weapon. His face is twisted with rage—raw, unfiltered anger.

"A cam girl? Are you fucking serious right now?" Jeremiah's voice booms, filling every corner of the room. He snatches the laptop and hurls it across the room. It smashes against the wall, fragments flying everywhere. The sound of it breaking echoes in my ears, mixing with the pounding of my heart.

"Jeremiah Blackwood, what the hell?" My voice shakes, but there's steel beneath the shock. "What are you doing?"

"Stripping for strangers on the internet? Really, Oakley?" His eyes burn with accusation. He advances toward me, and I instinctively step back, my bunny mask feeling suddenly ridiculous and useless.

"That's not—" I start, but he's already towering over me. A giant hulking mass that is eclipsing me. His presence is suffocating, his rage palpable.

"Don't lie to me!" he shouts. His hands grip my shoulders, shaking me slightly. "I saw the photos being passed around the locker room. I know what you've been doing."

"You're being a judgmental prick right now. It's not what you think it is. It's not sexual."

"Then explain why you're prancing around in that bunny mask?" He gestures wildly at the mask that is still covering my eyes and nose. "You don't think every guy in that chat isn't thinking about you naked and the things—" Jeremiah goes silent like his brain is short circuiting. "I will kill every fucking one of them."

My breath hitches in my chest when he gently slips the mask off of my face and tosses it on the floor on top of my shattered laptop. Before I can speak, Jeremiah is cupping my face in his large palm.

"Let go of me!" I snap, trying to wrench free from his grasp. But his hold tightens. His green eyes, usually so thoughtful, are now wild with something dark and possessive.

"How long?" His voice drops, becoming dangerously quiet. "Do you touch yourself for those bastards? Answer me!" He's well past the border of psychotic behavior at this point, and yet I'm not scared of him.

"None of your business," I spit back, defiant despite the fear coursing through me. "You had no right to break in here and destroy my stuff! I'm not doing what you think I'm doing. Even if I was..." I poke his massive chest with my index finger, "...I don't have to answer to you. I don't care what you think of me anymore." That last part is a boldface lie.

"Your stuff?" He laughs bitterly, conveniently latching onto only one thing I said. "Is that all you care about? Your damn laptop?"

"Better than accusing people of things they're not doing," I retort. My gaze locks with his, electricity arcing between us. His grip loosens just a fraction, enough for me to step back but not escape the intensity of his presence.

"You don't get it, do you?" he murmurs, almost to himself. "I don't want anyone else looking at..." Jeremiah stops, gesturing his hands up and down my body. His jaw flexes as he takes in my short dress and white knee-high socks. I can see the possessive heat rising in his face.

"I don't really care what you want," I counter, my voice rising. "You think smashing my computer and barging in here is protecting me? You're out of your mind, Jeremiah. Get out of my room."

He takes a step closer, closing the distance. His breath is hot on my face when he confesses, "I'm not going anywhere until you do give a fuck what I think. I'm not trying to hurt you, bunny." It's only on the last word that his tone softens and he sounds like the Jeremiah that I used to know.

He's invading my space with his towering frame. His green eyes blaze with anger and hurt. "Not that I owe you an explanation, but I went through some stuff and I'm trying to work through it. Just because you aren't hurting me doesn't mean no one has."

"Who? I want a name," he growls, his breath hot against my face. "I'm not playing twenty questions, bunny. Who was it?" He doesn't bother asking me what the person did and by the look in his eyes, I don't think it would matter if I said the guy breathed in my direction. He's off the rails.

CHAPTER 10
JEREMIAH

My chest is heaving, and a small ache resides in my gut and in my fucking leg from kicking this goddamn door in without any boots on. Sneakers don't really give you the support you need. And then my girl opens her mouth and I know whatever comes out next will set me into a spiral.

"Someone put hands on me before," Oakley spits out, her voice trembling but defiant. The words hang in the air, sharp and jagged, slicing through the tension between us.

"Wait, what? What do you mean someone put hands on you?" My voice drops, anger and concern fighting for dominance. I take a step closer, trying to catch her eyes, but she turns her head away. "Who fucking touched you, Oakley?"

"Back again to play the hero?" There's so much anger in her tone, so out of place with the softness of her usual speech, it stings. "You weren't here when I needed you."

"Fuck," I mutter under my breath. Confusion and frustration swirl in my gut. "I didn't know—I would've been there."

Her eyes flash with pain, tears threatening to spill over.

She's shaking, her usual composure shattered. "You don't get it, Jeremiah. You left me, remember? Royce left me. No one was there."

"Oakley, look at me." I reach out, gently placing my hands on her arms, feeling the tremor in her body. "Tell me who did this. I need to know."

Her gaze finally meets mine, a storm of emotions swirling in those crystal blue depths. "I don't know who it was. He came out of nowhere, took me by surprise." Her voice breaks, barely more than a whisper.

"Fuck," I mutter under my breath, frustration and rage boiling inside me. "I need to know what that bastard did to you. I won't rest until I make him pay." My grip tightens slightly, full of protectiveness and desperation.

"Sure, Jeremiah," she scoffs, pushing back a lock of hair with a hand that's too steady for the rest of her trembling form. "Just like you and Royce used to protect me? Just how easy was it to push me to the back of your mind?"

The accusation hits like a physical blow, and I feel my face contort into a snarl. "That was different, Oakley. This—" I gesture vaguely at the setup around her, "isn't you."

"Isn't me?" Her laugh is hollow, devoid of humor. "And what do you know about me, huh? Since when do you care?"

"Since always," I snap back, anger and concern warring for dominance inside me. "Since before your brother decided I was the enemy."

Her blue eyes flash, nothing but storms brewing in their depths. "You left me alone, Jeremiah. All alone."

The air between us crackles, heavy with unsaid words and pent-up emotions. I fight the urge to reach out, to pull her away from this dark spiral, but I know if I touch her right now, without permission even just to wrap her in my arms it will set her off. Not after everything. Not right now.

"Oakley," I say, and my voice is raw, stripped of any pretense. "Talk to me."

She turns her head away, and I can almost hear the walls slamming up around her. But I'm not going anywhere—not this time.

"Jeremiah, let it go," she pleads, but there's no way I can. Not after hearing this.

"Not happening, Oakley. Not when someone hurt you."

Oakley's eyes well up with tears, her vulnerability on full display. She looks at me and I see the pain etched in every line of her face. "You left me. My brother left me. No one was there to protect me!" Her voice cracks, raw emotion spilling out. "Now I'm fucking broken and trying to put the pieces back together, and all you're doing is making it that much harder."

Her words hit me like a punch to the gut. I never wanted to abandon her. I never intended for her to feel so alone. Guilt gnaws at my insides as I take a step closer, reaching out to gently place my hands on her arms. She's trembling beneath my touch, but I need her to understand that I'm here now.

"Freaking fine, just to get you to stop nagging me," she whispers, finally agreeing to something. The room falls silent save for our ragged breaths, the weight of her unspoken pain hanging thick in the air between us.

I perch on the edge of a chair I dragged to sit right in front of her on the bed, my eyes fixed on Oakley's hunched figure. Fear seems to cling to the walls of her cramped room.

"Jeremiah, you don't get it," she chokes out, her voice brittle like thin ice. "Every day, it's...it's like I'm clawing my way through dirt just to breathe, just to feel something other than..." Her words trail off into a sob, and her hands flutter to her face, fingers trembling.

"Oakley," I start, voice low, desperately trying to bridge the gap between us. My skin itches to touch her. I reach out, my fingertips barely grazing the soft flesh of her arm. She flinches away from me as if scorched, her eyes darting up, twin pools of liquid pain.

"Please, don't," she whispers, wrapping her arms around herself like a shield. Her shoulders shake, and I can almost taste the salt from her tears in the back of my throat.

"Damn it, bunny." The words are a growl, torn from somewhere deep inside me. I ball my hands into fists, fighting against the urge to pull her into my arms, to erase every foul thing that's touched her. "I want to help you. Let me help you."

Her laugh is a sharp crack in the stillness, bitter and jagged. "Help me?" There's an edge to her voice that could draw blood. "What can you do, Jeremiah? Can you unmake the past? Can you—"

"Stop it." My voice cuts through the tension, hard and final. "Don't fucking push me away."

She bites down on her bottom lip, and for a heart-stopping moment, I think she might actually reach out to me, let me in. But then she's moving, scooting back into her pillows, putting more space between us. She's not even two years younger than me, but right here she looks so small and defeated. I've never seen her look this way before and it makes me want to burn the world down, starting with her fucking brother. I don't care what shit happened between us, how fucking dare he abandon her.

"Oakley, look at me," I demand, determination burning in

my eyes. "Tell me anything you can remember about who did this. I won't let them get away with it."

She hesitates, her gaze dropping to the comforter as if the weight of the world rests on her shoulders. The silence stretches between us, heavy and suffocating. Finally, she lifts her head, her eyes meeting mine full of fear.

"Why does it matter?" she whispers, her voice barely audible. "You're just going to leave again. And then where will I be? I need to take care of myself."

"That's not true," I counter, tightening my grip slightly to keep her from pulling away. "I'm not going anywhere, Oakley. Not until I make sure you're safe."

"Safe?" she scoffs, bitterness lacing her tone. "There's no such thing as safe anymore."

"Then I'll create it for you," I insist, my voice firm. "But I can't do that unless you help me figure out who hurt you." I pace back and forth before finally stopping.

"Oakley." I utter, my own need raw and demanding. "Look at me. Please."

For a long second, there's nothing but the sound of our breathing, ragged and uneven. There's a haunted look in her eyes that makes my chest ache, makes me want to tear down the whole damn world to make her whole again.

"Rem," she breathes out, and it feels like a surrender. "I'm so tired. So lost..."

Fuck, this girl. This brave, broken girl who has always been my undoing. I lean closer, close enough to see the golden flecks in her blue eyes, close enough to feel the heat of her skin.

"Then let me be your compass, Oakley," I say, fierce and unwavering. "Let me guide you home."

But even as the words leave my mouth, I know they're not

enough. Not yet. Because the darkness that's latched onto her soul won't let go without a fight. And neither will I.

"I don't know anything about him," she admits, her voice trembling.

"Fuck," I mutter under my breath, trying to control the rage boiling inside me. Someone dared to lay hands on her, to hurt her, and I will find him. I will make him pay.

"Jeremiah, please," she says, her voice breaking. "Just let it go."

"Not happening, Oakley," I repeat, my jaw clenched. "I need to know what that bastard did to you. I won't rest until I make him pay."

"Why?" she asks, her eyes searching mine. "Why do you care so much?"

"Because you're my girl," I admit, my voice low and intense. "And I can't stand the thought of anyone hurting you."

Her shoulders shake with silent sobs and if I was a better man I'd comfort her, but I can't shake the anger in me long enough to do that.

"Goddammit, Oakley," I snarl, my voice dripping with frustration. The air between us crackles with tension. "I need to know what that sick fuck did to you." My jaw clenches so hard I can feel the pressure in my skull. "I won't rest until I find him, torture him and then kill him." Crossing my arms over my chest, I take a step closer, crowding her space. "I'm not leaving until you give me the answers I need."

Her eyes dart away from mine. She takes a shaky breath, her tears glistening in the dim light. "Why can't you just let it go?" Her voice trembles, but there's a steel edge to it. "Why do you need to know every fucking detail?"

"Because," I growl, barely keeping my rage in check, "I

need to understand how much pain you're carrying. I need to know so I can find this bastard and make sure he feels every inch of the hurt he caused you."

"Fine," she spits out, her eyes blazing with fury. "You want to know? He grabbed me, yanked me down, and forced himself on me." Her voice cracks, raw with emotion. "He didn't care that I was scared, that I couldn't breathe. Is that what you wanted to hear? Are you satisfied now?"

She doesn't even give me time to say anything. My mind is going faster than I fathom, trying to piece it all together.

"Go on." I'm pacing now, my hands clenched into fists.

"I was walking back to my dorm freshman year after having gone to one of those dumb freshman mixers. I was on campus and walking right by the library." Her words fracture, broken shards of memories cutting the air between us. "That's when he...he grabbed my hair, pulling me into the alley and pushed me against the wall. His hands...everywhere. Tearing at my clothes. I tried to scream, but he covered my mouth."

"Fuck." The venomous word slips out before I can stop it. I want to smash something, anything. To unleash this beast raging inside me.

"Jeremiah." Oakley's hand shoots out, grabbing my arm. "I fought him—I did. But he was so strong, and when he..." she chokes on her tears, her body trembling like a leaf in a hurricane.

I wipe her cheek and plead with her to continue.

"It was so dark, and he—he was just too strong. He forced himself into my mouth." Her words are jarring as she spits out the poison of her trauma. "He didn't care that I couldn't breathe, or that I was fucking terrified. Someone spooked him before he could do anything else to me."

"Oakley..." My voice cracks, but she doesn't let me finish.

"So, now you know, and you don't get to judge me for anything I do to reclaim some of my power back." She says it so calmly, so matter of fact that I'm forced to look at her, really look at her. She's right, I know that, but she's mine and I'm not okay with others lusting after her.

"Fuck." I rake a hand over my hair, envisioning the faceless fiend who dared hurt her. "I swear, when I find him—"

"Jeremiah, stop!" Her plea slices through my thoughts. "You can't just...it's not that simple. You can't kill a ghost."

"Like hell it isn't and like hell I can't. Nobody stays a ghost when it comes to a Blackwood." I'm a caged animal pacing back and forth, every muscle coiled tight. "No one touches what's mine and gets away with it. I'll tear this city and the next apart if I have to."

"Yours?" There's a spark in her gaze now, a flash of that sass I know so well. "Since when do I belong to anyone?"

"Since always, bunny." My words are hot and possessive. "And don't try to distract me. I'm not playing around."

Oakley's breath hitches and she gets off the bed standing before me, all five-two of her. "You think you can just march in here, all high and mighty, and fix everything?"

"Damn right I do." I step closer, close enough to catch the scent of strawberries in her hair. "Because I'm not letting you go through this shit alone. Not now, not ever."

She looks up at me then, those crystal eyes searing into my soul. And in that moment, I know. I'll burn the world to ashes for her if I must.

"Stop," she says, her voice gaining strength as she pulls herself together. "Just stop."

"Why?" I demand, frustration boiling inside me. "Why won't you let me help you?"

"Because it's too late!" Her words cut through the air like a knife. "You can't fix this, Jeremiah. You can't fix me."

"Who says I can't?" I snap, my fists clenching at my sides. "I can fix anything, damn it!"

"Try all you want," she retorts, her eyes blazing with something between anger and sorrow. "But I've already started rebuilding my life." She looks around the room. "I don't need your help anymore."

"Like hell you don't." The words are out before I can stop them. "Goddammit, Oakley! You think you can just do this alone? After everything?"

"Yes," she snaps back, not missing a beat. "That's exactly what I'm doing."

"Why?" My voice softens, a desperate edge creeping in. "Why won't you let me in?"

"Because letting you in means risking getting hurt again," she replies, her voice breaking slightly. "And I can't handle any more pain, Jeremiah. Not from you."

"I don't accept that and while we're at it, you're not safe here, Oakley. You're coming back to my place—now."

She recoils, her blue eyes wild as cornered prey. "Jeremiah, you can't just barge in and—"

"Can't I?" I cut her off, my heart thrashing like a caged beast. "After what that bastard did? Hell no. I'm not letting you out of my sight."

Her lips tremble, and she's this beautiful, broken thing that I'm desperate to piece back together. "Your house isn't my home. It'll be a prison."

"Prison, sanctuary—it doesn't matter." My tone is unyielding. "It's where you need to be."

"God, you're so...controlling. So Blackwood," she spits out, and it stings, but I don't have the luxury of hurt feelings.

"Maybe," I concede, my voice low and rough. "But someone needs to protect you, and I don't trust anyone except for myself."

She's shaking now, and every instinct screams at me to hold her. Instead, I step closer, our breath mingling.

"Your door's busted. You can't lock it. Anyone could walk right in and..."

"Stop it!" she yells, cutting me off. "Just stop and my door would be just fine if you hadn't come in here like the Boondock Saints."

"I'm not leaving you here alone. It's not safe," I insist, my voice low and unyielding.

"Jeremiah, please," she pleads, her voice cracking. "I need to do this on my own."

"Fuck that," I growl, my hands itching to pull her into my arms and never let go. But I know she'd resist. "This isn't about your independence or your pride. This is about your safety. And I won't take no for an answer."

"You're impossible," she mutters, looking away.

Oakley's lip catches under her teeth, a nervous habit that I remember all too well. I reach for her then, my hand trembling as it finds the softness of her golden hair. It's like silk through my fingers, and for a moment, I allow myself the luxury of just feeling her.

"Jeremiah..." she whispers, her voice barely audible. She's fighting hard to keep her composure, but I can see the cracks forming. This isn't easy for her. Hell, it's not easy for me either. But I can't let her stay here, vulnerable and unprotected.

"Your safety comes first," I say, my voice low. "We can argue later, but right now, you're coming with me."

She opens her eyes, staring at me with frustration. "Fine,"

she finally concedes, her shoulders slumping in defeat. "But don't think this changes anything."

She throws a couple of things in her bag before I grab it and lead her out of her dorm room, nodding at the wide-eyed RA just loitering in the hallway.

"I'll have someone come by and handle this. No need to tell anyone, right?" I ask the RA and all they can do is gulp and nod their head. The Blackwood name. Instilling fear in others since 1969.

CHAPTER 11
OAKLEY

The night air wraps around me as I follow Jeremiah out to his bike. He stops and turns, revealing something in his hand—my old helmet. It's worn, sporting a few scratches, but unmistakably mine.

"Wow, you kept that?" I quip, raising an eyebrow.

Jeremiah chuckles, a sound that sends a shiver down my spine. "Well, you're the only one who has ever worn it. Figured you might want it back."

My heart does a little somersault at his words. Damn him. "Yeah, well, I'm surprised you remembered," I say, trying to play it cool. But the tension between us is palpable. It feels almost like a coiled spring ready to snap.

"I remember every single thing about you," he says softly, almost to himself. The way he looks at me, it's like he's seeing right through all the walls I've put up. I hate how easily he can still get under my skin.

We mount the bike, and I can't help but feel a pang of nostalgia. The rumble of the engine, the smell of gasoline—it all brings back memories I'd rather bury because they're so bittersweet. They make me want to go back to a time when hiding my crush on Jeremiah Blackwood was my only problem.

"Remember those late-night rides?" Jeremiah's voice breaks through my thoughts. "When you couldn't sleep and I'd wait up until you texted me?"

I stiffen. Of course, I remember. Those nights were like our secret escape, a refuge from our world where only he and I existed. But now, they feel tainted, like everything else between us. On those rides, I'd let myself sink into his back, wrap my arms around him. I can still feel the thick muscles of his chest and abdomen contracting under my light touch. I've craved that feeling for the last two years, but I can't let myself go back there. I can't fall back into his world.

"Yeah, I remember," I say, placing my hands lightly on the side of his ribcage almost like I'm touching something so delicate. I keep myself as far away from him as possible, even though we're on the same bike. The physical distance mirrors the emotional chasm between us.

"Those were good times," he says, and there's a wistfulness in his voice that makes my throat tighten. "I've thought about those rides, bunny. Every. Single. Night." There's a sexual undertone to his voice that strikes a chord in me and I'm not sure if he means it that way or if he's just being naturally flirty.

"Sure," I reply, my tone flat. The memories flood back, unbidden. The thrill of the ride, the wind in my hair, the feeling of being free; and then reality crashes back in on me.

"Why aren't you holding onto me? Put your hands under my shirt, bunny. You know how cold your hands get." His question hangs in the air, heavy and loaded with the years we've been apart.

"Why do you think?" I snap back, unable to hide the bitterness. "Two years have passed, Jeremiah. Things are not the same."

He doesn't respond immediately, and I wonder if I've struck a nerve. Good. Let him feel some of the pain I've carried all these years.

"Things didn't have to end the way they did," he finally says, his voice low. "That was my fault and I own that."

"It's not that simple, Jeremiah," I admit, more to myself than to him. But it's too late for what-ifs.

The bike roars beneath us, the cool night air whipping past, and I know that calling him by his first name again is probably why he revved the engine. I can probably count the times I've called him his actual name in the years that I knew him.

As we ride, the memories continue to swirl around me, each one a stark reminder of what we've lost. And yet, there's a part of me that can't help but yearn for those simpler times, when it was just this pretty boy and me.

"Hold on," Jeremiah says again suddenly, snapping me out of my reverie as his voice comes in through the helmet comms.

"To what?" I ask, sarcasm dripping from my words.

"Me," he replies, and there's a challenge in his eyes. "Or I'll make you."

I hesitate, but then reluctantly wrap my arms completely around his waist. The warmth of his body seeps into me, and despite my best efforts, I can't ignore the familiar scent of him—leather, musk, and something uniquely Jeremiah.

"Don't let go," he murmurs, and there's an edge to his voice that sends another shiver down my spine.

"Just pay attention to the road," I mutter, tightening my

grip, but I refuse to put my hands under his shirt like old times.

Jeremiah's hand grabs mine. His touch is firm but not forceful. Slowly, he guides my hands under his shirt, pressing them flat against the hard, warm planes of his abs. My breath hitches for a moment as the heat of his body seeps into my palms.

"I need your hands on me, bunny," he turns his head slightly as he murmurs. His voice is low, almost a growl, and it sends an unexpected shiver down my spine.

"Fine," I mutter, more to myself than to him. Reluctantly, I tighten my grip around his waist, but I'm stiff, afraid to let my guard down.

The engine roars to life beneath us, vibrating through my entire body. The scent of the exhaust fills my nostrils, dragging me back to nights long past. Nights when it was just the two of us, lost in the dark roads and each other.

"That's my girl," Jeremiah says, his voice praising me in a way I don't expect.

I don't reply because I'm trying to mask the whirlwind of emotions inside me. He speeds off; the wind whipping at my face, and for a moment, it's like we're racing away from our broken past.

When we finally arrive at the Blackwood house, the sprawling land looms before us, as if we aren't just off campus. I'm surprised Mr. Blackwood didn't try to claim eminent domain on the entire college. Walking inside, I see Penn lounging casually on the couch, a smirk playing on his lips. "Hey there, little brother!" he calls out to Jeremiah, his voice oddly chipper and grating.

"Shut the fuck up," Jeremiah snaps back. The tension between them is palpable, crackling like static electricity.

Penn bursts into laughter, seemingly unaffected by Jeremiah's hostility.

"Same old Penn," I mumble, shaking my head slightly. That infuriating, unflappable demeanor of his never changes. If anyone can get under the other Blackwood brothers' skin, it's Penn.

"Jerry. Jerry, Jerry," Penn drawls, his hazel eyes sparkling with mischief. "You always were a drama queen."

"Keep running your mouth, Penn," Jeremiah retorts, his voice cold enough to freeze fire. "I'll beat the fuck out of you in front of Oakley. I've done it before."

"Touchy, touchy. And did you beat me, though?" Penn chuckles, leaning back further into the couch, completely at ease like he doesn't have a care in the world. All the Blackwood brothers are dangerous and have no qualms about being violent, but Penn is the most unhinged. He's the type to slit your throat while telling you a knock-knock joke. His gaze shifts to me, and I feel exposed under his scrutiny.

"Don't start," Jeremiah warns, stepping closer to his brother, his presence looming. It's a silent threat, one that Penn seems to relish rather than fear.

"Wouldn't dream of it," Penn replies smoothly, his grin widening. "Welcome back, *bunny*."

"Thanks, pennywise," I reply dryly, not really knowing what else to say. It feels like I'm caught in the crossfire of their sibling rivalry.

"Don't fucking start your shit," Jeremiah growls at Penn, probably for using the pet name Jeremiah gave me. "Ignore him," Jeremiah says, his tone hardens ever so slightly as he turns to me and realizes that I'm trying not to laugh at Penn's antics. "Let's go."

Jeremiah's anger is a tangible thing, almost suffocating in

its intensity. Without warning, he scoops me up, slinging me over his shoulder like I weigh nothing. My world tilts as I clutch at his shirt, my fingers digging into the fabric instinctively. Adrenaline pumps through my veins.

"Rem, what the hell?" I gasp, my heart pounding against my ribs. His muscles are taut beneath my touch, coiled like a predator ready to strike. Each step he takes reverberates through me, the tension rippling through his frame.

Instead of answering, he just growls, his voice a low rumble that sends shivers down my spine. "Just hold on and stop asking questions you already know the answer to."

And I do. Against my better judgment, I cling to him, feeling the heat radiating from his body once more. I'm like a fiend for it and I kind of hate myself for it. We ascend the stairs, each step bringing us closer to his room, away from prying eyes and mocking brothers.

When he finally sets me down on the bed, his hands are surprisingly gentle, a sharp contrast to the fury simmering in his eyes. His gaze locks onto mine, raw and unyielding, pinning me in place.

His voice is rough with determination when he says, "I'm going to find the person who hurt you, ya know? I don't care how long it takes, or what I have to do. I'm going to find them, and you know what I say is true. No one truly is a ghost. They will have left at least some minuscule thread for me to find and tug on. Once I find it, their life is over."

I look away, my throat tightening. The memories still feel too fresh, too painful. I can still feel the phantom ache, the violation that lingers in the corners of my mind. Vulnerability washes over me, mixing with the fear I can't quite shake. I should have known that he was too calm after I admitted to him what happened. He just wanted to get me here without much of a fight.

"Stop," I whisper, my voice barely audible. "Just...don't."

"Look at me," he commands, and I reluctantly meet his gaze. There's a fire there, a promise of retribution that both terrifies and comforts me.

"You're not alone in this," he continues, his tone softening just a fraction. "I won't let that bastard get away with it."

"Rem..." My voice cracks, betraying the turmoil inside me. But he's relentless, his determination unwavering.

"This won't be the first time I killed someone because of you," he says, stepping closer and I think my brain has short-circuited because...WHAT?

"You're joking," I sigh, the words heavy with resignation because he has to be. Right?

"Jeremiah," I start, my voice barely above a whisper. The weight of the confession sits heavy on my chest, but I force it out. "There were no cameras where it happened. I never saw his face. I have nothing to give you."

The words hang in the air like a dark cloud. Jeremiah's jaw tightens, and I can see the muscles in his neck strain as he processes what I've said. His fists clench tightly at his sides, knuckles turning white with the force of his anger. It's almost palpable, the anger radiating off him in waves.

"Fuck," he mutters, stepping back, his eyes blazing with an intensity that makes my heart race. "Fuck!" he repeats, louder this time, the word echoing off the walls of his room. For a moment, I think he's going to punch something, anything, just to release the rage that's consuming him. But instead, he exhales sharply, trying to regain control.

"Jeremiah..." I begin, unsure of what to say, how to

comfort him when I'm still grappling with my own fear and vulnerability.

"Don't," he snaps, though there's no real bite in his voice. He paces the room, running a hand through his short-cropped hair. His movements are restless, agitated, like he's searching for an escape. "I can't stand the thought of someone hurting you and getting away with it."

His words cut through me, and all I hear is pain and something else—something that feels dangerously like longing. Before I can respond, he stops suddenly, pulling off his t-shirt with a swift motion. The sight of his bare chest, sculpted and familiar, sends a jolt through me. My breath catches in my throat as he tosses the shirt at me, the fabric soft and worn from countless washes.

"Here," he says, his voice softer now but still tinged with that underlying tension.

I catch the shirt instinctively, the scent of him filling my senses. Memories flood back: late nights curled up in his bed, wearing his shirts that always seemed too big on me, feeling safe and cherished in a way I hadn't with anyone else. It's a bittersweet comfort, a reminder of what we once had and what we've lost. Just childhood dreams remain crumbled at the back of my mind.

"Are you sure?" I murmur, clutching the cotton to my chest.

His eyes lock onto mine with an intensity that leaves me breathless. "Just put it on, bunny."

"Thank you," I finally say, my voice trembling slightly. It's not enough to convey the depth of my gratitude, but it's all I can manage in the moment.

"You're welcome," he replies, stepping closer until the

space between us is almost non-existent. His hand reaches out, brushing a strand of hair away from my face. The touch is gentle, almost reverent, and it stirs something deep within me.

"Don't leave the room," Jeremiah commands, his voice low and intense as he points around the dimly lit space. "There are cameras everywhere. They'll catch any movement if you try to leave the property. Plus, Penn will snitch. You know he loves telling everyone else's business, so don't think you can trust him."

"Great," I mutter, rolling my eyes. "Big Brother's watching."

"Seriously, Oakley," he continues, ignoring my sarcasm. "Stay put. You can go wherever in the house, but enter one of my brother's rooms at your own caution."

"Fine," I sigh, crossing my arms over my chest. A strange mashup of vulnerability and curiosity stirs within me at his concern. "Just don't take forever."

He nods, his eyes lingering on me for a moment longer than necessary before he turns and walks out. The door clicks shut behind him, leaving me alone in the sprawling room that reeks of his presence.

I sink down onto the bed, the mattress firm beneath me. Jeremiah's shirt is still clutched in my hands, the fabric soft and worn. A part of me wants to toss it in the corner just out of spite, but a larger part is desperate to put it on and feel that safety net.

The safety net wins, and I tug my dress off before slipping on the t-shirt, some leggings, and my favorite pair of slouchy socks.

My stomach grumbles a little bit, but finding the kitchen

means interacting with Penn and I don't have the energy to deal with him right now, so I crawl into the covers on the bed and feel my eyes start to droop closed before sleep claims me.

CHAPTER 12
JEREMIAH

I shut my bedroom door behind me and lean against the wood separating us now. My breath comes fast and heavy, my fists clenched so hard my knuckles turn white.

I shake out my hands before knocking my knuckles against the door.

Once.

Pause.

One, two, three, four times.

Pause.

One, two, and the final knock.

One. Four. Three. A thing I saw once scribbled in Oakley's journal after her fascination with 90s movies.

I bound down the stairs, my feet pounding against the hardwood. In the living room, Penn is still on the couch, absorbed in his phone. He looks up as I approach, one eyebrow raised.

"Keep an eye on her." I say, trying to keep the desperation

out of my voice. "Don't let her step outside. If she so much as tries, call me."

Penn raises an eyebrow, his tone dripping with sarcasm. "Why yes, Jeremiah, since you asked so nicely instead of demanded, I would love to have a fucking bunny sleepover as if I don't have shit to fuckin' do."

"Fuck off, Penn. Just do this for me aight," I snap back, not in the mood for his games. My hands are already itching for something to hit.

"Okay, but what am I your personal hostage negotiator? Do I get a badge and little mount me hat like the wack ass sheriff's wear?"

"I'm not fucking around, Penn." I step closer, invading his space.

"Chill, brother," he smirks, the sly grin never reaching his hazel eyes. "Oakley's safe with me. Go punch some sense into yourself or whatever you pretty boys do."

Ignoring his jab, I grab the keys to my bike and head for the door, desperate for an outlet. The echo of the front door and Penn's insane cackles follow me as the cool night air slaps me across the face, trying to soothe the heat itching to escape from underneath my skin.

I straddle my bike, the engine roaring to life beneath me. The vibrations travel up my legs, a familiar sensation that usually brings me a semblance of calm. Not tonight. As I speed toward the boxing gym right off campus, the wind whips around me, but it does not offer me a reprieve from anything that's bothering me.

The gym's neon sign flickers as I pull up and throw down my kickstand. Removing my helmet, I set it on the tank and just stare at the brick building before me. A place where pain is expected, even welcomed. The gym is almost a dive, reeking of sweat and blood, but right now, it smells like fucking redemption. I push open the door, the sound of fists slamming into bags and grunts of exertion greeting me like a twisted lullaby.

The gym is surprisingly empty right now compared to usual. I clock just a few guys and squinting my eyes I see a woman in the far corner.

"Blackwood!" someone calls out, but I don't even bother looking up. They're just background noise. I'm here for one thing only—to drown out the chaos in my skull with the pure, straightforward pain of physical exertion.

I make a beeline for the heavy bags, my hands already curling into fists. I don't bother with gloves or wraps. I want to feel the impact. I want the pain.

I take a swing, channeling every ounce of my anger into the blow. The bag moves wildly; the chains rattling with the force. But it's not enough. It's never enough. I hit it again and again, grunting with each impact. Sweat pours down my face, stinging my eyes, but I don't stop. I can't stop.

Fucking Royce—where the hell is he? I'll beat the fucking shit out of him too for not protecting Oakley like he should have. She was off limits to me because of him, and he didn't do his fucking job.

I throw my first punch hard enough to rattle my knuckles, the impact a kiss against leather. "That's for not being there," I hiss through clenched teeth. Another hit, harder, faster.

My fists are already clenched, knuckles white, as I imagine the faces of those who've dared to hurt Oakley. Me. Her brother. The sick fuck who I'm going to castrate. They're going to regret ever crossing paths with her—with me. Because when it comes to that girl, I don't play by any rules. I write them. And right now, the first rule is to let the beast inside me loose. Let it wreak havoc until there's nothing left but the wild, unrestrained parts of who we are meant to be.

The sound of footsteps behind me breaks my concentration. I whirl around, fists raised, ready for a fight.

A figure emerges from the shadows, a cocky grin plastered on his face. He's young, probably a freshman, with the kind of swagger that comes from being too dumb to know better.

"Well, well, well," he drawls, sauntering closer. "If it isn't the Jeremiah Blackwood. Looks like you've been going at that bag pretty hard. Tired yourself out yet?" Definitely a freshman who's heard my name and thinks he's going to be the jackass to finally take down a Blackwood.

I don't answer, just watch him warily. He's muscular, I'll give him that, but he's no match for me. Not with the rage coursing through my veins.

He takes my silence as an invitation, circling me like a shark. "You know, I've always wanted to take on a Blackwood." I roll my eyes, but he keeps talking. "See what all the fuss is about? And here you are, all tuckered out from beating up a defenseless bag."

A harsh laugh escapes my throat. "Trust me, kid. You don't want any part of this."

But he just smirks, rolling his shoulders back. "Oh, I think I do. In fact, I insist."

He lunges at me then, throwing a wild punch that I easily dodge. He's fast, I'll give him that, but he's sloppy. Untrained. I could end this in seconds if I wanted to.

But I don't want to. I want to make him hurt. I want to make someone bleed for what happened to Oakley. And this arrogant prick just volunteered.

"Hope you can keep up," he says, bouncing on the balls of his feet like this is some sort of game.

"Keep up?" I echo, stepping into his space again, my voice low and dangerous. "Try not to drown."

I let him come at me again, his fists flying in a flurry of motion. I block each blow effortlessly, toying with him. Let him think he has a chance. Let him taste the false hope of victory.

And then I strike, a vicious uppercut that snaps his head back. He staggers, dazed, and I press my advantage. A jab to the ribs. A hook to the jaw. Each impact sends a jolt of satisfaction through me, the beast inside me roaring its approval.

He's on the ropes now of the ring we didn't even get a chance to step into, barely standing. One more hit and he'll go down. I raise my fist, ready to end it when he comes at me again. I sidestep, feeling the air shift where my head was just a moment ago.

"Is that all you've got?" I growl, the taste of violence alive on my tongue.

His eyes narrow, and he comes at me again, throwing combinations that might impress someone who has more to lose than I do. But not me. I block, I weave.

"Come on, Blackwood, show me—" His words shatter against my fist, connecting with his jaw, the sound echoing off the high ceilings like a siren call.

"Showing enough for you, now?" I spit out, my knuckles screaming because this fucking kid is too goddamn cocky for his own good.

He tries to rally, to summon some hidden reserve, but it's useless.

"Fuck," he gasps, staggering back. His guard drops. Rookie mistake.

"Language," I tease with a smirk, even though my blood

sings with the same profanity. I advance, and he's flailing now, drowning in the deep end.

My foot arcs through the air. It connects against his side, and he folds like a bad poker hand, hitting the floor with a thud that vibrates through the soles of my shoes.

"Lesson's over," I announce, my chest heaving, my fists still hungry for more. But it's not satisfaction I feel—it's emptiness, because no amount of fighting here can put a fucking band aid on what I actually need to be doing.

I want to protect her, to claim her, to make sure she's never marked by anyone's hands but mine. And God help anyone who stands in my way.

A hand clamps down on my shoulder, yanking me back. "Enough, Blackwood."

I whirl around, ready to unleash my fury on whoever dared to fucking touch me. But I falter when I see who it is.

Declan Reed. The top MMA fighter at St. Charles. He's not someone to mess with, even for me.

"Let it go, man," Declan says, his grip on my shoulder tightening. "You've made your point."

I glance back at my opponent, who's slumped on the mat, blood dripping from his nose and mouth. The sight jolts me back to reality. Fuck. I nearly killed him.

I shrug off Declan's hand and step away from the ring, my chest heaving. The adrenaline is still pumping through my veins, making my hands shake.

"I just...I needed to blow off some steam," I mutter, not meeting Declan's eyes. "He ran his damn mouth and got exactly what he asked for."

Declan snorts. "Yeah, well, next time maybe don't do that shit in front of people who can snitch. Bad form, bro."

I nod, because he's right. I let my anger get the best of me. It's a mistake I can't afford to make again.

Declan's got that look. You know, the one that says he's seen too many guys like me lose it over less.

"Nice right hook," Declan drawls, leaning against the ropes with all the casual arrogance of a king in his court. "Though I've heard pillow talk that's less aggressive."

"Then you're doing it wrong," I snap back, the sarcasm thick in my voice. My knuckles ache, longing to feel flesh give way beneath them again. Anything to silence the roar in my head.

"Or maybe I just choose better company." He arches an eyebrow, unimpressed by my glare.

"Better than your hand?" My voice is brittle, almost as fractured as my self-control.

"Touché," he chuckles, pushing off the ropes and signaling to a group of rookies gaping from the doorway. "Get in here! Clean-up on aisle four."

The rookies scramble forward, hesitant glances tossed my way like they're waiting for the next round of fireworks. The poor bastard I thrashed is still sprawled on the floor, groaning like a ghost condemned to haunt this gym.

"Make sure he doesn't choke on his own spit," I toss at them, trying to reign in the hurricane I've become. "I'm gonna head out before my brother fucks with what's mine."

"Watch yourself, Blackwood," Declan warns, releasing me but not dropping his guard. "Obsession makes for sloppy fighting."

"Thanks for the tip," I say, my voice laced with sarcasm as thick as the bloodlust that still hums beneath my skin.

"Anytime," he replies, a knowing smirk playing on his lips

as he steps away, leaving me to gather the shattered pieces of control I'd tossed aside the moment my fists started flying.

I grab my stuff and head for the door, my mind already racing ahead. I need to find out who hurt Oakley. I need to keep her safe.

And God help anyone who gets in my way.

I slam the gym door open, the cool night air hitting my sweat-slicked skin. The parking lot is empty, just a few scattered cars glinting under the streetlights. I pause for a moment, trying to get my bearings, my mind still reeling from the fight.

Pulling out my phone, I shoot a quick text to Ramsey.

> Need you to dig into Oakley's life. Find out everything that's happened since I last saw her. Leave no stone unturned.

The response is immediate.

> RAMS
>
> On it. I'll hit you back when I've got something.

I shove the phone back in my pocket, my jaw clenching. Whoever hurt Oakley, they're going to pay. I'll make damn sure of that.

I'm halfway to my bike when I hear footsteps behind me. I whirl around, fists clenched, ready for another fight. But it's just Declan, his hands raised in mock surrender.

"Easy, killer," he says, his tone dry. "Just wanted to make sure you weren't going to do anything stupid."

I scowl at him. "Like what?"

"Like going after whoever roughed up your girl." He gives

me a knowing look. "I've seen that look before, man. The one that says you're out for blood, and only one thing can make a man look like that."

I don't bother denying it. "She's not just some girl. She's..." I trail off and glare at him before finishing, "mine. She's fucking mine." I give him a terse nod, then turn back to my bike. "I gotta go. I'm needed elsewhere."

"Just remember what I said," Declan calls after me. "Be smart. Don't let your anger make you stupid."

I wave a hand in acknowledgment, then start my bike before peeling out of the parking lot.

I don't go straight back to the house. Instead, I ride around town, letting my bike take me in and out of the city limits while I try and unpack and repack everything. Trying to compartmentalize so I can get my fucking shit together.

I glance down at my gas gauge and notice it's just above the E, so I turn around and head back.

I pull up to the house, tires crunching on the gravel driveway. The engine's barely off before I'm swinging myself off the bike.

Penn's waiting for me on the porch, flipping his lighter open and closed, his expression wary. "She's still here," he says, answering my unspoken question. "Hasn't tried to leave."

I nod, brushing past him into the house. "Then I guess you did your job."

He rolls his eyes. "You got it, boss."

I ignore the sarcasm in his voice, throwing over my shoulder, "Don't start any fucking fires tonight. I'm tired," before taking the stairs two at a time. I just need to lay eyes on her, make sure she's actually still here.

I quietly open my bedroom door and there she is, curled up in the middle of my bed, under my blankets.

Exactly where she fucking belongs.

CHAPTER 13
OAKLEY

A dim glow sneaks through the curtains, casting shadows along the walls of the large bedroom. I blink, trying to shake off the fog of sleep that clings to my mind. Where am I?

I turn my head, and everything comes flooding back. Jeremiah Blackwood, asleep beside me. His freshly showered skin glistens in the faint light, dark eyelashes resting against his cheeks as he breathes deeply. His hair is so short, basically buzzed completely off, and I miss the little curls that would hang over his forehead when we were kids. A pang of longing surges through me as I realize that I fell asleep on his bed in his t-shirt and now his scent is fused to my skin. I must have kicked my leggings off at some point because I'm currently swaddled in the soft, worn fabric with only my panties underneath. Glancing around and off the side of the bed, I see the gray fabric bunched up on the floor near the foot of the bed.

"Shit," I mutter under my breath, my heart hammering in my chest. I try to slip out of bed quietly, but Jeremiah stirs, his strong arms wrapping around me and pulling me back into the warmth of the blankets. I need to get out of here because I can tell I'm not strong enough. It would not take much for me to fall back into his arms and let him hurt me all over again.

"Where do you think you're going?" he murmurs, his voice low but determined. His green eyes lock onto mine, holding me captive.

"Jeremiah, I...you need to let me leave. If you want to follow me around campus and act like a caveman, fine. But I can't sleep in your bed and cuddle with you like everything is fine," I admit, my voice wavering. The vulnerability in my word's surprises even me.

"Oakley," he says softly, his grip tightening around me. "I promise I'll make things right. I'll protect you. It's early. Come here." Jeremiah's hand slides down my back and over my ass in a maneuver that he's never done before in all the nights I spent in his bed as a lovesick girl. I expect him to shift again to my back, but instead, he grips my ass cheek hard enough to make me gasp as he pulls me into the heat of his naked chest and abdomen. His fingers only move to grip my leg, forcing me to wrap my leg over his hip. "Get some rest," he groans, pressing his face into the side of my neck, seemingly breathing my scent in.

A shiver runs down my spine as his breath ghosts over my neck. There's something thrilling about his possessiveness, about the promise of being cared for so fiercely. But at the same time, a nagging voice in the back of my head whispers doubts and fears. The dichotomy isn't lost on me. It's always going to be two vastly different sides of a coin.

"Who will protect me from you?" I ask, my voice barely a whisper. The weight of everything that's happened—my assault, Jeremiah's disappearance, the tumultuous emotions between us—feels overwhelming.

"No one," he snaps, his voice a low growl that sends a shiver down my spine. "No one will ever come between us again, bunny."

I start to shove him away, but he rolls us over, pinning me beneath him and for the first time I feel for myself that the jokes about how big Jeremiah must be everywhere aren't actually a joke. He's thick, hard and hot, pressing against my hip. It would barely take a twist of my body for him to be pressing between my thighs instead. God, is this how other girls feel? Is this how it's supposed to feel?

"Oakley," he murmurs against my skin, his voice thick with desire. "Let me show you how much I care. Let me prove to you that this is real."

Tears prick at the corners of my eyes and it's not because I'm afraid of him or the intimacy he's sprung on me. It's because he's the only one I'm not afraid of touching me, and he's probably the most dangerous to my mind and heart. I blink, trying to hold them back, but they spill over, streaming down my cheeks like raindrops on a windowpane.

"Jeremiah," I whisper, my voice cracking with emotion. "You left me. You just...vanished without a word. I thought...I can't go through that again. It almost killed me. I don't know why you won't hear me when I keep saying it."

He remains silent, his grip on me unwavering. The room feels heavy, suffocating, and yet I can't bring myself to break free from him. My heart pounds in my chest, fear gripping me like a vise—fear of abandonment, of losing him again.

"Bunny," he says, his voice barely audible above the sound of my ragged breaths. "I don't ever want you to feel that way again. I'm here now, and I'm not going anywhere."

"Please," I choke out, clinging to my independence like a

lifeline. "I can handle things on my own. I don't need you to protect me."

His grip tightens around me, and I feel the resolve in his touch. "You'll stay at the Blackwood house with me now. You can take as much or as little time as you like to process that, but nothing you say or do will change it."

My mind races, torn between the desire for safety and the fierce need for self-reliance that has fueled me for so long. But as Jeremiah's words sink in, a flicker of hope ignites within me, illuminating the darkness that has burdened my heart.

I decide I need some space to think about everything, and there's only one way to do that. "I'm going to be late for class."

Jeremiah groans in annoyance, but ultimately lifts his weight off of me. "You won't be late. I'll take you." He leans down, kissing me quickly on the forehead and then on the nose. "But if you think I'll forget about what I said about you living here, you're in for a surprise, bunny."

The moment Jeremiah's bike roars to life, I can't help but feel a sudden surge of excitement mingling with the lingering apprehension in my chest. Clinging onto him as we speed through the crisp morning air, I'm torn between wanting to pull myself closer and craving the independence that has been stripped away from me.

"Are you okay back there?" he calls over his shoulder, concern lacing his voice.

"Fine," I reply, trying to sound nonchalant despite the way my heart races in my chest. It's not the bike or the speed that scares me; it's the knowledge that I'm willingly placing myself in his hands when I've been fighting so desperately for control.

As we pull up to the entrance of the building where my first class takes place on the other side of campus, I take a deep breath, steeling myself for the inevitable stares and whispers that will follow us into the building. It was the same back in high school, being seen with a Blackwood guaranteed you were going to be the topic of conversation. The gaudy architecture looms overhead, casting long shadows on the cobblestone paths as we make our way toward my classroom. Jeremiah's long arm swoops around me, tucking me against his side as if he knows what's about to happen.

"I've never seen him with a girl," a male voice snickers from behind us. I cringe inwardly, knowing that our arrival has not gone unnoticed.

"The Blackwood brothers don't do public dates. She's gotta be a cousin or something. No way they're fucking, and he'd bring her out in public," a female voice answers her friend. She's half right.

"Shut your whore up or I'll snap your neck in front of her," Jeremiah says, and he stops abruptly to look back at the couple. The guy turns, walking away without a word or a backward glance at the girl with him. She scurries to catch up with him and Jeremiah glowers down at me like this interaction has set the tone for the whole day.

"Sorry," I mumble, feeling my cheeks heat up with embarrassment. "I almost forgot how you guys are campus royalty."

"Hey," he says, tilting my chin up to meet his eyes. "Don't worry about them, alright? You're here with me, but you're not something to be gawked at."

I nod, touched by his genuine concern for my well-being, even as I struggle with the weight of my dependence on him. I don't say anything, mostly because I don't have the wherewithal to form any coherent thought about what's going on with Jeremiah and me.

The classroom is in sight, and he must realize I'm in my head because he stops abruptly, grasping my jaw in his big hands, forcing me to look at him. "Don't listen to anything you hear. I'd never keep you a secret. I will burn this whole campus to the ground to let every last person know that I am owned by only you," he blurts out, and I'm unable to conceal the shock that is undoubtedly showing on my face. I wasn't expecting him to say something like that to me, but his words hit me right in the chest.

Jeremiah must realize what he's said in the heat of the moment, because he masks his expression with a more neutral one. "Come on, you're gonna be late, bunny."

As we enter the classroom, I can feel the gazes of my peers following our every move, their curious whispers filling the air like static. Ignoring them is impossible, but I focus on the familiar sensation of my pen between my fingers as I slide into my seat. Penn is already in his seat, grinning at me like he's about to announce to the class that I'm pregnant and he knows which one of his brothers is the father. I would not put it past that funny fucker.

"Thanks for the ride," I say quietly to Jeremiah when he makes no move to leave the room, trying to find some semblance of normalcy in this strange new reality.

"Anytime, bunny," he replies, his hand resting on the top of my head for a moment before he drops a kiss to my forehead. The warmth of his lips lingers on my skin, igniting a flush that spreads across my cheeks. "I'll be here to pick you up when class is over."

"Damn, baby bro, I want a forehead kiss too!" Penn

exclaims from a few rows back, causing the tension in the room to dissipate as laughter fills the air. The playful banter brings a smile to my face, momentarily easing the turmoil inside me.

"Get in line, pennywise," Jeremiah retorts with a smirk, playfully flipping him off. For a moment, I almost forget about the lingering uncertainty and dread within me.

"Alright, alright, settle down everyone." The professor attempts to regain control of the classroom. "If the Blackwoods would be ever so kind to wrap it up, we have a lot to cover today."

As Jeremiah makes his way toward the door, he casts one last glance over his shoulder at me. I can almost feel the weight of his gaze, a look of protectiveness and desire that seems to anchor me to my seat. He offers me a small nod before disappearing into the hallway, leaving me both relieved and bereft at the same time.

I shift my attention back to the lecture, trying to focus on the professor's words. But it's no use; my thoughts are a whirlwind of conflicting emotions and unanswered questions.

My hand trembles slightly as I scribble notes, the pen scratching against the paper like a whisper of doubt. I can't help but wonder if accepting Jeremiah's offer to ride with him this morning was a mistake, or if allowing him back into my life will only lead to more heartache. I don't know who I'm trying to fool, heartache and the Blackwood name go hand in hand.

Like I had a choice. I roll my eyes at the thought. Jeremiah Blackwood is not easily swayed.

As the minutes tick by, the laughter fades, and the atmosphere in the room returns to its usual studious calm.

Professor Whittier concludes his lecture and leaves us to quietly work on our assignment.

I glance up from my notebook, only to find the professor standing by the door, his eyes wide in surprise as he holds it open.

"Delivery for Oakley Ashford," says the delivery person, a young woman dressed in a crisp uniform, her hands full with an extravagant bouquet of pink and white flowers.

My heart skips a beat at the sound of my name, and a wave of heat washes over me as every pair of eyes in the room turns toward me yet again. The weight of their gazes feels heavy on my skin, and my cheeks flush with embarrassment.

"Uh, yeah, that's me," I stammer, raising my hand hesitantly.

"Looks like someone has a secret admirer," Penn teases, his voice breaking through the silence. His playful grin is infectious, and I can't help but smile back at him, despite the anxiety clawing at my chest.

"I have no idea who they could be from," I say.

"Maybe Jeremiah's just trying to outdo himself after that forehead kiss," Penn adds with a wink.

"Alright, settle down everyone," the professor chides, carrying the bouquet through the sea of desks toward me. My heart pounds in my chest, a wild rhythm that seems to mirror the chaos of my thoughts.

"Here you go, Miss Ashford," he says, handing me the flowers with a quirk of his eyebrow. "Let's try to keep the distractions to a minimum for the rest of class, shall we?"

"Thank you, professor," I reply, my voice barely audible above the clamor of my racing thoughts. The flowers are stunning—their petals soft and velvety beneath my fingertips.

Before I can gather my thoughts, Penn reaches over and

snatches the card from the bouquet. "Let's see what the pretty boy has to say for himself."

"Give that back!" I protest, but he's already unfolding the small piece of paper, his eyes scanning the message inside. I hold my breath, waiting for the punchline, but instead, his smile fades.

"Uh, little Ashford," Penn says, suddenly serious. "This isn't from Jere."

"What?" My heart sinks. "Then who's it from?"

He hesitates before reading aloud, his voice low and uneasy. "I've been watching you, Oakley. Do you miss me as much as I miss you? Soon, we'll be together again."

A chill runs down my spine, and I feel sick to my stomach. This cryptic message, filled with longing and menace, is far from the romantic gesture I had imagined. The room seems to close in on me as fear takes hold. Is it from the man who attacked me?

I'm going to puke all over Penn Blackwood, and that's literally going to be my legacy.

My heart hammers in my chest, the sound echoing in my ears as I try to process the menacing message. "I don't know who could've sent this," I stammer, shaking my head helplessly.

"Are you sure?" Penn presses, his eyes searching mine for any hint of recognition. "Could it be some kind of prank? A boyfriend you're hiding from us from your old school?"

"Who would think this is funny?" I snap, anger flaring through me. The classroom is silent, everyone's gaze fixed on us, and I suddenly feel very exposed.

"Alright, alright," Penn says, holding up his hands defensively. "Just asking."

I swallow hard, forcing myself to breathe as I try to

untangle my thoughts. Who could be watching me? Who would want to scare me like this? My mind races through a list of names, but none make sense.

"Little Ashford, you know I know a guy who knows a guy..." Penn trails off.

"Thanks, Penn," I say softly, my eyes flickering around the room. The bouquet feels heavy in my hands, a tangible reminder of someone playing a sick joke on me. "I just...I need to think."

As the professor continues with the lecture, I find it impossible to focus. The chilling words of the card haunt me, wrapping their icy fingers around my heart. I glance at the empty seat beside me, wishing Jeremiah was here. Despite our complicated history, I'd feel safer with him by my side. It doesn't matter that Penn is here. It's different. The only thing I know is that I need to toss these before Jeremiah shows up to pick me up after class because I need to figure out who they're from and what they want before Rem goes berserk on every male on campus.

I can only hope Penn keeps his big mouth shut until I can tell him myself.

CHAPTER 14
JEREMIAH

I can tell something's off the moment Oakley steps out of the classroom, her shoulders hunched like she's carrying the weight of the world or some shitstorm. Her eyes are fixed on the ground and her hands clutch her books like a lifeline. She doesn't even notice me at first, lost in whatever hell is going on inside her head.

"Oak," I call out, my voice slicing through the buzz of students spilling into the hallway. She jumps, those blue eyes snapping up to meet mine, and there it is—that flash of something raw and edgy before she slaps on a too-quick smile.

"Hey, Rem," she says, voice soft but not fooling me one bit. Rem, haven't heard that nickname since she's dropped back into my life but anytime she's said it now it feels good. No one calls me that but her.

"Cut the crap, bunny," I press, closing the distance between us. "You look like you've just seen a ghost. What's eating you?"

She shakes her head, waves of golden hair catching the dim light of the corridor. "It's nothing, really—"

I just stare at her because she'll crack, she has to.

"I swear, it's nothing. I'm just tired today," she says too quickly, shaking her head. The lie is obvious.

"Don't bullshit me," I growl, stepping closer. "Tell me what's wrong."

"Can we not do this here?" she whispers, a plea in her gaze.

"Oakley." My tone brooks no argument, and I see her resolve waver.

I grab her hand, ignoring the current that zips up my arm, and lead her outside.

The fall air of October hits us as we exit the building, the buildings of St. Charles casting long shadows across the courtyard as the yellowing, rotten leaves lay across every surface. I guide her over to where my bike waits. She's seen more than her share of confessions, from both myself and Oakley.

"Talk to me," I insist, stopping by the bike and turning to face her. Her scent wraps around me, and it takes everything I have not to get sidetracked.

"Jeremiah, I—" She hesitates, chewing on her lower lip.

"Out with it," I growl, my patience fraying.

"Okay, well..."

I don't give her a chance to dodge again. In one smooth move, I back her against the bike, my hands planting firmly on the metal on either side of her hips. The motion cages her in, and our bodies are so damn close I can feel her every breath.

"Jeremiah," she gasps my name breathily, caught between the bike and me, and damn if it isn't the hottest thing I've heard all day.

"Tell me," I demand, my voice dropping an octave, the words vibrating between us.

Her chest rises and falls rapidly, her eyes locked onto mine. In this space where it's her and me and the thing we used to do together, I see it—all the want, the fear, the need. It's a heady mix that has my blood singing, and the urge to close the gap, to taste her cherry-kissed lips, to stake my claim, is almost unbearable.

"It's nothing, please," she pleads, and the tremor in her voice is like a siren song.

"Please what, bunny?" I lean in, my lips hovering just above hers, my breath mingling with hers. "Tell me what you need."

"Just to get out of here," she breathes out, but her body tells a different story, pressing ever so slightly against mine. And fuck, I'm only human.

"Is that really what you want?" I tease, my mouth brushing against the corner of hers, not quite a kiss. "Because your body's saying something else entirely."

"Please," she moans, and the sound sends my senses spiraling.

"Please what, Oakley?" I murmur, letting my lips brush her ear. "Talk to me. Tell me why you're so scared and then maybe I'll take you for a ride."

"You're too close," she says, her voice trembling.

"Am I?" I smirk, enjoying the way she shivers. "Maybe this is exactly where I need to be."

"Stop it," she pleads, hands pushing weakly against my chest, but there's no real force behind them. "Not everything has to be a quid pro quo."

"I can't help if you keep shutting me out.," I demand, my tone softening just a fraction.

"Fine," she bites out, frustration flashing in her eyes. "You want to know? Everything about physical touch freaks me out.

It sends me into a panic. I can't...I can't handle it. Too many people in class were too close today and it just got to be too much."

"Why didn't you tell me sooner?" I ask, frowning. My hand instinctively reaches for her hip, thumb brushing over the fabric of her dress. Her breath hitches, and I feel a surge of protectiveness.

"Because I'm broken," she says, tears welling up. "And I didn't want you to see how messed up I am."

"Oakley," I say, my voice low and intense. "You're bent but not broken. You're stronger than you think. And do you really think I would judge you on how messed up your life is? In case you forgot, my life is full of fucked up things."

"Promise?" she asks, looking at me with those big, vulnerable eyes.

"Promise," I reply, sealing the vow with a kiss to her forehead. Her skin is soft, warm under my lips, and I feel an overwhelming urge to shield her from every hurt.

"Now," I say, lifting her chin with a finger so she meets my gaze again. "Are you going to let me in, or do I have to fight my way through those walls you've built?"

She nods, a small, vulnerable movement that does funny things to my chest. I fight the urge to pull her into my arms further.

"Yea, I know you'll keep me safe from certain things. But you're not safe for me." Pain lances through me because as much as I want to fight against her statement, it's true. I've already proven that.

"C'mon," I murmur, my thumbs tracing idle patterns on her hips. "I'm taking you for a ride."

"Okay," she agrees, her voice steadier now.

She shoves her books into her backpack, and I go to take it from her, and she shakes her head.

"It's gonna be heavy, Oak. I can put it between me and the tank or I'll have someone come grab it." I tell her, but something about the look in her eyes tells me that's not happening.

"No, thank you. I'd really rather have it with me and on my back. Just please don't push me on this." Considering everything, I concede even though it annoys me knowing she's gonna have that heavy shit on her back.

Grabbing the helmet off my right handlebar, I tug it on her head, tucking all the wisps of hair in so they don't get caught. Flipping the visor up so she can see me, I lean in, my fingers grazing her neck and chin as I fasten it on her. She's not smiling, but she's now scowling at me either, so I'll fucking take it.

"You ready?" I tell her, giving her the chance to speak. To give voice to anything else she might need to say in this moment, but all she does is nod, looking adorable in her dress, cardigan, and this clunky helmet that makes her look like a bobblehead. My little bobblehead, but still.

I grab her by the waist and lift her up and put her directly on the back of my bike. Could she swing her little, short self on, yes, but this way gives me a fucking hard-on and clearly, I'm a goddamn masochist.

"Always such a gentleman," she says, a hint of sarcasm lacing her words.

She grabs the back strap as I climb on and lift the bike up and off the kickstand. Settling into our seats, I feel her grip around my waist tight and familiar. I haven't had anyone else on the back of my bike in years. Just her. Always her and since she's been back in my life and on my bike, I've finally realized it's a comfort I hadn't realized I missed.

I rev the engine, the deep rumble vibrating between us,

and we take off, leaving the campus behind. The wind whips past us, carrying away the weight of words, history, and everything between. Oakley's grip tightens as we speed up, her soft hair whipping against my neck.

We ride for what feels like hours, letting the bike take us away from the present. It's just two wheels and the asphalt and us. My favorite place to be, between her thighs. Finally, I pull over at an overlook that offers a view of the valley below. A food truck sits off to the side, its neon sign flickering invitingly.

"Feeling hungry?" I ask, glancing back at her. Her cheeks are flushed from the ride, eyes sparkling with excitement.

"Starving," she says, her lips curving into a smile that could light up the darkest night.

"Stay put," I tell her, though part of me doesn't want to let go just yet. I walk over to the truck taking off my helmet, order us some food, and return to find her gazing out at the horizon. The setting sun casts a golden glow over everything, painting a picture so perfect it almost hurts to look at it. I take out my phone and snap a picture of her sitting on this damn picnic table. She sparkles just like a fairy, and I'm tempted to call her Tinkerbell, but I'd like to keep my balls intact today.

"Food's here, bunny," I say, placing the food on the picnic table. She spins around and moves to sit on the bench. Silence wraps around us comfortably. The only sounds are the distant hum of the food truck's generator, the few other people that stop to enjoy the view or food, and the occasional rustle of leaves in the breeze.

"It's beautiful," Oakley finally says, breaking the silence. Her voice is soft, contemplative.

"Yeah," I reply, though I'm not looking at the scenery. My eyes are fixed on her, taking in every detail—the way her hair catches the light, the delicate line of her jaw, the way her lips part slightly as she breathes.

"You're staring," she says, catching me off guard.

"Yep," I tell her. I have no need to deny it. I'll stare at her as much as I want and never be fucking ashamed of it.

She looks down, a faint blush creeping up her neck, and I wonder if every part of her can turn that color. How easy would it be? Does it spread quickly or is it a slow flush?

Guess I need to fucking address the elephant in the room. "You know what happened with Royce wasn't what it looked like," I start. "You need to know that."

Her eyes flash with something. Hurt, anger, maybe even hope, and she looks away.

"It doesn't matter," she says softly but firmly. "Whatever it was or wasn't, it still happened and look at us. We're all splintered. I don't have my brother or my best friend."

"We can't go back," I admit. "But I want...I need us to figure out how to move forward."

"I miss this," she whispers finally, breaking the silence. "Being with you. You always were so hard to say no to and yet so easy to hang out with. You were like sunshine to me."

Her words fucking sting because I'm not sunshine, but she is, and the fact that she called me her sunshine rips at my insides.

Claim her. Lock her up and never let her go. She's yours, always has been and always will be.

"Do you know what it feels like to have your body seize up and alarms scream in your head whenever someone gets too close or looks at you too long?" She shudders, her small frame wracked with the effort of confession. "It's panic, Jeremiah. Raw, unfiltered panic that takes hold of me and—and I hate it. It chains me down, stops me from being normal, from—"

"From what?" I push, needing to understand her torment as I round the picnic bench and sit down next to her.

"From being with someone. I tried telling my parents, but they just waved me off and sent me to their doctor. All he wanted to do was write me a prescription for Xanax and told me to go shopping." The last words come out as a choked sob, and she buries her face into my chest.

"Fuck," I swear, the word slipping out before I can catch it. Her honesty guts me, leaves me reeling.

"Jeremiah, I've tried to drown it out, the fear. I mask it all and try to be the fun party girl who people like, but it makes everything worse." Her admission is barely audible against the cotton of my hoodie, but it cuts through me, sharp and clear.

"Jesus, Oakley." My frown deepens, concern etched into every line of my face.

"Are you still...have you ever been with anyone?" The question is blunt, raw. I need to know the depth of what I'm dealing with.

"Not before or after. Just that." She shudders and I feel like I could puke.

"Fuck," I swear softly, my hand pausing from rubbing along her back. A virgin. My girl. The thought sends another surge of protectiveness through me.

"Jeremiah, I don't want your pity." Her voice is a plea that wraps around my heart and squeezes.

"Are you still comfortable around me?" The question hangs heavy between us, even as I fight to keep my tone nonchalant. "Even after everything, even when you're pissed at me?"

She hesitates, then nods, and it's like a shot of adrenaline straight to my heart. "Yes, but it's infuriating," she confesses, and I can sense the frustration boiling.

"Good," I breathe out, a smirk tugging at the corner of my mouth. "Because if you weren't mad at me, I'd think I wasn't trying hard enough."

"Trying to do what?" She sasses back at me, letting her melancholy linger away for now.

"Trying to get under your skin." My words are deliberate, each one carefully chosen to rattle the bars of the cage she's trapped herself in. "Trying to be the one you can't push away."

"Jeremiah Blackwood, you're impossible," she huffs, but there's a smile teasing at the edges of her lips.

"What if I had a solution? It might not work, but it's worth a try," I counter, watching her reaction like a hawk. "You said you feel comfortable with me."

Oakley nods, but she's eyeing me suspiciously.

"Listen to me," I start, my voice low and steady. "I've got a proposition for you."

She looks up, her interest clearly piqued.

"Go to my football games. Let me keep an eye on you from the field." The words tumble out before she can interrupt, each one deliberately calculated. "In exchange, you get something too. You practice whatever you want on me." My offer lingers between us. I want this and so does she, and if she needs to do it this way, then we can. She feels stuck, like she's never going to be able to escape that night. I think a positive experience could help her forget, and I sure as fuck am not going to let her do this with anyone else. I dig my nails into my palms at the thought of someone else touching her. I need to keep my head on right now, so I don't scare her.

"Jeremiah," she whispers, and there's that soft sass, her voice a caress and a slap all at once. "You can't just offer me sex lessons in exchange for knowing where I am at all times." I am annoyed and impressed that she saw through my request for her to come to my games. Games are the only time I can't keep an eye on her.

"But I can," I interject, a little rougher than I intend. "Because when it comes to you, Oakley Ashford, there isn't anything I can't or won't do."

There's a flicker of something in her gaze then.

"Let me be the one who helps you face those fears," I plead.

"Fine," she finally murmurs, and the single word is a victory. "But Jeremiah, I'm in charge."

A grin splits my face, all teeth and predatory satisfaction. "Bunny, I wouldn't have it any other way."

"Well, since we are just talking about everything today..." My words trail off as I gauge her reaction. "I've already had your stuff moved to the house."

Her eyes widen, definitely in anger. "You did what?"

"Consider it part of the deal." My hand slides to her waist, fingers branding her through the fabric of her dress. "Your safety isn't up for negotiation, Oakley. At the house, I can keep an eye on you, make sure you're okay. And if I'm not available, one of my brothers is or my cousin."

"Jeremiah Blackwood, you are infuriatingly presumptuous," she snaps, but there's no real bite to her words, just the flush of her cheeks betraying her.

"Maybe so," I concede, smirking at her flustered state. "But tell me you don't like the idea of waking up safe, knowing I'm there."

"Damn you," she whispers, the fight leaving her as her body subconsciously leans into my touch.

"Every night if you want," I murmur against her ear, lips

grazing her skin, the words a sinful caress. "But only if you say yes."

Oakley's response is a shudder that ripples through both of us.

"Fine," she breathes out, defeat laced with anticipation. "But, Jeremiah, this is my game now."

"Oh, love," I assure her, a dark promise dripping from every syllable. "I don't play any game I don't intend to dominate."

CHAPTER 15
OAKLEY

The roar of the crowd is almost too much. I stand at the edge of the bleachers, gripping the cold metal railing so tightly my knuckles turn white. Jeremiah's on the field, all six-three of him towering above the other players. His green eyes are sharp, his movements calculated and predatory. The familiarity of it all hits me like a wave—his presence, the game, the rush of nostalgia.

"Go Spartans!" someone yells behind me, but my focus is solely on Jeremiah. Memories flood back: the motorcycle rides, the secret smiles, the way his laughter used to echo in my very soul. Back then, it felt simple. Effortless. Us against the world.

He moves with the grace of a panther, every muscle in his body coiled, ready to strike. Watching him, I feel an odd sensation of longing and bittersweet joy. It's almost painful. He tackles an opponent, bringing him down with a force that makes me wince. The crowd goes wild. It is hard to see him and not remember everything.

The game wraps up, and my heart races because I know

what comes next. There's no turning back now. The anticipation and nervousness about the upcoming "sex lessons" gnaw at me, a constant undercurrent to my thoughts. I remind myself why I'm doing this—learning, reclaiming, healing. But doubts creep in, whispering insidious questions. Is this really the way? Letting Jeremiah back into my life will land me spiraling worse than I already have been.

My cheeks flush as Jeremiah glances in my direction, his gaze locking onto mine. A smirk tugs at the corner of his lips, and at this moment, it feels like old times. Just us, no complications.

As the players start heading off the field, I catch one last glimpse of Jeremiah. He disappears into the locker room, and I feel the knot in my stomach tighten. It's not just nerves; it's something deeper. Anticipation laced with fear. Desire mixed with uncertainty.

"Just breathe," I whisper to myself. "You can do this." I walk slowly as I make my way toward the hallway where the locker rooms are located. He told me to meet him there after the game.

I'm barely down the hallway and he emerges from the locker room, still damp from his shower. His eyes lock onto mine, and for a moment, I'm caught in those piercing green depths.

"You ready to go, bunny?" he asks, his voice smooth, almost too smooth. He can see my mind is spinning and I hate that he's so hyper-aware of my moods, and all I can do is nod. Following him out to the parking lot.

The drive to his house is tense but short. I'm not sure why he has the Escalade instead of his bike and honestly, I can't find my voice to ask. The interior smells of leather and Jeremiah's aftershave, a scent that stirs memories I thought I'd buried. We don't speak. The silence is thick, and I can't help but wonder why he's not talking as well.

Jeremiah is silent as he leads me into the house, not uttering a word, but he reaches out to hold my hand. My stomach somersaults at the gesture. If I'm melting at something as small as his hand enveloping mine, I'm going to be a freaking mess if I go through with these lessons.

Once inside his room, I take a deep breath. "Jeremiah, I don't know if I can do this. It's easy for you. You've got groupies falling down at your feet and it all just comes effortlessly to you," I declare, my voice steady despite the trembling in my hands.

He looks at me, something unreadable flickering in his eyes. "Oakley, you have no idea how much I've thought about this—about you." He steps closer. The tension between us almost feels like a living, breathing thing. "During our lessons, I won't be touching anyone else but you. No need for jersey chasers when I've got the sweetest girl in my bed, every damn night."

"I don't know if I believe that." I say, skepticism lacing my tone.

"Why the fuck would I lie about it?" he says, his voice firm. He reaches out, his hand hovering near my face but not quite touching. "You set the boundaries. You call the shots. You want to feel safe and learn. I can provide you with that, Oakley."

"Safe," I murmur, the word tasting foreign on my tongue. Safe with Jeremiah? Is that even possible?

"Yes, safe," he insists, his eyes never leaving mine. "Because I know I've fucking hurt you before, but you and I both know I wouldn't lay a fucking hand on you in pain. Well, unless you keep fucking defying me and then maybe I'll spank your damn ass until you finally listen."

I challenge, stepping closer until we're nearly chest to chest. "I'm not the same girl that fawned all over you and if you said jump, I'd say how high."

"Oh, bunny," he says, his voice low, almost a growl. "You've always had me wrapped around your pretty little finger. It was me that was jumping for you."

Jeremiah steps closer, his presence overwhelming. His hands cup my face, the touch both tender and commanding.

"Oakley," he murmurs, his voice a low growl that sends shivers down my spine. "It's just you and me. Other women do not exist to me, and I've already made sure you're untouchable on campus."

"Untouchable?" I echo, confusion threading through my words.

"Yes," he replies, and there's a dangerous glint in his green eyes. "No one will dare lay a finger on you. Unless they want the wrath of me and my brothers reigning down on them, they won't even glance in your direction."

The weight of his words hangs heavy in the air, a promise and a threat all at once. My heart races, pounding against my ribcage. "You threatened to beat people up if they talked to me?"

"Or break their kneecaps," he corrects, his thumb brushing over my cheekbone.

"Are you unwell? What are you—" I start, but Jeremiah cuts me off.

"I am protecting what's mine," he says with an intensity that makes my knees weak. "Because anyone who dares harm what belongs to a Blackwood faces consequences they can't even imagine." He pauses, letting the menace linger. "And you have always been Blackwood owned, bunny."

"What's yours?" I repeat, my voice barely more than a whisper. The word tastes foreign, thrilling, terrifying.

"Exactly," he says, his smile almost predatory.

I tremble, my body betraying my confusion and fear. Jeremiah's eyes narrow, a glint of amusement dancing within them. "You're shaking," he notes, his tone shifting to something playfully curious. "But is it fear...or because you want me as much as I want you?"

"Jeremiah," I begin, but he cuts me off, his voice dropping to a seductive murmur.

"Do you want to start our lessons with something as innocent as kissing?" His question is laced with teasing, a challenge for sure.

"Maybe," I say, my breath hitching.

"Maybe?" he echoes, leaning in closer, his lips hovering just inches from mine. "Or definitely?"

"Definitely," I admit, my pulse quickening. The space between us crackles with tension, the anticipation almost unbearable.

"Good," he whispers, his breath warm against my skin. His lips curl into a smirk, that familiar arrogance seeping through.

A twinge of heat creeps up my neck. Jeremiah takes in an unsteady breath, and I say, "I'm not the only one who's shaking"

"Yea, because you make me nervous, bunny," he says roughly. "I know what it's like to live without you." Jeremiah's eyes darken as he steps back, sitting on the edge of the bed. He motions for me to join him, and despite my racing heart, I move toward him. His presence is magnetic, drawing me in even as every instinct screams that he's the hunter and he'll swallow me.

"Come here," he says softly, patting his lap. I hesitate for a moment before moving closer and straddling him, our bodies close but not yet touching, at least not in a lewd way.

I lean in. Our lips meet tentatively at first, almost in a cautious way. Like wading into the ocean and waiting to see if a shark is going to eat you as soon as you dip your toes even once inch into his domain. His mouth is warm, tasting faintly of mint. My fingers dance across his short hair, and I feel his hands settle on my hips, firm but oddly gentle.

The kiss deepens. I can feel myself growing bolder as our breaths mingle. My desire sparks and I can't help but feel a little surge of power, my own power and I give voice to it.

"Wrapped around my finger, huh?" I murmur against his lips, my voice laced with teasing. Just the thought of Jeremiah bending to anyone's will is so funny to me.

"So tight...around your finger," he teases, gripping my hips harder and pulling me down on his lap until I feel our centers connect. He's hard and I don't know what I was expecting, but even through layers of clothes, I've decided that Jeremiah Blackwood is entirely too big for me. He's big everywhere. Not that I have really anything to compare it to. I feel a gasp leave my mouth, unbidden.

I can feel his chuckles, a low, rumbling sound that sends shivers down my spine as they shake me up and down on his lap. "It will fit, bunny."

Our kisses become more urgent, more demanding. My body presses closer, feeling the solid warmth of him beneath me. His hands slide up my back, pulling me tighter against him, but still maintaining a restraint that I wish wasn't there.

Which is stupid of me because I know I'm not ready for the full scope of his seduction.

"Jeremiah," I gasp as his lips trail down my neck, leaving a burning path in their wake. His lips barely leave my skin, each whisper of breath sends shivers down my spine. His hands are in my hair, and he pulls roughly. It feels *so* good. The bite of pain makes me wet, and my nipples harden. But something else is happening. I feel a sharp stabbing pain in my chest and the urge to vomit.

"S-stop. STOP!" I manage to choke out, my voice a strangled whisper. The rough yank on my hair has sent me spiraling into a dark corner of my mind, one I've tried so hard to forget. I can feel the man who grabbed me, ripping my head back, pulling my hair, and shoving me to the ground. My whole body is trembling.

"Bunny?" Jeremiah's voice is instantly filled with concern, hands freezing in place. "What's wrong? Talk to me."

I swallow hard, fighting to steady my breath. This isn't easy, but it has to be done. "When you pulled my hair... it...he pulled my hair that night. I'm sorry-"

"Stop. Stop apologizing. You did nothing wrong." Jeremiah's eyes search mine, confusion giving way to realization. "Are you sure you don't remember anything else about him, even something you think small or insignificant?" he urges softly, his grip loosening but not letting go, grounding me in the present.

"No. It's all so blurry," I admit, my voice barely above a whisper.

"Oakley..." He says my name like it's a prayer, a promise. Gently, he cups my face, his thumbs brushing away tears I hadn't realized were falling. "If you remember anything else, I need you to tell me."

I nod and he moves his hand back to my hair, but this time his touch is tender, fingertips massaging my scalp with gentle, soothing strokes. The tension starts to melt away under his care, replaced by a warmth that spreads through my body.

"Is this okay?" he asks, his voice low and filled with genuine concern.

"Yes," I breathe, closing my eyes and leaning into his touch. "This is perfect."

"Good," he murmurs, his lips brushing my forehead. "I promise I'll always listen to you. You say stop and we do."

"Thank you," I whisper, feeling a weight lift off my shoulders. "I needed to hear that."

"That's enough," Jeremiah says, pulling back. His green eyes lock onto mine with such concern. "We're done with the lessons for tonight."

"Wait, what?" My voice comes out sharper than I intended. The abrupt end leaves me suspended in a haze of confusion and relief. "Just like that?"

"Yes, just like that." He groans, pulling me down on his lap one last time before he lifts me off of him and stands up, towering over me, every inch the imposing figure I've known him to be. "I don't want to push you further than you're ready to go, and I need to make sure I'm not going to lose control. It would be so easy to take things too far."

"Jeremiah..." I trail off, unsure whether to feel grateful or frustrated. But before I can sort through my tangled emotions, he's already moving.

"Go to the bathroom," he commands softly, but there's no mistaking the authority in his tone. "Change into the pajamas I got for you." He tosses me a shorts and tank top set made out of white eyelet and tiny pink bows.

"Seriously?" I raise an eyebrow, trying to mask the flutter

of excitement mingling with disappointment. "How very...thoughtful of you. Which pom-pom waving girl helped you order these?"

"Trust me, Oakley," he smirks, a flicker of amusement dancing in his eyes. "You'll look perfect in them. And I am quite capable of ordering them on my own, you little smartass."

I scoff, not even thinking about the flashback I had, but more annoyed that Jeremiah isn't touching me anymore. There's an undeniable thrill coursing through me. "You really think you have everything under control, don't you?"

"Always," he replies, his gaze never wavering. "Now go."

"Fine," I mutter, pushing myself off the bed.

I close the bathroom door behind me, the cool tile against my bare feet grounding me momentarily. "God, he's infuriating," I whisper to myself, stripping out of my clothes. The cool air brushes against my skin, sending shivers down my spine. As I slip into the pajamas that Jeremiah apparently deemed mine. The soft material caresses my body, igniting a sense of comfort and vulnerability. I mentally note that red silk lingerie is probably not what Jeremiah would like. He likes me in soft things.

"Ready or not," I murmur, taking a deep breath before stepping back into his room.

Jeremiah's eyes are on me the moment I re-enter. For a heartbeat, the world narrows to just us.

"Perfect," he murmurs, his voice low and velvety. "Absolutely perfect."

"Flattery will get you nowhere," I retort, though my heart hammers violently in my chest.

"Who said anything about flattery?" His gaze darkens, and for a moment, I'm lost in the intensity of it. "You look perfect, just like I knew you would." There's something in the way he's looking at me that says he wants to eat me alive right now, but he won't.

"What's next?" I ask, my voice barely above a whisper, anticipation and dread threading through my words. "You said no more um..."

He steps closer, his presence overwhelming, magnetic. "Next, you're going to bed and getting some sleep."

"I'm not tired?" I blink, thrown by the unexpected gentleness in his tone and the way my statement comes out as a question.

"Yes, you are," he repeats firmly. "We'll continue when you're ready. No rush, remember?" He reaches out, tucking a stray strand of hair behind my ear. "Now, get into bed."

"Bossy much?" I quip, but there's no real bite to my words. Just a strange sense of acquiescence, a willingness to follow his lead.

"Yes, when necessary," he counters, his lips quirking into a half-smile.

"Fine," I sigh, climbing into his bed. The sheets are cool, the mattress firm yet yielding beneath me. "Goodnight, pretty boy."

"Goodnight, bunny," he replies as he tucks me in almost as if I am a child, before turning and I watch him walk toward the bathroom. I can't help admire how his butt flexes. I never considered myself someone who looked at men's asses, but he's got a nice, firm one.

CHAPTER 16
JEREMIAH

The water's hot enough to scald, but I don't give a damn. I lean my forehead against the cool tile, water cascading down my back, each drop trying to wash away the burn Oakley's touch left on my skin. It beats back the urge to storm out of the room and drag Oakley until she's naked and underneath me, where I know we both want her.

I've taken more showers since she appeared at that fucking party than ever before. I'm surprised my skin isn't chaffed. Jesus, I took one not even two hours ago after practice.

"I need to have some damn self-control," I mutter to myself, gripping the shower handle like it might anchor me in this steam-filled haze. My expensive shower gel—-some woodsy, musky scent that clings to skin, does nothing to clear my head. Just reminds me of her, how she smells mixed with me. Now, I'm picturing how she'd look with droplets slipping over those curves I'm trying so damn hard not to think about.

I close my eyes, letting the shower's roar drown out everything else. My hand moves almost unconsciously, seeking relief and as I touch my cock, I know it'll pale in comparison to what it would feel like to sink inside her. I'm stroking myself, damn near torturing myself until I'm half-way to forgetting her for the night when the faintest creak of the door gets my attention.

My heart kicks up a notch, and I freeze. No one else should be creeping in here. My head tilts, ears straining, as the sound of soft footsteps creeps over the tile. The smirk that spreads across my face is enough to cause just a bite of pain as it splits my face. It's her. I know even before I see the silhouette through the frosted glass. None of my brothers are coming into my bathroom, and if they were, it wouldn't be this quietly.

"Couldn't stay away, bunny?" My voice cuts through the steam, sarcastic but laced with that damn desire I can't shake. I can almost feel her hesitation, the tension between us thick enough to choke on.

"Not really..." Her whisper floats to me, tentative but determined. It hangs in the air, a challenge and an invitation all wrapped into one.

"Enjoying the show?" I ask, though I don't stop what I'm doing. I can't stop, not now that she's here, watching. It gives me a thrill, urging me on to finish chasing my release.

"Yes," she breathes out, and I can hear the smile in her voice—the wicked curve of her lips that promises sin and salvation all at once. I know I should send her away, but hell if I don't want her right where she is.

I stare at her as I keep stroking myself. My body turned into her view and her eyes are locked in on the movement. Her chest is flushed in her frilly little tank top and heaves as she watches.

Her nipples pebble and it would be so fucking easy to pull

the clear glass door open and tug her to me. I could sit down on the shower bench, and it would be the perfect height for me to latch on and lave each peak through the silk camisole.

I give myself one more tug before I let my dick go and we both watch as it bounces back up against my stomach.

"I think you saw enough, yea?" I ask, swallowing down the urge to mark her right now.

"Maybe you missed something. I could check. Just in case," she teases back, but there's an edge to her words, like she's not really sure what she's saying or doing. My girl is trying to run without learning how to walk first. It's cute.

"Like hell I did. You've seen everything there is to see tonight." The words scrape out rougher than I intend. My chest tightens as our eyes lock, and I can feel the weight of her gaze on my wet skin. It burns hotter than the water ever could.

"Everything?" There's that sass, the one that gets under my skin and wraps around me like ivy.

"Play your games with someone else, bunny. I'm not in the mood, I know damn good and well I told you to get some rest and from where I'm standing, you're trying to jump headfirst into waters you can't yet swim in."

"Could've fooled me," she murmurs, and shit, she's right. My body betrays me, responding to her proximity without my damn permission.

"Oakley," I warn, the name feeling like a plea and a reprimand all at once. "Don't start something you can't finish."

"Who says I can't finish it?" she grumbles.

"Me. I'm saying it. Now get out before—" I cut myself off, because what? Before I lose control? Before I do something we'll both regret?

"Before what, Jeremiah? Before you show me just how

much you want me? I've got a pretty good idea." Her voice is soft and yet seductive, wrapping around me, pulling me taut.

"I don't think I need to show you any more ways to prove to you how much I want you. The evidence is goddamn clear."

My hand moves of its own accord, slow, deliberate strokes that match the throb of my pulse. I pull the shower door open so there's nothing between us.

"Since you're here begging, why don't you give me a proper show? It's the very least you could do and baby I now know you love to perform." The command rolls off my tongue, smooth and heavy with implication.

For a second, she doesn't move, and I wonder if she'll balk. But then her hands, trembling slightly, reach for the hem of her top. She pulls it up, inch by agonizing inch, revealing skin that glows like moonlight. Her compliance is silent, but it speaks volumes, echoing in the small space between us.

"Higher, bunny," I urge, my voice rough with lust as my hand matches the rhythm of my heart—fast, unyielding. She obliges, fabric bunching above her ribs, and the sight of her, so willing, so utterly mine in this moment, tightens something deep inside me.

I can see the soft under swell of her chest and my eyes lift to meet hers, burning my gaze into her skin. I don't even have to give another command. She knows what to do. What I want from her, as she pulls it up further until her pretty little cherry-tipped breasts are a feast for my eyes.

Steam curls around me, and her compliance is a heady drug, one that sends a bolt of desire straight to my core. "You're such a good girl," I say, and my voice is like dark chocolate—rich, smooth, and wicked.

I don't even guide her with words. It's like my mind is

playing directly into hers as one hand travels down into the little shorts, and I know as soon as her fingers hit nirvana.

"Fuck..." Her voice is a whisper, strained with need, but all I can offer her is a cruel chuckle. Her saying that word will never fail to make me laugh and make me hard.

"Keep going, bunny. You're doing so well for me." I growl, the hunger in my tone almost feral. Her gasps and moans spur me on, and I punish my dick, it's red and tight and leaking and the only cure is Oakley, but I can't fucking do that right now. So, I settle for this.

Her movements become more frantic, more desperate. There's a flush creeping down her neck, spreading over her chest, and I watch with a ravenous fascination as her body responds to my every word, my every command.

"How does it feel to have your small little hands rubbing that wet pussy? Imagine what it would feel like if it were mine. If I spread your lips and dipped my fingers in and out of you, pulling every drop out until your thighs are sticky?"

The water pounds against my back as I watch each hitch in her breath, each flutter of her lashes. I can hear how wet she is, and she's so lost in the feelings she's giving herself that she can't hear it. If she did, I know she would be embarrassed. I want to lick up every drop covering her pretty little cunt. Never even seen it, but I just know without a doubt that it'll be the prettiest one I'll ever see.

"Jeremiah, please," she whimpers, teetering on the brink of ecstasy.

"Stop."

Her hand stills instantly, and her eyes fly open, wide and disbelieving. A whimper escapes her as she looks at me. Frustration pools in those crystal blue depths.

"Wh-why?" she stammers out, her voice breaking on the single syllable.

"Because I said so," I reply, my words clipped. The water sluices down my front.

"Jeremiah, that's cruel..." Oakley begins, but her protest dies on her lips.

"You don't get to come. Not until I say."

"But—" I cut her off by reaching out and pulling her hand out of her shorts. I bring her fingers up to my face, inhaling the sweet, musky scent of her pussy makes my eyes narrow. I need a fucking taste and I'm not going to deny myself any longer.

I suck her two digits into my mouth, wrapping my tongue around each one and savoring the way she tastes. I'll never be able to stop thinking about it, dreaming about it, demanding it. When it's all said and done, I'm going to have her riding my face every damn night and twice during the day.

Fuck, I can't wait to see her legs spread obscenely around my shoulders as she rocks her cunt against my face until she drowns me.

"Bed. Now."

I expect her to snap at me, but she doesn't. She pulls away from me, pulls her tank top down and turns around and walks her pert little ass right out the door.

"Goodnight, Oakley," I call out after her, and she gives me the middle finger over her shoulder and all I can do is chuckle.

My fingers worked at my cock, pumping furiously, Oakley's image seared into my brain. The memory of her taste floods my senses, her fingers soft and sweet, her body warm and pliant and just within reach. My balls tighten, and my cock throbs in my hand. The way she moaned as she rubbed her needy little clit. It was enough to drive even the sanest man mad.

My mind takes me on a fantasy as I slide one hand down her body, dipping my fingers between her legs, and confirming what I already knew to be true. Warm and wet, just for me. Fantasy me thrusts my hips forward in between her soft thighs as I feel her lips caress the top of cock. Her soft little moans filling my ears.

"Jesus, Oakley," I groan loudly, unable to help myself as I send myself over the edge. My orgasm crashing into me, spilling into my fist as I have to lean against the shower tile. I feel my cum dripping off my hand and dick.

I'm fucking spent, willing my heart to slow down to a normal rhythm. It takes a few moments, but once I can stand steadily, I make quick work of actually washing my body before turning off the shower and stepping out.

Grabbing a towel from the rack, I wipe off my damp skin and run it over my buzzed head before wrapping it around my waist.

Looking into the mirror, I can see my pupils are still wider than normal. I can't go into my bedroom right now, see her in my bed and not fucking take advantage of the situation. I pull on a pair of basketball shorts, throw on some deodorant, and brush my teeth before using the other door and stepping out into the hallway. Christ, I'm avoiding her like one of us has the plague.

I step out of the bathroom; the door clicking shut behind me. My heart is still pounding from that intense moment with Oakley—her touch, her scent, her everything. I take a deep breath, trying to shove those thoughts into a box far in the back of my mind. Easier said than done.

I head downstairs and as I approach the living room, I can

hear Penn and Graham's voices mixed with the sounds of explosions and gunfire from whatever video game they are playing.

"Come on, come on!" Graham's voice is urgent, competitive. Typical.

"Don't choke now, Grammy," Penn teases, his voice smooth and sing-songy.

I step into the room, taking in the scene. They're both on the couch, controllers in hand, eyes glued to the screen. The smell of buttery popcorn lingers in the air.

"Hey, J," Graham says without looking up. "Wanna join or just gonna stand there brooding?"

"Just soaking in your shitty gameplay," I shoot back, pushing off the frame and walking over. "How many times have you died already?"

"More than you'd like to know," Penn smirks, not missing a beat. His eyes flicker toward me briefly before returning to the game. "But at least I'm not hiding in the bathroom."

"Yeah? At least I'm not getting my ass handed to me by a twelve-year-old online," I counter, grabbing an empty spot on the couch and a controller.

"Touché," Penn chuckles. He knows how to get under my skin, and he relishes it.

"Alright, enough bullshit," Graham grins. The game resumes, bullets flying, characters shouting. It's chaos, but it's exactly what I need right now.

"Bring it on," I say, settling into the rhythm of the game. For now, the flashing images and rapid-fire action drown out everything else—the tension with Oakley, the confusion, the desire. But I know it's only temporary.

"Did you and Oakley enjoy a nice, well whatever it was that you two were doing up there?" Penn's voice drips with mockery as he dies and is ejected from the game. His smirk is infuriatingly smug.

"Shut up, Penn," I snap, feeling my cheeks flare with heat. "Worry about your own love life, if you can call it that."

"Aw, come on, pretty boy. Did she finally tell you how much she can't resist your brooding charm?" He wiggles his eyebrows, clearly enjoying himself.

"Maybe she just likes guys who don't wear slippers that look like a stuffed animal massacre," I retort, nodding toward his feet. The absurdly fluffy slippers really are an eyesore, even for him.

"Hey, these are comfortable," he defends, but I see the flicker of annoyance in his eyes. "Besides, they're not as tragic as your love life."

"Better tragic than nonexistent," I shoot back, gripping the controller tighter. The plastic creaks under my fingers. "How many people did you strike out with last week?"

"None," he says smoothly, shrugging. "But nice try."

"Focus on your game, Penn, or you'll be the one getting embarrassed," Graham interjects, leaning into the screen with fierce intensity. His hair bounces with each rapid movement.

"Ha! Nice try," Penn crows as he takes down both me and Graham. "Better luck next time."

"Come on, Jeremiah, step it up," Graham chides, his competitive streak flaring. "I can't carry you all night."

"Who's carrying who?" I retort, managing to take out two of Penn's characters in quick succession. "Looks like I'm pulling my weight just fine."

"Touchy, touchy," Penn laughs, his teeth flashing in the dim light. "Maybe you need to get laid. Oh wait, you're too busy pining over Little Miss Perfect."

"Watch your six!" I warn, spotting an ambush forming around Graham's character as I ignore my dipshit of a brother.

"Got it," he acknowledges, swiftly evading the trap.

We play round after round, taking turns having each other's back and also killing one another.

"Okay, last round," I announce, feeling the fatigue setting in but unwilling to show it. The adrenaline is wearing off, replaced by a dull ache of unresolved tension.

"Game over!" Penn's voice slices through the tense silence as my character collapses on the screen one final time. The defeat stings, but his smug grin is worse.

"Nice try," he drawls, leaning back, controller dangling from his fingers. "But you know what really made my day?"

"Don't want to hear it." I glare at him, but he's already rolling on, unstoppable.

"Two co-eds. One mind-blowing blow job." He emphasizes each word with a lazy smirk. "Blonde and brunette. They were insatiable."

"You're such an asshole," I mutter.

"Love you too, bro," Penn says, his laugh ringing out as his character respawns. "Love you too."

CHAPTER 17
OAKLEY

Sunlight filters through the curtains, waking me up slowly. I'm cocooned in the comforter, my body heavy with contentment. Turning my head, I see Jeremiah asleep beside me. His strong features are softened by slumber, and I can't help but smile. Careful not to disturb him, I slip out of bed and pad down the stairs toward the kitchen.

I'm only in the kitchen for ten minutes and I already have the familiar scents of coffee and bacon swirling around, instantly warming my heart. Cooking breakfast for the Blackwood brothers has become a comforting routine, one that makes me feel like I belong. I set about preparing their favorite dishes, humming softly under my breath. The aroma must be swirling down the halls because Penn comes stumbling through the door, his face scrunched up like he's pissed that his empty stomach woke him up.

"Pancakes are the price for waking me up this early. And don't forget the butter," Penn says cheekily, opening up the newspaper. I roll my eyes at him because out of all the Blackwood brothers he's the one who doesn't treat me any differently than he always has. Also, who still opens an actual newspaper? Penn Blackwood must be single-handedly keeping them in business. He acknowledges that I exist because he happens to like the way I make fluffy pancakes. "I see Jeremiah has you dressed up like his weird little wet dream. Vanilla ass."

"Good morning to you too, Penn," I reply, my sass sneaking into my tone. "They're just pajamas."

He chuckles and leans back in his chair, his eyes never leaving the paper. "No luck," he says, curiosity piquing my interest in his annoyed tone. He must notice because he adds, "I always check the obituaries to see if anyone I hate died."

"You're...kidding." I reach under the counter, looking for all the things I'll need to make the king of the manor his pancakes.

"Would I joke about that?" Penn says, his casual demeanor unnerving, so I decide to just focus on his food while he... checks his list.

The sizzle of bacon fills the kitchen, drawing me out of my thoughts as I flip it with practiced ease.

"Hey," Penn asks casually, and I turn to see him pouring enough sugar in his coffee for twelve people. "What was the deal with those creepy flowers you got in class the other day? Seems to me you've got a lot of creepy little things popping up and considering Jerry didn't fucking mention it yet...that means someone's been a naughty little bunny and hasn't told him."

My eyes widen, not expecting such a straightforward question from him. Before I can respond, Jeremiah suddenly appears in the doorway, his green eyes narrowed with curiosity and concern. They still have that bleary just woke up look and he's only in his sweatpants. It's hard to focus with his tanned abs and muscled arms on display. "What flowers are you two talking about?" he demands, his tone surprisingly sharp.

I look between Penn and Jeremiah, a flicker of anxiety crossing my features. Taking a deep breath, I decide to be honest with them. "The other day, I received a delivery of flowers in class," I explain, my voice tinged with frustration. "They were wrapped in a ribbon and accompanied by a note I couldn't understand. It was strange and embarrassing, and I honestly just want to forget about it. It was probably someone playing a prank because of you telling everyone they can't come near me."

"Embarrassing?" Jeremiah's voice is low, almost a growl, as his eyes darken. "Who the fuck were they from?" I realize he's talking to Penn, not me. "You knew about this and didn't tell me?"

"First of all, I'm an unpaid stalker and my shift is one class, so don't snap at me like you're paying my bills," Penn says, shrugging. My fingers twist the hem of my shorts, feeling uneasy under Jeremiah's intense gaze. "I didn't know she wasn't going to tell you about them."

"It creeped me out, so I threw them away and I knew you'd overreact. Which you just did," I say to Jeremiah who glowers at me like he has no idea what I'm talking about. I plate Penn's pancakes that I have half a mind to throw out for the birds to eat since he wants to tattle on me.

"Maybe they thought it was romantic," Penn suggests, an amused smirk playing on his lips. "You know, some people like that kind of shit."

"Romantic, my ass," I mutter, rolling my eyes. "It was more like a scene from a horror movie."

"Regardless," Jeremiah interjects, bringing our attention

back to him. "We need to find out who sent them and why." His protective nature, though endearing, only serves to heighten my anxiety.

"I really am convinced it was just a prank. Can we just eat breakfast without something causing mayhem?"

Jeremiah's jaw clenches tight, his eyes flashing with anger. "Just who the hell would be this stupid? I made it clear that you're off-limits," he growls, pacing the kitchen like a caged animal.

"Jeremiah, I don't think it's that serious..." I try to reassure him, but his anger is infectious, and my own pulse quickens. The air feels thick with tension, making it difficult to breathe.

"Excuse you, but I love mayhem with my pancakes. Thank you. Prefer murder and mayhem with them, but if I can only get mayhem, I'll take it."

"Shut up, Penn." Jeremiah and I both say at the same time while we have a stare down with each other.

"Where are the flowers now?" he demands, his gaze piercing me with an intensity that sends shivers down my spine.

"I told you, I threw them away before you picked me up from class," I admit, feeling a pang of guilt wash over me. "They unnerved me, and I didn't want them in my space anymore." As an annoyed furrow forms between his brows, I realize my mistake. "Obviously, you would have seen them if I walked out with them. I didn't want you to get in trouble for—"

"Killing every motherfucker on this campus," Jeremiah cuts me off. He runs a hand over his hair, frustration etched across his handsome features.

"I can help, I don't have an appointment till..." Penn holds his wrist with the watch on it, glances down and then says, "Three this afternoon, so I'm pretty open."

"To kill an entire campus of people?" I turn the stove off and cover the food before turning back around to face the two deranged men.

"Since when do you have 'appointments'?" Jeremiah uses air quotes and rolls his eyes like Penn having an appointment is the most ridiculous thing he's heard today.

"Look, I'm sorry, alright?" I finally say, matching Jeremiah's confrontational tone. "It was creepy and invasive, and I just wanted it gone. I'm trying to destress my life and adding a stalker to the equation is not really on my list of things to do right now."

The room falls silent for a moment. Jeremiah's chest rises and falls with each heavy breath, his eyes still locked on mine. I can practically feel the heat radiating from him, fueling the fire within me.

"Mhm," he finally says, his voice low and controlled. "Whoever sent those flowers obviously has some twisted intentions, and I'm going to find the dumb fuck one way or another. Even if the most minute thing happens, I need to know about it."

The alarm on my phone going off snaps me back to reality, and I suddenly realize I'm running late for my shift at the library. "Crap, I need to get going," I say, mentally calculating how long it will take me to walk back onto campus and make it to the building.

"I'll give you a ride," Jeremiah interrupts, his voice firm but gentle. I'd argue with him, but to be truthful, I don't want to. I secretly like when Jeremiah escorts me everywhere.

"Alright," I agree, touched by his concern and unable to

resist another opportunity to be close to him. "Let me get changed."

Outside, the crisp air nips at my cheeks as Jeremiah guides me to the Audi sitting in the driveway. Our bodies are close enough that I can feel his warmth emanating from him, causing goosebumps to rise on my skin. I turn away, ready to climb into the car, but he pulls me back gently, his strong fingers wrapping around my wrist.

"Jeremiah, what—" My words are cut off as his lips meet mine in a surprising kiss. The world seems to stand still as every nerve in my body comes alive, the intensity of our connection sending shivers down my spine.

My cheeks flush with embarrassment as I become aware of people passing by, stealing glances at our intimate moment, but Jeremiah simply smirks and murmurs against my lips, "You look so pretty when you blush, bunny."

My heart is pounding in my chest. But the truth is, I don't want him to stop—not now, and maybe not ever. This is starting to feel real to me though, not just like lessons.

As we pull apart, the lingering sensation of his lips on mine sends a delicious ache through me, adding a layer of urgency to my thoughts. Jeremiah opens the car door for me like a true gentleman, and I slide into the seat, my mind racing with unanswered questions. "I thought this was just supposed to be..."

"I'll kiss you wherever and whenever I want. Let's get you to work," he says with a knowing grin, and I can't help but wonder if he's reading my thoughts, or if he's just as affected by our kiss as I am. As we drive away, the world outside blurs into a mixture of colors and shapes, but all I can focus on is the man in front of me—the man who has both broken my heart and has become the only one who can put it back together.

It's two hours into my shift and the library lobby is a sanctuary, quiet and peaceful as I walk around looking for misplaced books. The scent of aged paper and polished wood fills my senses, providing a much-needed respite from the chaos that's recently invaded my life.

"Oakley." My co-worker, Cindy, comes out from behind the front desk and pushes her glasses up the bridge of her nose, giving me a forced smile. "A delivery guy was here earlier. He left this envelope for you."

With trembling hands, I take the envelope and find a secluded corner to open it. As the contents slide into view, my heart lurches in my chest—disturbing pictures of women in bondage, their eyes pleading for mercy, then pictures of me. Me on campus, here in the library, and even in my dorm. There's a chilling note expressing anticipation of seeing me in that state.

Can't wait to see you like this

The scrawl reads, and bile rises in my throat. It's the same handwriting as the note that came with the flowers.

Panic courses through me as I clutch the envelope tightly in my hands. Without a moment's hesitation, I dial Jeremiah's number, because I need him with me. No one else will do. The click of the call being answered screams in my ear.

"Jeremiah," I choke out, my voice barely a whisper. "Someone sent me...pictures. And a note." My words tumble out incoherently, but he seems to understand the gravity of the situation.

As I stand in the library, surrounded by the familiar scent of books and the hushed whispers of my fellow students, I can't help but feel exposed—vulnerable in a way I've never experienced before. Instead of feeling at ease, fear gnaws at me, consuming my thoughts with the disturbing images from the envelope. Is the person who sent me these disturbing images watching me even now? Are they waiting for the perfect moment to strike, to turn their twisted fantasies into reality? I grip my phone tightly, my knuckles white as I listen to Jeremiah's voice.

"Oakley, just stay put, alright? I'm on my way and I'll take care of this shit." His tone is firm, yet gentle, a balm for my frayed nerves. "I won't let anything happen to you."

"Thank you, Jeremiah," I breathe out, my eyes stinging with unshed tears. "I don't know what I would do without you."

"Hey, none of that," he chides playfully, his warm laughter a stark contrast to the cold terror still gripping me. "I want you to go sit at the front desk where you have a clear view of who is near you. I'll be there in two minutes."

My heart swells with gratitude at his words, and I try to focus on the soothing cadence of his voice instead of the sickening dread threatening to swallow me whole. Reluctantly, I hang up the call and tuck my phone into my pocket, attempting to regain some semblance of normalcy.

As I make my way to the front desk, I look around to see if anyone is watching me. I don't see anyone out of place. No one seems to even notice that I'm here. I take a seat and try to fix my face to a more neutral and less horrified expression so not to alert Cindy of the situation. She's the type who would try to get me fired for receiving hate mail.

When she's busy dealing with someone who lost the book they checked out, I look through the contents of the envelope. Even though I know what's in it, nothing can prepare me for these vile pictures and the sinister note that accompanied them. The images haunt me, making my skin crawl and stomach churn.

Shaking my head to dispel the lingering fear, I have to trust that Jeremiah will handle it.

As if I made him appear, there he is shoving a student out of his way and stomping through the doors, his eyes locked in on me.

Oh, he looks mad as hell.

CHAPTER 18
JEREMIAH

I burst through the locker room doors, my heart pounding like a goddamn sledgehammer against my ribs. The air is heavy with the sweat and musk of post-practice exertion, but it's Oakley's safety that's got my blood boiling, not the workout. A goddamn stalker. Some sick fuck getting his kicks out of terrorizing her—is all I can think about as I storm across campus.

Fuck that. I'm gonna find the sick bastard and make them pay.

How much bad luck follows my girl? She needs a fucking break.

I push through the throng of students, the usual campus chatter becoming background noise. My boots pound against the cobblestones. I need to see her, need to know she's okay.

I shove open the heavy wooden doors to the library, the scent of old books and lemon oil polish slamming into me. It's too fucking quiet in here, just the shuffling of papers and clacking of keyboards.

I spot a flash of golden hair between the stacks. I move

quickly toward the front desk, my soles thudding against the worn carpet. I round the corner and there she is, looking small and frightened as she clutches her bag.

"Oakley," I call out, my voice battling between relief and urgency.

She jumps, startled, her bright blue eyes blinking up at me. Her lips part, ready with a greeting.

"You came." She whispers.

"You called."

Her eyes get teary, and I take two large strides until I'm right in front of her and sweep her up into a hug. I can feel the tremors in her body as relief, confusion, fear, and adrenaline all battle for space.

"Grab your shit. You're done here for the day," I interrupt, my tone brooking no argument. Oakley's eyebrows knit together, a silent question forming on her face. I don't give her the chance to voice it. "Someone else can cover this desk."

She frowns, a mixture of confusion and defiance flashing in her eyes. "But I have to—"

"Like hell you do," I cut her off, grabbing her hand. It's small and warm in mine, and I grip it tighter than I probably should. "I already said someone else can cover your shift."

I turn her head toward me. "You okay, bunny?"

She shakes her head, blonde waves tumbling over her shoulders. "N-no. But it was just some pictures and a note. Jeremiah, how did they—. Everything is okay."

"Does it look like everything's okay?" I snap back, sarcasm dripping from every syllable as I glance around the too-quiet library. It's not her fault, but my nerves are frayed, and there's no room for pleasantries. She's trying to act like she's okay, and I think that's more for my benefit than hers, but she's not thinking clearly.

"Jeremiah...can't you just go all Blackwood and take care of it?" Her voice trails off, a mixture of hurt and confusion painting her features.

"Look, Oak, I'm not trying to scare you, but until I can handle this, then you should be scared. Scared means you'll be alert. There's a bastard out there who's messing with what's mine." The words come out harder than I intend, possessive and raw. Her eyes widen at my statement.

"Yours?" she breathes out, the single word laced with layers of meaning we both feel but never say.

"Damn right." I reach out, grabbing her bag and sliding it over her shoulder. "Let's get out of here."

Oakley opens her mouth like she wants to protest, but I shoot her a look. I'm not budging on this. Her safety is the only thing that fucking matters. After a beat, she nods, clutching her bag tighter.

We walk out of the library and all I can focus on is Oakley's small hand in mine and the need to get her somewhere safe. Somewhere secure. Somewhere that I control.

Oakley stumbles slightly, drawing my attention. "Rem, slow down. Your legs are longer than mine," she protests, a little breathless.

"Sorry, baby. I just need to get you out of here." I try to temper my pace for her sake, but the sense of urgency is screaming at me. I should just fucking pick her up and throw her over my shoulder. It's so fucking tempting.

"Do you think this has to do with Lincoln?" Oakley's question cuts through the tense air, sharp and loaded with worry.

"Maybe. Just...let's get inside first." I don't want to think about Lincoln's shitstorm right now, but how fucking coincidental is it that someone's destroying his whatever the hell he's calling Iris' room and now I got some sick fuck toying with sweet Oakley.

The Blackwood house looms ahead, its silhouette dark and foreboding just like daddy dearest likes it. I practically drag Oakley up the steps, her small hand clutched tightly in mind, the door swinging open before us like the gaping maw of some beast.

"Jeremiah, Jesus—" Oakley stumbles over the threshold.

"Meeting. Now," I bark out the command the moment we're inside, where the rest of the brothers are already a brooding presence in the living room and the sound of their voices assaults us.

"What the fuck is going on?" Lincoln's baritone rings out, all traces of his usual cockiness replaced by an undercurrent of tension.

I shoot him a look, my jaw clenched. "Ask your girl. Seems someone's got a hard-on for fucking with her and it's bleeding over into my life."

Iris' eyes go wide at my words, but Lincoln just scowls, wrapping a possessive arm around her waist and pulling her against his side. "What did you do this time, angel?"

She scoffs and shoves him off, but I can see the fear flickering behind her eyes. "I didn't do shit, asshole."

"Both of you, shut up if you aren't going to fuck and give me a show," Penn cuts in, his deep voice slicing through their bickering. He turns to me, eyes narrowed. "What happened?"

I take a breath, reining in my anger enough to explain. "Some sick fuck has been sending Oakley pictures and notes at work. Stalker shit."

Graham's head whips around, his expression thunderous. "What? Who? When?"

"Today at the library," Oakley pipes up, her voice small.

"Just...pictures of me and some other things. And a note that said—"

"Don't repeat that shit," I growl, pulling her closer against my side. I can feel her trembling slightly and it ratchets my rage up another notch. "It doesn't fucking matter what it said. All that matters is finding out who the hell is doing this."

"You think it's the same person messing with the incest twins over there?" Penn's gaze is sharp, assessing.

I shrug one shoulder, my grip on Oakley tightening. "Maybe. Could just be some sick coincidence, but you know how I feel about those."

Lincoln snorts, rolling his eyes. "Because our lives are just filled with those, right? It's gotta be connected somehow."

"Well, we're gonna find out. I'll play Lt. Benson," Penn holds up the envelope, the pictures still inside. "I'm taking these to Ramsey, see if he can pull any prints or trace where they came from while I bang Stabler."

"Good idea," I grunt, not even bothering to comment on his weird SVU kink. I turn to Oakley, my voice softening despite the fire still raging in my veins. "You okay heading upstairs for a bit, baby? I'll be up in a few."

She bites her lip, her blue eyes shimmering with a mixture of fear and gratitude. "Yeah. Yeah, I'm okay."

I lean down and press a hard kiss to her forehead, letting my lips linger against her soft skin. "I've got you, bunny. You're safe with me."

She nods, the ghost of a smile tugging at her lips before she turns and heads for the stairs. I watch her go, my chest constricting with a confusing swirl of emotions. Protectiveness, for sure—the need to keep her safe is practically burning me alive from the inside out. But there's something else, too. Something deeper, more primal, that makes me want to pull her back and never let her out of my sight again.

I slam the photos down on the coffee table, a mosaic of obsession sprawling out under the lamplight. My brothers lean in, their faces etched with concern as darkness plays over their features.

"Look at this shit," I say, my voice a low growl.

Graham's fist clenches, the knuckles bone-white. Lincoln looks like he's ready to tear something apart, and hell, so am I. But it's Penn who moves first, snatching the pictures and rifling through them with eyes sharp as razors.

"This one," he mutters, his finger jabbing at a shot of Oakley in the library, oblivious and alone. "Taken from outside, through the window. That's brazen."

"Too close for comfort," I spit out, watching his analytical gaze devour each image.

"Angles are consistent," Penn continues, flipping to the next. "Our guy likes to keep his distance but not lose sight. He's methodical."

"Methodical and fucked up," I add, feeling the coiled spring of tension winding tighter in my chest. I glance at Oakley in one of the photos. Her face pale, her lips pressed into a thin line.

"Got a preference for close-ups," Penn notes, a picture of Oakley laughing caught mid-motion, a moment of joy turned sinister. "Likes her expressions, the details. Intimate."

I shake my head, forcing the thought away, and turn back to my brothers. "Okay, we need a plan to handle this shit."

"Well, no shit," Lincoln scoffs. "I'm ready to take this into our own hands. Fucking tired of sitting around playing grab ass while someone fucks with Iris. Only person fucking with her is gonna be me."

His words are laced with the same bitterness he's been harboring for days now.

"We're not doing shit until we know what we're dealing with," Penn says, ever the voice of reason. "Once Ramsey takes a look at those pictures and does his geek squad mass spectrometer type shit, we'll have a better idea of who might be behind this."

I nod, forcing myself to breathe through the rage still simmering inside me. "He's right. For now, we play it cool. But if this is the same fucker who's been messing with Iris..."

My hands curl into fists at my sides and I have to stop myself from putting one through the nearest wall. The thought of some sick pervert going after my girl, my Oakley, makes me see red.

Lincoln must sense my shift because suddenly he's in my face, his expression hard. "Easy there. If it is, then I'll be handling it since he fucked with my property first. "

I open my mouth to tell him to fuck off, but Graham beats me to it.

"Don't be a dick, Linc," he snaps, crossing his arms over his chest. "We all know how you are, but if it's the same guy, then you two can handle it together. Team effort, yay."

Lincoln's jaw tics, but he doesn't argue. He knows Graham's right—if the situations were reversed, he'd be ten times as volatile as I am right now.

"Okay, well," Penn says, his tone indicating he's about to say something to piss me off. "We're all on the same team here just like a gang bang. Let's just take a beat, get our dicks hard and let Rams do his thing, and start round two when we've got more intel. For now..." He looks at me, something utterly chaotic flickering in his eyes. "Go be with your girl upstairs and make sure she's good. I'll go do what I do best and that's frolic in the dark, obviously."

I give him a curt nod, grateful for his understanding despite the situation. My brother is crazy, damn near certifiable if Dad would have gotten him tested, but there's nothing he won't do for me or the others. He'd carve out his own heart for one of us, damn near has and there's no one I trust more to have my back than him.

I turn and head for the stairs, taking them two at a time. My heart is pounding in my ears, drumming so loudly with fear and fury that it's quickly becoming overwhelming. I need my calm.

By the time I reach my room, I can barely breathe. I shove the door open, my eyes instantly finding Oakley perched on the edge of my bed. She looks so small, so fragile, huddled in on herself like she's trying to disappear.

The sight of her like that, her bright spirit dimmed by fear and uncertainty, is like a physical blow to my gut. Before I can stop myself, I'm crossing the room in three long strides and dropping to my knees in front of her.

"Hey," I murmur, reaching up to cup her face in my hands. Her skin is soft and warm against my calloused palms, and I drink in the sensation like a man dying of thirst. "Hey, look at me."

Slowly, she raises her eyes to meet mine, and my breath catches in my throat. Those baby blues are brimming with unshed tears, the anxiety and confusion swirling in their depths like a storm on the horizon.

"It's gonna be okay," I tell her, forcing as much conviction into my voice as I can muster. "I've got you, Oak. I'm not gonna let anything happen to you, you hear me?"

She nods, her lower lip trembling, and I feel something

inside me break. Seeing her like this, so scared and vulnerable...it's killing me. All I want is to wrap her up in my arms and shield her from the world, keep her safe and happy and smiling that radiant smile that never fails to make light shine in my fucked-up life.

Without thinking, I slide my hands into her hair, cradling the back of her head as I pull her toward me. Our foreheads meet with a soft thunk, and I close my eyes, breathing her in.

"Rem..." she whispers, her breath fanning across my face. I can hear the question in that single syllable, the fear and uncertainty she's trying so hard to mask.

"Shh." I press my lips to her forehead, letting them linger for a long moment. "I said I got you, baby. You're safe with me."

She makes a soft sound in the back of her throat, something between a whimper and a sigh, and it resonates straight down to my soul. I pull back just enough to look into her eyes again, holding her gaze with everything I have.

"You know that, right?" I rasp, the words tearing themselves from my throat. "You know I'd never let anything happen to you. Not now, not ever."

Her eyes widen, shimmering with hope and disbelief. "Jeremiah..."

"I mean it, Oakley." I'm barely aware of the words tumbling from my lips, operating on pure instinct now. "You're everything to me. Fuck, I..." I trail off, swallowing hard against the lump rising in my throat. "I don't know what I'd do if anything happened to you again. I fucked up once and I won't be fucking making that mistake again."

She's staring at me now, her eyes wide and luminous, and for a long moment the only sound is our ragged breathing.

Then, slowly, she lifts a hand to my cheek, her touch soft and trembling.

"You mean that?" she whispers. "Jeremiah, I...I need to know you mean that."

The rawness in her voice, the naked vulnerability, is like a knife to the sternum. Without hesitation, I turn my head and press a searing kiss to her palm, holding her gaze the whole time.

"I've never meant anything more in my life," I growl against her skin. "You're mine, Oakley. Have been since the day we met, even if I was too fucking stupid to see it."

A soft gasp escapes her lips and her fingers flex against my cheek. I can see the longing in her eyes, the desperate need for reassurance after so long spent apart. Well, I'm about to give her that and then some.

I frame her face with both hands and crush my mouth to hers. She whimpers into the kiss, her hands fisting in the front of my shirt as I pour every ounce of pent-up emotion into the scorching slide of our lips.

These last few days have been a fantasy come to life for me. I've imagined her more times than I can count over the years, late at night with my hand wrapped around my aching cock. I've fantasized about the way her lips would taste, the little sounds she might make as I mapped every inch of that sweet mouth with my tongue. But reality is so much better than any dream, any forbidden fantasy. Reality is hot and slick and all-consuming, setting me on fire from the inside out.

Oakley kisses me back with a fierceness that steals my breath. Her nails scoring lines of delicious heat down my chest. I groan into her mouth; the sound vibrating between us and lift her up. She opens for me instantly, her thighs parting to cradle my hips as I wrap her legs around my waist.

The hard length of my cock is trapped between our bodies, the heavy ridge straining against the thin cotton of my sweats. I know she can feel me, hard and aching, because she gasps and arches up into me. Her damn dress offering no protection from me. The friction is pure sin, a burst of white-hot pleasure that has me seeing stars.

"Fuck, baby," I pant against her lips. "You feel so good."

"Rem..." She whimpers my name like a prayer, her hands sliding up to tangle in my hair. "Please..."

The naked need in her voice resonates straight through me and I growl, low and feral. I've waited too damn long for this, longer than I even realized. But now that I've had a taste, I'm not sure I'll ever be able to get enough.

I trail hot, openmouthed kisses along the line of her jaw, down the slender column of her throat, trying to rein myself in, but like a junkie I just need a hit. I need the feel of her, the taste, to be embedded in me. She tilts her head back, baring that sweet, sensitive skin to my questing lips, and I take full advantage. I lave my tongue over her thundering pulse, sucking hard enough to leave a mark that will show the whole damn world she's mine.

"You're mine," I rasp against the delicate shell of her ear. "My girl, my Oakley. You hear me?"

She nods frantically, her fingers tightening in my hair. "Yes...yes, Rem, I'm yours. Always yours."

CHAPTER 19
OAKLEY

I pull back from Jeremiah and unwrap my legs from his body, and he sets me down, but I hear the little grumble he lets out. I want to make sure he really hears me. Whenever I'm in his arms, I'm lust drunk, and I can't think straight. He says all the pretty words, but I know he's slick with his tongue. I need a level-head and to remember why I'm doing this.

"Pretty boy," I say, my voice wavering. "I know we have a lot going on right now, but I want to continue our lessons." I look at the room, not looking at him, because when I look at Jeremiah Blackwood, I show every card I have. "I'm ready to try the um...you know?" My heart races, and I know I'm blushing.

He looks at me with surprise and concern. "No. You're not." He deadpans.

I bite my lip, trying to hide my nerves. "I *am*. I trust you, Jeremiah. We damn near almost did it just now if I hadn't climbed down your gigantic bean stalk frame."

"If you were ready, you'd be able to actually say the word,

bunny." He takes a deep breath before saying the words I've been dreading. "We're taking this slow."

As he approaches me, I can practically feel the tension building as he reaches out and gently tugs at the hem of my dress. His touch sends shivers down my spine, and I find myself holding my breath, waiting for what comes next.

"Just...teach me." I hate how whiny I sound right now, but isn't that the whole point of these sex lessons?

"I'm going to make you feel good, okay?" he asks, his eyes searching mine for any sign of hesitation as his hand reaches out to tuck a strand of hair behind my ear.

I nod, swallowing hard. "Yes." My voice is so breathy I don't know if he even hears the word.

"Such a sweet girl." Jeremiah murmurs and I feel myself blush and my heart beats faster and I feel myself grow slicker in my panties. God, he's too good at this and he barely touches me. His words alone make me feel like I could come just from his praise.

Slowly, deliberately, he begins to undress me, taking his time with each stitch of my clothing. His fingers linger at the nape of my neck, then trail down to the collar of my dress. My breath hitches. The intentional nature of his actions heightens the anticipation and I shift, trying to press my thighs together for some relief.

"Je..." I whisper, but my voice is swallowed up by everything I am feeling.

"Shh," he soothes, his lips curving into that infuriatingly confident smirk. He undoes another button, his knuckles brushing against my skin, leaving a trail of fire in their wake.

The next button yields easily under his deft fingers. He pauses, fingertips grazing the swell of my breasts, teasing, testing.

And God, do I feel it. Each touch, each brush of his fingers sends electric shocks through me. He removes the last button, and my dress slips from my shoulders, pooling around my feet like water.

Standing before Jeremiah, my heart races as I feel exposed and vulnerable. I shiver, the air cool against my skin, and I look to him for guidance and reassurance.

"God, you are literal perfection, Oakley. Soft and sweet. I'm going to love dirtying up every inch of you. Making your pale skin glow bright red for me," he whispers, almost reverently. His hands roam, exploring the newly bared skin and If I blush anymore, I'm going to look like a lobster.

"Jeremiah," I stammer, my voice barely a whisper. "What —I'm not sure what to do."

"Hey," he replies softly, his eyes locking onto mine. There's a fire there, a possessiveness that shocks me to my core. Jeremiah isn't just saying the words when he tells me that I belong to him, he really believes it. "I'm guiding you through it all, yea?"

"Okay," I nod, feeling a bit more at ease with his support. He's always been there for me, and now, when my uncertainty sets in, I sense the shift of power just by his actions and words.

"That's my good girl," he praises me, and his words have a shiver running down my spine that has nothing to do with how naked and exposed I am. "You like that, don't you? You like when I praise you. When I tell you how perfect you are." I suck in a breath because I feel lightheaded in the best possible way. I don't know how to respond to my pretty boy, but the way he's smirking at me, he knows the exact effect he has on me.

He cocks his head before reaching out and gripping my

hips, "You good?" and all I can do is nod and I'm tossed on the bed. Jeremiah kneels before me; his movements deliberate and focused. I watch as his hands reach out, gently caressing my thighs, and it's as if his touch causes my body to seize up. Not in fear, but in anticipation and desire, yet he remains calm and composed.

"Relax, bunny," he murmurs, his lips brushing against my thigh. Just the top of one and I feel it all the way in my hair and my toes. The sensations overwhelm me. "Trust yourself, trust me."

"I do," I say, attempting to let go of my lingering anxieties. Inhaling deeply, I try to focus on his touch and the growing desire within me.

"Tell me how you feel," he encourages, his fingers tracing patterns on my skin as they inch closer to my pussy. Swirls and shapes but I can't focus enough to figure out what each is.

"So good," I manage to whisper, my breath hitching as his proximity intensifies the sensations coursing through me. "*Really* good." I mentally roll my eyes at myself for not being able to come up with anything more articulate to say. He's literally stealing my brain cells.

"Remember. Wrapped around your finger. You're in control," he says, his tone gentle yet firm. "If you want to stop or change anything, just open your cute mouth and say the word."

As his fingers continue to explore and tease, I feel my impatience growing. I want him more than I want anything else. I want him to touch me there, to make me come, and to come for me. I feel him sliding my panties down and I'm exposed.

As if my mind is disconnected from my body, I feel myself bow backwards at the first touch of Jeremiah's warm tongue against my sensitive center, and I can't help but gasp at the unfamiliar sensation. I force my back to meet his bed again before looking down and his eyes are locked onto mine as he continues to explore me down there.

"Does this feel good, bunny?" he asks, his voice low and controlled. "You taste so good. My new favorite flavor."

"Y-yes," I stammer, finding it difficult to concentrate on anything other than the waves of pleasure that are threatening to engulf me. "It feels so good. Please don't stop."

"Thank fuck, I have to tell you I've watched enough porn that I knew what to do but you're the first girl I've ever touched like this," he murmurs, his breath hot against my skin as his tongue utters those against my pussy.

His sudden confession catches me off guard, and I find myself holding my breath. He chose right now to tell me, when my legs are shaking to the point he grips my thighs, turning his head to kiss the soft flesh he finds there.

"Never?" My brows knit together, trying to reconcile the confession with the man who seems so sure, so in control.

"Never," he repeats, "Always felt too damn intimate, and it wasn't something I wanted to share with anyone. Just you, only ever you."

His lips press against the insides of my thighs, soft and reverent, and I shudder. When his mouth finally finds me, it's a shock of pure sensation. His tongue is relentless, exploring every fold, every hidden corner, and I'm gasping, gripping the sheets as if they're a lifeline.

"God, Jeremiah," I whisper, my breath ragged as I struggle to form coherent thoughts. My entire worldview narrows down to the feeling of his mouth on me. "I...don't know what to do."

"Shh, it's okay," he reassures me, his voice steady and calm as he guides me through this. "Just focus on how you feel and let me take care of the rest."

"Right there—don't stop," I manage through clenched teeth as he hits a spot that sends stars exploding behind my eyes.

"Fuck, Oakley," he groans against me, the vibrations sending another rush of pleasure coursing through me. I can tell he's reveling in this; in the power he has to unravel me.

"Jeremiah, please," I beg, no longer able to contain my need. The sound of my own desperation is almost embarrassing, but I can't bring myself to care. All that matters in this moment is the overwhelming desire for release.

"More," I plead, the urgency of my need coating everything spewing from my mouth.

"Let go, bunny," he encourages, his voice low and sensual as he pushes me closer and closer to the brink. "All over my tongue. I want to taste you."

With one final flick of his tongue and his words, I let myself go. Being pulled under by a wave that crashes over me, over and over again. Stuck in the undertow of this feeling. The sheer intensity wracking my body is beyond reason. It's a blinding white light behind my eyelids, and it robs me of speech, of thought, of everything but the raw feeling of his mouth on me. It's a rush of heat and wetness, leaving me helpless.

I watch as Jeremiah's eyes widen in surprise as he laps at my tight hole, and I can't help but feel a mixture of embarrassment and confusion. Oh God, I think I just peed on him. In his mouth. I'm never going to recover from this.

"Jeremiah, I'm so sorry," I stammer, my cheeks flushing with mortification. "I didn't know that could happen. I..."

"Oakley, don't apologize," he interrupts, his voice laced

with arousal. "That was incredible. You're incredible. You squirted because you let go and gave me everything I was asking for, baby." I feel warmth of a different kind invade me as he reassures me. I've heard of squirting. I do have an older brother and I eavesdropped on their conversations all the time. I just never knew what it actually was, but apparently, I can do it and it's not peeing on someone. So yay, I won't be dying of embarrassment right this second.

"What about you?" I ask hesitantly, still unsure of myself, but pushing to sit up, fully prepared to give him the best of myself, "I don't know how. Can you show me how to?"

"Hey," he says softly, placing a hand on my cheek and making me look directly into his eyes, and I can't help but notice how his lips glisten from my orgasm. "This is about you right now, bunny. Trust me, seeing you like this is more than enough for me. Besides, I came in my pants like a fucking schoolboy just from licking you," he says it so seriously, and I don't think he's exaggerating.

"Like a horny pretty boy?" I tease, though warmth blooms in my chest at the thought of him losing control because of me.

"Exactly like that. You always did underestimate the effect you have on me," he admits, the corner of his mouth quirking up before leaning down to press a gentle kiss to my lips and I can taste myself on him. "The sweetest, don't you think?" Jeremiah flicks his tongue out to swipe across mine. Before I can answer, he's suggesting, "Are you ready to try again?"

"A-again?" I ask tentatively, did I hear him right?

"I didn't stutter, Oakley," he confirms, his green eyes glinting with playfulness. "I want you to give me everything you've got, bunny. I know you've got a couple more for me."

With that, Jeremiah's lips find my neck, kissing and

nipping at the tender skin as his hands roam over my body, reigniting the desire that still lingers just beneath the surface. This time, however, I let go of my inhibitions and allow myself to fully embrace the sensations he's creating within me.

"Jeremiah," I gasp as his fingers tease me once more, the pleasure building rapidly. "It's happening again."

"Let it happen, bunny," he murmurs against my skin, his breath hot and heavy in my ear. "Come all over my fingers, baby."

And so I do. As the intensity of the moment reaches new heights, I lose myself in the ecstasy, grateful for the man who has shown me that even the most unexpected experiences can be beautiful and breathtaking when shared with someone you trust.

"I can't take anymore." I reach down, trying to push his hand away from my pussy, but he's wrenching my legs open and pinning my hips down so that he can devour me with his lips once more. "Jere- I...oh my..."

"Give. Me. One. More," Jeremiah demands, his fingers pistoning inside me in tandem with his tongue that is now flicking across my clit once again. I feel like my entire body is short circuiting, but he doesn't relent until I'm coming all over his mouth again. "Mmm, that's my good girl," he praises me once again, making the orgasm tear through my body even harder.

"Oh my God," I whisper, my whole-body quivering from the waves still moving through me.

"I'm your God, Oakley?" Jeremiah's voice is light as he moves up on the bed to lie next to me, but there's a darkness in his eyes that tells me that there's only one right answer. Jeremiah cups my face, demanding my full attention be on him. "Tell me."

"I think you always have been, pretty boy," I say, and Jeremiah doesn't wait for me to say anything else.

"Good girl," he murmurs, his lips slick with my arousal, his praise more intoxicating than any drug. I'm spent, every nerve ending singing with overstimulation, my mind a haze of post-orgasmic bliss.

"Are you happy?" I ask, my voice barely there, a whisper against the adrenaline rushing through me. "Did I do good for you?"

"Oakley," he says, his eyes dark with something akin to reverence, "you did fucking incredible."

He's kissing me roughly, his hand moving to rest against my throat. He's not gripping me hard, but there's enough pressure there to let me know he's back to calling the shots. I like this feeling of being at his mercy, having to follow his every direction.

It's Jeremiah who pulls back when our kisses get too intense. I protest, needing more, trying to press closer to him. I've missed him for so long and now that I have him back, I want to savor every moment. I want to remember what every inch of his skin feels like beneath my fingertips.

"We need to stop, or I'm not going to be able to," Jeremiah's jaw tics with what can only be annoyance. He wants me as much as I want him, and I've never gleaned as much satisfaction from anything else in my entire life. Jeremiah must see the cheeky look on my face because he's quick to pull the sheet up over top of us and turn me to face away from him. He pulls me back, cuddling me against his chest with his arms locked around me. "I know that look, bunny. I'm not strong enough to stop myself, and I don't want you to regret anything."

"Fair enough. I'm exhausted anyway. I guess that's what

happens when someone goes for a...what do they call it?" I say on a yawn, the orgasms he pulled from me finally taking their toll on me. I smile once my eyes are closed because he's gripping my hips and groaning as my ass wiggles across his hard dick. "Oh yea, a hat trick. Hockey is such an amazing sport." I know my pretty boy, and it will be football only for me from now on.

"Don't make me punish you for that sassy ass mouth," Jeremiah growls, pressing his hardness against my ass and tightening his arms. "Goodnight, bunny."

"Goodnight, pretty boy."

CHAPTER 20
JEREMIAH

The late afternoon sun beats down on the practice field, making the air thick and heavy. Sweat pours down my face as I run another play, muscles straining against the weight of the offensive line crashing into me. My focus should be blocking out everything except the ball sailing through the air into my waiting hands, but that's not what's happening.

We're scrimmaging but my gaze keeps veering off-field. I'm supposed to be focused on the next play, but hell, for a split second, I let myself look over at the bleachers where Oakley sits, legs crossed, and bottom lip caught between her teeth as she watches me intently. The cotton of her navy dress with cute little yellow flowers clings to her body, the soft swell of her tits visible through the delicate fabric. My cock twitches in my compression shorts at the thought of peeling that flimsy material off her, baring her perfect tits to my hungry gaze. After last night, I know that I will never see anything more deserving of the title of perfection than her.

Fuck, she's so goddamn beautiful. God, she looks like she

stepped out of some old movie—soft waves of golden hair cascading around her face and bright blue eyes. Delicate and damn near angelic. Except I know better. And she's all mine, whether she fights me about that or not. There's a lot of baggage to unpack, and I'm just going to keep shoving that shit in the closet.

The shrill sound of Coach's whistle snaps me back to reality as the defense breaks formation. I shake my head, clearing the hazy lust, and get back into position for the next play. Can't let my mind wander, not when so much is on the line. I fucking hate losing, and my brothers feel the same way.

"JB! Eyes on the game!" Coach bellows, and I snap back, grunting an acknowledgment but it's fucking hard to play right now with my dick like steel.

Still, I can't resist stealing another glance at Oakley. She's fanning herself with one delicate hand, chest flushed a pretty shade of pink from the sun shining down on her. Christ, she's going to be the death of me. I adjust the hard bulge in my shorts, trying to ignore the throbbing need building between my legs.

"Fucking focus. Christ, I expect this shit from your brother, but not you!" Coach barks, and I snap my head back toward the field, jaw clenched. Fucking prick. I know he's talking about Penn, because Penn is always doing something to irritate him.

"I'd let myself be distracted by Betty Crocker over there also," quips one of the linebackers, smirking as he jogs past. My teeth grind and I step forward to go after him when Graham steps in front of me, shaking his head. I grumble to myself but choose my fucking battles right now.

The rest of practice is a blur of sweat and exertion as I force myself to focus. Every time I look Oakley's way, she's watching me with those big eyes, lips slightly parted. She knows exactly what she's doing to me, the little tease.

By the time the final whistle blows, I'm a wound-up ball of tension, every nerve ending thrumming with arousal and adrenaline. I rip off my helmet and make a beeline for the locker room, needing a cold shower before I do something stupid.

Like grab Oakley and fuck her senseless right there on the bleachers for the whole team to see.

I look over at her and mouth 'stay put' before heading into the locker room. I already scared the equipment boy to keep her in his fucking eyesight until I'm done.

Stripping off my soaked jersey and pads, I turn on the shower and let the icy spray pound against my overheated skin. I need to get rid of this fucking hard-on, but I'm not about to do it in this full ass shower and no one has the balls to comment on my hard dick, anyway.

Except for my fucking brothers, which is why I'd like to be out of the fucking shower before they're done shooting the shit and stroll their asses in here.

Doesn't matter how many times I jerk off, it's never enough. I need Oakley like I need air to breathe. She's become my obsession, my reason for existing. Without her, I'm just an empty fucking shell.

I wash myself quickly, so I don't fucking smell like a pigpen, but I don't have time to let the water soothe me. I need to go snatch up my bunny.

After toweling off, I tug on a clean pair of sweats and a t-shirt before heading out to the parking lot. Oakley is leaning against one of the pillars with the water boy not far behind, scrolling through her phone with a little furrow between her brows that makes me want to smooth it away with my thumb.

She looks up as I approach, lips curving into a soft smile that has me melting from the inside out.

"Hey," she murmurs as I pull her into my arms, nuzzling my face into the sweet-smelling curve of her neck. She giggles, the sound like music to my ears. "I see you're no longer grumpy."

"I see you're done being mad at me for making you come to practice today. Missed you, baby," I mumble against her skin, inhaling the strawberry smell of her hair.

"Watching you out there," Oakley's voice breaks through my stalker ass behavior of trying to inhale her into my lungs, "it's like stepping back in time." Her eyes catch the light, shimmering with memories. "Remember when Royce and I used to watch all your games? You were unstoppable, even then."

I smirk at the memory, but something twists inside me. "Yea," My grip tightens on her hand. "Guess I've always liked putting on a show."

My hands roam over the soft fabric covering her back, dipping down to graze the swell of her perfect ass. "You look so fucking good in this dress."

She pulls back with a teasing smile, eyes sparkling with mischief. "Oh yea? You like it?"

Instead of answering, I yank her flush against me so she can feel the hard ridge of my cock digging into her belly. Her pupils blow wide, lips parting on a soft exhale as she grinds against me instinctively. Christ, she's so responsive, so perfectly attuned to me.

"Does that answer your question?" I growl, nipping at the delicate shell of her ear. A shiver races through her, and I can't resist adding, "You have no idea how much I want to rip this thing off you and put your pussy in my mouth right here in the parking lot, baby."

Her breath hitches, and she bites that plump bottom lip in a way that makes my cock throb insistently. "Jeremiah..."

The sound of my name on her lips in that breathy, wanting tone is like an electric jolt straight to my dick. Grabbing the sides of her face, I angle her head back and crash my mouth against hers in a searing, possessive kiss. She mewls softly, melting into me as our tongues tangle.

When the need for air becomes too great, I tear my lips from hers with a ragged groan. Oakley's chest is heaving, lips swollen, and eyes glazed with naked desire. Fuck, she's perfect.

"You know you're only a quick tug away from being naked for me, right?" I rasp, smoothing my thumb over the slick, kiss-swollen curve of her bottom lip. "One little piece of fabric between me and that gorgeous body of yours."

A delicate shiver wracks her frame, and she gives me a look that could set me on fire from the inside out. "Is that a promise, Mr. Blackwood?"

Christ, the way she says my last name, all innocently and yet sin-laced, has me aching. I growl deep in my chest and haul her up, her legs automatically winding around my waist as I walk us to my bike. She gasps at the sudden movement, arms looping around my neck as I grind my rigid length against her core, her soft little delicate panties hardly a fucking barrier. I could fucking spear right through them with how hard I am for her.

"You want it to be a promise, baby?" I snarl against the creamy column of her throat. "You want me to strip you down and fuck you right here until you're screaming my name?"

She whimpers, hips undulating in desperate little circles as she chases friction. "Yes, please, Jeremiah, I need-"

The shrill ringing of her phone cuts her off, and she lets out a frustrated groan as I reluctantly set her back on her feet. Fumbling in the little woven bag hanging from her shoulder, she fishes out her cell with shaking hands and frowns at the screen.

"It's Ro...Royce," she stutters out his name, and just like that, the hazy lust clouding my brain clears like someone dumped a bucket of ice water over my head.

Royce. Her brother, my former best friend, the guy who tore us apart all those years ago with his jealous, possessive bullshit. The irony of that isn't lost on me, as I now am a walking billboard of possessiveness when it comes to his sister. The memory of that night two years ago slams into me with the force of a freight train, bitter resentment and regret burning like acid in my veins.

Seeing the name on her phone screen now is like a kick to the teeth, all the old anger and bitterness rushing back in a tidal wave of emotion. I curl my hands into fists, nails biting into my palms as I struggle to contain the storm of rage swirling inside me.

Oakley answers the call with a resigned sigh, shoulders slumping, but I don't miss the excitement shining in her eyes. "Hey, big brother. What's up?"

There's a brief pause as she listens. Her brow furrows, lips turning down at the corners in that way that makes me want to pull her into my arms and chase all her troubles away.

I shove my hands into the pockets of my sweats and rock back on my heels, jaw working furiously. I want nothing more than to snatch the phone from her hand and ream Royce a new one, to remind him what a piece of shit brother he is.

A minute goes by.

Then another.

Until finally, she pulls the phone away from her ear and jabs at the screen with one manicured nail, effectively ending the call. For a long moment, she stares at the device clenched in her hand, chest heaving with harsh breaths. When she finally looks up at me, her eyes are over-bright with unshed tears.

"He...he uh, Rem," she whispers, voice cracking with emotion. "There was no one there. He didn't actually call me. Just a stupid fucking pocket dial. Two fucking years and then this. Why am I not worth it for the people I love to stick around?"

The anguish in her tone, the naked vulnerability shining from those beautiful blue eyes, has the anger draining out of me in an instant. I step forward and gather her trembling body into my arms, cradling her against my chest. She melts into my embrace with a soft, broken sound, burying her face in the hollow of my throat.

"Shhh, it's okay, baby," I murmur, pressing a lingering kiss to her silky hair. "I know, I know."

We stand like that for long moments, her slim form shaking with quiet sobs as I rub soothing circles over her back. The urge to hunt down her asshole brother and bash his face in wars with the need to comfort Oakley, to shield her from any more pain and heartache.

"I'm so sorry," she mumbles again when her tears have subsided. Pulling back, she swipes at her damp cheeks with one hand, offering me a watery smile. "God, you must think I'm such a mess."

"Never," I growl fiercely, cupping her delicate jaw and brushing away the last lingering tear tracks with the pad of my thumb. "Don't ever think that, okay? You're the strongest, bravest person I know, Oakley. Look at what life has thrown you and you're still here, still standing, still giving me a fucking run for my money."

A muscle ticks in her jaw, and she gives a jerky little nod, pressing her face into my palm like she's drawing strength from my touch. "I just...I hate that I was ready to cave. To forgive him as if he didn't abandon me. He's my big brother and the one person above all else I should be able to count on. To have in my corner, to protect me from the monsters under the bed and in real life. But all he did just now was make me feel like a desperate, helpless little girl."

White-hot rage lances through me at her words. The thought of that idiot making Oakley feel anything less than cherished and adored makes me want to put my fist through a wall. She deserves so much better, so much more than his shitty, manipulative behavior. I gripe about my own brothers, but none of them would ever disappear and leave me when I needed them. She definitely deserves better than me and the sinister life breathing down my neck.

"Listen to me," I say roughly, tilting her chin up so she meets my stare. "You're not helpless anymore, you hear me? You're a grown woman, beautiful and strong and so fucking incredible."

She just nods but doesn't say anything and I swear to fuck when I see Royce Ashford again, I'm knocking his ass out.

Oakley's breath hitches, a sound so fragile it fractures the air between us. Suddenly, she steps back, her hand slipping from my grip as if it burns her.

"Take me home, Jeremiah," she says, voice laced with an edge I can't decipher. It's not the soft plea from moments ago; it's resolute, like she's severing a lifeline.

"Oakley?" The confusion claws at my gut, a dull ache spreading through my chest.

"Please, just get me out of here," she insists, and there's a tremor in that one word, a shiver down her spine that doesn't escape my notice. I read the conflict in her eyes, blue storms raging in depths I'm suddenly barred from entering.

"Alright, let's go," I agree, though every muscle in my body screams in protest. I slip on our helmets, but it's like she's oceans away.

The ride back to the house is silent, tense, and now I'm mad and annoyed at this entire situation. She doesn't even wait for me to get off first and help her off. She's already trying to undo the helmet herself, but her fingers are trembling too much. I unlatch it for her, and she gives me a small smile before heading toward the front door.

"Look, I can't help if you don't let me," I admit to her retreating back. "One minute you're all in, the next you're sprinting for the hills and putting behind a damn brick wall."

She winces. Good.

But just when I thought she'd turn around and fucking talk to me, she surprises us both by straightening her spine and walking away from me and right through the front door.

Oh no, baby bunny. You got me fucked up.

CHAPTER 21
OAKLEY

I can do this; I tell myself as I stand outside of the study for lack of a better term. It's fine. I only completely shut down, ignored him, and walked away a few hours ago. He hasn't come up to his room and has left me completely alone staring at these four walls and picking at this navy-blue blanket. I need to just do it.

That stupid phone call from my brother that wasn't even supposed to happen threw me back into the reality of this situation.

The scent of dark wood and leather fills my nostrils as I step into the dimly lit room, my heart pounding in my chest like a wild animal trapped in a cage. I can barely contain the anxiety that threatens to consume me, and I clear my throat, trying to steady myself as I face Jeremiah.

"Jeremiah," I begin, my voice wavering slightly. God, why do I have to sound so weak right now? "We need to talk."

He looks up at me, his green eyes piercing right through me, and I take a deep breath, gathering the strength I'll need to express my decision.

"About what?" His tone is measured, almost detached. It infuriates me how he can be so calm when I'm a tornado of confusion inside.

"I can't do this anymore," I say, forcing the words out. "Us. The lessons, I mean." I wave my hand between us, frustration bubbling up. My eyes meet his, searching for any sign of understanding, any hint that he's not about to hate me for what I'm saying. All I find is amusement like he knows I'd never be able to walk away from him.

"Bunny," he replies, his voice tinged with a note of sarcasm. "What exactly do you want to stop?"

I bite my lip, resisting the urge to snap back at him. This isn't a joke, and I need him to understand that. "It's just...it's too hard to compartmentalize my feelings. It's fake. You're doing it to help me. I guess because you feel bad for—" I look away. "Never mind. But it doesn't feel fake when we're together, so I just think—"

"Fake?" He raises an eyebrow, his tone incredulous, as if the very suggestion is an insult. "You think what we have between us is fake? When have I given you that impression and do you think I just call you mine for the fun of it? You fucking know better than that, Oakley." His words create an echo chamber in my head as I watch him stand up from the chair he's sitting in and take a step toward me.

"Yes. They're lessons...not—" I admit, feeling my cheeks heat up with embarrassment. "It feels real for me, and I don't want to end up feeling like I did when you left and—"

I take a deep breath and pace a few steps.

"I'm not explaining myself clearly," I say, my voice barely above a whisper. "I appreciate you helping me get over my fear of being touched or being close to someone, but when you touch me, I want it to be because you *want* to touch me. Not because you feel bad that someone hurt me. It's all just too much for me."

"Too much?" His voice drops, low and dangerous. Before I can react, he's across the room, touching my arm and spinning me around to face him. His breath is hot against my cheek, and I feel his fingers burning an imprint into my skin even though they aren't even gripping me.

"Baby, touching you is the only thing I think about all damn day," he says, reaching out to touch my cheek, his fingertips grazing my skin with a tenderness that sends shivers down my spine, "You don't ever need to worry about that. I struggle to *stop* touching you. What you do need to worry about is walking away from me like earlier. I won't have that, you need a fucking moment then you say so. You don't get to just shut me the hell out."

A shiver runs down my spine as I watch Jeremiah's face, searching for any hint of emotion in his strong features. He remains silent, stoic, but I can't help but feel like I'm caught in a trap. Jeremiah's eyes flicker toward me, and for a moment, I think I see a flash of vulnerability before he quickly looks away. My heart clenches in my chest, a weird feeling of sorrow taking hold. I take a deep breath, steeling myself for the next part of my confession. I just need him to let me go.

"You've helped me so much in overcoming my trauma," I tell him softly, reaching out to gently place a hand on his arm. The warmth of his skin against mine calls to me, wants me to give in and feel his arms wrapped around me. "And I'm not afraid anymore."

He finally meets my gaze, his eyes filled with a raw intensity that makes it hard to breathe. I can see the struggle behind them, the weight of his own emotions threatening to shatter his own walls. My heart lurches in my chest, and for a moment, I fear that I might have pushed him too far.

Suddenly, he rushes toward me with a fierceness I've never seen before. His eyes burn into mine, a fiery determination blazing through them. "You don't understand," he growls, his voice low and filled with pent-up frustration.

"Jeremiah," I stammer, struggling to find the right words. My breath hitches in my throat as I take in the raw desperation etched across his face. It's disconcerting to see him like this, stripped of his usual composure. But it also ignites something deep within me. Isn't this what I always wanted? Am I not just trading once fear for another?

"Please," I whisper, my voice shaking slightly, "you have to understand that I didn't mean to imply that you were a liar." I pause, searching his face for any sign of understanding. "I just...it's been so hard for me to separate our lessons from what's happening between us."

"Look," he says, running a hand over his head back and forth, clearly agitated. "If you don't think this is real for me, you don't know me at all. Every single thing I've said and done for and to you is real," he says more softly, his voice losing its edge as he takes a step closer. "If you think I don't care about you or that this is just some game for me, you're wrong. This was never meant to be fake. I just said that fucking tit-for-tat shit, so you'd agree, and I didn't have to lock you up like a caveman. It was always gonna be real—for both of us."

I want to say something, but his expression softens ever so slightly as he studies my face. The air around us is thick with tension, as though we're both holding our breath, waiting for the other to make a move. He grabs my face in his hands, forcing me to look at him. "I've never felt anything like this before," he says, his words laced with passion and possessiveness. "You're mine. Every part of you belongs to me."

A desperate urge to resist him wars with the undeniable pull I feel. I know I should be frightened by everything that comes with Jeremiah Blackwood.

"I'm trying to protect myself." He just shakes his head at me before leaning forward and pressing a kiss to the top of my head.

"Bunny," he whispers hoarsely, his voice thick with need. "That's not your job anymore, it's mine. If we're being honest, it always has been, and we just went on our own little side quests for a moment. You're mine, and I need to show you that. I need you to hear it, to see it, to feel it and know it."

His lips crash into mine with a force that steals my breath, something he does so frequently I should be dead. His kiss is rough, demanding, leaving no room for doubt. My body responds instantly, traitorously. I melt against him, our tongues clashing in a frenzied dance of need.

"You're impossible," I manage to gasp out when we break apart for air. His eyes bore into mine, dark and wild.

"And I'm done fucking talking about this with you," he growls, his hands gripping my waist possessively as he lifts me up. I can tell he's about to throw me over his shoulder like a freaking caveman again, so I lock my legs around his waist instead.

I can feel his grin stretched wide across his face on the skin of my neck as he cups my ass and walks us out of the study, taking the long hallway before we climb the staircase and reach his room. I can feel him peppering kisses on my pulse point and it makes me squirm, my center rubbing across his hard cock each time I do.

I jolt when he shifts me so he can lift one leg and kick the bedroom door closed behind us.

"Rem, I want you. I want to feel you. All of you. I'm ready, so show me what it means to be yours," I breathe out. If he denies me right now, I might spontaneously combust.

"Yea baby, and just how bad do you want me? Bad enough to realize this is it? I'm telling you right now, Oakley, we do this, and you'll never get another moment of peace. I will invade every bit of you, and you won't even have one damn sliver of a chance to walk away. So, think very carefully before you decide." He sets me down on the edge of his bed and I lean back on my arms, gazing up at him as I travel up his body and to his face. The damn pretty boy smirk firmly there and his eyes feel like they are burning my clothes away.

I tug my dress over my head, tossing it aside like it's nothing. My fingers make quick work of my bra, and then I lay back down and shimmy out of my panties and toss them past him. He snatches them out of the air before bringing them up to his nose and inhaling deeply. I should be embarrassed, but even though I'm exposed, vulnerable, the hunger in his eyes tells me that he loves it.

"Isn't this enough of my answer? I'm here, bare before you without hesitation," I tell him, and he just scoffs.

"I want your words, Oakley Ashford. Drip each syllable from your lips like your cunt is going to drip honey down my cock," he mutters, lowering his mouth to my chest as his arms bracket either side of my body. His lips close around a nipple, and I arch into him, a moan escaping my lips. He sucks harder, his teeth grazing sensitive skin, sending my core into spasms.

"God, Jeremiah," I breathe, my hands grabbing and pulling him closer. He grunts in response, his mouth moving to my other breast, lavishing it with the same intense attention. Every touch, every lick and bite, is all-consuming.

"Do you feel this?" he murmurs against my skin, his voice thick with need. "This is real, Oakley. This is us."

"Yes," I pant, caught in the whirlwind of sensation he's creating. His hands roam over my body, exploring, claiming. He trails kisses down my stomach, each one leaving an imprint on my flesh.

"Fuck," I gasp as his tongue finds its target, teasing, tasting. My hips buck involuntarily, seeking more. He chuckles darkly, his grip tightening on my thighs, holding me in place as he devours me.

"Look at you," he says, his voice dripping with satisfaction. "So responsive. So perfect." His words only heighten the pleasure, pushing me closer to the edge.

"Please," I beg, needing release, needing him. His mouth never stops its relentless assault, driving me higher, faster. My world narrows to just this moment, just him.

"Come for me, bunny. I gotta get you nice and wet for me," he commands, his voice rough and authoritative. And I do, shattering under his ministrations, crying out his name as waves of ecstasy crash over me and spill onto him.

"That's it, soak me, baby," he murmurs, his tone almost tender now. "Good girl." His words wrap around me as I try to catch my breath.

He moves up my body, settling himself between my legs and I can feel him, hard, thick and throbbing. When the hell did he take his clothes off and how didn't I notice? He must see the confusion written all over my face because he's laughing at me as he bends down to whisper in my ear, "You went to the moon for a minute there, baby. Plenty of time for me to get naked and between your legs before you came back to me here on earth."

Gosh, how freaking embarrassing. I feel the blush spreading across my face immediately. He just stares at me, pushing the hair out of my face. What is he waiting for? A freaking invitation.

Shit, of course he is. He said he wanted my words.

"Rem, please. I'm ready. No fear, no flinching. I want to feel it and I want it to be you. Didn't you say it was always me and it was always going to be me? Well, Jeremiah Blackwood, it's you, and it's always been you, and it's always going to be you. So are you going to claim me or am I getting up and walking out of here? Because there's no way we could go back, only forward." He gives me no words, no affirmation that he hears me, but he grips my chin and presses our noses together and I know he hears me.

He hears me and he sees me and he freaking believes me. I don't need his words. He leans back on his knees, and I see his cock and my mouth speaks before my brain can even stop it.

"There is no way that's going to fit. Are there steroids for dicks because there is no way something that size is supposed to fit into someone's actual body?" Jesus.

"Christ, you're good and bad for my ego, bunny. It'll fit. Why do you think I had you come already? You get so fucking wet, it'll help me slide in."

"That feels like something you're just saying to me to try to ease my very real concern of you impaling me." I'm not wrong.

"You give me too much credit baby. It's average but never speak of it to Penn because I'll never hear the end of it. Now it's gonna hurt and I'm sorry about that," he murmurs against my ear, one hand pinning my wrists above my head while the other guides himself to my entrance. "I can go slow or..."

"I'd rather you not torture me with it."

Without warning, he thrusts into me, filling me completely. The sudden intrusion steals my breath away, pain shooting through me as he stretches me wide.

"Fuck, Oakley," he groans, his voice gravelly. "So tight. So perfect." He's not moving, not even a twitch, and how does he have this much control?

I squirm, trying to move, trying to get him to move, but he just shakes his head at me.

"Let your body adjust, bunny. I don't need to be a fucking neanderthal right now." So, I take a deep breath and we lay there for what feels like forever before my body slowly relaxes. I'm still stretched wide; I still find the sting of pain from having him in me, but something else is happening.

I want more; I want to ease the ache building up in me and I want to come. It has to be written on my face and in my body language because he reads me so easily.

He pulls back slightly before driving in again, harder this time. Each movement is deliberate, controlled, asserting his dominance over me.

"Fu—" I try to form words, but they dissolve into moans. My body responds instinctively, hips arching up to meet his every thrust.

"Such a good girl taking it," he demands, his tone brooking no argument. "Take what I'm giving you."

"Yes," I manage to choke out, my voice trembling with need. His eyes darken, a possessive gleam shining through.

"That's my girl," he praises, his pace quickening. "Feel that? Every inch of me inside you, claiming you."

"Please," I beg, though I can't tell if I'm pleading for mercy or more. The line blurs, leaving me helpless under his command.

"Fucking cunt is wrapped so goddamn tight around me," he groans, his grip on my wrists tightening. His movements become more urgent, each stroke driving deeper, pushing me closer to the edge, but I need more.

My world is reduced to our bodies moving together, and the last barrier I was trying to hold on to is obliterated by him.

"Say it," he orders, his voice a raw whisper. "Tell me you're mine."

"Yours," I breathe, surrendering completely. "I'm yours, Jeremiah."

"Good girl," he mutters, his lips crashing down on mine in a bruising kiss.

He releases my wrists and trails his fingers down my arms, making me shiver. His hands find their way to my hips, gripping them tightly as he grinds against me, eliciting a gasp from my lips as the friction on my clit increases.

"Pretty boy," I moan, my back arching off the bed as pleasure courses through my veins, my heart pounding wildly in my chest.

"Say it again," he orders, his voice thick with need, and I comply without hesitation.

"My pretty boy." It's like I said the magic words he was longing to hear because he finally touches me there, fingers pinching and circling and I can feel my orgasm building. He isn't even fucking me, just holding his cock in me as I clench and tremble all around him.

"Come for me. I wanna feel what it's like when your little body squirts all over me. You gonna mark me, bunny? Would you like that, huh?" Yes, yes, I would like that. Half-embarrassed at the thought, but the other half is winning when I feel it building. It's like my embarrassment is a dam holding me back and he knows it. He pulls out quickly, making me gasp and before I can grumble, he's sharply thrusting in me again, angling upwards as he pinches my clit and I tumble over.

Wave after wave I ride as I feel my orgasm leak out of me and he starts fucking me through it. Each slap of his body against mine is sharp, but it feels like I'm underwater.

"Fuck, that's so goddamn hot. Listen to how wet my pussy is. My pretty little waterfall pussy. Every day I'm gonna want you to come all over me just like this, baby. Fuck, I can't wait to drink you down again." I want him to stop. His filthy words have my nipples hard and I can feel it building again. I can't do it again. It's too much.

He looks up at me, his green eyes darkened with lust and desire, a wicked smile tugging at the corners of his lips. "Speechless, baby?" he murmurs, his voice low and commanding. "I want to hear you scream my name."

"I can't—I need a break," I finally tell him, and he must sense I really do need it because he stops teasing me. He doesn't pull out though, he just strokes my hair and my face. I can hear him whispering, but I honestly have no idea what he's saying. I'm just trying to come back into my body and catch my actual breath. Everything is so much more than I expected it to be.

My head is finally clearer when I realize something.

"Wait," I gasp, pushing against his chest with as much strength as I can muster. My heart hammers wildly in my chest, my voice trembling with urgency. "We forgot to use a condom."

God, how could we have been so stupid? Isn't that what

they drill into us from all angles? How many times has he not used one before? My imagination runs wild.

"Hey! Stop it, right now. I've never not worn one before and none of them matter, anyway. You've known I wasn't a saint for a very long time, bunny. And I know you're on birth control, I'm gonna fuck you bare. Over and over and spill my cum into you every chance I can get. One day, you'll have my little dirty blonde-haired babies, and I can't fucking wait. But for right now, I'm gonna practice knocking you up every chance I get."

I don't even know what to say. All I can picture is him holding a baby now and Penn fighting with the others over who's the favorite uncle. I want that, not now, not anytime soon, but yea one day. I can't help the thrill that runs through me that I'm the only one who's felt him like this.

"Stop snooping through my things!" I tell him when I realize he's obviously gone through my makeup bag and seen my pills. All he does is roll his eyes because of course, everything that is mine is his or however they run their lives in this family.

"That will be a no. Now, do we need to talk about this more or can we fuck so I can nut in you and watch it run out? You let me know if you want to come again." He shallows starts thrusting in and out of me in a teasing manner.

"Next time, we talk first because being with you makes me lose all my brain cells I swear. But yes, I very much would like to come again, pretty boy. Please." My plea at the end is barely a whisper as heat builds and pools between my legs.

"Let me show you how much I need you," he murmurs before capturing my lips with his own.

Jeremiah's grip tightens on my hips, his breath hot against

my ear. My mind races, my legs wrapping around his waist like a lifeline.

"That's it," he growls, thrusting deeper.

I moan, my fingers digging into his back. "Please," I beg, not even sure what I'm asking for.

"Come for me," he orders, his hand slipping between us to find that perfect spot. "I want to feel your cum on me one more time before I let go." He reaches between us, rubbing my clit and continues pounding inside me, taking everything he can. Heat and pressure build inside me, making it harder to breathe, and I can feel my legs shaking. "Fuck." Jeremiah groans as my pussy tightens around him as my orgasm rips through me.

"Christ, bunny...you're so fucking perfect," he groans into my ear, his breath sending shivers down my spine. "I can't get enough of you."

"Neither can I," I admit, my voice barely more than a gasp as he moves inside me. His thrusts are slow and deliberate, but soon they become more forceful, almost animalistic. And with each stroke, I feel myself slipping further and further under his spell, watching as he chases his own release using my body.

"Rem," I moan, my fingers digging into his back as he continues to drive into me. "You can go harder. I can take it. I was made for you, right?"

"Fuck. I don't think I can hold back much longer," Jeremiah gasps, his eyes locked onto mine, searching. His grip tightens around my legs as he pulls them up to his shoulders before stroking hard and fast in between my thighs.

"Goddam I...I—" a guttural roar escapes his lips as he spills inside me, refusing to pull out.

"Mine," he mutters, collapsing onto me. His weight pins me down, our bodies still joined.

"Yours," I echo weakly, my heart pounding in my chest. The room is filled with the scent of sweat and sex. Gosh, I am definitely going to need to clean this room myself because I cannot have the cleaners smelling all this.

He rolls off me, but not far as he takes me with him. Just enough so I can breathe again. His hand remains on my hip, possessive, insistent. He's still in me and how is he still semi hard? I thought it would, you know, shrink and slip out.

"You're a possessive bastard, you know that?" I tease, but there's no heat behind my words.

"Mhm. Now go to sleep and keep my dick in you. He's quite fucking happy to live there now, covered in both of us."

"There's something wrong with you." I tell him but his eyes are already closed, and his breath is evening out, so I give up trying to argue with him and just lay down against his chest as I feel my own eyelids begin to flutter.

No one tells you how utterly exhausting sex is. They should have led with that.

CHAPTER 22
JEREMIAH

I wake to the soft caress of Oakley's breath against my chest, her body curled into mine like she was made to fit there. Trailing my fingers along the delicate curve of her spine, I savor the warmth of her bare skin.

Last night's memories flood back in vivid detail—the desperation in her eyes as she confessed her feelings, the taste of her lips, the velvet heat of her cunt stretching around my cock. A possessive growl rumbles in my throat. She's mine now officially, branded by my touch, her innocence devoured by me and my feelings for her.

She stirs, her thick lashes fluttering open to reveal those piercing blue eyes that have haunted my dreams for years. A soft whimper escapes her lips as she shifts against me, no doubt feeling the lingering ache from the way I fucked her.

Claimed her.

"Good morning." My voice is a low, gravelly purr as I brush the tousled blonde locks from her face. "How are you feeling?"

A rosy flush blooms across her cheeks, those plump lips

parting in that irresistible pout. "S-sore," she whispers, unable to meet my gaze. "But...good. Really good."

Chuckling, I tilt her chin up to hold her captive with my stare. "You were incredible last night, bunny. So tight, so fucking perfect for me." I lean in, nipping at the tender flesh of her throat. "The way you took every thick inch like you were made for it."

She trembles against me, those tantalizing little breaths fanning across my skin. I can smell her arousal, sweet and musky, mingling with the lingering scent of sex from last night.

Oakley melts into me, her nails raking down my arm as she whimpers into the kiss. I could drown in her, the scent and feel of her surrounding me until I can't breathe anything but her essence. Growling, I roll her beneath me, pinning her deliciously small frame with my weight as I grind my already throbbing dick against her slick heat.

She gasps, her back arching as I trail scorching kisses along the graceful column of her neck. "Jeremiah." My name is a breathless plea on her lips, driving me to sink my teeth into that spot where her neck meets her shoulder.

"I know you're sore, baby," I rasp against her skin, rocking my hips in a slow grind that has her writhing and panting beneath me. "But I can't get enough of this perfect little cunt." Reaching between us, I brush my fingers through her dripping folds, reveling in the way her eyes flutter and her lips part on a broken moan.

With a wolfish grin, I guide the thick head of my cock to her entrance, catching on that plump rim before easing just an inch inside her. Oakley keens, her nails scoring lines down my back as I fuck that same inch in and out of her.

I pull out and slide the underside of my cock between her

two lips, letting her wetness provide for us as I use her body for my own.

"That's it, baby," I growl against the swell of her breast, laving one dusky nipple with my tongue. "Gonna fuck you anyway I can."

We're both trembling and slick with sweat, as I rain open-mouthed kisses along her collarbone and the tops of those perfect tits.

"You feel so goddamn good, Oakley," I grate out, fighting the urge to start pounding into her with reckless abandon. "Like you were made to take my cock."

She whimpers, her thighs quivering on either side of my hips as she tries to grind up against me. "Please..." The broken plea has me shuddering, my control stretched to the breaking point.

With a rumbling growl, I hook my arms beneath Oakley's knees and push them up toward her chest, spreading her further open for me. Her back bows off the mattress as I rut between her legs, my cock head catching on her entrance every now and then as I dip into it just a bit. Her eyes rolling back in her head as her mouth drops open on a broken wail.

"That's it, bunny," I snarl against the slick skin of her calf, nipping at the tender flesh. "Take what I'm giving you. Every... fucking...bit." I punctuate each word with a brutal thrust, savoring the way her tight little cunt flutters and clenches around me, desperate to feel me bottom out in her and fill her hungry little snatch with my cum.

Oakley's hands fist in the sheets, her head thrashing from side to side as I ruthlessly chase my own orgasm, using her body for my selfish gratification. But I know she's loving every second, her cries spiraling higher and higher until they're broken sobs of bliss.

With a growl that damn near sounds inhuman, I brace my weight on one arm and reach between us to rub tight circles over her swollen little bundle of nerves. Oakley's back bows almost unnaturally, her mouth dropping open on a shrill scream as her orgasm slams into her with the force of a freight train.

"coming for me so good, baby. I'm gonna give you all of mine now."

Her cries, her nails digging into me, and the flutter of her cunt's spasms around my cock is my undoing. Snarling like a feral beast, I notch myself at her entrance once more and let go, my release tearing through me in hot spurts that seem to go on forever.

I watch as I paint her with my cum, some of it dripping out of her puffy little pussy and the rest of it covering her. I let her other leg go and then I scoop some of it up and shove it back into her abused hole before rubbing the rest into her pussy and upper thighs.

Fucking marking my girl.

For long moments, the only sound is our harsh pants and the thundering of my pulse in my ears. Slowly, I peel myself off of her, rolling to my side and gathering her pliant form against me. She burrows into my chest with a contented sigh, her eyes drifting shut as I trail my fingers through her sweat-damp hair.

"I know you said you don't want to do the lessons anymore," I murmur against the crown of her head, "and that's fine. We don't need the guise of them, but a deal is a deal, and I'm still going to protect you from anything and everything. So, you'll be in my bed every night from now on. No arguments."

Oakley stiffens slightly, those captivating blue eyes

flicking up to search my face. I meet her gaze steadily, letting her see the implacable resolve burning there. I won't be denied, not when it comes to her.

To her credit, she doesn't flinch from my dominance, that small spark of sass flickering behind her eyes. "Sure, pretty boy," she murmurs, a teasing lilt to her tone.

Growling, I nip at her plump lower lip, delighting in the way she shivers. "Such a brat," I chide gruffly. "But you're truly mine now."

We lay together in bed for another hour as I trail my hands through her hair, down her back, over and over. Only interrupted by the occasional kiss I place on the top of her head as she swirls her fingertips across my chest. Drawing random patterns that only she can see.

Eventually, the real world can't be ignored any longer. With a weary groan, I force myself out of the tangled sheets and Oakley's arms to grab clothes out of my dresser. I can feel her eyes tracking my movements as I dress, searing a path over my skin.

"Where are you going?" she asks, propping herself up on her elbows to gaze at me with doe eyes.

"Practice," I grunt, tugging my shirt over my head and trying not to focus on the delicious way she looks in my rumpled bed, all tousled hair and kiss-swollen lips. "Coach will have my ass if I'm late again."

Oakley's brow furrows into an adorable pout that makes me want to drag her back beneath the sheets and never leave this room. "Do you have to go?" she asks, her voice taking on that breathy, needy tone that has become my undoing.

"Baby." She knows I do and if I could skip it I would.

"Cough, cough. I think you're sick. Let's take your temp."

She's so fucking cute at her attempt at trying to get me out of football practice.

Gritting my teeth, I force myself to grab my duffel bag and head for the door before I give in to the temptation writhing in my bed. "I'll be back as soon as it's over," I toss over my shoulder. "Don't go anywhere."

Her soft laughter follows me down the hall. "Yes, teach."

By the time I reach the practice field, I look down at my phone to check the time and see I'm actually going to be on fucking time. Maybe even early. Thank fuck, because I did not want to hear Coach bitching at me. He does enough of that with Lincoln and Penn.

I'm so lost in my thoughts that I almost don't hear the raised voices carrying across the empty field. Frowning, I slow my steps, straining to make out the words over the pounding of my pulse from my trek across campus.

"...getting out of hand, Robert." Coach's gruff tone is laced with a weariness I've never heard from the hard ass before. "Your boys are a nightmare to deal with, and their behavior is becoming a serious liability."

"Those 'boys' happen to be the best players on your pathetic little team," a familiar, oily voice sneers. My jaw clenches at the sound of my father's disdain. "You're lucky to have them, you insignificant prick."

"Enough!" Coach's bellow makes me flinch, a growl rumbling in my chest. "I don't give a fuck how much money you throw at this team. Your sons are completely out of control, and I'm at the end of my rope with dealing with their bullshit with this fucking school!"

My brow furrows as I inch closer, peering around the corner of the equipment shed to see Coach squaring off with my father. Robert Blackwood is leaning back against the brick wall, his expression one of bored disdain as he examines his nails.

"Are you quite done with your tantrum?" he drawls, those cold eyes flicking up to pin Coach with a look of utter contempt. "I don't pay you to whine about disciplining my boys. That's your job. If you can't handle it, I'll find someone who can."

Coach's face is mottled with rage, his fists clenched at his sides. For a moment, I think he might actually take a swing at my father. But then his shoulders slump in resignation, and he shakes his head with a bitter scoff.

"You know what?" he grits out through clenched teeth. "Fuck you, Robert. I'm done putting up with your bullshit, Blackwood. Get your sons to keep their shit under lock and key, and this wouldn't even be a problem."

With that, Coach storms off into the field, his heavy footsteps fading into the distance. For a long moment, my father remains utterly still, his expression unreadable. Then his lip curls into a cruel sneer.

"Idiot," he mutters, shoving off from the wall and straightening his suit jacket. "People don't tell me what to do. I simply end them."

Rage boils through my veins at his callous dismissal. Coach has been with the Spartans for years, pouring his heart and soul into this team. And my father just cast him aside like a used rag as if he hasn't made me and my brothers better football players.

Before I can stop myself, I'm storming out from behind the shed, my footsteps heavy on the grass. "What the fuck was that all about?" I growl, glaring at the man who spawned me.

Robert's eyes narrow as they land on me, that familiar look of disdain curling his lip. "Jeremiah," he sneers. "I didn't realize you were here. Eavesdropping again?"

"Where else would I be? Didn't realize I had to hide from my own father," I shoot back, shoving my hands into the pockets of my shorts to keep from clenching them into fists.

He scoffs, rolling his eyes as he turns on his heel and starts to walk away. "I don't have time for your teenage angst right now. Go run laps with your idiot brothers and stay out of my business."

"I'm fucking twenty-one now, not that you remember shit about any of us. Not unless it's something you need from us."

Robert freezes, his spine going ramrod straight. When he turns to face me again, his expression is as cold and implacable as a slab of granite. "You don't know what the fuck you're even talking about. I don't care how old you are, if you act like a teenager then you are one."

"Jeremiah!"

The bellow cuts through the tension, both of us whipping around to see Coach storming back across the field toward us. His face is thunderous, a vein pulsing at his temple.

"What the fuck are you doing just standing there?" he roars, jabbing a meaty finger toward the track. "Get your ass out there and do your sprints with your goddamn brothers! I'm tired of dealing with all these fucking Blackwoods!"

He turns that furious glare on my father, his shoulders squaring like he's bracing for a fight. "And you," he growls, "keep your nose out of my practices. This is my team, and I'll be damned if I let you keep undermining me in front of my players!"

To my shock, Robert doesn't rise to the bait. He simply levels Coach with a look of pure loathing before smoothing his hands over the lapels of his suit jacket. "We'll see about that," he says in that soft, deadly tone that has always made my blood run cold.

Then, without another word, he's brushing past me, the scent of his expensive cologne making my stomach churn. I watch him stalk away, that familiar sense of dread pooling in my gut.

Whatever shit my father is trying to pull, none of us are going to come out unscathed.

CHAPTER 23
OAKLEY

Jeremiah is off at practice, so instead of staying put, while all the Blackwood dictators are away, I'm here at work. My second home. The hushed silence of the library envelops me as I drift between the towering shelves, my fingers gliding over the worn spines of countless books. The scent of aged paper and ink fills the air, comforting in its familiarity. My eyes catch a rare book nestled among the others, and I carefully retrieve it, cradling it in my hands like a precious artifact. I don't know how it got here and I'm not going to ask, but I'm in no mood for the lecture the entire staff is going to get if the head librarian sees this.

"Guess you're off to the basement later," I murmur to the book, placing it on my desk with a mental note to store it away properly. I'm not even scheduled to work right now, but I can't help it. I wander back through the stacks with my cart, collecting discarded books that students left on the study tables. The only sounds in this sanctuary are the soft rustling of pages and the creaking of ancient floorboards beneath my feet. I often wonder what this place looked like when St.

Charles was first built. What were the people like? What books did they read the most?

When I finally return to my desk, my heart lurches in my chest as I realize the rare book is gone. Confusion and concern wash over me, leaving a bitter taste in my mouth. My eyes dart around the room, searching for any sign of the missing tome. It's not like Cindy is the type to do extra work that she isn't asked to do. She's more of a self-appointed supervisor whose only job is to delegate the work amongst the rest of us.

"Where the hell did it go?" I mutter under my breath, trying to shake off the growing tension that coils in my stomach. It would be just my luck that I'd be the one to lose an expensive heirloom donated to the college.

"Looking for something, Oakley?" a voice asks from behind me. I jump, startled by the sudden intrusion. It's just Cindy, but her innocent question only serves to fuel my unease.

"Uh, yeah," I reply, swallowing hard. "There was this book here on my desk, and now it's gone."

"Maybe someone took it by mistake?" she suggests, shrugging nonchalantly. But I know better. No one picked that book up by mistake and the only thing I can think of is that maybe she's setting me up so she can get me in trouble for something. She's a known tattle tale, but she's never been able to catch me slacking at work.

"Is something wrong?" Cindy asks, her face pinched up like she's smelling something absolutely rank. I don't think it was her. She'd love nothing more than to wave it in my face and taunt me as she made a report for a missing book.

"Never better," I lie, plastering a fake smile onto my lips. "Just...let me know if you need any help today?"

"Sure thing," she agrees, disappearing back into the labyrinth of shelves.

My heart pounds as I approach my coworkers who are huddled around the front desk, trying to stifle the anxiety bubbling within me.

"Hey, uh, have any of you picked up a book I left on my desk? It's one of the ones that belongs down in the freezer. I stepped away for a moment and now it's gone," I ask, my voice wavering slightly.

One by one, they shake their heads, denying any knowledge of the missing book. The air hangs heavy with suspicion, and I can't help but feel like I'm walking a tightrope above a pit of vipers.

"How did it even get up here? Does Cindy know?" Kevin asks, adjusting his glasses nervously. "She'll write a report on it if she finds out."

"I didn't see anyone go near your desk," chimes in Marissa, her eyes darting around the room as if the book might magically appear.

I nod, swallowing hard. "I'm not sure, found it in the Mystery stacks. Thanks, anyway." My fingers drum against my thigh, my mind racing with possibilities. I have that weird feeling again like I'm being watched, which makes me annoyed at myself because as I look around, no one is here that shouldn't be. A stalker didn't sneak into the library and leave a book for me to find just to snatch it off my desk.

Right?

I'm going insane.

As I listen to my co-workers chatter about their schedule and who can take whose shift, Cindy's condescending voice slices through the air like ice on glass.

"Maybe your little fling with Jeremiah Blackwood is

affecting your focus, Oakley. You know, distracting you from your work," she sneers, a cruel smile playing at the corners of her lips. "I overheard you all. Losing one of the heirloom books is a huge deal. Like fired and kicked out of school. Big deal."

A surge of anger washes over me, and I narrow my eyes, ready to defend Jeremiah and his family. The nerve of this woman, thinking she knows everything about my life, my feelings. I won't let her get away with it.

Suddenly I'm sixteen again, ready to take a bullet for Jeremiah because he's the only thing that really truly matters to me.

"First off, *Cynthia*, my relationship with Jeremiah is none of your business. And secondly," I continue, my voice cold and sharp as if I'm channeling one of the Blackwoods, "the Blackwood brothers have nothing to do with this. So keep your snide remarks to yourself."

"Touchy, touchy," Cindy scoffs, clearly taken aback by my sudden assertiveness. "Just trying to help, Oakley. No need to bite my head off."

"Help? Is that what you call it?" I retort, my chest heaving with the effort of keeping my emotions in check. "You're not helping, Cindy. You're just stirring up trouble where there isn't any."

Cindy is used to everyone cowering down to her because she kisses the head librarian's ass.

I stare down Cindy, my heart pounding in my chest as I muster the courage to stand up for myself and those I care about. My hands clench into tight fists at my sides. I've taken her shit and everyone else's for far too long. I snap, my voice trembling with barely contained rage, "I don't want to hear another word from you about Jeremiah or his brothers."

"Oakley," Cindy stammers, her eyes wide in shock, "I've never seen you talk back to anyone like that before." Her tone is begrudgingly respectful, but I couldn't care less about her opinion right now. All that matters tonight is finding that missing book.

"Maybe it's because I'm tired of being pushed around," I retort, my eyes never leaving hers. "Now, if you'll excuse me, I have things to do." Her mouth gapes and it's so fucking satisfying. I know I'm putting a target on my back, but I don't regret it. With a dismissive flick of my wrist, I turn away from her and return to my task.

As I sift through the remaining books on my cart, my mind races with thoughts of the mysterious disappearance. The faint creak of floorboards and the low hum of the fluorescent lights above do little to calm my frayed nerves.

I shove the last book onto its designated shelf, my fingers trembling with frustration and anxiety. The hushed atmosphere of the library only amplifies my unease, as if the silence is a living thing, waiting to swallow me whole.

"Pull yourself together, Oak," I whisper under my breath, forcing a shaky smile onto my face. It's just a missing book. There's a reasonable explanation. No one is out to get me. I hate that I'm this shaken up, but I can't help but feel like it was put there as bait for me to find. It very much feels like someone is toying with me right now.

As I turn to leave the aisle, a shiver races down my spine. My heart thuds wildly in my chest as I glance over my shoulder, scanning the dimly lit aisles for any sign of life.

"Hello?" I call out hesitantly, my voice barely audible even to myself. "Is anyone there?"

No response comes, save for the sound of floorboards—taunting me, mocking my fear. I let out a frustrated sigh, rubbing my temples as I try to convince myself it's just my nerves playing tricks on me.

Oh my God, I need to get a grip. I force my legs to carry me back to the main reading area. I can't help but feel like I'm being ridiculous.

But as I weave through the maze of shelves, the soft rustle of pages turning echoes around me, the sound grating against my ears like nails on a chalkboard right now.

"Uhh, Oakley, you look a little on edge," one of my coworkers states as I pass by, making me jerk back. Their concerned gaze bores into me as I try to calm down.

"I'm fine," I snap, the word coming out harsher than I intended. "Just...worried about that book."

"Okay," they murmur, clearly unconvinced, but not willing to push me further. "Let us know if you need anything, alright?"

"Sure," I mutter, offering them a hollow smile before continuing on my way.

"I'm as paranoid as freaking Penn now," I mutter under my breath, forcing my shaking hands to steady themselves. Jumping out of my skin because a co-worker approached me *at work* isn't cute.

I'm about to head across the aisle when I'm grabbed from behind. I instantly go ridged, kicking until I hear Jeremiah's soothing voice. "Bunny, you okay? I didn't mean to scare the shit outta you." Jeremiah's big arms wrap around me, pulling me back into his hard chest and abdomen.

"Of course, just...I was just in my head," I say, leaving out the fact that I've felt like someone has been watching me my entire shift. I'm unwilling to admit the depth of my unease because I don't want to worry him. The urge to lean into him, to seek reassurance and comfort from the one person who seems to truly understand me, wars with my need to prove my strength and independence.

Something deep within me tells me that Jeremiah is here for keeps, that he'll never let anything happen to me.

"Do you want to let me in on what?" He offers, his eyes searching mine for any hint of the turmoil churning within me as he turns me around to face him. His skin is still damp from his after-practice shower. He takes more showers than anyone else I know and always has. That's why I started calling him pretty boy. He was always determined to be clean and look like he walked off a freaking photo shoot.

"Thanks, Rem, but just thinking about classes and midterms," I say, injecting false confidence into my words. I can't rely on him to fix everything, no matter how tempting the thought may be. "What are you doing here? I thought Coach wanted you to review game tape?"

"I couldn't stop thinking about you," he says, a grin spreading across his handsome face. "And nothing but feeling you in my arms would fix the craving."

"You're ridiculous," I tell him, and I feel the heat flushing my cheeks as he cups my face and leans down to kiss me too roughly for the backdrop of our school library.

"And you're fucking sexy when you blush, bunny," he says as he pulls away from my lips long enough to drop a kiss to my forehead. Jeremiah grins when he sees Cindy walk by the aisle to glare at us. "My fan club is showing up. I guess that's our cue to leave."

Cindy huffs and stomps away, which makes me burst out in laughter, causing Jeremiah to cup the back of my head, pulling my face into his chest so I don't get fired for being too loud in the sacred St. Charles library. When I sober up, I look up at Jeremiah Blackwood and realize that there's nowhere else I'd rather be than in his arms.

CHAPTER 24
JEREMIAH

The heavy thud of the package hitting the doormat makes me jump. I glance at the grandfather clock in the hallway. It's only noon, way too early for the mail, and he knows better than to throw our shit carelessly onto the porch.

I toss aside the textbook that's been siphoning my attention for the past hour and stride to the door with an annoyed huff.

Furrowing my brow, the old wood creaks as I swing open the front door. A battered cardboard box sits innocuously on the deck. No return address, just my name scrawled in thick black marker.

"The fuck?" I mutter, scooping it up.

My sneakers clunk against the hardwood floors as I head for the kitchen. A couple raps with my knuckle reveals it's definitely not clothes or anything soft inside. Solid and weighty.

I grab a steak knife and slice through the tape, my curiosity getting the better of me. Flipping open the box, I'm met with a ratty old book, its leather cover cracked and faded. The scent of aged paper and leather wafts up to greet me.

"Jeremiah?" Oakley's soft voice drifts in from the living room. "Everything okay?"

"Yeah, just some weird ass package showed up." I turn the book over in my hands, searching for any kind of inscription or note tucked inside. Nothing.

Oakley pads into the kitchen, eyes going wide when she sees what I'm holding. She lets out a strangled gasp, both hands flying to cover her mouth.

"Oakley?" I frown, setting the book on the counter. "What's wrong?"

She doesn't answer, just stares at the book with her big blue eyes damn near bugging out of her head. Her chest rises and falls rapidly with panicked breaths.

"Baby." I cross the room in two strides, hands cupping her face. "Breathe. Talk to me."

"That...that book," she stammers, pointing a shaky finger. "It was on my desk. At the library. I had it yesterday, then... then it was just gone."

"Gone?" I repeat, stomach sinking. "You're telling me this just showed up on my doorstep after vanishing from work?"

She nods, worrying her plump lower lip between her teeth. "I didn't want to tell you about it because I felt stupid, like I was overreacting. But now..."

"Dammit, Oakley, why the hell wouldn't you tell me something like this?" The words burst from my lips before I can reel them back in. My hands clench around the leather-bound spine of the book, knuckles whitening.

Her eyes are brimming with apprehension, and it's like I can see the wheels turning in her head. But she doesn't have to say anything; the fear written all over her face says plenty.

"Jeremiah, I—I just..." Oakley stammers, her voice a hushed whisper swallowed up by the spaciousness of the room. "I didn't want to make a big deal out of nothing."

"Nothing?" I scoff, tossing the book onto the coffee table. It lands with a thud, echoing against the walls of my family's ridiculously oversized living room. "You think a book that by accounts looks old and probably valuable as shit just disappearing from your desk is nothing? Shit Oak, if you can't call or tell me these things, then what the fuck are we even doing?"

"Please, I didn't mean it like that." Her plea wraps around me, soft but urgent, and I can almost feel the tug of her worry.

"Christ, bunny," I mutter, rubbing my neck as I wrestle with the anger boiling inside me. "Do you have any idea who could be behind this? We're talking about a rare-as-hell book just popping up after going missing. This is a fucking taunt. Whoever is fucking with you is taunting us, which means he was too fucking close to you at that goddamn library, again."

She blinks rapidly, like she's fighting off tears or worse, total shutdown. And damn it, the sight of her trembling lip and those fingers twisting into the fabric of her dress—it does something fierce to my heart.

"Hey." I breathe out, closing the distance between us in two long strides. My hands find her shoulders, gentle despite the thunderstorm raging in my chest. "I'm sorry. I shouldn't have snapped at you."

Oakley's gaze lifts to meet mine, vulnerability naked in her eyes. "You're right to be mad. I just got scared, and—"

Her breath hitches, eyes glistening with unshed tears. I pull her against my chest, tucking her head under my chin. She clings to me, her slender frame trembling against my body.

"It's okay, baby," I murmur, stroking her silky hair. "I've got you."

On the inside, I'm fucking raging. Someone is fucking with her, toying with me, and it makes me want to put my fist through a wall. No, worse than that. I want to find the sick fuck responsible and bury him alive with a camera so I can watch his panic.

Footsteps thunder in the hallway, cutting off my darkening thoughts.

"Jeremiah!" my dad's gruff voice bellows. "Where the hell are you, son?"

Oakley stiffens in my arms at the sound of him. I shoot her a reassuring look, pressing a kiss to her forehead.

"In here," I call out flatly. No fucking way am I telling him about any of this shit going on. He'll just make things a thousand times worse.

Robert Blackwood storms into the kitchen, his face like a thundercloud of doom about to add to the bullshit that is my day. I straighten to my full height, keeping Oakley tucked against my side.

"Didn't expect to see you today, or ever without a summons," I say, injecting a casual note into my words. "To what do we owe the honor?"

"Can't a father visit his son?" He tilts his head slightly, eyes sharp, missing nothing.

"Of course, but you and I both know 'visits' aren't really our thing. What's got your panties in a twist this time?" I sneer, unable to resist riling him up. Oakley squeezes my hand in silent warning, but I barrel on. "Did you lose a deal because they couldn't put up with your ego?"

"Watch your fucking smart mouth," Dad growls, dark eyes

narrowing to slits. "Your brother went and got himself arrested for assault so I don't have time for your shit."

A muscle ticks in my jaw. "I don't see why you're here throwing a fit with me, Dad."

"I swear, you boys will be the death of me." Dad rakes a hand through his silver-streaked hair, letting out a blustery sigh. "I swear, you boys will be the death of me.

His gaze shifts past me, landing on Oakley, and I feel her stiffen. "Miss Ashford," he says, his voice dripping with a politeness that doesn't quite reach his cold eyes. "A pleasure."

"Mr. Blackwood," Oakley replies, her voice a tremulous whisper that somehow still carries the weight of her courage.

"Robert," he corrects with a hint of command. "We're practically family, after all."

"Practically," I echo, the single word laced with a lifetime of unspoken battles. I'm not about to let him rattle us—not here, not now.

"Jeremiah," Oakley whispers, her fear a tangible thing pressing against my side.

"Everything's under control, Oakley," I assure her, though the tension coils tighter within me, ready to spring.

"Good to see you putting those protective instincts to use," Robert comments, his eyes gleaming with a challenge. His mouth curls into a sneer. "Of course, the two of you would be joined at the hip. The end of the world wouldn't have kept the two of you apart, would it?"

White-hot anger surges through me. I open my mouth to unleash the storm brewing inside, but he just keeps going.

"The Ashfords," he drawls from the doorway, lips twisted in a smirk that could curdle milk. "Always had more dollars than sense, didn't they? But I suppose crushes—or whatever you kids are calling it these days—know no bounds."

The words hit me like a punch to the gut. My fingers curl into fists as his sneer crawls under my skin. He's always known exactly how to needle me, and mentioning Oakley, sweet, innocent Oakley, in that tone...it's a low blow even for him.

"That's enough," I say, voice low but firm as steel. I arch one eyebrow at my father. "If you've got a problem with me, say it to my face instead of dancing around with petty insults. She's got nothing to do with this."

"You need to learn some fucking respect, boy!" he roars, rounding on me again.

"Jeremiah!" Oakley cries, darting forward to put herself between us.

"Get out of my way, you little bitch," Dad snarls, pushing her backwards.

That's it. I snap, seeing red, every rational thought blown out of my brain.

"Don't you fucking touch her!" I lunge for my dad, hands closing around his throat.

We go down in a heap, trading blows and grunts of pain. Dad gets in a solid punch, rocking my head back. I taste copper, thick and metallic in my mouth.

"What the fuck is going on?" Graham's voice booms from the doorway.

Before I can react, he's on me, arms like steel bands locked around my chest. With one massive heave, he hauls me off Dad, pinning me against the wall.

"Let me go!" I thrash wildly, hell-bent on ripping my father's throat out.

"Jeremiah, you need to shut the fuck up and go cool off," Graham growls in my ear, leaning his weight into me. "We've got enough chaos with Lincoln right now. Don't make this shit worse by boxing Dad in the fucking living room."

I sag against the wall; the fight draining out of me. Graham's right. As much as I want to beat Dad's face in, that won't solve a damn thing.

Oakley has backed herself into a corner, shoulders hunched, eyes wide with fear. She looks so fucking small, so fragile. Like a scared little rabbit.

The sight of her like that hits me harder than any of Dad's punches. I shove Graham off me, ignoring his warning glare.

"Oakley," I say, keeping my voice soft and level. "Let's go, baby."

She doesn't hesitate, darting across the room to my side. I wrap an arm around her, pulling her close as we leave the kitchen. Dad and Graham's angry shouts follow us down the hall, but I block them out. Graham can be Dad's golden boy right now because I'm fucking done.

Once we're in my room, I shut and lock the door behind us. Oakley immediately burrows into my arms, face pressed against my chest. I stroke her hair, murmuring soothing nonsense against the crown of her head.

"Jesus," I exhale, leaning back against the door. "Is it just me, or does he get worse every time?"

Oakley laughs, the sound brittle but real. "It's not just you," she says, squeezing my hand.

"I'm sorry you had to see that, bunny," I whisper, guilt gnawing at my insides. "I never wanted you to be around that kind of ugliness."

She tilts her head back, eyes shimmering but determined. "Don't apologize for him, Rem. You were just protecting me."

"Christ, I'd kill for a moment of peace."

CHAPTER 25
OAKLEY

"I can't stand to be in this house while he's here," Jeremiah spits out, rage and anguish twisting his features as he enters his bedroom. "Come on, we're going to go for a drive." His voice cracks under the weight of his emotions, eyes burning with anger and sadness that cuts through me like a knife.

I can't just stand by and do nothing. His father is an ass, always has been and most likely always will be, but I still don't want to be the reason he and Jeremiah are fighting. I step closer to Jeremiah, reaching out to touch his arm gently. "Pretty boy," I say softly, trying to infuse my voice with as much understanding and concern as I can muster, "you don't have to do this for me. I don't want to be the reason—"

Jeremiah cuts me off by covering my fingers with his own. He looks down at my hand on his arm, then back up at me. The torment in his eyes makes my heart ache. He's always been so strong, but right now, he looks like he's barely holding it together.

My breath hitches as I look into his eyes, feeling the

weight of his emotions pressing against me like a tangible force. His gaze is filled with so much love, it feels like it's branding itself onto my soul. The world around us fades away, leaving just the two of us in this moment.

"The reason for everything I do," he continues, his voice gaining strength, "is you. Every single thing. I promise you, bunny, nothing else in this world matters to me." His words wrap around me, and for the first time in years I actually feel what love feels like. My parents were just there, existing, and my anger with Royce has eclipsed my emotions. The room seems to close in, making every word, every breath shared between us as one.

Jeremiah's lips crash into mine with a force that leaves me breathless. The taste of him floods my senses—warm, intoxicating, and utterly consuming. His hands, strong, slide down to grip my waist, pulling me closer. Every second our lips are locked together, I feel this all-consuming love. His large hands cup my ass, pulling me into his body like he wants to mesh us together.

"Jeremiah," I gasp against his mouth, but he doesn't let up. He kisses me like he's trying to etch himself into my very soul. I have to push up on my tiptoes even though he's leaning down to my height. My hands find their way to the back of his neck, fingers linking together right beneath the stubble of his hair that's starting to grow out. The world outside fades into obscurity; it's just us.

"C'mon Oak, we gotta get outta here," he murmurs, his voice husky with need and urgency. With a gentle yet firm hold on my hand, he pulls me away from the room.

"Where are we going?" I ask as we briskly walk down the dim corridor of the house, the opulence of it now feeling more like a gilded cage than a home. The Robert Blackwood effect.

"Back to where it all began," he says ambiguously, glancing at me with anticipation in his green eyes. A small, enigmatic smile plays on his lips, and it sends a shiver down my spine.

"Jeremiah, you can't just say something like that and not explain," I press, my curiosity getting the better of me. "How long have you been planning this?" I ask skeptically, because I don't buy for a second that he thought of this just because his dad showed up and made him mad.

"I've wanted to take you somewhere for a while," he replies, his tone teasing but tinged with something deeper. "Today's the perfect night."

We emerge from the mansion into the cool fall air with Jeremiah holding both of our jackets. The sky is a hazy gray, and you can almost sense the impending rain. Jeremiah's bike waits for us, sleek, black and green Ducati Streetfighter Lamborghini. I only know that's what it was because Penn was bitching about it the other night. I just knew the color and how it feels to be on the back of it previously.

He grabs my helmet and places it on my head, his fingers brushing against my skin as he secures the strap. Always taking care of me, even little tasks that I'm perfectly capable of doing myself. I let him though, because I truly think he does enjoy it. My breath catches as his eyes lock onto mine for a beat before he pulls back, strapping on his own helmet with practiced ease.

"Ready?" he asks, his voice a low rumble that sends shivers down my spine.

"Always," I reply, my heart pounding in anticipation as I slip into my black leather he left for me on my seat.

Jeremiah swings his leg over the motorcycle with a fluid grace that leaves me momentarily breathless. He glances back at me, holds his hand out with the invitation clear in his eyes. I grab hold of him and climb on, wrapping my arms around his waist, and slipping my hands underneath the leathers and his shirt, feeling the solid strength beneath my palms. The engine roars to life, a powerful vibration that reverberates through my bones.

As we speed away, the world blurs around us. The wind whips through my hair, carrying with it the scent of decaying pine and asphalt. My grip tightens around Jeremiah, pressing myself closer to him, feeling the heat of his body seep into mine.

"Where are we going?" I shout over the roar of the engine, my voice tinged with exhilaration.

"Just trust me, Oakley," he calls back, his voice barely audible over the wind.

The city lights fade behind us as we ride, the landscape shifting to familiar territory. My heart skips a beat when I recognize the route. Our high school looms ahead and memories flood my mind, bittersweet and vivid. The place where it all began, indeed.

"Jeremiah..." I whisper, the name a blend of nostalgia and longing.

"Hold on tight," he says, his voice softer now, laden with unspoken promises.

We pull up to the school; the bike coming to a smooth halt. The silence is almost too much to handle after the rush of the ride. Jeremiah dismounts first, offering me his hand. As I take it, our fingers intertwine, grounding me in him. We leave our helmets and jackets on the bike and stand there staring at Bridgehead High.

"Why here?" I ask, my voice trembling with so many emotions, I can't possibly pick just one.

"Because this is where everything changed for me, bunny," he replies, his eyes dark with intensity. "I knew there would never be anyone other than you for me all the way back then."

"You did?" I ask, confusion mingling with curiosity.

"It's always been you. I keep trying to tell you that," he repeats, pulling me closer, his breath warm against my ear.

His words wrap around me like a protective cocoon, and despite the uncertainty, I feel a flicker of hope. We stand there for a moment, locked in each other's gaze, the weight of our past pressing down on us.

"Let's go," Jeremiah says finally, his voice a gentle command.

"I'll let you lead," I reply, my heart pounding with anticipation as he tugs me toward the back of the school.

Jeremiah's fingers work the lock, each click and clack echoing, and I glance around, waiting for us to be caught. The air is cool, but my skin tingles with anticipation. I watch him, biting my lip as he works. His intense focus is almost hypnotic.

"You're pretty good at this," I whisper, my voice barely audible in the stillness. The echo of our high school days surrounds us, both comforting and eerie.

"I'm a Blackwood, after all," he shoots back with a smirk, not taking his eyes off the lock. A final, satisfying click, and the door swings open. "Penn taught me," he finally admits with a shoulder shrug, and I'm not surprised at the revelation.

"After you," he says, stepping aside and sweeping an arm in a mock-gentlemanly gesture.

"Such a charmer," I murmur, slipping past him. The darkened halls feel different, shadows stretching long and memories lurking around every corner. My heart pounds louder than our footsteps.

"Where to?" I ask, glancing back at him. I don't even feel the jittery need to ask if he thinks this is okay, if we'll get caught, if we'll be in trouble. With Jeremiah, I don't have to worry about anything. He wouldn't let anything happen to me.

"Follow me," he replies, his voice low and magnetic. He grabs my hand, and we move together. We ascend staircases and Jeremiah's grip on my hand steadies me, anchors me.

"Almost there," he says, pushing open a door that leads to the roof. The sudden gust of wind makes me shiver, but the sight before me steals my breath.

The football field and then the crop of trees that surround Bridgehead span in front of us and you can just barely see the tops of houses on the other side of the woods. I hear music start to play and I glance back to see he's set his phone up on one of the ledges. The sounds of Chappell Roan reach my ears and I'm shocked he's playing pop music, but I guess I shouldn't be. He knows she's my favorite artists' favorite artist.

"Wow," I breathe, stepping forward.

"Figured you'd like it," Jeremiah says, coming up behind me. His hands find my waist, pulling me close. His warmth seeps into me, making my heart race.

"You're full of surprises," I say, leaning into him. His scent —earthy, musky, familiar—wraps around me, grounding me.

"Just wait," he murmurs, his lips brushing my ear. "I've got more in store."

"Promises, promises," I tease, turning in his arms to face him.

"Oakley," he says softly, his voice deep and raw. "I need you to know everything I do is for you. To protect you."

I don't say anything in return because I don't have the words. I lean back against him, fully allowing him to hold my weight. I need him to know that I trust him now in a way that I didn't before. I trust him with my life, and I can't say that about a singular other soul in this world.

"Remember how we used to sneak up here during school hours?" I ask, tracing the lines of the skyline with my eyes. "We thought we were invincible."

Jeremiah replies, his breath warm against my neck, "Back when things were simpler. Or at least seemed that way."

"Who would've thought we'd end up here again?" I continue, a wistful smile playing on my lips. "So much has changed since those days."

"Everything's different now," he agrees, his voice tinged with a hint of melancholy. "But some things never change."

"Like what?" I turn to look at him, curiosity flickering in my eyes.

"Like how I've always needed you," he says, his gaze intense. "How I'll *always* need you."

"Jeremiah," I whisper, my voice catching in my throat. The weight of his words hanging heavy in the air between us.

"Oakley," he says, pulling me closer. "You don't have to say anything. Just let me hold you."

He lets me go before he sits down, back up against the roof's short wall, and he tugs my hand until I stumble and settle on his lap. Our bodies fit together perfectly, as if we were made for each other. The sensation of his strong arms around me, his heartbeat steady beneath my ear, fills me with a sense of completeness I've never known before.

"Is this real?" I murmur, my fingers tracing the contours of his face. "It feels like a dream."

"It's real," he assures me, his voice a soothing balm. "And I'm not going anywhere."

"Promise?" I ask, needing to hear it again.

"Promise," he says, sealing it with a kiss that makes my heart flutter.

As we sit there, the world fades away. All that matters is this moment, the feeling of being right where we belong.

"Let's stay here forever," I say, knowing it's impossible but wishing for it all the same.

"Forever might be a long time," he teases, a hint of a smile curving his lips. "But I wouldn't mind trying."

"Yea, me neither," I reply, my heart swelling with hope and love.

As we lean in for another kiss, the clouds above seem to part letting small rays of sunshine in, as if they too are witnesses to the magic of him and I. And for the first time in a long while, I feel truly, deeply happy.

I see the pain in his eyes, a mirror of my own. "I made mistakes," he admits, each word trembling. "Leaving you...it was the biggest one. I want to spend the rest of my life making that up to you."

It feels like I'm caught between wanting to console him and needing to hear more. He cups my face, his touch sending electric chills down my spine. "I'm so sorry, bunny. I need you to believe it."

"You're here now," I murmur, pressing my forehead against his. The warmth of our closeness, the mingling of our breaths—it feels like reclaiming something lost.

"I love you. I need you to know that. You don't have to say

it back, but—" his fingers dig deeper into my flesh, almost as if he's afraid I'm going to run away from him.

"Shut up," I cut him off, my voice choked with emotion. "I love you too, pretty boy."

The confession bursts from me, raw and unfiltered. It's as if we're pouring all our pain, love, and promises into this moment.

His hands roam my body, pulling me closer until there's no space left between us. The world fades away, leaving just this.

That's the thing about Jeremiah Blackwood. He always knows what I need.

CHAPTER 26
JEREMIAH

She fucking loves me.

Jeremiah. Just Jeremiah, not Blackwood, not leading defensive back for the state.

Not because of my money or status. Definitely for my big ass dick, though.

I'm gonna marry this girl and put babies in her one day. Fuck, just the thought of it has me bricked up and ready to start now.

My hands grip Oakley's waist, pulling her closer, flushed hard against me. Her body is such a contrast to mine—petite, almost fragile. But there's nothing delicate about the way she's looking at me right now. She looks like she could devour me, and I'd let her.

"Jeremiah," she breathes, desire and desperation coating every syllable. There's something in the way she says my name, like it's a prayer or a curse.

I push her back against the rough surface of the school's roof, relishing the way her soft curves press into the hard lines of my body. The sky opens up and rain soaks through our clothes, plastering fabric to skin, but I can't get close enough. My fingers tangle in her long golden hair, pulling gently to expose the slender column of her neck.

"God, baby, you're perfect," I groan, tracing the blue veins visible beneath her skin. She arches into my touch, and I can't help but feel like some obsessed artist driven mad by his muse.

"Pretty words from a pretty boy," she teases, her eyes bright under the darkened sky, "keep talking like that, and we won't make it to bed."

But the water dropping on us is relentless, thrumming in a steady rhythm, as if it's urging us on. I drop my head to her shoulder, inhaling the earthy scent of rain mixed with her floral perfume. It's intoxicating, and I lose myself in the sensation, in the taste of her skin against my tongue as I lick up and down her neck and jaw.

"Always so quick-witted," I say against her lips before claiming them with mine.

She responds with equal fervor, her nails digging into my back as if she's trying to pull me inside her soul. And I'd go willingly; I'd drown in the depths of her without a second thought.

"Want you so much," I murmur, moving urgently against her feeling her dress sticking to my hands.

"Show me," she challenges, sass wrapped in sweetness, her hands demanding as they explore my own drenched form.

I drag myself down her body, lifting the now sheer fabric of her dress up and pull her panties down and tucking them into my pocket so I can feast on her sweet cunt.

I wrap my hands around her small legs, watching as they damn near cover the whole thing and spread her open for me. Burying my face into her pussy, I breathe her in and her taste, her scent, it's better than I remember. She's soaked for me, her arousal coating my lips and chin as I lap at her center like a man starved of water. I can't get enough of her.

My tongue burrows into her tight heat, seeking out her clit and teasing the bundle of nerves until she's damn near incoherent. Her cries of pleasure muffled only by the rain pelting the tin roof of the entrance.

"Ah fuck," she moans, her sweet little voice sounding so dirty with the fuck word on her lips as I tease her clit with my tongue, swirling around it before gently sucking it into my mouth. As I run my tongue over her folds, I can taste the sweet tang of her arousal, and it's like a drug, making me want more.

Her hands grasp at my outgrown hair, nails dragging through the short stubbly strands as she arches her back.

"Look at you, under me like my own personal fucking Tinkerbell, folded like origami. I own you, Oakley Ashford. Your heart, your body, your soul, and your womb. I'm gonna fuck my cum into you so hard one day it'll take root and your little body will birth my big Blackwood babies."

I devour her, using my lips, teeth and fingers to wring every last ounce of pleasure from her trembling body. She's so wet, so goddamn wet for me and it's all I can do not to dive in right then and there. Instead, I tease her mercilessly, circling her clit with my tongue before plunging two fingers inside her tight heat, curling them inside her as I worship her with my mouth. Oakley's taste is addicting, like honey and sin, and I don't know how I ever went without it.

The sight of her before me, the taste of her on my tongue, and the wet sounds of my fingers plunging in and out of her have me ready to start humping this fucking roof.

"Oh God," her legs shake around my shoulders as she cries out as she comes apart in my mouth, showering me with her release. I relish in the power I have over her, the way she falls apart under my touch.

I pull away, glancing up at her flushed face and glazed over eyes. "You taste like what I imagine pixie dust tastes like," I growl, licking my lips before standing up and lifting her into my arms. Her legs wrap around my waist willingly, as if she was made to be here with me.

"Your turn," I growl against her neck as Oakley bites down on her lip, arousal clouding her eyes. Reaching down, I push my joggers until I can free my rock-hard cock. Sitting down on the drenched roof, I sit her on my stomach. "Ride me," I order through clenched teeth, unable to hide how badly I want her now.

She doesn't hesitate, wrapping those sexy thighs around me as she slowly lowers herself down onto my waiting length. A low moan escapes both our lips at the contact; it's everything we both needed and not nearly enough.

Oakley's delicate hands brace against my drenched chest as she slowly rocks up and down; her wetness and the rain helping her descend. The sight of her taking me so willingly, so hungrily is enough to make me come undone right then and there.

"That's it, baby girl," I growl, claiming her lips in a bruising kiss as she bounces on my cock. "You missed me, didn't you?" I growl against her lips.

"I did," she whimpers, biting down on her bottom lip in ecstasy. "You have no idea."

"Fuck, you're so tight," I groan as she grinds against me, taking me inch by inch. "You feel so fucking good, Oakley," I moan against her skin.

Oakley moans into my mouth as she finds her rhythm, bouncing up and down on my cock. The sound of our wet skin and her little mewls are the only thing breaking the silence between us. Her hands grip my biceps, digging in as she leans back, heading for another orgasm.

"That's it baby, take it all," I growl my praise as she impales herself over me. "You've always belonged to me, even when you didn't know it," I say, thrusting upward as she bottoms out on me.

Her pussy clenches around me like a vise grip, covering me in her juices and the rain making us even more slippery than before. "I've missed this pussy so much," I pant out as I pull her hair so her blue eyes meet mine.

"You just had me. How can you even miss it?" she moans before biting my bottom lip hard enough to draw blood, but I don't even care.

"Because I left it, even if it was only for a few hours," I growl as I drive myself deep inside her again and again, trying to get closer to whatever it is that makes her who she uniquely is. And fuck if it isn't the best fucking thing I've ever had, as the rain pours down around us like some sort of biblical cleansing.

There will be no washing away this sin, I'm a goddamn sinner and she's the one I'll sin over and over for.

"Jeremiah," she moans, her nails digging into my chest as she forces me deeper inside her tight pussy.

"Oh fuck," I moan as she milks my length with every ounce of skill she possesses. This girl was made for this; she was made for me. "I'm gonna-"

Before I can finish, Oakley's body tenses around me, milking the cum right out of my fucking balls. My orgasm rocks through me like lightning arcing through my veins as I fill her with everything I have to give; my body shudders violently underneath hers as we both call out in unison.

Her legs begin to shake as she collapses against my chest, my cock still buried deep inside her. I hold firmly onto her hips as our breathing even out. There's a part of me that doesn't ever want to let her go, that wants to feel the warmth of her body against mine for an eternity.

"I love you," I say, brushing a strand of wet hair away from her face.

Oakley looks down at me, eyes glassy with lust and something else I can't quite place. "I love you too," she whispers before kissing my jawline.

My heart swells with emotion that I thought had long ago been dead.

I pull her up off my cock and slide her up to sit on my lower abdomen as my cock hangs spent between my legs. Drawing my legs up, I grab her panties out of my pocket, balling them into my fist before pushing her backward to rest against my bent knees.

I watch as her senses come back to her, and she tries to push the wet, frilly dress down to cover her pussy and one searing look from me stops her.

"You're pretty little pussy is leaving such a mess on me, baby. We're gonna have to do something about that. Such a messy girl." She blushes bright red and if my cock could stir enough to fuck her again it would.

I wipe up the puddle of our combined cum from my stomach with her pastel green panties and then slowly drag them up and down her slit. Her body switches and her eyes widen at my action until I stop at her entrance and slowly force the silky used material into her until she swallows it up.

"Gotta keep my cum in you, baby. It's gotta brand every inch of you from the inside and out, and we don't want to waste a drop, do we?"

All she can do is shake her head before I lean up and help her to stand up. She shuffles her legs as she gets used to the feeling of being stuffed full of something that's not my dick.

Tugging my wet fucking pants up and tucking my cock back in is fucking annoying, but it's time we get off this roof before I decide we can just live here.

The rain's turned cold as hell, and Oakley's shivering in my arms. "We should get inside," I suggest, half-dragging her toward the roof door, my voice rough with concern.

She shakes her head, those bright blue eyes defiant even as she quakes. "No, stay here with me." Her lips are tinged blue, but they're stubborn. "This is perfect, Jeremiah. Just us."

"Perfect doesn't include you catching pneumonia, bunny," I argue, but it's half-hearted because goddamn if I don't love her just a little bit more because of it.

It's a heady thing, having someone love you like that. Having them put that much faith in you, even after all the bullshit I've put her through.

I'm not sure I deserve it. But I'll be damned if I don't plan to spend every day proving myself worthy of it.

I take her hand and lead her toward the door that'll take us back down into the school. Only to find it firmly locked, the handle not even budging when I rattle it.

Frowning, I crouch down to inspect the lock. It doesn't take long to realize something is very wrong. There's a piece of metal jammed into the locking mechanism, clearly intentionally placed to block the door from opening.

A cold sense of dread washes over me as I straighten, automatically pulling Oakley against my side. She must sense the shift in my mood, her brow furrowing in concern as she looks up at me.

"What is it? What's wrong?"

"Someone's here," I murmur, casting a wary glance around the rooftop. "I can feel it."

Keeping a tight grip on her hand, I guide us toward the far edge of the roof. My breath catches at the sight of my bike lying on its side, tires slashed and the glossy paint keyed to shit with what looks like a name carved deep into the metal.

Rage surges through me, bitter and caustic on my tongue.

Pulling my phone from my pocket, I quickly hit Penn's number and push call. It rings twice before that smug voice answers.

"Well, well, if it isn't my favorite little brother calling me for a favor. What'll it be this time, Jere? Need me to-"

"Can it, asshole," I growl, cutting off his snide remarks. "I need you to get your ass over to Bridgehead High, and I need you here yesterday."

There's a pregnant pause before he speaks again, his tone shifting to something more serious. "What's going on?"

"Someone's been here," I grit out, gaze roving the rooftop again as I tighten my grip on Oakley. "They fucked with my bike, and now I'm stuck up here with a blocked door. I need you to get here and help me get Oakley out safely."

"Well, well, Jere, you sly dog. Should've known this had something to do with that blonde bombshell of yours. A little high school role play. Kinky. So tell me, what'll you give me if I get my ass over there to play white knight?"

I grit my teeth, fighting the urge to put my fist through the nearest wall. Trust Penn to try and squeeze something out of this for his own amusement. The fact that Oakley's safety is on the line doesn't seem to matter to that selfish prick.

"How about I don't beat the ever-loving shit out of you the next time I see you?" I growl. "Would that be enough incentive for you?"

He lets out a low whistle. "Damn, baby bro, you've got a hell of a way of asking for favors. Fine, I'm on my way. But you owe me one. This isn't something I'll be forgetting anytime soon."

The line goes dead, and I resist the urge to chuck my phone over the edge of the roof. Instead, I pocket it and turn to Oakley, my free hand coming up to cup her cheek.

"Penn's on his way," I murmur, holding her gaze. "I'm gonna get you out of here safe, bunny. I swear it on my life."

Whatever shit is about to go down, I'll be ready. No one takes from me and gets away with it.

Not anymore.

Time stretches, thins out. Every minute is an hour, waiting for Penn's arrival, but at least it's finally stopped raining. The overhang was just barely big enough to fit Oakley under it to keep her from getting hit with anymore droplets.

The faint sound of footsteps, a silhouette emerging from below. Penn.

"Brother!" I call down, relief flooding through me, washing away some of the dread. "It's about damn time."

"Keep your panties on," Penn's voice floats up, that trademark slyness interlaced through his tone despite the gravity of the situation. "You owe me big for this one."

"Put it on my tab," I shoot back, but my hands aren't shaking anymore, and my breath comes easier. With Penn here, the odds shift back in our favor.

"Let's get you two off this rooftop before you turn into a couple of drowned rats," he says, looking between us, taking in the scene. "Or worse."

"Thanks, Penn," Oakley says, her voice steady, her sass undiminished even now. "Your chivalry is noted."

"Chivalry's my middle name, lil Ashford," Penn quips, but

the tight line of his lips tells me he's taking this seriously. "Now, let's figure out a way to bust this door open and get the hell out of here."

Penn tinkers with whatever the fuck is on the other side of the door before finally it pops open.

"Shame I couldn't use fire. It would have been like senior year all over again." I don't even bother responding.

"Once we're down, we need to check out my bike." I can't keep the anger from seeping into my voice, thinking about the vandalized mess waiting below. Someone's sending a message, and it's written all over my ride.

"Whoever did this has a death wish. You just don't mess with a man's bike," Penn states, echoing my thoughts. His jaw clenches, a muscle ticking in his cheek. "We'll find them, and I'll light their asses up."

I grab Oakley up in my arms and carry her down the stairs and away from the roof, trusting my brother to watch our backs for whoever is fucking lurking.

We pause at my bike and look at the damage. It's going to need cosmetic work for sure, but it's salvageable. The gouges I saw from up above are clearer now. Bunny.

Someone is definitely fucking paying too much attention to us.

"Can you call Weston and have my bike picked up?" I ask my brother.

"Already did. It'll give me an excuse to go over there and let him suck my dick, also. He's got a mouth like a vacuum sealer." And there it is. I could do without knowing the merits of everyone's blowjob skills.

I see he's brought the Escalade and left it idling at the turnabout in front of the school. I open the back door and set

Oakley inside before having her scoot over and climbing in to sit next to her.

Penn slides into the driver's seat with a casual ease that belies the tension radiating through the vehicle. He glances back at us through the rearview mirror, his smirk returning. "You two look cozy back there. So happy to be driving Miss Daisy."

"Shut up and drive, Penn," I snap, my patience wearing thin. Every second we waste is another second whoever did this could be getting away.

"Alright, alright," he mutters, putting the car into gear. "No need to get your undies in a twist."

"Uh, what's this?" I glance over and see Oakley holding up a screaming ghost mask, and I literally want to reach forward and smack the shit out of my brother.

"Ayy lil Ashford, that's mine. Don't you worry about it, but you tell me if you ever want a break from that one next to you and to take a ride on it mkay." he cackles, swear to fucking God an evil cackle escapes his mouth.

Jesus, fuck, he's psychotic.

CHAPTER 27
OAKLEY

Jeremiah's called a meeting with two of his brothers to try to figure out who is stalking us. His hands are steady as he presents a stack of papers to Graham and Penn.

"Are there snacks? Do we have hats? Like, what can I expect from this team meeting? Where's the round table? I have fucking questions Jerry and the least you could do is provide libations especially after I just played captain save-a-hoe for you and my bestie like less than an hour ago?" I'm more convinced now than ever that Penn was switched at birth.

"What's this?" Graham asks, leaning forward with his brow furrowing and stopping whatever argument was about to happen between the other two Blackwoods, sucking up all the air in the room. He takes the stack from Jeremiah, his broad shoulders tense with a restless energy.

"More evidence," Jeremiah replies, his voice tight. "Who-ever this is, followed us up to Bridgehead and trashed my bike,"

"Jesus Christ," Graham mutters, his eye twitching already.

"I want to know who this fucker is," Jeremiah continues, his voice steady. "Watching her every move, sending threats... It has to be whoever attacked her back when..." I hear the waver in his voice, like he feels like I was only attacked that night because he wasn't there to protect me.

I cut in because I don't want him to carry that burden any longer, "when I was at St. James, someone attacked me. I don't remember much of it, but Jeremiah thinks this is the same person."

"How the hell does this just happen, and no one knows shit?" Graham's voice is taut with anger, his piercing brown eyes locking onto mine.

I swallow hard, my mind racing. The memories of the past flood back, each moment of fear and paranoia amplified by the dark, oppressive thoughts swirling around me.

"Bunny, it's going to be okay. You have me. You have my brothers too," Jeremiah says softly, his gaze shifting to me before shooting back to Graham and Penn. Graham nods in affirmation.

"I'm down to fuck some shit up," Penn says, grinning, leaning back on the recliner and crossing his arms over his chest. "Any idea who it is? If not, no worries. I have no problem just picking off random dudes till we get the right one." He shrugs and I want to laugh, but I don't because I know he's not kidding. Penn Blackwood is psychotic.

I shake my head slowly, my fingers intertwining and twisting together in my lap. "He got spooked when he heard someone coming and he knocked me out. When I woke up, he was gone. I don't remember what he looked like."

"Was it on campus?" Penn asks, his eyes still fixed on the disturbing photos before his gaze moves up to me. I nod and he asks, "At a party?"

Jeremiah nods yes for me, his expression grim as he pulls me on his lap. He can see I'm shutting down and I'm grateful he knows me so well.

Graham leans forward, eyes like ice chips boring into me. "Oakley," he says, voice low and rough-edged. "Do you have any idea who it might be? Anybody at all? Anyone you talked to that night? Did he live at the house where the party was?"

My hands twist together in my lap, fingers knotting and unknotting like a nervous dance.

"I wish I did. Rem has asked me countless times, but there's nothing up here." My voice is barely more than a whisper, but it feels like it's echoing in the vast room. " I didn't really have any friends at St. James. I was so used to tagging along with you guys—" I can feel the weight of their stares pressing down on me. "I thought maybe by getting out, I'd meet some new people. Turns out not everyone is as nice to me as the infamous Blackwood brothers." I try to joke, but no one laughs. Jeremiah presses his face against my hair, pulling me tight against his chest.

"Dammit, Oakley," Graham growls, his frustration palpable. "You cannot trust random people."

I feel Jeremiah take a deep breath like he's about to lay into Graham for blaming me, but it's Penn who snaps at him. "It's not her fault. Royce wasn't there to protect her, and neither were any of us. So shut the fuck up before you shut her down completely. You're the least in tune with emotions, Grammy and so let your big brother take the lead. We need to figure out who the fucker is so we can rip his dick off and make him swallow it."

I glance at Jeremiah, hoping for some sign of reassurance, but his face is a mask of grim determination. Penn's smirk is gone; his usual sarcastic edge replaced by a rare seriousness.

For once, we're all united by the same goal, the same need to end this nightmare.

"I'm scared," I say, trying to keep my voice steady. "I don't know who it is. I wish I did. But I don't want to put any of you in danger. Because I live here, I feel like that's exactly what I'm doing."

Penn twirls his finger in the air as if to say, 'big whoop'. "I'd like to see them fucking try to come in here. I hope they do, actually. I wouldn't have to worry about public cameras, moving bodies, you know the usual shit that gets little piggies sniffing around."

"Did your mom drop kick you when you were a baby?" Graham snaps at Penn before turning to me, "No one will touch you here. We'll figure it out. I'm sorry that happened to you." Graham isn't one to express emotion and the words come out clipped and straight to the point, but I know he means what he says.

"I'm gonna get punched in the dick for bringing this up, I'm sure." Penn's voice slices through the quiet like a knife. He leans back in his chair, eyes glinting, and I just know whatever he says next is going to be bad. "But let's not forget there might be other reasons someone would want to keep tabs on you, Oakley."

I stiffen, already knowing where he's going. At least my new laptop is not within arm's reach of Jeremiah.

"Maybe one of your...viewers?" He raises an eyebrow, the implication hanging heavy in the air. "From your stripper shows."

My stomach churns. The room feels smaller, suffocating. My hands fidget in my lap, fingers twisting together as if they can somehow hold me together. I force myself to meet his gaze, then look away just as quickly when I feel Jeremiah jerk forward. "It's okay," I say, but Jeremiah's eyes are zeroed in on his brother.

"I never stripped, first of all," I tell him, my voice steady but low. "But I blocked and reported any of the guys who gave me a hard time. I was careful to use a backdrop, and I never gave any identifying info, so they'd know where to find me."

"Yes, yes, I'm sure you did all the things but little Ashford, when it comes to crazy baby, none of that matters. One small slip up and they can find you. I do it all the time," Penn says, sarcasm dripping from every word. His eyes are fixed on me, challenging.

"I'm telling you I didn't slip up," I snap, frustration bubbling up. "But being a cam girl was therapeutic for me. It gave me control after...after everything."

The room goes silent. I can feel every eye on me, judging, questioning. The weight of their scrutiny presses down, making it hard to breathe.

"Therapy, huh?" Penn's tone is mocking, but there's something else there too—curiosity, maybe even understanding. "Interesting choice."

"Yeah, well, we all have our ways," I reply, my voice sharp. "And mine helped me reclaim my body, my autonomy."

"Okay, okay, chill," Penn says, holding up his hands in mock surrender. He's snickering and I realize then he only brought up the cam site thing to irritate Jeremiah. It wasn't this side of five minutes ago he was admonishing Graham for victim blaming me. "Just putting it out there."

"Well, put it back," Jeremiah snaps, glaring at him. I can tell that he's trying to hold himself back for my sake. He doesn't want to upset me by pummeling Penn right now. Penn wouldn't go down without a knock down drag out fight and it would be a whole thing none of us have time for right now.

"Enough," Graham's voice cuts through our exchange, firm and authoritative. "This isn't helping."

"Fine. Bunch of wet fucking blankets. Did I upset you, Oakley?" Penn mutters, leaning back again. But his eyes never leave me, studying, calculating. I just shake my head no, because he didn't.

Graham leans forward, elbows resting on his knees, eyes moving from Jeremiah to me. "Oakley, can you remember anything—anything at all about the assault? Even the smallest detail might help." His voice is gentle, yet there's a steely edge to it, a promise of protection and vengeance.

I swallow hard. Memories flash like broken glass in my mind, sharp and painful. "I—I don't know," I stammer, my fingers twisting together in my lap. "It's all so fragmented. I don't even know if any of the fragments are actually real."

"Think, Oakley," Graham urges, his tone softening as he reaches out, almost touching my hand but stopping short probably because he knows how territorial Jeremiah has become with me. "Anything might trigger something useful. We need to find this bastard."

I look up, my gaze drifting to the gold necklace around his neck. His football number glints in the dim light, catching my eye. Suddenly, it's like a switch flips in my brain. My breath catches in my throat as the memory floods back, vivid and horrifying.

"That necklace," I whisper, my voice trembling. "The guy...he wore one, too. But it had letters on it. 'KA.'"

Graham's eyes widen, and he leans in closer, his expression intense. "Kappa Alpha? Are you sure?"

"Yes," I nod, my heart pounding in my chest. "Positive. It's burned into my memory. The letters were bright against the dark background. I could never forget them."

The room falls silent again, the air thick with tension. Graham's jaw tightens, and I can see the wheels turning in his mind. He stands abruptly, pacing the room with restless energy. Graham's eyes narrow, his jaw clenching as he processes my revelation. Every muscle in my body is taut.

"Fantastic," Penn drawls, breaking the silence with his trademark sarcasm. His eyes narrow into slits. "You know what we should do? Burn the entire Kappa Alpha house down while they sleep. Quick, efficient, problem solved."

For a moment, the room hangs in shocked stillness, as if everyone collectively forgot how to breathe. My heart pounds so loudly I can hear it echoing in my ears.

"Are you insane?" I manage to choke out, feeling horror and disbelief. He is in fact insane, I'm not sure why I even said that in shock.

"Penn, this isn't a joke," Jeremiah snaps, his voice tinged with anger, his protectiveness hanging around us like a dark cloud. His eyes lock onto mine for a split second, sending a jolt through my body.

"Who said I was joking?" Penn retorts, a sly grin creeping across his face. "Desperate times, desperate measures. Besides, it gets the job done."

"You can't commit a mass murder because you don't feel like figuring out which fucker hurt Oakley," Graham interjects, fists clenched at his sides. His frustration is shared.

"Call it what you want," Penn shrugs nonchalantly, leaning back in his chair. "I call it justice."

"Justice?" The word tastes bitter on my tongue. "There's got to be another way. We can't just go burning buildings down."

"Don't worry, little Ashford," Penn says smoothly, leaning forward. His voice lowers. "We'll make sure you're far away when it happens. Wouldn't want you getting singed."

"Enough!" Jeremiah's voice cuts through the room, commanding everyone's attention. He rises from his seat, eyes blazing with anger. "We'll find the motherfucker and make him talk. Then make him fucking pay."

"Whatever you say, brother," Penn replies, raising his hands in mock surrender. "Just remember, sometimes the simplest solution is the best one."

"Enough of this bullshit." Graham's voice cuts through the tension like a whip. He's been silent up until now, but the frustration is evident in his furrowed brow, his clenched fists. He steps forward, his broad shoulders casting a shadow over the room. "We're going to play this smart and you two can even follow along or go fuck off. Neither of you are actually helping Oakley or this situation right now."

CHAPTER 28
JEREMIAH

The roar of the crowd is hyping everyone up, a roar of cheers and chants reverberating through the stadium. But there's an emptiness to it, a hollowness that seeps into my bones. Lincoln's absence is a gaping void, his energy and swagger missing from the sidelines.

I catch a glimpse of him in the stands, but it's not the same. He should be out here with us, leading the charge, not relegated to the role of a spectator because of some bullshit accusations.

"Blackwood! Defense!" Coach's voice cuts through the clamor, a sharp command that has me surging forward.

My gaze drifts to the row of seats directly behind our bench again, Oakley, my girl, sitting ramrod straight with her hands clasped tightly in her lap. Even from here, I can see the tension in her shoulders, the way she gnaws at her plump lower lip.

Iris is next to her sandwiched between my brother and my girl, leaning back with one arm slung over the seat beside her.

She murmurs something to Oakley, and my bunny gives a small nod, her ponytail swishing with the movement.

Just seeing her settles something inside me. She's here for me. With me. No matter how crazy shit gets, that's what matters. I've got two quarters to go, and I need to block out Oakley's stalker, Lincoln's assault charges, and how the fuck am I going to help fix either one?

Gritting my teeth, I force my focus back to the game. Can't let distractions fuck with my head right now. We need this win, and I need to be locked in.

The whistle blows, signaling the start of another play. I tear my eyes away from Oakley, forcing myself to re-focus. Graham is in position across from me, giving me a subtle nod as we line up. Coach has him playing tackle since Lincoln is out. We aren't winning this game on our offense. We have to cinch it with the D.

Hike.

I launch myself into the fray, cleats biting turf, every sense strung tight. My breath comes in ragged pulls, and I can tell—this is the play, this is the moment where everything tilts.

Bodies collide with a sickening crunch of pads and helmets.

Then it happens—a crack of pads, the gasp of the crowd, and a sudden, searing pain that rips through my leg like a goddamn train off its tracks. Pain is no stranger; it's an old friend, but this...this is something else.

"Fuck!" I hit the ground hard, my hand instantly flying to my thigh, fingers probing for damage. Shouts and whistles blare around me, but it all fades into a dull roar.

I grit my teeth, trying to push through it, but there's no mistaking the raw agony that tells me I'm gonna be benched the rest of this game.

"Eighty-seven, you okay?" The ref's face swims into view above me, concern etched into his weathered features.

"Does it look like I'm okay?" I snap, sarcasm a weak defense against the frustration boiling up inside me.

Gritting my teeth, I start to push myself upright. But a meaty hand clamps down on my good shoulder, holding me in place.

"Stay down, JB." The gruff voice of Coach cuts through the chaos. "We're getting you looked at."

I open my mouth to protest, but he silences me with a glare. Grinding my jaw, I force myself to nod again. No point arguing when he uses that tone.

Footsteps approach, and I glance up to see the team doctor kneeling beside me. His mouth is moving, but I can't make out the words over the pounding in my ears. I catch the gist though—up you go, to the locker room.

Graham helps haul me to my feet, keeping a steadying grip on my good side as we make our way off the field. I glance over my shoulder at the stands, at Oakley watching me with those big blue eyes, her brow furrowed with worry.

Our eyes lock, and I give her a reassuring nod. Mouthing 'I'm fine. This is nothing.'

Those words are meant for her, but they're just as much a reminder for myself. I've played through worse. Shaking it off, I turn my focus forward again.

My leg screams with each step, but I push through, leaning on my brother to help me in this fucking tunnel.

The locker room is mercifully quiet when we enter, the door swinging shut to block out the roar of the crowd. Graham guides me over to one of the benches and eases me down onto it.

"I got it from here," the doctor says, already pulling out his stethoscope and other gear. "Thanks, Graham."

I stare at my brother, not saying a word, but his slight nod tells me everything. He gets it. Gets me. And more importantly, he gets what Oakley means to me. Because if anyone touches a hair on her head, there'll be hell to pay. And not even the old man would be able to rein in the hurricane I'd unleash.

Doc lays me down on the table and one of his assistants comes over and they work my fucking game pants down so he can prod at my thigh and as soon as he does, I grit my teeth against the flare of pain.

"Looks like you took a good hit out there," he mutters. "We'll get some ice on it, but I want you to hit the showers first. Rinse off and change out of those clothes."

I open my mouth to argue, but he cuts me off with a shake of his head.

"You're not going back out there today. Not with that leg. You're too important. So rinse off and I'll take another look before you head out."

Clenching my jaw, I give a terse nod. He's not wrong. There's no way Coach will let me back on the field after that hit. Not with so little time left in the game, anyway. It's not worth the risk of further injury.

The sound of the shower is a welcome relief as I step under the steaming spray. I tilt my head back, letting the heat soak into my aching muscles. Grabbing the soap, I work up a lather and start scrubbing away the sweat and grime.

"Jeremiah!"

The shrill cry cuts through the rush of water, and my head whips around at her voice.

I barely have time to react before she comes barreling

through the door, eyes wide and frantic as they find me. A member of the stadium staff is hot on her heels, face pinched in disapproval.

"Miss, you can't be in here! This is the players' locker room!"

But Oakley pays him no mind. She crosses the space in a few quick strides and reaches for me, her small hands roaming over my chest and arms as if to reassure herself that I'm in one piece. I step out of the spray so she doesn't get all wet.

"Are you okay, baby?" she breathes, those blue eyes searching mine. "I saw you go down and I...I got so scared."

The panic in her voice, the genuine concern etched across her delicate features. It's like a soothing balm on my riled-up soul. She's really fucking worried about me.

My arms come around her without thought, pulling her against my damp skin in a fierce embrace. She melts into me with a shuddering sigh, her fingers clutching at the muscles of my back.

"I'm okay," I murmur against the top of her head, breathing in the sweet, familiar scent of her shampoo. "Just a little banged up, that's all. No one can touch me now that I have you back, bunny. I know what it's like to live without you, and because of that nothing else could ever hurt me."

"You're sure?" She pulls back just enough to look up at me, eyes searching my face. "You went down so hard, I thought..."

Her voice cracks, and I tighten my arms around her, a low rumble building in my chest.

"I'm sure, baby. It'll take more than that to keep me down for long."

"Miss, really, you need to leave." The staff member tries again, tone growing more insistent. "This area is off-limits to—"

I cut him off with a look that could cut glass, holding Oakley closer as if to shield her from the intruder's words.

"She can be wherever the fuck I am," I growl, low and dangerous. "Don't let me catch you speaking to my girl like that again."

The man's eyes go wide, but he doesn't argue further. With one last disgruntled look, he turns on his heel and stalks out of the locker room.

Letting out a long exhale, I turn my attention back to Oakley. She's watching me with surprise and fuck, that's definitely love. I'll never get tired of seeing that.

"I love it when you call me your girl," she murmurs, one delicate brow arched.

I smirk, leaning in until my lips are a breath away from hers. "Just how wet did that make you?"

Her tongue darts out to wet her lips, and I can't stop my gaze from dropping to trace the movement. "None at all."

"Liar."

"Where does it hurt?" There's a tremble in her question that I feel down to my bones.

"Here." I point to my thigh, then up to my chest. "But mostly here when you look at me like that."

The words are barely out before I'm kissing her, hard and hungry. She rises up on her toes to meet me, kissing me back with eager desperation. My hand slides up into her hair, cupping the back of her head to angle her how I want.

We're both panting when we finally break apart, chests heaving. Oakley blinks up at me with hooded eyes, lips parted and slick from our kisses.

"Ahem."

The doctor's pointed cough shatters the moment, and I

turn to glare at him over my shoulder. He's got one brow raised, looking distinctly unimpressed.

"If you two are done?" He gestures to the exam table behind him.

Grinding my teeth, I give him a curt nod. Right. I still need an official diagnosis.

"Everyone out," I growl, turning my glower on the few scattered staff members still lingering by their lockers. "Give us some privacy."

They don't need to be told twice. In a matter of moments, the locker room is empty save for me, Oakley, and the doctor.

"Up on the table," the older man instructs with a sigh. "Let's get you checked out and iced."

Oakley steps back, giving me space as I ease myself up onto the padded vinyl surface. She hovers nearby, worrying at her plump lower lip.

The doctor works in silence, prodding and manipulating my leg through a series of tests. I grit my teeth against the flashes of pain, but otherwise don't make a sound.

"Well, it's not broken," he declares at last. "Just a sprain or contusion. You'll need to ice it and take it easy for a few days."

I open my mouth to argue, but he cuts me off with a look.

"That's not a suggestion, Blackwood. You push it too hard, and you'll be out for weeks instead of days. So take the rest while you can get it."

Grumbling under my breath, I nod my reluctant agreement. He's not wrong. I know if I try and push too much it'll only end up worse in the long run.

"Good." He pats my good shoulder. "Now get dressed and get out of my locker room. You're done for the day."

Swinging my legs over the side of the table, I get down and make my way over to my locker, limping to avoid putting too much pressure on my left leg. Oakley trails behind, her presence a comforting warmth at my back.

I tug on a clean pair of joggers, then reach for a t-shirt to pull over my head.

"You about ready to head back out there?" I ask, keeping my own voice casual despite the way my pulse is kicking up a notch. "Watch two of my brothers finish demolishing these chumps?"

Oakley's tongue darts out again, swiping slowly across her full lower lip. "Lead the way."

I don't need to be told twice. Reaching for her hand, I tug her close and head for the door that will take us back out to the sidelines. I only stop and grab an ice pack so I can kill two birds with one stone.

As we emerge from the tunnel, the sound of the crowd washes over us in a wave of noise and energy.

Slinging an arm around her shoulders, I pull her snug against my side. She nestles in easily, that plump lower lip caught between her teeth in the most delicious way.

I may be out the rest of the game, but now I get to sit with my girl and watch the sport I love even if I can't play it right this minute.

Somehow, I'm perfectly fine with the outcome.

CHAPTER 29
OAKLEY

The cheer of the crowd is basically a wall of sound that vibrates through my bones. I barely hear Jeremiah's voice as he talks to Ramsey, his cousin. Their deep laughter cuts through the chaos, but barely. The scent of sweat and grass fills my nostrils. It's November, but the heat generated by all these people in the stands makes it warm. My heart races, not from the game, but Jeremiah being here with me. It's non-existent to watch a football game with my boyfriend. Wait, is he my boyfriend?

My pretty boy slides his hand up the back of my skirt, fingers grazing my skin with possessive ease. I feel every nerve ending light up, a rush of butterflies exploding in my stomach. His touch is thrilling and comforting, a reminder of who he is and what we mean to each other. Despite the noise around us, I lean into him, seeking safety in his dominance.

"Sorry, baby. Did you miss me, bunny?" His voice is low, almost a growl, and it sends shivers down my spine.

"Wouldn't you like to know?" I manage to whisper, my voice barely audible over the roaring crowd. I grin up at him, unable to keep up the sassy facade. I tell him, "I didn't mind you were talking with Ramsey. I just like being able to be here with you."

"Good." His hand moves to my ribcage and then even higher, teasing, almost cupping my breast. It's a bold, claiming assertion, one that makes my pulse quicken and my breath hitch. He knows exactly what he's doing, and the power dynamic between us is intoxicating. He wants everyone around us to know that I belong to him, and that makes me want to melt into a puddle of goo right here at his feet.

The final whistle blows, signaling the Spartans' victory. The crowd erupts in a thunderous wave of cheers. Their movements are like a tidal force that sweeps everyone onto their feet. Jeremiah doesn't let go of me, his grip tightening as he turns to face me fully. He's focused on me and only me in this moment. His green eyes lock onto mine, blazing with triumph and something darker.

"Come here," he commands, pulling me closer. There's no room for hesitation or defiance; his need is palpable, that I couldn't fight off even if I wanted to. Before I can react, his lips crash against mine in a kiss that's anything but gentle.

It's raw, possessive, a very public declaration that I belong to him. If he wasn't so possessive I'd be concerned he'd try and eat me out right here. His mouth moves hungrily over mine, claiming me in front of everyone. I can taste the salt of his sweat, feel the roughness of his stubble against my skin. My hands clutch at his t-shirt, desperate for something to anchor me to this man who means everything to me.

"Jeremiah—" I try to speak between kisses, but he silences me with another fierce kiss. The world fades away, leaving only the two of us. I couldn't care less who is watching or what they think. Jeremiah is the only thing that matters to me now.

"You're mine, Oakley," he murmurs against my mouth, his words searing into my soul. "Don't ever forget that. I want the whole fucking world to know that you belong to me."

"Never," I breathe, my voice trembling with bittersweet happiness. "I could never forget."

His eyes flash with satisfaction, and he finally pulls back, just enough to look at me. The intensity in his gaze is overwhelming. The crowd may be cheering for the Spartans, but all I can hear is the pounding of my own heart.

The cheers begin to die down, the crowd's euphoria ebbing slightly as they talk amongst themselves and start to trickle out of the stadium. Jeremiah's eyes lock onto mine, and I can tell right away that he's telling me it's time to go. He needs to be alone with me. There's a fire in those green depths.

I whisper, breathless, "What are you thinking?"

He doesn't answer me with words. Just a gaze burning through me, speaking volumes. My curiosity piques. He's always been good at this—leaving me hanging, wanting more.

I think maybe he's going to grab my hand and pull me with him, but I'm so wrong. In one fluid motion, he scoops me up into his strong arms. It's like I'm weightless, cradled against the hard planes of his chest as he starts heading toward the parking lot.

"Put me down, you oaf. You literally just got injured on the field." He grumbles, but doesn't say anything else as we walk right out of the Spartan crowd.

"It's bruised, not broken. Besides, I need you," he murmurs when we reach his bike, his voice a husky growl. As soon as my feet hit the ground, Jeremiah's hands have their own agenda, roaming over my body with unabashed desire. One moment he's gripping my waist, the next he's sliding under my skirt, fingers exploring, teasing. "Fuck, baby. I knew you'd be this wet for me. I'm practically salivating to taste you."

Jeremiah's thick fingers push inside my tight pussy, and I gasp, trying to keep my composure. "What—" Making out at his football game in front of all his teammates is one thing, but we're in the middle of the parking lot and he's knuckle deep inside me.

"Shh," he whispers, his breath hot against my ear. "I love this outfit on you. Makes me want to bend you over my bike and fuck you raw. I want to watch my cum leak down your thighs right now, bunny."

Arousal floods through me, mingling with the remnants of adrenaline from the way he carried me out of the arena and the chance of us getting caught. The world fades to a blur of sensations—the roughness of his stubble against my cheek, the scent of his soap and sweat, the way his fingers curl inside me, hitting just the right spot.

"Someone might see," I manage to stammer, though my protest sounds weak even to my own ears.

"Let them," he replies, a wicked grin curling his lips. "I want everyone to know how wet you are for me."

His words send a shockwave through me, and I can feel the heat pooling between my thighs, undeniable and overwhelming. He doesn't mean them, but I know he said them because he knew it would push me toward the edge. He bends me over the bike, the cold metal pressing against my stomach, contrasting with the feeling of his warm hands on my skin.

"God, baby," he murmurs, his voice dripping with desire. "You're so perfect like this."

My breath hitches as his fingers find their way under the lace of my panties again, exploring with a slowness that drives me wild. Every touch sets me up, every stroke pushing me closer.

I moan, unable to hold back. "Please."

"Patience," he whispers, his lips brushing against my ear. "I want to savor this."

His fingers delve deeper, and I grip the pegs of the bike, knuckles white. It feels like I might combust. He pulls back just as I'm about to come, it's like he knows my body better than I even do.

"Come for me."

My body arches into his touch, trying to get closer to him, but also wanting to run away from his assault to my senses.

Right now, nothing else exists. Just Jeremiah and me, locked in a bubble with one another that no one else could penetrate.

"That's my good girl," he murmurs, his voice filled with satisfaction. "So good for me, baby."

My breath comes out in shallow gasps as his fingers explore.

"Does that feel good, bunny?" he murmurs without hesitation. His green eyes lock onto mine, unwavering, filled with a determination that sends shivers down my spine. "I'm selfish when it comes to you. I want to hear you say it."

"Oh my G-god," is all I can get out. My legs feel like they're going to buckle under me, but Jeremiah holds me, keeping me steady.

"That's right," he replies, and I just know by his tone that he's got that mischievous smirk on his face. He quickens his pace with his fingers pistoning in and out of my body.

"I'm going to come," I whisper, pleasure flooding through me. But before I can tumble off the cliff, he pulls his fingers out, bringing them to his lips and depriving me of the orgasm I was soaring toward. His gaze never leaves mine as he sensually licks them clean, every movement deliberate, calculated. He lets out a low hum of approval, letting me know that he very much enjoys the way I taste.

"I'm insatiable for you," he says, his voice dripping with satisfaction. The way he looks at me, as if I'm his most prized possession. "I'm not ready to let you come yet. I think I want to play a little longer."

I open my mouth, ready to whine that he's denying me what I so desperately want from him, but he holds a finger up to cut me off.

"Get on the bike," he commands, his tone leaving no room for argument. I don't know what's gotten into Jeremiah, but I can't say I dislike it. He's demanding, like a man obsessed. I comply, straddling the seat while still trying to process the whirlwind of sensations he's stirred up.

"Where are we going?" I ask, my voice trembling slightly, though whether from excitement or apprehension, I can't tell.

"Wherever the fuck I want," he says, a small smile playing on his lips as he puts my helmet on for me before tugging on his own.

"I'd follow you anywhere," I manage to say, the words feeling inadequate to describe how I'm feeling right now. My body is humming, and it's only partly because of the pleasure that was coursing through me. He mounts the bike, reaching for my hands and guiding me to hold on to him. I could tease him right now by not slipping them into his shirt, but I feel like I've pushed the limits enough with him lately and I really don't want everyone to see me having sex in the parking lot.

We leave campus and if I was with anyone else, I would be worried about where we were going. I don't have that same compunction when it comes to him. He's not dragging me to any freaking alley ways.

It's only when we round the bend that leads to the founding families cemetery of Whispering Ridge that I pause.

"Are we...?" I start to ask, but Jeremiah's hand grabs mine, pulling it up to rest over his heart.

"Yes," he whispers in my ear, his breath hot against my skin.

My pulse quickens at the thought. The bike roars beneath us, but all I can think about is what happens next.

"I hope you know how much you mean to me, bunny. Because I'm about to fuck you so hard you might forget," Jeremiah says, his voice a promise of what's to come.

We pull into the cemetery, the bike's headlights casting shadows on the tombstones. Jeremiah kills the engine, and the sudden silence is deafening. He dismounts first, then turns to me, eyes blazing in a way that steals my breath away.

"Come here," he commands, his voice coiling around me. I slide off the bike, my legs trembling as I stand before him. He cups my face, his touch both tender and possessive.

"You're all I think about. All I dream about," he says, his voice husky.

I want to say something, but my voice falters, overwhelmed by the sheer force of the way it feels like he's looking into my soul. His eyes lock onto mine, and the world narrows down to just us, standing by the archway of the cemetery.

"Do you have any idea what you do to me?" he asks, his hands roaming down my body, leaving a trail of fire in their wake. "How much I crave you? I feel like I'm going insane when I'm away from you for even the shortest periods of time."

"Show me," I challenge, my own voice trembling with need. "Show me how much you want me."

His hands are everywhere, exploring, claiming. He lifts me effortlessly, pressing me against the cool steel bars on one side.

"C'mon, baby. Time to go do something scandalous," he demands, his voice rough with urgency as he unlocks my seat and grabs his gun before tucking it into his pants and dragging me through the gates.

CHAPTER 30
JEREMIAH

The scent of wet earth and decay fills my nostrils as we walk through the cemetery.

Oakley's hand is warm in mine, her fingers laced tight with my own. I glance down at her, taking in the flush of her cheeks.

We weave through the tombstones until I find one sturdy enough to support us both. My thigh protests with every step, but I ignore it, more focused on the pulse quickening beneath Oakley's pale skin. I guide her to sit on the cold stone, my hand firm on her shoulder, possessive. She flinches but doesn't resist.

"Cover your mouth," I order, leaning close. Her crystal blue eyes widen, catching the moonlight.

"Jeremiah, why—" she starts, but I cut her off.

"Don't argue. Do it." My voice is low, commanding. It sends a shiver down her spine that I can practically feel.

The marble angels are now the specters to what I'm going to do to little Oakley Ashford here in this old graveyard.

"Cover your mouth, bunny," I whisper harshly, my breath

hot on her neck. "We can't have you screaming out here and waking the dead."

She hesitates for a heartbeat before raising her hand to her lips, her delicate fingers trembling slightly. Satisfaction unfurls in my chest at her obedience. I can see the rapid rise and fall of her chest; hear the shallow breaths she's trying to control. It's intoxicating.

"Good girl," I murmur, my own breath hot against her ear.

Her eyes lock onto mine, filled with trepidation and something that mirrors my own obsession. My hand moves to her jaw, thumb brushing over her soft skin, feeling the rapid beat of her pulse beneath.

But it's a lie. A tease. I want her noises raw and untamed, a symphony for the dead and the living hidden in the dark. I grab her wrist, pull her hand away, and press my body harder against hers. "Actually, forget it. Let them all hear. Let them know who you belong to."

"Jeremiah..." she breathes, a tremor in her voice that tells me she's riding the same precarious edge I am.

"Say it louder, Oakley," I growl, each word laced with possessiveness—the kind that speaks of something primal and inviolable. "I want the ghosts to envy me."

Cupping her face, I tilt it up so I can gaze into eyes as blue as the sky on a clear summer day. "Who do you belong to, Oakley?" My thumb traces the fullness of her lower lip, teasing and promising. "Tell me, and I'll give you exactly what you need."

A faint whimper sounds from behind her hand. I can see the struggle in her expression, the way she wars between proprietary and the aching need coursing through her veins. Just as I'm about to repeat my demand, she gives me what I want, what I crave.

"You," she breathes, eyes shining with emotion. "I belong to you, Jeremiah."

Triumph surges through me at her admission. I crush my mouth to hers in a searing kiss, all teeth and tongue as I claim what is mine. Oakley melts against me with a soft moan, her fingers tangling in my hair to keep me close.

We're both panting when the kiss breaks, our breaths mingling in the space between us. I trail my lips along her jaw and down the pale column of her throat, nipping and sucking hard enough to leave marks.

My hands roam freely over her body, greedy and possessive, mapping every dip and swell through the thin fabric of her skirt. She arches into my touch, silently begging for more, and I'm all too happy to oblige.

My hands grip her hips and tug, settling her on the edge of the gravestone. Her skirt rides up further to pool around her waist, baring her to my hungry gaze. I lick my lips as I take in the sight of her, beautiful and wanting and all for me. She's wearing a scrap of pale blue lace that could barely be considered underwear and the sight of it has my mouth going dry.

"Christ," I growl, dragging my knuckles up the soft skin of her inner thighs. She shivers beneath me, her lips parting on a soft whimper. "You're fucking killing me here."

"Please," Oakley whimpers, squirming under my intense stare. Her hips rock forward in a silent plea, seeking the friction she so desperately craves.

I grin, sharp and feral, at her pleading. "Don't worry, baby. I'll give you exactly what you need."

And with that promise lingering in the air between us, I sink to my knees before her.

I bury my face between her thighs, breathing the scent of her deeply. Before ripping her panties at the seam. Oakley cries out at the first swipe of my tongue through her slick folds, her fingers tightening against my scalp. I groan at the taste of her, sweet and tangy and exhilarating, lapping at her with broad strokes of my tongue.

Her hips buck against my mouth as I zero in on her clit, flicking and swirling my tongue over the sensitive nub. We've done this so many times now, I know exactly which moves get her there the quickest and I'm nothing if not a gentleman that makes sure my girl comes. Well, as long as I okay it. "Jeremiah!" Oakley keens, her thighs trembling on either side of my head. I wrap my arms around them to hold her in place, feasting on her as she comes undone for me.

"Gotta get you nice and wet for me baby otherwise it's gonna hurt. You know I don't wanna hurt my pretty pussy. You can come now."

I plunge two fingers into her clenching heat and crook them, searching for and finding that spot inside her. Oakley shatters with a strangled shout, her inner walls clamping down on my fingers in rhythmic pulses.

I lick her through the aftershocks, gentling my touch as she comes down from her high. Only when Oakley relaxes bonelessly against the gravestone do I withdraw, licking my fingers clean again with a satisfied hum. I sink my teeth into the flesh of her inner thigh, marking her.

"You're not done yet," I warn her, standing to shed my pants. I set my gun on top of the tombstone next to us as my dick springs free as I shove my clothes down, hard and aching for her.

Oakley's eyes widen at the sight, but she makes no move to flee. Instead, she reaches for me, her touch reverent as she wraps her fingers around my length. I hiss in pleasure, thrusting into her grip, but that's not where I need to be.

"Flip over, baby," I command. Oakley obeys without question, presenting herself to me in offering. I kick her feet apart wider with my sneakers. The sight of her bare and bent for me, has lust searing through my veins.

I palm her ass, squeezing the firm globes and parting them to reveal her slick entrance. Still glistening from my mouth, her hole flutters at the brush of my thumb and I groan.

"You're so wet for me," I praise, lining myself up. I slide into her welcoming body with one hard thrust, burying myself to the hilt.

Oakley cries out, trembling around me, and it's all I can do not to come right then. I grip her hips hard enough to bruise, holding us both still as I regain control.

When I'm no longer in danger of coming too soon, I start to move. Long, deep strokes that have Oakley mewling beneath me, her fingers clawing at the dirt, unable to reach with her short ass arms. Helluva time for my girl to be a short stack. I drive into her again and again, chasing my own pleasure as I claim what is mine.

A twig snaps in the distance.

Oakley tenses, her muscles clamping down around me. She tries to twist away, but I hold her in place, grunting as I sink into her clutching heat.

"Shh, it's nothing," I soothe, running a hand down her spine. My thrusts don't falter for even a second. "Just relax. Let them watch. My gun is right there baby, ain't no one stupid enough to come over here. Not man or bear."

The thought of prying eyes on us, witnessing this raw and primal claiming, has pleasure coiling tighter in my gut. I fuck into Oakley harder, needing to mark her as mine in a way that can't be mistaken.

"You're mine," I growl, fingers digging into her hips so

hard she will have bruises before we even leave this cemetery. "Say it."

When Oakley doesn't respond quickly enough, I slap her ass, squeezing the reddened flesh. "Say it," I demand.

"Yours," Oakley gasps out, trembling beneath me. "I'm yours, Jeremiah."

Satisfaction and greediness surge through me at her words. I groan, burying myself to the hilt and spilling inside her with sharp, erratic thrusts. The sounds of our harsh breathing and the slick slide of her cunt around my cock echo in the air, underscored by the occasional snap of a branch as the wildlife flits in and out of the area.

The danger of discovery and the thrill of exposure heighten every sensation, my release seeming to go on and on. By the time I'm spent, Oakley is limp beneath me, held up only by my grip on her hips.

I ease out of her with a groan, watching in satisfaction as my cum trickles down the inside of her thigh. The primal, possessive part of me thrills at the sight, content in the knowledge that I've left my mark on her in a way that can't be erased. She is mine, now and forever. No one will have her the way I have.

"Get up and stop showing my pussy to anyone else," I say, already pulling up my pants. I tuck myself away, glancing over to find Oakley still motionless.

Irritation flickers. I snap my fingers sharply. "Now, Oakley."

I know I'm being a fucking dick, but I'm starting to spiral about all the fucking shit going on in my life.

Oakley and her fucking stalker and her goddamn rapist.

Linc, the team, his fucking charges.

Royce and where the fuck did he disappear to?

I don't have everything under control and while I enjoyed the thought of someone seeing her under me, I can't fucking stand the thought of them actually seeing any part of her that only my eyes have seen.

She's staring at me, seeing right through me and seeing all the things swirling in my head as she steps until she's toe to toe with me. Her head barely coming to my collarbone.

Her fingers clutch at my shirt. "I'm yours, Jeremiah. Always." There's a vulnerability in her gaze that tugs at something deep within me. "I could never belong to anyone else."

I press my forehead to hers, "Fuck, I love you so goddamn much."

"I love you more, pretty boy."

"This is only the beginning," I murmur, my voice rough with emotion. "I'll never be satisfied, never be full of you. You'll be the death of me, Oakley Ashford."

A small, tremulous smile tugs at her lips. "I won't. I just want you. The boy I knew and the man you are now. My protector."

I crush her to me, one hand fisting in her hair to angle her mouth against mine as I bend down. Our kiss is desperate, hungry, a clash of teeth and tongues. I plunder her mouth, savoring her taste, her whimpers of need.

Oakley clings to me, her nails scoring lines down my back that only fuel me on. I grind against her, my half-hard cock meeting the softness of her body once again. She gasps into my mouth, and I swallow the sound, consumed by an insatiable hunger.

"Again," I growl when we part for air, my hands roaming over her curves. "I need you again. Need to be inside you, buried so deep you'll never forget who you belong to."

"Yes," Oakley breathes, her eyes dark with want. "God, yes, Rem. Take me, I'm yours."

A feral sound rumbles from my chest as I back her up against the brick wall of the mausoleum behind us, pulling the cotton fabric down just enough for my cock to slip out. I hike up her skirt without preamble, bunching the fabric around her waist. She's still slick and swollen from moments ago and the sight has me throbbing and now I'm fucking completely hard again.

"So fucking perfect," I grate out, lining myself up and sinking into her with one hard thrust. We both groan, her inner walls fluttering around me in a velvet vise.

I set a punishing pace, driving into her again and again as her cries make a melody for me. My name falls from her lips in a breathless litany, each cry only fueling me further. I tilt my hips, changing the angle until I'm hitting that one spot inside her that has her keening.

"That's it," I growl against the curve of her neck. "Let me hear how good I make you feel. Let me know exactly who this sweet cunt belongs to."

My release coils low in my gut, building with every slick thrust into her welcoming depths. I tear my mouth from Oakley's, baring my teeth against the fragile skin of her throat.

"You're gonna have my babies. All this practice we have, I'm gonna make sure I knock you up soon," I demand, my voice wrecked with pleasure and need. "I want to feel you come all over my cock. My dick is only ever gonna find home in you. You fucking own me bunny."

Oakley's back bows, her inner walls fluttering and clenching around me. I grit my teeth, fighting against my own peak as she shatters apart with a broken cry. Only when her shudders begin to ease do I allow myself to follow, burying myself to the hilt as I come inside her for the second time tonight.

Fuck, my thigh is killing me, and this definitely isn't what Doc meant by taking it fucking easy, but this was worth it.

She's worth it. She's worth everything.

I pull back enough to meet her gaze, struck again by how beautiful she is at this moment. "Come on," I murmur, brushing a stray curl back from her face. "Let's get back to the house before the ghosts come up and bite your ass cheek."

"Jeremiah Robert Blackwood!" She screeches as me, and all I can do is fucking grin.

CHAPTER 31
OAKLEY

As I sit at one of the library's ancient wooden desk, surrounded by towering shelves of books I can't wait to read, I feel a sense of calm wash over me. I really do love working here. It's almost dusk, and the golden light filters through the stained-glass windows, casting vibrant hues across the room. The musty scent of old books mingles with the faint aroma of my chai tea. My fingers trace the embossed letters on the cover of a worn-out novel as I attempt to focus, but my mind keeps drifting.

A sudden creak of the heavy door pulls my attention away. My heart does an involuntary flip when I see Jeremiah standing there, his tall frame silhouetted against the dimming light.

I'm unable to hide the smile that tugs at my lips. For a moment, the world feels right again. He strides toward me, each step deliberate and confident. His expression is serious, yet there's a softness in his eyes that's reserved only for me. When he reaches me, he gently takes my hand in his, his touch sending comforting vibrations straight to my core. I exhale a breath I didn't realize I was holding.

"I missed you," he murmurs, his voice low and reassuring. "I have to leave campus for a bit, but I wanted to see you before I do." He pauses, squeezing my hand. "But listen, we found the person who hurt you."

The words hit me like a tidal wave, washing over the jagged rocks of fear and uncertainty that have plagued me since that night. Relief floods my senses, making my knees weak. Tears well up in my eyes, blurring my vision as I realize I can finally take a full breath.

"Thank you," I manage to choke out, my voice trembling. "Thank you so much, Jeremiah." I don't ask him who it is, because I'm too focused on how this nightmare is going to finally end soon.

His thumb brushes against the back of my hand, a simple gesture that speaks volumes. "I don't want to be away from you, but I think you understand why I need to be the one to take care of this," he says, his tone full of admiration and a feeling that stirs a longing within me.

"Your biggest qualm about what you're about to do is that you'll miss me?" I reply, attempting a light-hearted tone but failing to mask the emotion in my voice. I want to ask him what he's going to do to the guy, but I don't really need to. He'll kill him, it's just a matter of how. If I know my pretty boy the way I think I do, he'll make sure it's a painful enough retribution for what he did to me.

I lean into Jeremiah, our bodies melding together as he kisses me. His scent wraps around me, and for a moment, the world outside ceases to exist. I wrap my arms around his waist, seeking solace in his arms.

"Hurry back to me, Rem," I whisper against his lips, feeling the steady thrum of his heartbeat against mine. It's a rhythm that promises safety, something I've never felt with anyone else.

"You know I will," he replies, his voice a gentle rumble. He strokes my hair, each touch sending waves of comfort through me as he groans, dipping his head to kiss me again.

But then, the moment shatters.

"Isn't it inappropriate to be making out while on the clock?" Cindy's snippy voice cuts through the intimacy like a knife. Her tone reeks of judgment, each word dripping with disdain.

I pull back from Jeremiah, my face heating with embarrassment and anger. My eyes dart to bitchy Cindy, standing there with her arms crossed and a smug expression plastered on her face.

I snap back, my voice trembling with barely contained fury, "Do you ever mind your own business?"

"Just saying," she says, raising an eyebrow. "Some of us are trying to work here."

"Seems like you're more interested in watching us than actually working," I retort, my cheeks burning hotter, and I feel Jeremiah's chest bounce with the laugh he wants to let out.

"Honestly, Oakley," Cindy sighs, adjusting her glasses. "It's unprofessional."

"Unprofessional?" I laugh, but there's no humor in it. "Last I checked, you're not my boss."

"You should save the PDA for after hours," she insists, her voice grating on my nerves.

Jeremiah stays silent, allowing me to have my moment, but I can feel the tension radiating from him, coiled and ready to defend at any moment.

"Don't worry about it, Cynthia," he finally says, his voice calm but edged with steel. "We'll handle our relationship. You just focus on your own job. *If* you have one tomorrow, that is."

Cindy's eyes narrow, but she doesn't say anything more. She turns on her heel and walks away, her footsteps echoing in the suddenly too-quiet library. The fact that she doesn't give him a hard time tells me all I need to know. She's aware that Jeremiah could have her airlifted off campus if he wanted to. I think she realizes that he would do anything for me, including having her fired, maybe even maimed.

"You did good, baby," Jeremiah praises me, kissing the top of my head as I wrap my arms around him, not quite ready to let him go.

"I'm a real shark," I joke, pressing my forehead against his chest. The anger slowly ebbs away, replaced by the comforting steadiness of his heartbeat.

"Hey," he says softly, lifting my chin so I meet his gaze. "Don't let her get to you. She's not worth it."

When we pull apart, I finally ask him, "Are you going to tell me who he is?" The words are barely out of my mouth and Jeremiah is shaking his head in the negative.

"He's nobody. He doesn't deserve for you to know his name," Jeremiah says darkly, his jaw twitching with the anger that's running through him.

All I can do is nod because I trust him and if he thinks this is what's best, I'm going to believe him. What would be the sense of knowing his name? Looking him up so I can see his putrid face? I want to forget what little I do remember about that night.

"I love you, bunny. I was gonna have Ramsey take you home, but they have a game out of town. I've got the water boy coming to be your escort. Do not leave without him," Jeremiah tells me, and I parrot his I love you, meaning every single word. He kisses me quickly before leaving to go handle the man who set my world upside down.

It's almost closing time, and the library is quiet now, the soft hum of the overhead lights the only sound breaking the silence. I move through the aisles, checking that all the books are in place and the chairs are pushed in. The familiarity of the routine is soothing, a stark contrast to the chaos that Cindy always seems to bring to my shifts.

As I make my way back to the front desk, something catches my eye. Cindy's car is pulling out of the parking lot. I roll my eyes when I see her purse, abandoned and forlorn under the counter. Typical. She probably left it behind in her huff. My curiosity piques, and I think about picking it up and looking through it. She's so uptight and snobby, I'm curious how she lives. Is it neatly organized? Or a haphazard mess because she focuses so much on trying to control other people.

I decide to just leave her purse where it is instead of taking it to her dorm when I leave tonight. My luck she'll claim I stole her identity or something. I can't believe she just left me alone to shut and lock up this place. What a bitch.

I'm only a few feet away from the counter when the creak of the main door sounds. Cindy must have realized her bag wasn't with her. I turn slowly, every muscle tensing as I see Mr. Bryant, a teacher from my old high school, standing there. His lips twist up in a smile, making my stomach churn. Definitely not Cindy.

He was always a nice teacher, meek even, from what I remember, but something isn't right. I feel icy dread from all over and my gut is screaming at me that I need to run as far away from him as I can get. His brows are furrowed, and his eyes are so much darker than I remember.

"Good evening, Miss Ashford," Mr. Bryant says, his voice dripping with an unsettling tone. He sounds colder, harder, like he's angry at me.

"Mr. Bryant," I reply, forcing my voice to remain steady. "I was just about to head out. My boyfriend is waiting for me." It's half a lie. This is why we're supposed to always have two people closing together at night, but I guess Cindy doesn't care about being unprofessional in this situation.

My former teacher seems to ignore everything I'm saying and steps closer as if I've said nothing. "I've been wanting to talk to you, Oakley. Alone. I've been trying to get a private chat with you for a long time." It doesn't register at first, but then it clicks. He's the viewer I kept blocking for asking for a private cam show.

My heart pounds in my chest. This isn't right. Why would he be here and how did he know about my cam shows? I decide that if he's capable of all of this, there's no guarantee that he doesn't have a weapon on him. I don't know why, but my instinct is telling me that I need to placate him until I can figure out how to slip away. "I'd love to catch up. I'm sure my brother and boyfriend would love to see you again," I say, trying to keep the fear out of my voice. Royce may have disappeared out of my life, but this guy doesn't know that and even back in high school, everyone was afraid of my brother. Except for the Blackwoods.

"Now, Oakley," he murmurs, stopping just a few feet away from me. His eyes gleam with something dark and dangerous. "You see, I've been watching you for a very long time."

"That's...can I ask why?" I manage to ask, taking a step

back. My hand instinctively moves toward my phone, hidden in my pocket.

He tilts his head, smiling wider. "I found your little cam shows quite captivating. You have no idea how much joy they brought me."

A wave of nausea hits me. I was right. He knows. He really was the pushy guy who wouldn't take no for an answer. He must have sent the flowers and the creepy pictures. I can't have two freaking stalkers, my karma isn't that bad. "What are you here for? I mean what do you want?" I ask, though my voice wavers now.

"Don't play coy, Oakley. You know exactly what I want from you." His smile fades, replaced by a look of pure obsession. Smirking and reaching out to stroke his hand down my hair, he says sternly, "I was disappointed to see that you threw away the flowers I sent you. Did you know I was the one who sent you them? What about the photos I left for you?"

"You're sick," I whisper as the confirmation slaps me across the face, and I back up further until I bump into a bookcase. The room seems to close in around me and I feel like I'm being strangled.

"Am I?" he asks, moving closer. "Or am I just someone who appreciates beauty? Someone who sees you for who you truly are?"

"Stay away from me," I warn, though my voice sounds weak even to my own ears.

"Why would I do that?" His expression hardens, his eyes boring into mine. "I've waited so long for this moment, Oakley. So very long."

"Jeremiah will be here any minute," I bluff, hoping to scare him off. "You don't want to fuck with him."

"Jeremiah Blackwood," he sneers, the name twisting in his

mouth like a curse. "He can't protect you from me. No one can. He's a fuckboy with too much money and sucking on daddy's teat."

"Get out," I demand, feeling desperation clawing at me. "Now."

"Not until I've said everything I need to say," he replies, stepping even closer, "and done everything I need to do to you."

"Please," I whisper, my voice breaking. "Just leave me alone."

"Alone?" He laughs, a chilling sound that echoes through the empty library. "Oh, Oakley. You have no idea how alone you really are."

I grasp my phone tighter, praying for a miracle, for anyone to come through that door. But deep down, I know it's just me and him. And the night has only just begun.

"You're nothing but a little girl, Oakley," Mr. Bryant sneers, his eyes narrowing in disgust. "Running to that Blackwood brat like he's some kind of knight in shining armor."

"Shut up," I snap, the words coming out harsher than I intended. But I can't let him see my fear.

"*Oh, pretty boy,*" he spits out the name, rolling it around his mouth like its poison. "He's just a boy playing hero. He doesn't even know you, not like I do."

"You're delusional," I whisper, trying to keep my voice steady. "You don't know anything about me."

"Don't I?" His laugh is chilling, echoing through the empty library. "I've seen you, Oakley. I've watched you. I know every move you make, every thought that crosses your mind. You're mine, not his."

I clutch my phone tighter, my thumb hovering over Jeremiah's contact. I need to act fast, but I can't let him see me do it.

"He is going to kill you," I say, forcing myself to meet his gaze. "Jeremiah and I...we have something real. Something you'll never understand."

"Real?" He steps closer, his breath hot against my face. "Your so-called 'boyfriend' is nothing more than a distraction. A toy you've been playing with. But that's all over now. It's time you face reality, my dear."

My heart pounds in my chest, each beat beating against my skull. I can't wait any longer. As he rants, I subtly unlock my phone and hit Jeremiah's number. The screen lights up, and I drop it behind the desk, praying he doesn't notice.

Mr. Bryant slams his fist on the desk, and I jump, thinking he saw what I did, but he's still mid-rant. "Are you listening to me, Oakley?"

I manage a bitter laugh. "The only reality here is that you're a pathetic old man who can't get over a teenage fantasy." I need to keep him angry and talking because the louder he is, the better chance I have of Jeremiah hearing what's going on.

"Watch your mouth," he hisses, stepping closer until his face is inches from mine. "Or I'll make sure your little fuckboy sees what happens when someone gets in my way."

"You're not going to touch him," I say, my voice trembling but defiant. "He'll be here any minute. This is your last chance to walk away."

"Brave words," he mocks, his hand brushing a lock of hair away from my face. "But we'll see how long that bravery lasts once your little hero is out of the picture."

I flinch at his touch, nausea rising in my throat. Every

second feels like an eternity, but I hold on to the hope that Jeremiah will come through that door at any moment.

"Until then," he continues, his voice dripping with malice, "you're all mine."

I swallow hard, my eyes darting to the door. The seconds tick by like hours, and the air feels thick with tension. My breath hitches as Mr. Bryant pulls out a knife from his coat pocket. Its blade catches the dim light, reflecting a glint of madness in his eyes.

"You're not going to get away with this," I mutter, trying to keep my voice steady.

"Get away with what?" He chuckles darkly, twirling the knife between his fingers. "All I'm doing is taking what's rightfully mine."

My skin crawls at his words. "You were always so nice. What happened?"

"Was I?" He steps closer, the knife now pointed at my throat. "Or was I invisible? A doormat everyone stomped all over?"

I ignore him because I have no idea what he's talking about. "You're wrong about him," I say, though my voice wavers. "He'll come for me."

"Perhaps," he concedes, his smile twisted, "but not before I have my fun."

He grabs my arm roughly and drags me toward a chair. The scent of his cologne—overpowering and sickly sweet—fills my nostrils, making me want to retch. He forces me down, the cold metal of the knife pressing against my skin as he ties my wrists to the arms of the chair. The rope digs into my flesh, abrasive and unyielding.

"Just relax," he croons, tightening the knots. "It'll be easier if you don't struggle."

"Go to hell," I spit, but my bravado feels thin, like paper against the storm.

"Such fire for a pretty, sweet-looking girl," he mocks, stepping back to admire his handiwork. "It's no wonder you've captured my heart."

"Heart?" I laugh bitterly. "You don't have one."

"Maybe not," he shrugs, "but I do have plans for you."

"Plans?" A chill runs down my spine.

"Yes, plans," he continues, his tone almost conversational. "I've watched you for so long, Oakley. Tick Tock, while I bided my time. Your every move, your every smile. And now, you're finally here with me."

"I'm going to enjoy watching Jeremiah gut you like the spineless bastard you are," I say, clinging to the hope that he's on his way even though I know he's not nearby. I could have called 911, but I'm afraid if they roll up with lights and sirens that this psycho will take us both out rather than be captured.

"By the time he finds you," Mr. Bryant's grin widens, "it'll be too late."

"You're wrong," I hiss, feeling the tears prick at the corners of my eyes.

"Your defiance is adorable," he says, leaning in close enough that I can feel his breath on my cheek. "But it won't save you. Trust me, sweetheart. Nothing will save you from me. I've waited entirely too long."

"Please," I whisper, desperation creeping into my voice. "Don't do this."

"Shh," he soothes, brushing a stray lock of hair from my face. "Just let it happen."

My heart races, my mind screaming at me to do something, anything. But with each passing second, the reality of my situation sinks in deeper and deeper. I'm trapped, bound, and at the mercy of a madman.

"Just remember," he murmurs, his lips curling into a sinister smile, "this is all because you chose him over me. I would have quit my job to give you whatever you wanted, but you always wanted him, even back then. Robert Blackwood's heathens were always the bane of my existence. They never had to work for anything, just because of who their daddy is."

I don't even know what to say to his admission. I never realized what a sick, demented man he was, and he's right. All I cared about back then was Jeremiah. I must have missed so many signs, and now all I can do is hope that Rem makes it to me in time.

CHAPTER 32
JEREMIAH

My heart's pounding like it wants to burst out of my chest as the engines of our bikes growl beneath us, announcing our arrival to the shitty town that houses St. James University. The rapist's house looms ahead, its windows flickering with the light of late-night. The fact he doesn't live at the frat house is serendipitous. Off-campus housing means it makes it so much easier for us to get in and out. Penn's laughter cuts through the noise, dark and jagged as a broken bottle.

"Ready to dance, baby bros?" he hollers over the rumble, his voice dripping with that twisted anticipation of his. He thrives in the chaos that comes with hunting, maiming, murdering. I'm not naïve, my brother is likely considered a serial killer. If we kept a log of whoever he's ever killed, it would be long, but that's what happens when Robert Blackwood picks you to do his most heinous bidding.

"Of course I am," I shoot back, pushing my bike harder. The night air is thick with the smell of wet asphalt of the late-night crew fixing potholes throughout the city.

As we skid to a halt down the alley of this guy's fucking house, gravel crunches underfoot as we almost in sync get off our bikes. I could have done this myself, but they wouldn't have let me. Like the three musketeers, well five because of Linc and my cousin Ramsey. All for one and one for all. They would be here if I asked or told them, but Linc is dealing with the Nicole and Iris shit and Ramsey is still young. Not as damaged by the Blackwood name yet, since his dad isn't nearly as demonic as mine. I envy him a bit for that, except for times like now where I'll need every ounce of ruthlessness I've gained.

"Well, well, I do feel an urge coming on. You ready to get your hands dirty?"

I shoot him a look, my jaw clenched. Graham trails behind, silent but steady. Ready to jump in at any moment if needed. This motherfucker is going to pay for what he did to my girl.

We pull masks over each of our heads before entering through the kitchen back door; the porch creaking under our boots.

The house reeks of sweat and spilled beer as we shove into the front room. A crew of drunken idiots' gawk at us like we're aliens, but I don't have time for their bullshit. Their eyes are so blown they are definitely high on something and there's only three of them. I scan the dim room, my eyes narrowing when I spot him. Henry Butkis, the piece of shit who dared to lay his hands on Oakley.

He's surrounded by his equally moronic buddies, oblivious to the danger crashing through the door. Stalking toward him, every muscle tensed, fingers curling into fists. Penn falls into step beside me, no doubt with that twisted grin found on his face when he's about to fuck some shit up.

"You know, I was almost jealous," he drawls. "But you have friends, so I get to have fun also."

The guy looks up, his eyes widening as I loom over him. Fear bleeds into his expression, but it's too little, too late.

Penn and Graham zero in on the three degenerates who can't even process what's happening. I watch as Penn pulls something out of his pocket, giving it to each of them, and these idiots take it and swallow it before shuffling down to the basement.

"You made a big mistake touching what's mine," I growl, grabbing a fistful of Henry's shirt.

One of his friends turns and goes to open his mouth, but Penn's there in a flash, grabbing the guy by the throat.

"I wouldn't do that if I were you," he purrs, his gaze glittering. The guy nods sluggishly before turning back around and descending the stairs.

"P-please, man. I don't know what you—" Henry stutters out before his words choke off as my fist slams into his gut, doubling him over. I grab a fistful of his hair, yanking his head back to stare into his pathetic, watering eyes. I lift my mask so he can see my face now that no one else is around.

"You don't get to spew lies," I snarl. "You don't get to act like some golden fucking boy. You picked the wrong fucking girl to assault, you disgusting piece of shit." The words spill out of me.

The frat boy's lip curls, and I can see the flicker of fear in his eyes. Good. He should be fucking terrified. "Talk," I command, each syllable dripping with the promise of pain.

"Shit, man, I didn't know she was your—" he starts, but I cut him off.

"You didn't know? Bullshit. Everyone knows Oakley is

mine." My hands are shaking, not with fear, but with the sheer force of my rage.

"Oakley? You mean the quiet library nerd? Did not think that's who you were talking about. Bro, she wanted me. She was giving me those 'fuck me eyes' every time I saw her in the library. Practically begged for it with those little dresses she wore." I lean in, a predator closing in on his prey. He did not just call my girl a quiet library nerd or say she was asking for it.

"Just how many fucking women have you assaulted, butterball?"

My fist connects with the fuck boy's jaw, a satisfying crunch that rattles around in my head. For Oakley, I'd burn the world to ash.

His head goes flying to the side as he falls back into the cheap, nasty couch he was sitting on.

Penn crouches down, arms dangling across his thighs as he plays with the rings on his fingers, murmuring too quietly for even me to hear.

His hands lash out quickly until his grip tightens around the guy's throat, his knuckles white and sinews taut. The guy gasps, eyes bulging, as Penn leans in closer, a sinister smile curling his lips.

"Look at you," Penn hisses. "This is what happens when you cross the Blackwoods. I can smell you pissing your pants right now. Do I scare you? I should, we all should. Daddy dearest taught me to be the scariest thing that goes bump in the night."

He pats him on the cheek before standing up and fucking bowing to me, "Your move, brother. Let's get this show on the road. I have a hard-on now and would like to go get my dick wet...and no one here is appealing enough for that."

I don't have words; I don't need them. I start pummeling the sniveling little weasel as he sits. My knuckles splitting his flesh and my own as I take every ounce of Oakley's pain and shame and deposit it back on him.

Another punch, this one cracking against his jaw with a sickening crunch. Blood sprays from his split lip, but I'm not done. Not even close.

"Shit, that sounded expensive," Penn observes, a twisted smile playing on his lips. "Hope he had insurance. Actually, it doesn't even matter. You won't be making it out alive Butkis. Terrible last name by the way. I definitely wouldn't let you eat my ass."

Hit after hit rains down on him until he's a crumpled, whimpering mess at my feet. Still, it's not enough. I want to hear him scream, to beg for the mercy he'll never receive.

I draw back my fist, feeling the rawness of my knuckles, the wet warmth of his blood mixing with mine. His eyes, swollen and barely open, peer up at me with a mixture of fear and resignation.

But I don't stop. I can't. My fist crashes into his face again, and the impact sends a sickening thud through my arm. Henry's breath is ragged now, wheezing like a deflating balloon, each exhale saturated with blood.

A death rattle is what they call it.

It's a wet sound, a cross between a wheeze and a gurgle from a dying person's throat when saliva, mucus, and blood are all built up in their trachea with nowhere to go.

"You're fucking pathetic. Get up," I growl, yanking him to his feet by his collar. His legs wobble uselessly beneath him, barely sustaining his weight. He reeks of fear, sweat, and urine and the pungent scent churns my stomach.

Henry gurgles something unintelligible through broken

teeth, spitting out blood and fragments of whatever excuse he was about to offer. It doesn't matter. His words are lost in the void between us.

"You're gonna regret ever laying a hand on any woman." My voice is low, each word dripping with venom.

Penn leans against the couch, arms crossed and that infuriating grin on his face. "Don't kill him here," he advises lightly, as if we're discussing dinner plans.

I pause, briefly considering Penn's words before delivering one last punishing blow to Henry's ribs. He crumples to the ground like discarded trash, gasping for life.

A shrill ringing cuts through the chaos, and I freeze, my chest heaving. Oakley's ringtone. I fumble for my phone with bloodied hands, pressing it to my ear.

"Bunny? Baby, what's—"

The words die in my throat as her cries reach my ears, shredding what's left of my control. Grunts and muffled shouts sound in the background, driving icy tendrils of dread through my veins.

"Oakley!" I roar into the phone, but there's no response, only the sounds of a struggle.

I drop the phone, the frat boy forgotten as I whirl toward Penn and Graham.

"She's in trouble. We have to go. Now."

Penn arches a brow, somehow managing to look bored despite the violence swirling around us. "What, you mean your stalker magnet found herself another admirer?"

I surge toward him, but Graham's hand clamps down on my shoulder, holding me back.

"Finish this, quickly," he says, his voice a low rumble of reassurance in my ear.

I pick up my right leg and press my black riding boots into

Butkis' throat until I feel his windpipe give way and there's nothing left but to clean up this mess.

A noise draws all three of our attention and we turn to see a flash of a tall, dark-haired girl walking through the alley with a direct eye line into the kitchen window and what we've just done.

"Just fucking go. I'll clean this shit up and go deal with little red riding hood out there. I can't deal with you spiraling anymore tonight." Penn tells me and I nod before Graham, and I head out of the house and leave Penn to do what he does best. The grimiest brother I have.

CHAPTER 33
OAKLEY

"Stop it!" I scream, my voice piercing the thick, suffocating air. Mr. Bryant's knife slices through the ends of my dress, his eyes gleaming with sadistic pleasure. My kicks and struggles are useless against his iron grip. Each taunt from his lips fuels my desperation to get away from him. Why is he doing this to me?

"Such a pretty little thing," he sneers, his breath hot and foul against my ear. "Too bad your pretty boy isn't going to save you." Rage runs through me at the mention of Jeremiah. I can't fathom how he was watching me all the way back then. I never really noticed him. He was always a teacher that didn't give anyone trouble. I don't really even remember anything about him, just those little bow ties he wore every day.

"Get off me!" I cry, my voice cracking as I twist and kick. The room feels like it's closing in, trapping me in this nightmare. His hand inches closer to my exposed skin, and panic claws at my insides. I can barely breathe. "What is it that you want?" He brings his hand up to my mouth, pressing his finger against my lips. I don't know if he's trying to shush me or thinks he's being sexy. I know it's only going to hurt me, but I'll do anything to delay his sick plans for me. I bite down hard on his finger, causing him to jerk back and slap me hard in the face.

"You little bitch!" he yells, soothing his finger with his other hand. It's not long though before he's smirking at me again, the rage he conveyed now subdued. It clicks then that he doesn't want this to be quick. If that were the case, he could have done me in with his knife already. Slit my throat, stabbed me, anything. He wants this to be worth all the time and effort he's put into obsessing over me. He's going to make this as slow and painful as he possibly can.

"You're all mine. And that's all I have ever wanted," he whispers, his hands brushing my skin, sending shivers of revulsion down my spine. But then, headlights flash through the window, illuminating the room in a sudden burst of light. Mr. Bryant freezes, his eyes wide with panic. Could it be Jeremiah? Maybe my call actually went through and it's him riding up.

"Shit!" I try to pull away from him, but even though he's so much smaller than Jeremiah, he's still too strong for me to get away from him with any sort of ease.

"That's Jeremiah. I told you he was coming for me," I lie. I have no idea who it is, but I need to distract this monster so I can gain some sort of ground. He wastes no time cutting me from the chair and dragging me toward the basement stairs. I stumble, my heart racing, fear and adrenaline pumping through my veins. The basement is cold and musty, the concrete walls mirror my dread.

"Move!" he hisses, shoving me forward. The smell of damp earth and decay fills my nostrils as we descend into the darkness. My mind races, desperately searching for a way out, but the shadows seem to swallow every glimmer of hope.

"Please," I whisper, my voice trembling. "You don't have to do this."

"Shut up," he snaps, his grip tightening on my arm. The basement is a maze of boxes and flickering fluorescent lights, each corner hiding old furniture and other long-forgotten relics. My body shakes with fear, my breaths coming in shallow gasps. It's never felt this scary before to be down here.

"Someone's going to find us," I say, trying to keep my voice steady. "They'll come looking."

"Not before I'm done with you," he growls, his eyes burning with rage and a sick satisfaction that turns my stomach.

"Now move!" Mr. Bryant's fingers dig into my arm, dragging me deeper into the basement. My heart pounds, each beat a desperate plea for escape.

Footsteps echo above, a glimmer of hope sparking within me. "Jeremiah! I'm down here. He has a knife!" I scream, desperation clinging to every syllable.

"Shut up!" Mr. Bryant hisses, jerking me forward through the basement toward the freezer where we keep the most prized books of the St. Charles collection.

"Hey, Oakley, did you forget to lock up again?" Cindy's indignant voice cuts through the tension, oblivious and irritatingly casual. She must have come back for something and clearly is completely unaware of the nightmare that is unfolding for me.

"Help me!" I scream, but it's drowned out by Mr. Bryant's laughter. His grip tightens, his cruel smile widening.

"She's not going to help you," he sneers, shoving me toward a small door. He yanks it open, revealing a freezer where we keep some of the antique books. The air inside is stale, the metallic scent of the freezer hitting me hard.

"Get in," he orders, his eyes burning with twisted pleasure.

"Please, no," I beg, my voice cracking. But he shoves me inside, the cold hitting me like a physical blow. The walls close in, the space suffocating and unbearably cold.

"Don't worry, little VelvetVix," Mr. Bryant's voice slithers through the freezing air, a hiss that makes my skin crawl. "I'll deal with your coworker upstairs." His eyes bore into mine. He seems to relish the power he holds over me, the helplessness no doubt reflected in my wide, terrified eyes.

"Don't do this to me," I manage to stammer, my voice breaking. The cold bites at my cheeks, my breath forming icy clouds in the confined, suffocating space.

"Begging already?" He chuckles, a sound devoid of any warmth or humanity. "How sweet. I bet Jeremiah loves that about you. You're so soft and gentle. Do you think the bitch upstairs will beg me too?"

"Leave her alone! She doesn't deserve whatever you plan on doing!" Desperation claws at my throat, every word feeling like a futile attempt to grasp onto something solid in this nightmare.

"Maybe I'll carve her up a bit, teach you a lesson about keeping quiet." He leans in closer, pushing me further into the freezer. He grabs me roughly by the throat, leering down at my exposed breast that I've tried my best to cover. "Do you know how long I've fantasized about this? How long I've thought of tying you up and fucking you senseless?" I gag at his words, bile rising in my throat, and for some sick reason this seems to make the whole situation better for him. It's almost like he *wants* me to be grossed out by him.

"You're a sexy little thing, Oakley. But that wasn't what drew me to you. It wasn't because I could dominate you, twist you up and do the vilest things to you. It was because that Blackwood kid had you wrapped around his finger. He had everything. You would have let him do anything he wanted to you, and he didn't appreciate it." His words are like a punch in the gut. "And then I was hooked. I followed your every move and when you stopped doing the cam shows, I needed my fix. You gave me the courage to finally do what I'm meant to do to you." Then, with one last smile, he slams the freezer door shut, locking me inside the oppressive darkness.

"NO!" I scream, the sound tearing from my throat, raw and primal. My fists pound against the metal door, each impact sending shockwaves of pain up my arms. The walls of the metal coffin press in on me, the musty stench of old books mingling with the acrid tang of my own fear.

"HELP!" I cry out again, but the sound is swallowed by the thick, heavy silence. It's as if the darkness itself is mocking me, wrapping around me tighter with every passing second. The cold seeps into my bones, making me shiver uncontrollably.

"Jeremiah." My voice echoes back to me, distorted and hollow. Tears spill down my cheeks, freezing quickly, leaving icy trails across my skin. Each sob feels like a knife twisting in my chest, the weight of my helplessness pressing down on me. I know he's not even on campus, but I was hoping he would have gotten my call and rushed back to find me. To save me. I'm suddenly transported back to the night I was attacked. My hair being pulled, the assault, and right before I was knocked out, Jeremiah's name was the only thing on my lips.

The air grows thinner the longer I'm in here, and every

breath feels like a battle. My lungs burn, each inhale more desperate than the last. The realization hits me like a sledgehammer—I'm running out of oxygen. Panic surges through me, its icy grip tightening around my heart. I forgot that after so many minutes the system starts depleting it. We only ever have ten minutes max down here when we have to do anything with these items.

"Shit," I gasp, my voice barely a whisper. "Shit, shit, shit."

My breaths come faster, shallower. I clutch at my chest, feeling it tighten with each passing second. The cold is relentless, invading every part of me, making my movements sluggish, my thoughts hazy.

"Jeremiah," I murmur, his name a lifeline in my suffocation. "Please...I need you."

I'm going to fucking die down here, but I'm not going without a fight. I'm gonna go all Blackwood on Mr. Bryant as soon as he fucking shows his rat face again.

"Fuck!" I slam my fists against the walls again, feeling the sting, the warmth of blood. But it's no use. The walls are unyielding, just like the fear that grips me.

But my strength is waning. I need to conserve as much of it as possible because I'm taking him down with me, but all I want to do is pound relentlessly on this door. The exhaustion creeps in, a heavy weight dragging me down. My legs buckle, and I slump to the floor, feeling my vision blur, dark spots dancing before my eyes.

"Help," I murmur again, my voice a broken plea. "Someone, please..."

I press my hand against the freezing floor, trying to push myself up, but my body feels heavy, unresponsive. The cold is a vise, squeezing the life out of me. Each breath is a struggle, a fight against the inevitable. I claw at the hinges. There's no glass window to break, no handle to pull on. I'm truly stuck with no way out. I'm trying to count like Jeremiah taught me, to keep myself from panicking. I know the more worked up I get, the quicker I'll use up the remaining oxygen left. Chills are all over my body and my lips are starting to go numb. I know that even if he does make it back to the library, there's a slim chance he would look down here. My fingers are stinging and I try to rub them together, but that only makes the burning sensation worse.

I try to focus, to cling to a sliver of thought, but everything feels distant, slipping away like grains of sand through my icy fingers.

My eyelids grow heavy, fluttering shut despite my desperate attempts to keep them open. My senses dull; the once piercing cold now feels like a distant memory, a dream fading into oblivion.

CHAPTER 34
JEREMIAH

Red lights, stop signs—they all blur together as I push the bike to its limits, weaving through traffic with recklessness. I can't lose her again. Thank fuck I shared her location months ago.

The campus edges into view, and I grit my teeth, leaning harder into the turns. Just hold on, baby. I'm coming for you. And God help anyone stupid enough to get in my way.

We screech to a halt outside the library, and I'm off the bike before it's fully stopped. The doors are locked, but that's not about to stop me. I hurl my shoulder into the glass, and it shatters with an ear-splitting crash.

Shards rain down around us as we charge inside, but I barely register the stinging cuts. Inside, it's like we've stepped into a waking nightmare. The main hall is trashed, books and furniture strewn about. My boots crunch on broken glass as I move deeper, scanning the wreckage for any sign of where my girl is.

My gaze sweeps through the lobby, landing on a crumpled form near the front desk. A cold fist closes around my heart as

I take in the blood pooling beneath the body. The world tilts violently, nausea clawing at my throat as I fight down the scream building in my chest.

"Oh God. Oakley," I choke out, staggering forward.

But Graham grabs my arm, his grip like iron as he pulls me back.

"That's not her," he murmurs, his voice grim. "Look closer."

I blink, forcing myself to focus, and realization slams into me like a sledgehammer to the chest. It's that nosy bitch from the library, Cindy, or whatever her name was. She was always snapping her fucking gum and leering at me. She's lying in a twisted heap, her eyes open and glassy, throat brutally torn open.

"She was just shitty collateral, I guess," Graham mutters as his eyes access the same scene as me.

A low growl rumbles in my chest as I turn in a slow circle, scanning every inch of the lobby. There's no sign of Oakley, but a scuffed trail of blood leads deeper into the stacks.

"She's gotta be here somewhere," I mutter, more to myself than Graham. "Who the hell is this fucking guy? And where the fuck is the water boy I sent to fucking keep an eye on her?"

As if in answer, a muffled thump echoes from somewhere below us, like something heavy hitting the floor. My head whips toward the sound, zeroing in on the door marked *Employees Only* near the back corner.

"Oakley?" I call out, the name ripping free before I can stop it. Stupid, reckless, giving away our position to God knows what's waiting around the next corner.

But I don't care. If she's here, if she can hear me...I'll risk anything for that chance.

There's no response, just that endless, labored breathing.

It's coming from up ahead, from the direction of the study rooms. A cold fist clenches in my gut as we approach.

I'm moving before I can think, Graham hot on my heels as we barrel through the door. A harsh voice drifts up from the darkness.

"...won't be getting away this time, my dear."

A feral snarl rips from my throat as we reach the corner and see a cracked door. The storage room is dimly lit, boxes and shelves casting long, twisted shadows along the walls. And there, huddled in the far corner was some tweed and glasses wearing motherfucker.

Goddamn Giles wannabe turns just as I reach him, his piggy eyes widening comically behind his glasses. But he doesn't have a chance to react before my hands are around his throat, slamming him back against the concrete wall.

"You're gonna pay for this, you sick piece of shit," I snarl, leaning until our faces are inches apart. "I'm gonna make you beg for death before I'm through with you. Already got one body on my hands tonight, might as well add to the count."

He struggles, clawing at my hands, but I don't budge. I could snap his neck with barely any effort at all. Part of me wants to, wants to watch the life fade from his eyes and know he'll never hurt her again.

I want Oakley to watch. I want her to see him suffer, to see what I'll do for. How I will protect her and slay all her demons?

Graham is there in an instant. He shoots me a look, a silent question in his eyes.

Kill him or not?

Every ounce of strength and weight in my body slams this fucker against the brick wall, over and over until I let go of his throat. He grapples for air, but I steal it from him with a kick to the gut. He did something to my girl, so now he's gonna feel my ire.

Don't fuck with what belongs to a Blackwood.

Don't fuck with what belongs to me.

I turn back to the sick fuck, taking in his mottled, purpling face and the stark terror in his bulging eyes. The rage is still there, burning through my veins. But there's something else, too. Something darker, more vicious.

This bastard doesn't deserve the mercy of a quick death.

A cruel smile curves my lips as I lean in close, my voice a low, deadly purr.

"You're not getting off that easy, asshole. You're gonna wish you were dead by the time I'm done with you."

I feel the wet spray of blood hit my cheek as he spits at me and I wipe it off, knowing that's the last thing he'll get to do.

"Where is she?" I demand, not caring if he can understand me or not. I need to hear it.

His eyes find me, reddened slits in the ruin of his face. His lips move again, shaping words I can't make out. I crouch beside him, uncaring of the blood soaking into my jeans as I lean in close. He tries to speak, jaw working like a landed fish, but all that comes out is a wet, gurgling cough that splatters even more crimson across his own face.

"Oakley," I growl, so close I can smell the copper tang of his life leaking away. "Where?"

"Freezer."

He took her to the one place she couldn't fight back from. Couldn't scream or run or be heard. A cold, silent vault to leave her trapped and helpless.

"You sick fuck," I snarl, grabbing him by the front of his ruined shirt and hauling him up until our faces are almost touching. "What's she doing there, huh? What'd you do?"

"Tell me!" I roar, giving the man a vicious shake that has his head lolling bonelessly. "If you've hurt her, I'll—"

"N-no..." It's barely more than a gurgle, but it stops me cold. "Didn't...she's mine..."

"Motherfucker!" I hurl him away from me in a burst of rage and frustration, his broken body slamming back into the floor with a meaty thud.

"Jeremiah, we need to go." Graham's voice cuts through the red haze, fogging my vision. "If she's in the freezer..."

We turn and head for the stairs that will take us down into the belly of this place.

Finally, we reach the bottom, moving past the basement storage until we reach a corridor opening up into a wide space lined with heavy steel doors—the library's archival freezers. My breath fogs in front of me as I scan them, dread and urgency warring in my chest.

"Which one?" Graham's voice is hushed.

I open my mouth to answer, but the words freeze in my throat as another sound reaches us. A faint, muffled whimper, little more than the barest of sound, but it ignites the nerves in my body like a lightning strike.

"Bunny?" I call out, heart in my throat as I strain to trace the noise to its source.

There it is again, a little stronger this time. My feet are moving before I can think, carrying me down the row of freezer rooms until I'm standing before the largest of them all.

"Oakley, baby, I'm here!" I shout, grabbing the latch and wrenching it open with every ounce of desperate strength I possess.

The door swings wide to reveal the black void within, a cloying wave of icy stale air billowing out to swallow us whole.

There, huddled in the far corner, a shivering lump of fabric that turns itself into the shape of a person as I move closer. A whimper, weak and trembling, escapes those shapeless folds.

"Oakley?" I breathe, daring to hope.

"J-Jerem..." Her voice is little more than a cracked whisper, the breath pluming from her lips in vaporous clouds. "Is it... really you?"

"Yeah, bunny," I choke out, dropping to my knees in front of her and reaching out with a trembling hand. "It's me. I've got you now."

She makes a small, wounded noise in the back of her throat, like a broken thing trying to become whole again. Then her fingers are tangling with mine, shockingly cold and fragile in my grip.

"Thought I was...going to die." Her words are slurred, heavy, and it's all I can do not to gather her up and crush her against me.

"You're not going anywhere, you hear me?" I growl, leaning in until our faces are inches apart. I can see the fear swimming in her eyes, the disbelief and relief warring there.

"J-Jeremiah..." It's half a sob, half a sigh of surrender as she crumples forward into my arms.

CHAPTER 35
OAKLEY

"Holy fuck," he says, and I don't think I've ever heard panic in his voice the way I do now. "Come here," Jeremiah's voice is clipped, and I know it's because he's worried. My teeth chatter violently, and all I see is rage in his eyes. He moves with purpose, closing the distance between us in quick strides, and he has me in his arms, cradling me against his chest.

"Are you hurt?" His tone is measured, but there's an edge of urgency. He looks down at my torn dress, but I've managed to cover my breast. I know what he's thinking, and I need to put his mind at ease.

"He didn't get a chance…" I trail off before telling him, "I'm okay, just cold," I mutter, feeling the sting of tears I refuse to let fall. "Really fucking cold."

"Hang on." His words are a promise, and for a moment, the fear ebbs away, replaced by the certainty that with Jeremiah here, I'll make it out of this.

"Thanks for coming for me," I add, attempting another shaky smile. I don't need to ask him if he's found Mr. Bryant or if I'm still in any danger. I know with Jeremiah I'm always safe. He's always got my back. He always shows up.

Without a word, he scoops me up, lifting me effortlessly. My body curls against his chest, seeking out the warmth that radiates from him. His grip is firm yet gentle, holding me tightly against him.

"Of course I did, baby. You called. You're going to be fine," he murmurs, his breath warm against my ear.

The freezer door closes behind us with a soft thud. Jeremiah's steps are sure, as he moves us further away from my would-be tomb. I cling to him, my fingers digging into the fabric of his shirt. A chill still bites at my skin, but his presence is all I need.

"I'm going to fucking kill him," he says, his voice low and edged with concern. I think that he's mostly talking to himself, because by the tone of his voice, he's already made up his mind.

We emerge into a slightly warmer room, the oppressive feeling left behind us. Jeremiah sets me down carefully on what I assume is a tote full of books. I don't look around. All I want to focus on is the man in front of me. Jeremiah's hands linger for a moment longer than necessary as they brush down my sides and I lean into him. I need this. I need him. Jeremiah pulls back, his green eyes locking onto mine, seemingly searching for any signs of distress.

"That dress has to go," he says, already reaching for the hem.

"Excuse me?" I quip, raising an eyebrow despite my shivering.

"Trust me," he replies, his tone brooking no argument. "I need to get you warm. We'll deal with everything else later. You're my priority, bunny."

He strips the freezing cold dress from my body, his movements quick and almost sterile. But there's a gentleness there, a carefulness that speaks volumes. As his hoodie envelops me, its scent and warmth seeps into me, chasing everything away.

"Better?" he asks, his hands rubbing my arms briskly to generate heat.

"Much," I breathe, feeling a flush of gratitude and something deeper, more primal.

"I want you to smell like me, so you'll remember I'm always watching." And then Jeremiah's arms are around me, warming me up even more. I need to ask him about Mr. Bryant and if he made it to where he was going before I called him, but I don't have it in me. I don't know if my eyelids or arms feel heavier. I feel like I've been dragged by a truck, and all I want right now is to crawl into bed, preferably with my boyfriend.

"Did he hurt you anywhere? Do you need to go to the hospital?" Jeremiah finally asks, his large hands sliding down my back and then back up in the most comforting motion.

"No," I shake my head, trying to steady my racing heart. "Cindy came back and spooked him before he could. And then I guess you showed up." I lean up, kissing him chastely on the mouth before saying, "Thanks for saving my ass, pretty boy."

"I always will, bunny," he replies. "I'm never letting you out of my sight again. I swear to fucking God."

"I'm going to hold you to that," I say, my voice softer now, filled with every ounce of love I have for Jeremiah Blackwood.

Jeremiah's voice cuts through the silence. "The fuckhead who attacked you that night is gone. He'll never touch you again. He'll never make you scared."

I pull back slightly, looking up at him. His emerald eyes are hard, resolute, and I see a flicker of something dangerous there.

"And that motherfucker who locked you in the freezer? He's injured. I didn't finish him off because I needed to find you, but I'm going to."

"He's gone..." I trail, my mind racing. The implications are clear, but I need to hear it. Need to know exactly what he means.

"Yeah," he nods, his gaze unwavering. "You're safe now, bunny. I promise." Jeremiah's warmth wraps around me like a blanket. "Baby, talk to me," he murmurs, his voice a comforting rumble against my ear. "What happened tonight? Is he the one who sent the flowers, and those fucked up pictures?"

"Do you remember him?" I ask, my voice trembling but gaining strength with each word. Jeremiah shakes his head no, and I'm not surprised. Jeremiah didn't pay much attention to anything in high school besides football and me. "He said he picked me because I was obsessed with you and—" I cut myself off because I don't even want to repeat it.

"Go on," Jeremiah prompts, his tone steady, encouraging.

"After I left high school, he found me online. When I stopped using the cam site, I guess that made him snap, and he found me here," I continue, shuddering at the memory. "He didn't get to touch me, not really, but God, the way he looked at me...it was like he thought I belonged to him."

"Son of a bitch," Jeremiah mutters, his grip tightening protectively.

"It's okay," I shake my head, feeling relief wash over me. "You found me in time."

"That bastard," Jeremiah growls, anger etching itself into

his tone. He pulls back slightly, just enough to look me in the eyes.

"We're okay," I assure him, my voice barely above a whisper. "I knew you'd come for me."

"He's not going to hurt you again," Jeremiah vows, his eyes burning with intensity. "I promise you that."

"I know you won't let anything happen to me," I manage to say, my voice cracking under the weight of my emotions. "I love you."

"I love you more than anything. I'd burn the whole fucking world down to protect you," he replies, brushing a stray lock of hair from my face.

"I know you would," I murmur, feeling a warmth that has nothing to do with being away from downstairs and everything to do with the boy I've loved in one form or another my entire life. We stay there, locked in a moment that I'll remember for the rest of my days.

"I just...I want to see him before you kill him," I manage to say, though my voice trembles.

"Trust me, bunny, you will get to say and do whatever you want to that fucker." His words are laced with a promise, a vow that he's made to himself as much as to me.

Finally, we reach the top of the stairs leading to the main level of the library. Jeremiah pushes the heavy door open with a rough shove, his other hand never leaving mine. Graham is leaning against the far wall and my breath catches in my throat as my eyes lock onto the figure slumped by his feet.

Mr. Bryant. The man who wanted to torture me before he killed me is now motionless. His once confident posture is now reduced to a pitiful, injured heap. Blood stains his khakis, and his glasses lie shattered on the ground beside him. A groan escapes his lips as he tries to lift his head, his eyes narrowing as they focus on us.

"Miss Ashford..." he rasps, his voice a twisted mockery of the authority he once held. "What...what's going on?"

"Shut up," Jeremiah snaps, stepping between us, his body a protective barrier. "Not a single soul alive here is going to fall for your attempt at being coy."

Emotions churn within me—fear, anger, disgust. Seeing Mr. Bryant so vulnerable, so powerless, stirs something deep inside me. I take a step forward, my legs trembling but resolute.

"Just why?" The words slip from my lips, sharp and accusatory. "Why did you do all this?"

"Oakley, please..." His voice is pathetic, pleading. "I never meant to hurt you. I just...I couldn't help myself."

"Couldn't help yourself?" I repeat, bitterness coating my tongue. "You stalked me, invaded my life, made me feel unsafe in my own skin. And you think that's an excuse?"

"He's not worth your time. He's a forked tongue," Jeremiah interjects, his voice hard.

I hold up a hand, my gaze never leaving Mr. Bryant's pitiful form. "I need to hear it from him. I need to understand."

"Oakley, I'm sorry," Mr. Bryant whimpers, his face contorting in pain. "I was obsessed. You were just so...perfect."

"Perfect?" The word feels like a slap. "I'm not your fantasy. I'm a person. And you have no power over me anymore."

He flinches at my words, the reality of his actions crashing down on him. I feel a surge of anger and a strange, liberating sense of justice. This man who had terrorized me is now nothing more than a broken shell. And I am no longer his victim.

"Oakley," Graham says, finally giving a voice to his presence. "Is there anything you want to say to him?"

I turn to Mr. Bryant, who still lies crumpled, his eyes flicker with fear and desperation. My breath catches; I can almost taste the bitterness of what's about to happen. I don't speak, I don't have time to before Jeremiah is moving in front of me, eyeing Mr. Bryant with so much scorn in the world plastered on his face.

I almost feel bad for the beady-eyed little man...almost.

CHAPTER 36
JEREMIAH

I stand over the middle-aged fucker, the scent of old books and blood mingling in the air. His face is a mess of bruises and gashes, courtesy of my fists. He whimpers, trying to crawl away, but I grab his collar and haul him back.

"Where do you think you're going?" I growl, tightening my grip. The bastard doesn't answer, just gurgles through a mouthful of blood. Desperation pulses through my veins. Oakley. My Oakley. The thought of her trapped, scared, makes my vision blur with rage.

"Answer me!" I shake him, and his head lolls like a rag doll's. Pathetic.

"Please. I didn't mean..." he stammers, blood bubbling at the corners of his mouth. Pathetic. This piece of shit dared to lay a hand on her, dared to think he could get away with it. The sight of his broken form should be satisfying, but it isn't enough. Not yet.

"Didn't mean what? Didn't mean to trap her in a goddamn freezer?" My knuckles are white from gripping his shirt, the scent of his fear mixing with the metallic tang of blood in the air. "You think you get to walk away from this?"

"Jeremiah, stop," a soft voice whispers behind me. I whip around, finding Oakley standing there, her blue eyes wide but not with fear—something else. Admiration? No, something darker, more complex.

"Baby, he hurt you." My voice cracks on the last part. "He deserves this."

"I need you to let me slay this demon," she says, stepping closer. Her presence calms the rage inside me, even as it stirs another, more primal need. Her delicate fingers brush against mine, and I release my grip on the man's collar. She kneels beside him, a strange calm settling over her.

"What are you doing?" I ask, head tilting, watching as my innocent girl sits in blood. I don't want her to see this side of me, but it's too late. She's already seen too much.

"Taking control," she replies, her voice steady and with such resolve in her eyes. She pulls the small knife I keep on me from my boot. There is only a slight hesitation before she lashes out. With a swift motion, she slits the man's throat, pushing her entire little body into it in order to sever the carotid. Blood pools around him, dark and viscous, staining the old library floor.

She stands, trying to wipe the blade on my sweatshirt, and looks at me with defiance and vulnerability. My pulse quickens, the sight of her strength intoxicating.

"You're full of surprises, baby," I say, stepping closer. I can feel the heat radiating from her body, the scent of blood and adrenaline mixing.

"Are you disappointed?" she asks, a challenge in her eyes.

"Never," I whisper, cupping her face with my hand. Her skin is warm, and she leans into my touch, closing her eyes.

"Hey! What the fuck is going on here? We're having a murder party without me, and that's just fucking rude." Penn's voice cuts through the haze.

"Can't you see we're in the middle of something?" My tone is ice; my stare, just as cold.

"Yea, I can. Still fucking rude of you, but we've got a fucking problem."

"Get to the point," I snap, feeling the adrenaline spike once more.

He strides into the room, his eyes looking between the lifeless body on the floor and the blood-splattered knife still in Oakley's hand. "Real fucking mess you've made here. Didn't know you had it in you, little Ashford."

"I was just channeling my inner Penn." My girl quietly says with a little smile on her face. She's always loved my brother and his quirks. She's never judged him for how off the fucking wall he is.

"The little peeping tom from earlier was a fine ass girl." Penn's words hang in the air, each one a nail being driven into our coffin. "And she slipped away from me."

"Fuck," Graham mutters, stepping forward with a scowl etched across his face. "You couldn't keep her under control?"

Penn shoots him a glare. "Oh, I'm sorry. Maybe if you weren't busy playing sidekick captain save a bro hero, you'd know how slippery she was. It was like trying to grab a butt plug covered in Crisco."

"How much does she know?" Oakley asks, her voice steady despite the fear flickering in her eyes.

"Enough to sink us all," Penn replies, running a hand through his hair. "I've gotta find her before she talks."

"Damn it, this is the last fucking thing we need," Graham growls from behind Penn.

"Right, well if you would rather handle it on your own then be my fucking guess lil bro," Penn snaps, sarcasm dripping from every word.

"Stop it, both of you!" Oakley's voice slices through the tension, and we fall silent. "Fighting between each other isn't going to help."

"Penn, find her and end it."

"Jeremiah," she pleads, her touch gentle against my arm, "let's not become monsters over this."

"Too late for that," I mutter, but my gaze softens on her. "We'll handle it. We always do."

"I get to play Magnum PI," Penn says. "We need to move fast, cover our tracks here."

"Agreed," Graham adds, all business now. "Gotta start thinking like Blackwoods."

"Fine." I take a deep breath.

"Jeremiah," Oakley's voice is a whisper, barely audible over the pounding of my heart. Her grip on my arm tightens, and I can see the panic starting to set in her crystal blue eyes. She's trembling, her breaths coming in short gasps. Damn it, she's having a panic attack.

"Hey, hey," I murmur, trying to keep my voice steady, soothing. "I've got you, bunny. You're safe."

"Jeremiah, I can't—" She chokes on her words, her body going limp against me.

"Fuck this," I mutter under my breath. Without another thought, I scoop her up into my arms, cradling her against my chest. Her head lolls onto my shoulder, and I can feel the rapid rise and fall of her breaths against my neck.

"Stay with me, Oakley," I command, more for my own sanity than hers. Her panic is contagious, and I have to fight to keep my own anxiety at bay.

"Jeremiah, we really don't have time for this," Graham's voice cuts through the fog of my mind. He's standing by the door, his expression a mask of urgency and frustration. His dark eyes lock onto mine, and we exchange a tense glance.

"Take her home," he says, his tone leaving no room for argument. "We'll figure out our next move."

"Fuck," I hiss, torn between wanting to stay and needing to protect Oakley. But one look at her pale, trembling form in my arms, and I know there's no choice.

Her grip on my shirt tightens. Panic rises in her eyes, and I can almost feel her slipping away back into herself.

"It's just me, bunny," I say, my voice firm but gentle. "You're safe now. I've got you."

"Jeremiah," she gasps, her body shuddering. "I can't... breathe..."

"Hey, look at me," I demand, tipping her chin up so our eyes meet. "You're okay. Just breathe with me, alright?"

"Fuck," Graham mutters, looking around at the dead body and the disaster that is the library.

"Yeah," Penn replies. "We've got ourselves a real fucking pickle here boys."

"Understatement of the century," Graham snaps, pacing back and forth. "Evidence is too strong. No way we can make this look like an accident. We're screwed, and I don't even know if Dad can sweep this under the rug."

"Oh, calm down," Penn says, his tone oddly soothing. "It's not like you two will pay the price he requires, anyway." His eyes darken, shadows creeping in, almost to the point it seems like his entire iris is black.

Oakley's fingers grip my shirt weakly, her voice barely above a whisper. "Burn it down," she breathes, each word trembling but resolute. "Burn everything to the ground."

Her statement silences us all, the gravity of her words settling like ashes after a fire. Even Penn looks momentarily stunned.

He recovers first, shaking his head with a laugh that seems to echo unnaturally in the silence. "Oh, what the fuck," he mutters, voice dripping with sarcasm. "Every time I suggest we burn shit down, I'm the problem. Little Miss Muffet here does it, and now we're all 'yay fire friends.' This is bullshit." He reaches into his pocket, pulling out a silver lighter and flicking it open with a flourish. The small flame dances.

Both Graham and I just deadpan stare at him. I cannot with his bullshit right now. Everything is always a fucking comedy show.

"Lucky for you guys," he says, waving the lighter theatrically, "I've got my trusty lighter and enough gasoline in the generator outside to light this place up like Burning Man. Good job, you little guardian devil. Thank you for this gift of setting this motherfucker up."

"Well, she's definitely one of us now," Graham says.

"Fuck yeah, she is. I need to get her home, though."

"Go," he orders. "We'll handle this." His tone leaves no room for argument.

I turn to walk away, leaving my brothers to take care of the library and everything in it when Oakley peeks over my shoulder.

"Everything, Penn," she repeats, stronger this time, her conviction searing through her fear. "Ashes can't tell tales."

Graham laughs, the sound devoid of any humor. "She's not wrong."

"Damn baby Blackwood! You just made my dick hard with that one." I'm going to kill him. What's it called when you kill your own sibling? Fratricide. I'm definitely doing that shit.

CHAPTER 37

OAKLEY

The moment we cross the threshold of Blackwood manor, I can feel the energy around us shift. The world outside fades away, leaving only Rem and me. No words are needed as he carries me down the hallway, the warmth from his touch seeping into my very core. I'm nuzzled into him, not really caring what his plan is for tonight. I just need him.

"No one is ever going to take you from me," Jeremiah murmurs, his voice a soothing balm to my frayed nerves as he opens our bathroom door. Suddenly, I'm worried that I'm going to be left alone with my thoughts. Even if Jeremiah is in the next room, it's not close enough. I need to be able to see him and feel him.

"Are you staying?" I whisper, unable to hide the trembling in my voice. He reads mind, shaking his head as he sets me down on the bathroom counter and leaning in to kiss me more roughly than I expected.

"I'm not leaving you alone. Ever, Oakley. I hope you understand that I'm so fucking serious. We'll clean up together." I instantly relax at his words. I thought maybe he'd want to shower separately to wash the blood off, lord knows he loves his showers. I watch him turn on the water and roughly dump way too much body wash into the stream. I guess my pretty boy likes bubbles, which makes me giggle. He turns to look at me, his eyes serious and brooding, a scowl fixed on his handsome face. I don't have the words to explain how funny it is to me that this man who killed not one, but two men for me tonight is drawing me a bubble bath and I suspect it's not only for me.

I watch as Jeremiah undresses, his gaze never leaving mine. His eyes are half-lidded, a clear indication that he's got more on his mind than relaxing. I can practically see the adrenaline pumping through his body, his shoulders stiff like he's holding himself back from ravaging me right here.

Jeremiah approaches me, and my eyes roam his gorgeously sculpted body as he takes his hoodie off of me roughly. He wastes no time caressing me as his hands slide over my shoulders before he lets me hop down. I'm clad only in my panties, but he doesn't leer or ogle. Instead, he meets my gaze, steady and unwavering, a silent promise of safety etched within those green depths.

"Ready?" he asks softly, extending a hand to guide me into the bathtub.

"Ready," I reply, taking his hand and allowing him to help me ease into the warm water. As I sink deeper, every muscle in my body relaxes, surrendering to the comforting embrace of the bath. My eyelids flutter shut, and I can't help but let out a contented sigh.

"Feeling better?" Jeremiah inquires, genuine concern lacing his voice as he gets in behind me and wrapping his arms around me.

"Much," I admit, opening my eyes to find him watching me with a tender smile. "I didn't realize how much I needed this."

"I didn't realize how much I needed you, until I didn't have you," he murmurs against my neck, pressing kisses there as he rubs his hands up my thighs and then over my belly. His hand rests there against the flat of my stomach. "I would have been a fucking menace if something had happened to you tonight. Bunny. Every person on this fucking planet would have had hell to pay."

"Not to point out the obvious," I begin with a little laugh, "but you did kill two people for me tonight. That's kind of a menace, right?"

"Bunny," he replies softly, his eyes darkening with emotion that I can't quite place. Love, affection, but something even further I'm not sure I've ever seen before. "I would have killed them all. Every. Single. Fucking. One."

The intensity of his words sends a shiver down my spine. I can feel my pulse quicken as our eyes lock, desire simmering just beneath the surface. The air between us grows heavy.

"Pretty boy," I breathe, leaning closer to him, turning around in his arms.

"Yes?" he murmurs, his voice husky with longing.

"I love you so much."

"Keep saying that and you're not leaving this room until I've put a baby in you," he whispers, his hands finding my shoulders. I'd argue with him, tell him that we're too young, but his fingers dig into the knots and tension, eliciting a moan from me as I surrender to the pleasure. I'm on the pill and we both know it, but with the way he's acted tonight, I wouldn't be surprised if he took down my birth control next. "I'm trying to be a gentleman. You've been through too much tonight. You need to relax, and I have a hard time controlling myself around you. I tell myself I need to be gentle, and then..." he trails off with a groan.

"God, that feels amazing," I breathe, my eyes fluttering shut. I feel him hard under me, and I purposely wiggle against him. He's right, I have been through a lot tonight, but somehow that just makes me want to be closer to him right now. I want him inside me, pinning me beneath this huge frame. I want to feel like I can't escape him, because with Jeremiah, I'm safe.

His green eyes are dark with concern as he tilts my head to the side, making me look at him. His dark brows are furrowed, as if he's trying to decipher the inner workings of my mind. I can't help but feel a thrill at the sight of him, his broad shoulders blocking out the glow of the bathroom lights.

"I can't fucking believe I've got you back, bunny." His voice is sincere and filled with a promise that makes my heart race. "God, you're so beautiful," he breathes out. The intensity in his eyes sends shivers down my spine, and I revel in the knowledge that he wants me just as much as I want him.

"Jeremiah," I say softly, my voice trembling slightly with the depth of my emotions. "I don't know how to thank you for everything you've done for me."

He reaches out and places his hand on mine, interlocking his much bigger fingers with my more delicate ones. The heat of his touch sends a jolt of electricity through me. "You don't need to thank me, bunny," he says, his voice taking on a husky quality that makes my pussy clench. I feel his cock jerk beneath me, and I know I'm not imagining things. Jeremiah Blackwood is doing everything in his power right now not to impale me. "Just knowing you're here with me, feeling safe and cared for—that's all I need."

I don't get a chance to respond because he's nudging me to look forward and I'm not sure what he's got in mind. "I love you so much," his deep voice breaks through my thoughts, the rasp in his tone sending shivers down my spine. Jeremiah's strong hands find their way down my back, his skilled fingers massaging my muscles. The sensation is an intoxicating combination of pain and pleasure that leaves me breathless. As he works his way down my back, he cups my ass, squeezing and lifting me off of him ever so slightly.

"Your muscles are so tight; it's like you've been carrying the weight of the world on your shoulders," he teases, and I know he's stalling.

"I have had a rough couple of years," I retort playfully, the sarcasm in my voice barely masking the truth behind my words. "It's not easy being Oakley Ashford, you know."

"It'll be easy now. Anything you want. I will give you anything, bunny," he replies, and he sounds so matter of fact, like anything else is not an option.

"I have everything I need right here," I tell him honestly.

His fingers dig deeper into my flesh, coaxing moans from my lips as the tension in my body unravels. I can feel the heat building between us, a pull that threatens to consume. I tilt my head back, allowing the exhaustion to drain from my body as Jeremiah's skilled hands work their magic on my shoulders.

"Jeremiah," I murmur, my voice barely more than a whisper, "I want you to know I knew you'd come for me tonight. I didn't doubt it for a second, and I just needed you to know that. I just prayed it was before I met my end."

He pauses for a moment, his fingers stilling on my skin. His breath is warm against the nape of my neck as he presses kisses there. "I'll always show up for you. You're my only priority."

"Jeremiah, I..." My voice wavers as I struggle to find the right words. "I was so scared. I don't know what would have happened if you hadn't shown up."

His eyes, filled with empathy and concern, hold mine captive. "You never have to worry about me not being there," he assures me, his voice steady and strong. "I'll sew you to my fucking ribs before I'll let you out of my sight again." He's just exaggerating, but something in the back of my mind tells me that Jeremiah does not joke when it comes to me.

"You know, pretty boy," I say, my tone teasing despite the vulnerability still coursing through me, "it's hard to believe one of the Blackwood brothers could be so caring." I need to lighten the mood and let us be us again.

He chuckles, a low sound that sends warmth flooding through me. "Well, not everyone can be as off the rails as Penn."

I reply with a grin, my spirits lifting as our conversation takes on a lighter tone, "Can't let the world know that pretty boy Blackwood has a heart of gold."

"God forbid," he agrees, his fingers resuming their gentle massage of my shoulders.

His fingers still on my shoulders, I feel a subtle tremor in his touch. I glance at Jeremiah's face and see something I've never witnessed before: fear. The stoic mask he usually wears crumbles, revealing the raw vulnerability that lies beneath.

"Oakley..." he whispers, his voice trembling with emotion. "You have no idea how scared I was. How scared I am of losing you again. It would be what I deserve for leaving you like I did. For trusting that Royce was looking out for you, even if he wasn't around."

My heart clenches at the intensity of his words, the desperation evident in every syllable. This side of Jeremiah, so open and vulnerable, is a sight I've not often been privy to—and it takes my breath away.

"Jeremiah," I murmur, reaching up to cup his cheek, "I'm here. You saved me, and I'm not going anywhere." I whisper against his lips, "As weird as it sounded, I'd let you sew me to your ribs if that meant never having to leave your side again."

He leans into my touch, closing his eyes for a moment as if trying to absorb the reassurance I offer. A heavy silence settles over us, punctuated only by the faint sound of water lapping against the tub's edges.

"Promise me," he says, his voice barely audible. "Promise me you'll always be here."

"I promise," I whisper back, because I don't intend on living a single minute without him right next to me.

A small smile tugs at the corner of his lips, and he opens his eyes to meet mine once more.

"Oak," he murmurs, his voice rough with need. "I want you so damn much..." His eyes darken with lust, and there's no mistaking the heat that passes between us.

"Look at me," I whisper, reaching out to gently touch his cheek. The heat of his skin burns against my fingertips.

Our breaths mingle, his chest rising and falling against me. The intensity of our physical connection is almost too much for my body to handle. I feel like I'm going to short circuit if I can't get closer to him.

"I need you," I whisper, my voice barely audible above the sound of our quickened breathing.

"Say it again." His voice comes out rough, and I can tell he's trying to maintain control, but it's slipping through his fingers like sand.

"I need you more than anything, pretty boy," I tell him. "I've never needed anyone the way I've always wanted you."

"God, Oakley," he groans between kisses, his voice laden with desire. "You have no idea what you do to me."

"Show me," I challenge, a newfound boldness surging through me.

Something about tonight, about what he did for me makes this all more important. As his hands explore my breasts, tugging on my nipples, his other hand slithers around my ribcage and down my belly. He moves lower still where his expert fingers find my clit, and I can feel my inhibitions crumbling away.

"Fuck me, Rem." I whisper, my voice trembling with passion. "I need to feel you inside me."

Those words are all it takes, and he's making quick work of getting me out of the tub. His hands never leave some part of my body as he grabs a towel and wraps it around his hips before covering me with another one.

"That tub isn't big enough for the things I'm going to do to you tonight," he growls.

CHAPTER 38
JEREMIAH

I bend down, starting at her feet, and slowly drag the towel upwards so I can dry her off from the bath. Her skin is soft and smells just like the new honeysuckle soap she bought and it's already fucking with my head.

Her breath hitches as I move the towel up her legs, taking my time to gently pat her inner thighs dry. She's completely exposed to me, but there's no hesitation or embarrassment anymore, just complete trust.

I stand, moving behind her to gently dry her back and shoulders. She sighs, leaning into me. My body responds instantly to her softness pressed against me. I brush her damp hair aside, pressing a kiss to the nape of her neck.

When I straighten up, her eyes lock with mine, dark and full of desire. She reaches for my hand and guides it to her hair. I twist my fingers into the damp strands, cradling the back of her head.

"I want you," she whispers. "One more lesson."

I groan, body already reacting to her words. "Baby, are you sure?"

She nods, a wicked little smile playing on her lips. "I want to use my mouth on you this time. Will you teach me how to make you feel good?"

"Anything you want, bunny." My voice is ragged, filled with longing. This is the ultimate gift she could give me. To know she trusts me enough to do this, to do something that once traumatized her to what she thought was beyond repair.

She's been fighting her own demons and claiming back the parts of herself that have been hiding, and I'm so goddamn proud of her.

A wave of possessiveness washes over me at the thought of those perfect lips wrapped around me. No one's ever made me feel the way she does. I guide her to the bed, heart pounding with need.

Oakley straddles my hips, the slick heat of her rubbing up and down my hard shaft. She pins my wrists above my head, her grip deceptively strong. I groan at the sensation, my body taut with anticipation. I want her to take control, to ravage me until I'm delirious with pleasure and pain.

"You're mine tonight," she whispers, her lips brushing against my ear. A shiver races down my spine at her words. I'm powerless to resist her, my body and soul hers to command.

"Baby, I'm yours every night."

Oakley releases my wrists and slides her hands down so her fingers can trace the lines of my abdomen, feather-light touches that set me on edge. I buck my hips, seeking friction, but she pins me in place with her lithe body.

"Patience," she chides as her gaze rakes over my bare chest, filled with her own lust and possessiveness. She lowers her head and presses a kiss above my heart. "You're so beautiful, Rem."

Her words ignite something deep within me. I wrap my arms around Oakley and crush her against me. Our lips meet in a bruising kiss, all the pent-up adrenaline, desire and longing pouring into that single gesture.

We break apart, breathless, our chests heaving. Oakley rests her forehead against mine, her eyes searching my face. I see the depths of her love mirrored in her gaze. In this moment, if she asked me to, I would walk away from it all. This life, my family, everything I know. I would do it without a second thought because this girl eclipses all of that for me. Cut me open and all that will bleed out is her.

She kneels between my legs, looking up at me for approval. I brush my thumb over her bottom lip. "Go slow, use your hands too. And if you need to stop..."

"I won't," she says.

And I know she won't. My girl's not afraid anymore.

"Spit on it." I demand.

Oakley's eyes widen, but she doesn't hesitate. She leans forward and spits, letting me watch as it drops from her pouty little mouth right onto the tip of my dick, her eyes never leaving mine. Slowly, she wraps her hand around my hard length, working the saliva along my shaft. The sensation is so fucking hot; I have to bite back a groan. She's an eager student, moaning around me as I begin to guide her movements. My hips rock up instinctively, and she gags slightly but recovers, hollowing her cheeks and sucking hard.

"Good girl," I praise, my voice raspy with desire. I grab her hair and gently tilt her head back. "Now suck me off like you mean it."

Oakley huffs, but she doesn't argue. She dives back down on my dick, her mouth warm and wet around me. Her tongue flicks along my head while her hand strokes the rest of my cock. My hips buck as pleasure courses through my veins.

"Fuck, Oakley," I groan, my grip on her hair tightening. "You're driving me insane."

She hums around my cock and runs her tongue along the sensitive spot just beneath the head. I curse as a shudder runs down my spine. My eyes rolling back in my head as she continues to suck and lick and tease every inch of me. Her hands roam up my stomach, leaving trails of fire in their wake. Oakley is killing me, but I'd never felt more alive in my life.

"Jeremiah," she says against my cock before taking more of me into her mouth. Her moans vibrate against my skin and it's all too much for me to handle any longer. My vision blurs as I feel myself getting dangerously close to the edge.

I weave my fingers into her silky hair, feeling the strands glide between my digits as her head bobs up and down. She takes me deeper with each pass, hollowing her cheeks and working me with her tongue in maddening ways that have my hand tightening in her hair.

"That's it, just like that," I groan through gritted teeth, pleasure coiling hot and tight in my core.

She glances up at me through her lashes, blue eyes darkened with desire. Something possessive and primal surges up in me at the sight. I slide my other hand under her chin, tilting her face up toward mine.

"You're so beautiful like this, on your knees for me," I murmur, swiping my thumb over her swollen bottom lip. Her eyes flutter shut, and she whimpers around my length, the vibrations shooting straight to my groin.

Oakley's sounds of pleasure grow louder as she takes me even deeper. The wet heat of her mouth and the sight of her on her knees before me have me right on the edge.

"I'm close," I gasp out in warning.

She responds by quickening her pace, her tongue doing incredible things as her mouth works me over. A deep groan rumbles in my chest.

I caress Oakley's cheek, running my thumb over her soft skin.

"I'm gonna come in this pretty fucking mouth of yours, baby," I rasp.

Her eyes widen slightly but she doesn't stop, quickening her pace. Everything about what she's doing has me seeing stars. With a choked groan, I come hard, spilling myself inside her mouth in hot pulses. She keeps sucking me through it, her tongue working me until I'm completely spent.

Finally, I pull her up to me, crushing her in a searing kiss, tasting myself on her lips. She melts against me; little mewls of pleasure escaping her.

My hands trail down her body, fingertips grazing over her breasts, making her shiver against me. I lavish attention on them, kissing each pert pink nipple before nipping at it just to hear the quiet little squeal in the back of her throat.

Her breath catches when my hand slips between her legs, finding her slick and ready for me. I tease her entrance before sliding two fingers inside, curling them until she arches off the bed with a cry.

"Rem, please," she gasps, clutching at my shoulders.

I latch my mouth onto her neck, nipping and sucking the delicate skin. Marking her as mine. Marking her as many ways as I can. Inside and out.

I work her relentlessly, fingers thrusting deep inside her. She's panting and shaking in my arms, completely lost in pleasure. I curl my fingers, hitting that spot I know drives her wild.

"Oh, fuck!" she cries out, walls clenching around my fingers as she comes hard. I watch her fall apart, mesmerized by how fucking beautiful she is as she lets go.

As she comes down, I withdraw my fingers, slick with her release. Our eyes lock as I bring them to my mouth, licking them clean with a low groan.

"Delicious," I rasp.

Oakley's eyes begin to droop as she comes down from the adrenaline high of her orgasm, and everything from earlier tonight hits her also. I pull her forward until we're both laying across the bed.

She curls into my side, her breaths coming out in soft, uneven sighs. I run my fingers through her hair, her silky strands slipping through my grip.

My heart swells with possessiveness and something dangerous—love. No one else will ever get to see this side of Oakley but me.

With one hand still tangled in her hair, I reach for my phone with the other. Bringing up my messages, I type out a text to my brothers.

Everything taken care of? No traces left?

It feels like an eternity before the screen lights up with a reply from Graham.

G-MONEY

All clear. You know we got your back.

A second later, another message pops up from Penn.

PENNYWISE

Relax pretty boy. I threw the best barbeque and everyone was grilled *flame emoji* I mean thrilled

I release a breath I didn't realize I'd been holding. Everything is as it should be—for now. Whatever it took to protect Oakley and keep us together, I'd do it without hesitation.

LINC

I don't even want to know but let me know if you need me

I go to respond when I feel my sweet fucking girl murmuring and then feel her slick body gyrating against me.

My phone drops as she uses my leg to try and get off in her sleep. I glance down ready to wake her up when I see her coy smile and her bright eyes peering up at me through her lashes.

I chuckle darkly as Oakley grinds against my thigh, her eyes glinting up at me through her lashes.

"Just gonna use me anyway you can to get off, huh, baby?" I murmur, rolling us over so she's pinned beneath me. I slide a hand between us, feeling how slick she still is.

"Please, Rem," she whines, writhing against me.

I capture her mouth in a demanding kiss, swallowing her moans as I feel the head of my cock resting against her and push inside her tight heat in one smooth stroke. She cries out, clutching at my back as I fill her completely.

"That's right, take all of me," I growl against her lips. I set a punishing pace, pounding into her relentlessly as the headboard slams against the wall.

"You're mine," I snarl, gripping her hips hard enough to leave bruises. "This pussy is fucking mine."

"Yes, yes, I'm yours!" she sobs, meeting my powerful

thrusts. I can feel her getting close, her walls clenching down on me.

I latch my teeth onto the delicate skin of her throat. “Come for me. I want to feel you come all over my cock.”

My words send her flying over the edge with a sharp cry. Her orgasm crashes through her, rippling around me as I continue to pound into her mercilessly.

“That’s it, milk my fucking cock,” I grunt through clenched teeth. I’m right on the edge, my balls drawing up tight. “I’m gonna come so deep in this pussy, put a baby in you. You’ll be a fucking Blackwood soon bunny, make you my wife...my Oakley fucking Blackwood.”

My words trigger my own orgasm, pleasure exploding through me as I spill myself inside her in hot pulses. I collapse on top of her, both of us panting and spent.

I nuzzle into her neck, pressing soft kisses over the marks I left. “You’re mine.”

Slowly, I pull out of her, watching with satisfaction as my cum leaks from her swollen pussy. The sight ignites something dark and carnal inside me. I slide two fingers through the slick mess, pushing it back inside her.

“Don’t waste a drop,” I demand huskily. “Keep it all in there.”

Her blue eyes widen, but there’s no fear, only trust and that potent desire she has for me. She nods slightly, biting her lip, “I won’t, Rem. I’ll keep it all in.”

I drag my fingers out of her entrance before pushing them back in, feeling our cum and hearing it make obscene squelching sounds. Fuck me, that’s so goddamn hot.

“You hear that, baby? Your sweet little cunt is talking to me. She wants all my cum, and who am I to deny her? I’m gonna feed her every drop you can take and then even more.

She'll be bursting at the seams and when she can't take anymore, I'll feed you the rest and you'll swallow it all."

Her eyes are wide, but the blush traveling up her chest tells me she loves every fucking filthy word I just uttered.

"Get some sleep baby, cause you and I, we're gonna be fucking just like rabbits. I'm gonna wake you up with my dick and put you to bed with it, also."

CHAPTER 39
OAKLEY

It's been a few days since Mr. Bryant attacked me, and no one has said a word about anything to me. I don't know who Mr. Blackwood has on his payroll, but it's been nothing but 'This is currently under investigation, but no foul play is indicated'.

I'm at Jeremiah's game, and I've barely taken my eyes off of him the entire time I've been here. I feel like it'll be this way in forty years. It'll be hard to pull my gaze from him because he's the only thing I see. The roar of the crowd fades into white noise as my eyes lock onto a figure standing just beyond the bleachers, leaning against one of the many pillars that make up campus. He looks utterly detached from all of the chaos around him. Royce. My heart skips a beat, not out of affection but shock. Two years. Two agonizing years without a word besides that one pocket dial, and here my brother is, like some ghost risen from the dead.

"Oakley?" Lincoln's girlfriend's voice cuts through the din, her eyes assessing and questioning.

"Give me a minute," I manage, my eyes not leaving Royce

while asking for understanding. I don't know how much she knows about the situation with my brother and Jeremiah, but I'd suspect she knows at least a bit. Lincoln likes to pretend that he stays out of everyone's business and that he couldn't be bothered to get involved, but I've seen the way he is with Iris. He tells her every little thing, just like Jeremiah does with me.

Without another moment spared, I rise from my seat and stride purposefully toward Royce, each step fueled by anger and curiosity. I know Jeremiah is watching me, even from the game. I'm safe as long as his eyes are on me. I can feel Iris' gaze burning into my back, also. Watching, waiting and willing to jump in if I need her. A girls' girl, well, at least to me. I appreciate it more than she'll ever know.

As I close the distance, his frame comes into sharper focus: taller, more muscular, and that scar. It slices across his neck, raw and jagged. A reminder that I have no idea what it's from because he cut me out of his life without a word. It stands out starkly against his rugged exterior. It's impossible to look away.

"Royce," I say, my voice barely a whisper yet surprisingly steady. His name tastes bitter on my tongue, memories of betrayal flooding back. He looks up, his piercing blue eyes meeting mine. For a moment, it's like looking at the brother who was always there for me until he wasn't. Then I realize that they're colder, harder, and darker than before.

"I should have known I'd find you here, little sister," he replies, his tone as rough as the scar that marks him. If he's not here for me, then he must be here for Jeremiah. Suddenly, I feel very protective. If he's here to start their feud up again, I won't be bulldozed this time. I have enough of a voice to tell him exactly where he can go.

"Two years," I start, the words catching in my throat.

Emotions too volatile to contain flood through my entire body. "Where the hell have you been?" My question hangs in the air. My fingers itch to reach out to touch my big brother. But something else gnaws at me, more urgent than his disappearance—the scar. "What happened to you?"

He smirks, but there's no humor in it. Just bitterness and old wounds. "Life happened, oak tree. Things you wouldn't understand." He uses an old nickname, and the look that he's giving me is like he's daring me to push further.

"Try me and don't call me that," I counter, stepping closer. He has no idea what I've been through, so right now we're a match made up of traumas.

"You're determined, I'll give you that," he mutters, his eyes flickering with something unreadable.

"Don't patronize me, Royce. Not after everything." My voice is sharper now, cutting through the pretense.

"Everything?" He scoffs, running a hand through his tousled hair. "You don't know the half of it, Oakley."

"Then enlighten me," I challenge, refusing to back down. "Or leave. But don't you dare stand there and act like you don't owe me anything."

His eyes darken, a shadow crossing his face. "You chose Jeremiah. Remember that."

"Is that what this is about?" I snap, anger flaring. "Two years gone, and you're still hung up on that night?"

"More than you know," he admits, voice low and dangerous. The scar on his neck seems to pulse with his words.

"Then why come back?" I demand, frustration bubbling over. "Why now?"

"Because," he says, stepping closer until we're almost touching, "some things can't be left unfinished."

The cheers from the game swell behind us, but they feel miles away. All that exists is this moment, this confrontation. And the answers I desperately need.

"Fine," I say, my voice trembling with determination. "Let's finish it. Where the hell did you disappear to?" I demand, my voice cracking with desperation. The words spill out before I can stop them, years of longing and confusion bubbling to the surface as water rims my lashes. I search his eyes for any hint of remorse or explanation, but all I see is a wall of bitterness.

"Does it matter?" Royce's voice is cold, almost detached. He leans against the stone column, arms crossed. "You made your choice when you didn't back me up, Oakley. Whether I was right or wrong, you should have taken my side. I'm your brother." Spoken like a man who was definitely wrong and knows it, but somehow, it's still my fault.

"Isn't it always like this with you?" I retort, the sarcasm biting. "Always running, never facing things head-on."

"You're still young. Still innocent. Don't speak on things you don't understand." I want to throttle him. He has no idea about any of the shit I've gone through. Things I've done.

"Don't give me that," I snap, stepping closer until I can smell the faint scent of sweat clinging to him. "Two years, Royce. You disappeared without a trace, and you expect me to ignore that? Do you have any idea what that did to me?"

"To you?" he scoffs, eyes narrowing. "You think this is about you? You chose Jeremiah over me. Remember?" His eyes flicker with something dark, something that makes my skin prickle with unease.

"Dammit, Royce!" I hit his chest with my fists, frustration boiling over. "I deserve to know!"

"Deserve? I owe you nothing, Oakley," he sneers, grabbing

my wrists and holding them tight. "Do you have any idea what it's like to be betrayed by your own sister?"

"Like hell you don't, and let go of me," I say through gritted teeth, trying to wrench free. But his grip only tightens, his eyes flashing with anger and pain. "Royce, please," I beg, tears now streaming down my face. "I need you to let go."

"Fine," he says, releasing me abruptly. I stumble back, my heart aching with the weight of his words. " I guess some scars never heal."

"You think you're the only one with scars?" I ask, my voice shaking. "Don't be so obtuse or conceited. You left, but life goes on and bad shit happens to people every day. The world doesn't revolve around you."

"It doesn't matter now anyway," he admits, his eyes softening for a split second before hardening again.

"Royce, enough," I snap, my voice sharp and unwavering. The weight of the past couple of years presses down on me and it feels like a boulder is sitting on my chest, but I channel that pain into resolve. "You don't get to waltz back into my life and stir up chaos. Are you here for Jeremiah? He didn't do what you thought he did. I don't know why you could never believe that."

"Chaos?" Royce scoffs, his eyes flashing with anger and hurt, maybe. "You think I'm the one bringing chaos? Look around you, Oakley. You've got Jeremiah wrapped around your finger while you're still trying to play peacekeeper. It's pathetic, and no matter how much I have on him it seems like he still got his hooks in you."

"Pathetic?" My laugh is bitter, and I can feel my tears of sadness drying up. "What's pathetic is disappearing without a word and then expecting everything to be just as you left it. I've dealt with enough pain in your absence, Royce. You have no idea. You don't get to judge me, not after everything. I was in pieces, big brother, and I picked them up. Without you."

"Pain?" He steps closer, invading my space, his breath against my face.

"Just leave, Royce." I harden my gaze, drawing on every ounce of determination I have left. "I can't deal with your unpredictable presence anymore. I have no room for it in my life. I would have given anything to have you back months ago, hell a year ago would have been even better. But now you just remind me of how decayed our relationship is. How broken our entire family is. Say what you want about the Blackwoods, but you can't deny that not a single one of them leaves another behind, regardless of what may or may not have happened."

"Oakley, you're—" His retort is cut off by the sudden eruption of noise from the crowd. The final play of the Championship game has everyone on their feet, cheers filling the air, drowning out our confrontation. For a moment, we're both distracted, caught in the fervor of the crowd. I fucking missed it and now I'm pissed about that.

Royce mutters, his expression darkening. "I want to talk to Jeremiah, and I need you to stay out of it. This isn't your business and I would have preferred you stay the hell away from everything Blackwood."

"Yes, it is. Jeremiah is my business," I reply firmly, turning away from him, my heart pounding in my chest. As the crowd's excitement gets louder, all I can think about is getting away from him and getting back to the field. I know Jeremiah has noticed I've been gone too long by now and any minute he's going to burst off the field, murder in his eyes.

"Oakley!"

Jeremiah's voice cuts though just like clockwork. I glance

over my shoulder just in time to see him striding toward us, his eyes displaying with anger and protectiveness. He reaches my side, placing himself between me and Royce, a human shield made of muscle and determination. It helps he's still got his uniform on, but no helmet.

"Get gone, Ashford. Stay away from her," he growls, his voice low and dangerous. "You've done enough damage to last a lifetime."

Royce's lips curl into a bitter smile. "Oh, look who decided to play knight in shining armor. Just another pretty boy, always swooping in at the last second. Might want to check your facts."

"Shut up, Royce," Jeremiah snaps. "Or I'll shut you up. And you're just as much of a pretty boy as I am. Lest you forget we used to be fucking brothers."

Royce chuckles darkly, a sound that sends shivers down my spine. "That's funny coming from you. Almost as if I heard those words from a Blackwood before."

"What's that supposed to mean?" Jeremiah's fists clench at his sides, ready for a fight.

"It means," Royce says, his voice dripping with bitterness, "that I know the truth now. Jeremiah, you didn't fuck around with Penny. It's your father who is a piece of shit."

The revelation hits like a punch to the gut. My mind races, trying to process what is actually happening right now. Royce steps closer, his gaze locked onto Jeremiah's. I have no idea what he's talking about, and I honestly don't want to know if it has anything to do with Mr. Blackwood. Knowing shit about him is dangerous.

"He wanted to break us apart, you and me. And it worked, he succeeded. I don't know why, but again I don't understand shit about you Blackwoods and how you operate." My brother spews out and my head spins.

"You're lying," Jeremiah snaps, though doubt flickers across his face. "Why the hell would he do that?"

"I don't have a fucking reason to lie. It doesn't change the fact that things can never be the same between us," Royce continues with a shrug, with what sounds like regret lacing his words. "Our friendship is beyond repair, and I know that. I made sure of it when I forced you to stay the fuck away from my sister."

"Yep," Jeremiah replies, his voice quieter now but no less firm. "You know Blackwoods never forgive blackmail, unless we're the ones doing it. But that doesn't mean you have to drag Oakley through your personal hell."

"Drag her?" Royce's eyes flash with pain. "I came back to set the record straight with you. She chose which side she was on a long time ago. I'm not the villain in this story."

"Consider it straightened. Now do us both a favor and leave her alone," Jeremiah says, his tone final. "That's the best thing you can do for your sister."

The tension between them crackles. I stand there, caught in the crossfire of these two boneheads. Royce's confession changes everything and nothing, all at once.

"Fine," Royce finally says, stepping back. "I'll leave. But I'll be around. I just transferred to St. Charles." There's mirth in his tone that I don't like one bit.

Jeremiah doesn't reply, wrapping an arm around me protectively.

As Royce turns and walks away, the weight of the encounter settles over us like a dark cloud. For a moment, we stand in silence, the noise of the crowd fading into the background as we process what just happened.

"Are you okay?" Jeremiah asks, his voice gentle now, his protective stance softening.

"Yeah," I whisper, leaning into him, finding solace in his embrace. "I think so."

"Let's get out of here," he suggests, his eyes filled with concern.

We move through the crowd, the noise fading into a distant hum. My heart pounds in my chest, the uncertainty that lies ahead for the three of us weighing on me. I don't know why my brother has transferred here, but I suspect it's not because he has a sudden interest in getting a degree when professional boxing was always his goal. He wanted to be the next great and to see his name in lights everywhere. But with Jeremiah's arm around me, I feel a flicker of hope. Whatever comes next, we'll face it together.

"Blackwood!" Royce's voice calls out behind us, and I realize that he's turned back around to us. His tone is raw, stripped of its usual confidence.

"Oakley needs you," Royce admits, his eyes locking onto mine with an intensity that makes me shiver. "I can see that now. It doesn't mean I like what happened, but I get it."

Jeremiah's grip on me tightens, as if he can shield me from the weight of Royce's words. I glance up at him, seeing the conflict tearing him apart. But there's an understanding there, a reluctant acceptance.

"I'll keep her safe. From everyone. Even you," Jeremiah begins, his voice low and dangerous.

"I know," Royce replies, stepping closer.

"You have no idea what she went through because you left her. Because *I* left her," Jeremiah snaps, his muscles coiled and ready to snap.

"You're right," Royce says, his voice softening. He raises his hand, rough and scarred, extending it toward Jeremiah. "Truce, for her sake?"

Time seems to freeze as Jeremiah stares at Royce's outstretched hand. He looks at his hand as if it's a viper poised to strike. Two former best friends, to enemies, to acquaintances as best. How freaking tragic.

"Fine," Jeremiah mutters, releasing his hold on me just enough to free one hand. He takes Royce's hand, their grips firm but wary. "But this doesn't mean you have any right to call her, text her, or be near her. I'm on the edge, Royce."

"Understood," Royce replies, a faint smile tugging at his lips.

"Just remember," Jeremiah warns, his voice dropping to a menacing whisper. "You, of all people, know what the fuck I'm capable of. Don't give me a reason."

"Noted," Royce says simply, letting go of Jeremiah's hand. The tension between them simmers, an uneasy understanding forged.

"Let's get out of here," I say, my voice trembling. The need to escape is overwhelming.

"Yeah," Jeremiah agrees, his arm wrapping around me once more. As we turn to leave, I catch a glimpse of Royce's face—haunted, regretful, yet determined. I'll find out where he's been and why he was gone for so long, but I know it won't be right now. As much time as I've spent hating the fact that he left the way he did, I do believe him about Mr. Blackwood. I can tell that Jeremiah does, too.

I want to know what happened, how he got that scar and why he looks so exhausted, but I know it's not my place anymore to ask those kinds of questions.

That's his story to tell when he's ready.

CHAPTER 40
JEREMIAH

I push open the kitchen door, and the scent of garlic and rosemary hits me like an olfactory overload. Oakley's there, apron-clad, hips swaying to some soft tune only she can hear, her small feet tucked into those damn cute shoes that do funny things to my heart rate.

"Hey," I offer, leaning against the doorframe, trying to keep my voice casual despite the sudden tightness in my chest.

She glances over her shoulder, a smile playing on her lips, "Keep your distance, pretty boy. Wouldn't want you tainting this masterpiece with your dirty football grip."

"Football hands, bunny. Get it right," I correct her, but I'm grinning, caught up in our usual banter now that things have finally calmed the fuck down.

"Right, because that makes them cleaner?" She tosses back at me, her tone light, but her eyes filled with humor.

From the corner, Ramsey, ever the tech gremlin, is hunched over his latest gadget with his glasses perched on his nose. His head snaps up at Oakley's next jab, "And you, Ramsey Blackwood? Keep those hockey mitts off the table till they've seen some soap."

"Harsh, Oaks. My hands are pristine," Ramsey protests, throwing up his hands, looking more amused than chastised.

Unable to resist, I sneak up behind her, wrapping my arms around her tiny waist and pulling her back flush against me. "Got ya," I murmur against the delicate shell of her ear.

She doesn't startle or flinch away. Something I wasn't sure was ever going to happen. Instead, she melts into me, her body molding to mine in a way that has me swallowing hard. The trust she has in me these days...it's fucking everything.

"Mmm, is that so?" she teases, craning her neck to meet my heated gaze. Her blue eyes are sparkling with mischief and love, it leaves my heart pounding against my ribs. She dances out of my grip, and I step back to lean against the counter.

"What's on the menu tonight?" I ask, pushing away from the granite and inching closer to the fridge, unable to resist the urge to see what she's already made that I can pick at. I'm fucking hungry.

"Wouldn't you like to know," she teases, turning back to her task before adding with a soft chuckle, "Patience, Rem. Good things come to those who wait."

"Never been much good at waiting, especially when it comes to you," I admit under my breath, hoping she doesn't catch the weight behind the words.

But she does. She always does. And that knowing smile she sends my way tells me she's fully aware of the power she holds. Damn, if that isn't the hottest thing.

"Quit bothering me, Blackwood," she orders gently, pointing at me with her wooden spoon, "And stay out of the fridge. Dinner is almost served."

"Whatever you say, chef," I reply, obeying with a mock salute, but not before sneaking a quick peek at the swell of her backside. This girl is going to be the death of me, and what a way to go.

I lurk in the kitchen, the sizzle of the pan distracting her from the fact I'm about to snag something, hell I'll even take a piece of cheese to quiet the gnawing of my belly.

"Penn's not gonna be here for dinner I don't think," I tell her, fighting to keep my tone even as her scent surrounds me. "He's been MIA."

Oakley frowns, her brow furrowing in that adorable way that makes me want to kiss the crease until it dissolves. "Everything okay?"

I shrug, not wanting to worry her. "You know how he gets sometimes."

Oakley turns in my embrace, eyebrows knitting together in concern. "Did something happen?"

"Who knows with Penn," I say, shrugging it off. "He's probably off charming some poor unsuspecting soul or plotting world domination. Ya know, normal Penn things."

"He's been gone more than usual. Should we be worried?" It's just like her to care, to consider every angle.

"Let's just enjoy the quiet while it lasts," I suggest, trying to mask the undercurrent of concern in my own voice. There could be something going on, sure, but right now, Oakley's here in my arms, and that's all the world I need. Not to mention I trust my brother and if he needed me, needed us, he would tell us and there's nothing I wouldn't do for him. Except for give up my girl, I'd tell him to eat shit.

"Alright," she concedes, her smile returning. "But if he doesn't show up by tomorrow, I'm sending a search party."

"Deal," I agree, pressing a quick, daring kiss to her lips before stepping back.

"Need a hand with anything?" Iris strides into the kitchen, her voice slicing through the lingering concern. Thank fuck, these two get along because if I had to kick miss bitchy law barbie's ass I would have. Their first meeting was less than stellar.

"Absolutely," Oakley responds, her tone full of relief and welcome. "Can you grab the salad from the fridge and toss it?"

Iris and I just look at each other and grin, but don't make a comment in order to not corrupt and embarrass my girl.

"Got it." Iris moves with purpose, headed straight for the stainless-steel monolith of a refrigerator.

"Jesus Christ, Iris! Keep your clacking ass down." Graham's at the table, grumbling about the staccato of whatever the fuck she's wearing on her feet while his attention is glued to something on his phone. His annoyance crackles like static in the air, and I feel Oakley stiffen beside me.

"Excuse you?" Iris shoots back, her words sharp as shards of ice. "I'll clack however I damn please, thank you very much. You're lucky I'm not stomping and putting my size seven up your grumpy ass."

"Yea, shove it, Graham," Oakley chimes in, her sass a surprising match for Iris'.

"Whatever," he grunts, eyes never leaving the screen. I catch a glimpse of furrowed brows and the clench of his jaw.

"Anyway," Iris continues, undeterred, her smirk widening as she slams the fridge door shut with more force than necessary. "Let's get this show on the road before the rest of the zoo arrives."

Nodding in agreement, "Let's eat before the food gets cold

and I start considering cannibalism. Graham, you might want to use some goddamn headphones if we're too much for your delicate sensibilities."

"Fuck off," Graham retorts without missing a beat, though there's a hint of a smile tugging at the corner of his mouth.

"Language, gentlemen," Oakley teases, playfully wagging a finger at us. The aromatic scent of whatever other herbs she's used wraps around me. I don't know what the fuck she's making, but it looks and smells like some bomb ass chicken.

The volume on whatever Graham's watching increases, the tinny sound of a news report filling the kitchen. "...fire at the campus library a few weeks ago, which officials are calling an accidental blaze likely caused by faulty wiring. Two casualties have been confirmed, though their identities have not yet been released."

Lincoln's gruff voice cuts through the noise as he walks in. "Thank fuck."

"Let's just...let's just eat," Oakley says, swallowing hard, her playful sass replaced by urgency. "We're all here, we're safe. That's what matters."

The room settles into a silence as none of us wants to utter what we all know. We dodged a fucking bullet and the Blackwood fucking luck once again saved our fucking asses.

My stomach clenches at the possibilities of how shit could have gone sideways, but before I can dwell on it, Penn's voice rings out from the hallway. "I'm getting marrrriiiieeeeddd!"

He saunters into the kitchen, that trademark twisted smile of his firmly in place as he sings the words, swaying his hips in an exaggerated fashion.

Graham's eyebrows shoot up, his face contorting into disbelief. "Where the hell have you been? And to who?"

"Going to the chapelllllllll," His voice lilts through the air, drawing a collective gasp from the room. "Gonna get hitched-dddd or however that song goes. My version is better."

"Spill it, motherfucker. What in the entire fucking hell are you dragging us into now?" My words are edged with a challenge; we're all on edge, and Penn's theatrics feel surreal.

"Patience, brother. It's fixing a little problem. Everything will be fine," he singsongs, wiggling his eyebrows before sidling past us toward the countertop where Lincoln's plate sits, loaded with food. He swipes a piece of chicken, grinning like the Cheshire Cat.

"Bastard," Lincoln protests, but there's no real heat behind it. We're all too caught up in the absurdity of Penn's announcement.

"See you at the altar! I'm gonna let you guys duke it out on who's best man." Penn calls over his shoulder as he bounds up the stairs two at a time, leaving a trail of laughter in his wake.

"Unbelievable," I mutter, the tension easing out of my shoulders as I exchange a look with Oakley.

"Don't look at me. You know how he is."

I do know, but that doesn't make Penn's antics any less bewildering. Or concerning.

Shaking my head, I grab mine and Oakley's plates and follow the rest of my family into the dining room. It isn't until we're all settled at the long, wooden table that Lincoln finally speaks up. "So...are we gonna talk about the fucking elephant in the room, or...?"

Before I can even speak, Graham is stabbing a piece of chicken, "You know Penn is bat shit crazy and honestly at this point the less we know the fucking better. I trust him, so whatever he's doing, he's definitely got a plan in place. Now, can we fucking eat in peace finally?"

And we finally fucking sit down and each dinner in fucking peace as requested by Graham.

Well, except for the maniacal laughter still floating down the stairs from whatever the fuck Penn is planning.

I'm gonna need to borrow Iris' fucking Xanax and maybe some tums.

EPILOGUE

OAKLEY

VALENTINE'S DAY

The flickering of fairy lights I had Iris help me put up dance across the dimly lit bedroom in the Blackwoods summer house. I can't help but feel a thrill as I adjust the camera just so, ensuring that every detail is perfectly captured. The faint scent of vanilla from the candles fills the air, replicating a setting just for him, my heart beating in time with the rhythm of the ticking clock.

"Okay, Oakley. Give him the show of a lifetime," I whisper to myself, taking a deep breath to steady my nerves. I smile when I see the only user's name that was invited to this stream. I slip on my bunny mask, the one I had custom made just for this. His football number etched on one ear. A proud mark of belonging to him.

prettyboyblackwood has entered the room

On the other side of the screen, I imagine Jeremiah's eyes locked on the feed, his heart better be pounding with excitement and nervousness because mine sure is. He asked me to give him a private cam show for his birthday since I stopped streaming after he barged in, broke my laptop and commandeered me into his house, room, and life. All of the above. I shake my head at the thought, thinking about how far we've come since that night. He wanted to FaceTime instead, but I thought a real cam show where he can only type to me would be more fun. I can tease him without him being able to say anything back to me. I just know that his thoughts are consumed by the desire to see me, to hear my voice, to connect with me in this way. And with each passing second, the power I hold over him in this small way grows stronger.

"Hey there, pretty boy," I say, flashing a flirtatious smile at the camera. My voice comes out soft-spoken and thoughtful yet laced with a hint of sass. "A little rabbit told me you're the birthday boy today."

Baby

Jeremiah's types, and I think he's going to be broody because that's exactly how Jeremiah gets when I'm not with him, even for a few minutes. We're in the same dang vacation house, with only a wall separating us, but he's going to act like I flew to outer space without telling him my plans. He surprises me by typing.

You have no idea how much I've been looking forward to this.

"Is that so?" I tease, my fingers grazing over the lace trim of my dress. The thought of the effect I have on him sends a shiver down my spine, and I can't help but feel a sense of pride. "Well, I promise you won't be disappointed."

You look beautiful

He types. And though I can't see it, I know his lips must be curved into that smirk that I love.

You should wear that dress more often. But only for me

He adds, and I can't help but giggle.

"As if everything I do isn't only for you," I reply, my laughter bubbling up out of me like champagne. "Hmm," I say finally, my voice a breathy whisper in the stillness of the room. "Let's get started."

Bunny

Jeremiah types my nickname, and I can *feel* how he's filled with longing right now.

I can't do this. I'm coming in, unlock the door

I giggle, shaking my head in the negative.

"Tsk, tsk, pretty boy. You asked for a show and that's what you're going to get. Even my most loyal viewers don't get to touch," I respond, my words dripping with playful mischief. I look over at the open window, because I have something else in store for Jeremiah that he doesn't know about.

Slowly, I let the straps of my dress fall, enjoying the sensation of fabric slipping from my skin. Every movement is graceful, deliberate, like a dance choreographed just for him. I let my hand fall to the necklace around my neck that holds his Blackwood ring. I know he'll enjoy seeing the B dangling between my breasts, marking me as his in yet another way.

I'm so thankful I practiced this part. The soft rustle of my dress falling to the floor in the dimly lit room is all I can hear except for my own breathing.

It's a sixth sense, but Jeremiah's reactions are unmistakable, even though the digital barrier separating us. He's outside the door, watching me on his phone and swear I can almost hear his breath hitching with every reveal, sensing the anticipation building within him. It's titillating, knowing that I hold such power over him, able to ignite him with even the simplest of gestures.

"Tell me what you want, pretty boy," I whisper, my voice low and sultry. "Guide me."

"I want you to open this goddamn door," Jeremiah yells, his fist pounding on the large wooden door, and it takes everything in me not to laugh. He's so unhinged and I love him for it.

"What would be the fun in that?" I reply with a teasing smile. "Don't you want to see what comes off next?"

I can't help but imagine his heart racing uncontrollably as he watches me, his breath ragged and desperate. The thought fans the flames of my own desire, and I lose myself in the performance, determined to push him to the edge as I twirl around in my pale green matching bra and cheeky panties with my mask on.

"I'll break the door down," Jeremiah growls the words. "It wouldn't be the first I've done it to get to you and won't be the last either, Oakley. You have no idea how much I want you right now." He has no idea that I have no intention of taking my bra and panties off. I fully intend on letting him rip them off in his vigor to have what is so rightfully his.

"Mmm I'm pretty sure I do," I tease, my heart swelling with affection for this man who's my entire world.

I drink in Jeremiah's irritation that he can't get his hands on me right now. I mean he could, but he's letting me play my little game and I have no doubt he gets just as much enjoyment out of it as I do. It's a heady dose of praise that sends shivers down my spine. My body hums with newfound confidence and power fueled by his reactions to my every move.

"Tell me," I say, my voice sultry and commanding, "what do you want me to do next?"

Jeremiah hesitates, and I can almost picture the conflict in his eyes as he battles between desire and restraint. Finally, he types out his response, playing along because he thinks that by adhering to my rules, I'll do what he wants and unlock the door.

I want to feel your touch, Oakley. I need it.

My heart skips a beat at his admission, touched by the depth of his feelings. We've come so far since those innocent days when our connection was forged with secret glances and whispered conversations.

"Jeremiah," I murmur, my voice soft yet tinged with mischief, "you have no idea how much I want that too."

"Show me," he pleads through the door, desperation lacing his words. "Open the door and let me see just how much you want me."

In that moment, I feel powerful, in control. With a wicked smile, I hold a finger up at him and then run that same finger between my breasts, down my stomach, and dip my hand inside my panties. "If only you were close by," I fake pout. "You know your fingers feel better than mine ever will."

Jeremiah kicks the door, rattling the whole frame. "Open this fucking door, bunny. You're going to pay for this when I get my hands on you. I'm not going to let you fucking come." He sounds like he's out of his mind when he snaps, "or maybe I'll make you come so many times that you pass out."

"Jeremiah," I gasp, my voice trembling with anticipation, pulling my fingers up to my mouth and licking them just the way I know he likes to. I need to pick my moment, and I know this is it.

Another kick. He's so worked up, he's not even thinking about walking down the hall and getting the key like I thought he would. Instead, he's going to kick the wood right off the frame so he can come in here and wreck me.

"When I catch you, I'm going to fuck you so deep and hard, you won't be able to walk for a week," Jeremiah promises.

"Maybe I want to be caught," I admit, my voice dripping with mischief. "Unfortunately, I have plans for your birthday, so you're going to have to play along pretty boy, if you want to open your presents." I blow him a kiss and end the cam show. I have only minutes before he's in here, having his way with me.

I head to the window and climb out, thankful that we're on the first floor. I'm running across the open field toward the tree line when I hear him call my name.

"I'll give you a head start," I hear him say. He's leaning out the window with an absolutely feral look on his face.

"I love you too, pretty boy," I call out to him, blowing him another kiss, which he makes a show of catching. "Now come get your present."

This is going to be the best birthday Jeremiah Blackwood has ever had.

AFTERWORD

Thank you so much for reading Jeremiah and Oakley's story!

Want to know more about Penn and just how and why is he getting married?

I'm happy to tell you that his book, Wicked Spite is currently being worked on and you can preorder here!

For a sneak peek into his story turn the page.

WICKED SPITE SNEAK PEEK

The alley is dark as shit, only broken by the occasional flickering streetlamp that looks like it's on its last legs. Just my kind of place—grungy, hidden from prying eyes. Perfect for getting into trouble, which I seem to have a knack for. My combat boots thud against the cracked pavement as I stride quickly, head down, minding my own damn business. Stupid? Maybe. Necessary? Definitely.

I can't shake the feeling that something's off tonight. The alley is too quiet—no drunk laughter or the usual shuffling of feet.

"Keep it together, Reagan," I mutter under my breath, my fingers brushing against the switchblade in my pocket—a habit, a comfort. It's just another shortcut home, one I've taken a hundred times. But the air smells like trouble, and I swear the darkness is thicker than usual, sticking to my skin. Like honey when I used to make my younger sister Reese tea to cheer her up.

I round the corner and my heart skips a beat. I freeze as three tall figures loom ahead, tall and dressed head-to-toe in black like some wannabe ninjas straight from the TV. Shit. Why the fuck am I always finding myself in these goddamn situations?

Leaning against the brick wall of the alley entrance my heart thumps in my chest as I watch them dismount from their street bikes, kicking down their stands and throwing one leg over, moving in perfect unison like a well-oiled machine. Are they triplets? No one could be that perfectly in-sync with someone. The loud clang of their helmets hitting their gas tanks sounds in my ears. In the dark, I strain to make out their features, but it's useless. It doesn't matter, anyway. I could give two shits what they look like and when I think back on this moment, I prefer the anonymity of their helmets, anyway.

Something about their presence sends a chill down my spine, and not in a good way. They radiate violence, barely contained and bubbling at the surface ready to spill over. Something I'm so goddamn intimately familiar with. My instincts start screaming louder at me—run, hide—but I'm frozen, caught in their invisible grip.

My heart starts pounding double-time as I size them up, trying to gauge how much trouble I'm in. They haven't seen me yet, too busy glowering at each other like they're in some kind of pissing contest. Typical men.

Their presence is suffocating, and for a moment, I'm back there—sixteen again, sold by the man who should have been my protector. My body remembers: the fear, the powerlessness. But I'm not that girl anymore. I'm steel wrapped in skin, and nothing can break me. I'm already broken, and all my little jagged pieces were dipped into the fire and cauterized. I'm just a sack of flesh going through the motions.

I debate turning around and getting the hell out of dodge, but something keeps me rooted to the spot. A morbid curiosity has me following them as they slink through the alley away from their bikes. The smartest thing to do would be to leave and act like I haven't seen shit, but sometimes I'm just a dumb bitch.

Just where the fuck are they going and what are they going to do when they get there?

They turn out of this alley and into another grimy one before slipping into a house door. I pause, waiting a couple of beats before creeping toward the small window about four feet to the right of the door they just entered and look inside. A plain kitchen with faded and cracked linoleum greets my eyes until I look further out of the open floor plan and into the living room.

Finally, I can get a good look at each of them, but it's the way the one slips something to a couple of guys and ushers them downstairs that makes him the most intriguing. The other two are in front of the blond sitting on the couch. Does he owe them money? Did he offend them? I have so many questions. I wish I could hear what they are saying. My fingers poke at the window to see if it opens at all, but of course I'm not that lucky.

Black t-shirts, dark jeans, and black motorcycle books encasing each of the guys. The only difference is their height, build, and their masks. The two have plain, non-descript ones, but it's the third that intrigues me the most. He's got a screaming ghost mask on. My center clenches because who the fuck hasn't thought about fucking a guy while he wears a hot, creepy mask like that.

I can't tear my eyes away from him—the one with the screaming mask sitting like a crown atop his head. His face is like stone, but his eyes are dark, unreadable, but they pull at me, drawing me into something I know I should avoid.

I may not be able to hear their words, but the thuds and grunts of flesh against flesh are visceral sounds that echo off the grimy brick walls. There's a brutality to the way number one is beating blondie. My heart hammers against my ribcage, like a morbid drum line desperate to join the music. The excitement in my veins is like a shot of adrenaline straight to my pussy. It's wrong, so fucking wrong to feel this way, but it's there, nonetheless. A thrill at the sight of violence, blood and splitting flesh invades my system.

I'm frozen, caught between the impulse to flee and the perverse desire to witness more. I know I should leave. I've seen enough and being a nosey bitch will only lead to trouble. The problem is that this right here is the stuff my fantasies are made of. It's what will help me come later tonight when I play it back in my head.

I can almost feel the next impact, imagine the burst of pain that must be exploding behind the guy's eyes. My body tenses, but then I watch as the guy is dropped to the ground. The leanest one that just beat the ever-loving shit out of this guy pulls his phone out of his pocket and I can watch his mouth open as he answers it.

A different type of tension lines his body as he starts yelling into the phone, pacing as whoever is on the other line doesn't answer. The line must disconnect because he starts yelling at the other two.

His boot comes down hard, the sole slamming into the guy's windpipe. There's this sickening crunch that cuts through the air, and I know that I'm going to be thinking about it for days. The dude on the ground—it's over for him. He goes limp like a rag doll.

"Fuck me," I breathe out, the words barely slipping past my lips as I clench my thighs together. My heart's doing double time, pounding against my ribcage like it wants out. Adrenaline's got a chokehold on me, and I'm not sure if I want to break free.

For a second—a messed-up, twisted second—I picture myself in there, throwing punches, jumping onto Mr. Tall, Dark and Twisted. It's a heady thought; control, dominance, something I crave but never admit out loud. I can almost feel the weight of someone under my own boots, every stomp an assertion of my own strength. Heat coils low in my belly at the fantasy, dark and vicious and mine.

Damn it, Rae, what the hell are you thinking? But the question's rhetorical because deep down, I know exactly what I'm thinking. It's like staring into an abyss and finding it staring back, recognizing a part of yourself that's just as feral, just as hungry.

I shuffle, trying to alleviate some of the pressure in my core when my boot connects with a heap of trash, and the racket it creates is like a goddamn dinner bell in the silence of the alley. Shit. The sound ricochets off the walls, a roar of my mistake. I freeze, heart sinking, as the guys halt their talking and three heads swivel toward me.

"Fuck," I whisper out loud. Like I said, I'm a dumb bitch. I should have never come down here. Like Alice in Wonderland following the damn white rabbit.

Time's a bitch, stretching out like some sick joke, each tick echoing louder than the last. My eyes lock onto that screaming ghost bastard who stands there like death's own warden. His head tilts slightly, as if he's trying to decipher the puzzle of my existence from where he's standing. There's curiosity there, but mostly fucking danger.

I don't think twice. The instinct to run, to survive, slams into me like a freight train. My boots slap the pavement, pounding out a desperate rhythm as I flee from whatever hell I've stumbled upon. I can feel my heart trying to punch its way out of my chest, each beat screaming to put more distance between us.

"Shit, shit, shit," I mutter, cursing the adrenaline that's both my savior and tormentor. It's like it's not enough to witness something so fucked up—I have to get caught, too?

The cold November night air whips past me, cutting through the thin fabric of my band tee and the flannel I wear. But I barely register the chill—it's nothing compared to the icy dread coiling in my stomach. I refuse to be caught and made a spectacle of. I'd rather kill myself. I navigate the maze of alleys moving closer to campus. I just need to get somewhere that I can disappear into a throng of people.

So fucking stupid when so much is on the line. Reese flashes in my mind. My little sister who just had her sweet sixteen and blissfully unaware of the monster lurking in our father. He'll sell her soul for a dime and power. Not while I'm breathing. She's the one pure thing left in my life, and I'll be damned if I let history repeat itself.

I gotta get my ass out of here.

Every step of boots is fueled by the need to shield my sister from the darkness that's already stained my own hands. The pain the hard leather gives me keeps me focused but fuck I wish I had sneakers on. I dodge a stray cat as it scampers across my path, it hisses as if I've just annoyed the ever-loving shit out of it.

"Fuck you too, kitty," I snarl, but there's no heat in it. I'm too wired, every sense dialed up to eleven.

I'm so close to getting my sister free. I'll burn down the world before I let him touch her. I've danced with devils before—I'm not afraid to do it again.

I can almost laugh at the twisted irony. Me, Reagan St. Pierre, the girl who makes a mockery of rules, now playing guardian angel. If that's not fucked up, I don't know what is. But maybe that's just it; we're all a little messed up, trying to find a scrap of redemption in the chaos.

I push my long legs to go harder, faster, until the burn in my thighs feels like sweet punishment. There's a sick part of me that craves the pain, the rush. But the stakes are too high, and I'm not looking to cash out early.

My lungs are heaving, each breath a ragged tear through the air. I've been running for a few blocks, but it's not just the cold biting at my heels—it's the prickle of a thousand eyes, the sense that they are tracking my every move. It's like I can feel their gaze, heavy and unrelenting against my skin. It makes me itch, my flesh feeling too tight.

The neon lights of the bar strip flicker in the distance, slicing through the alley's darkness. The thumping bass beckons from one of the brick buildings calls me. Two more steps and I'm there, my combat boots slipping on something slick—don't think about what that might be—as I bulldoze into the throng of sweaty bodies.

"Move!" I growl, not caring who I elbow aside as I shove my way through the crowd. Hands and bodies brush and grope, but I keep my switchblade tucked away—for now. No need to start a brawl when I'm this close to blending in.

"Excuse you," some guy slurs, his beer-sloshed breath hot on my neck.

"Fuck off," I snap back without missing a beat, ducking under his clumsy attempt to grab my arm. I don't have time for this kind of bullshit tonight.

I lose myself in the mass of gyrating bodies, letting the heavy scent of sweat and spilled alcohol fill my nostrils. It's disgusting, really, but it's cover. And right now, I'll take whatever I can get. With each step further into the belly of the beast, I feel my pulse begin to level out. Just have to keep moving, keep hidden.

"Hey, watch it!" A girl stumbles backward into me, her drink splashing across the both of us.

"Sorry," I lie, not giving a damn about her stained shirt as I sidestep and push onward. This place is a pit—a perfect pit to get lost in.

"Reagan?" someone calls out, but I don't stop. Can't stop. Whoever it is, they can find me later. I purposely chose "Bleachers" to slip into instead of "Whiskey's Place", two doors down. Even if they follow me in here, it's just another barrier for them to come back and find me again. I have no connection to this place except the proximity to my job.

The layout is similar on all of these buildings, so it's easy to find a back entrance to an employee's only area.

I slip into the room; the door creaking behind me. The air is stale, tinged with the smell of cleaning chemicals and something musky and raw.

"Fuck." I whisper to myself, catching my breath, before I realize I'm not alone.

My eyes adjust to the low light, and there they are—a guy and a girl, wrapped up in each other. They're fucking hard against the stacked boxes of liquor, oblivious to my intrusion. Every thrust, every moan, echoes off the concrete walls, filling the tight space with their wet, sloppy sounds.

I should turn around. Should leave. But I don't. I'm already on edge, adrenaline still pumping from the alley. Watching them, I feel the pulse between my legs again, a reminder of how horny I am.

I feel my lips curl into a smirk. My gaze locks onto them,

taking in every detail—the way his muscles ripple under his sweat-slicked skin, the arch of her back as she clings to him. They're both pretty, easy on the eyes and he's obviously got a good dick because those moans of hers aren't fake.

"Hey," the guy grunts, pausing mid-thrust. His eyes meet mine, dark and intense.

His girl peers over his shoulder, drinking me up from the tips of my boots, up my ripped fishnets, shorts, and the flannel tied right up underneath my tits. "You wanna join?"

"Not this time, babygirl," I reply, my voice dripping with sarcasm and desire. "But I'm gonna watch. So put on one helluva show like a good girl."

The girl giggles, a sultry sound that sends shivers down my spine. "Your loss," she purrs, but there's no real disappointment in her tone. She knows she's got an audience now, and that's enough.

They resume, even more fervent, and I lean against the wall, crossing my arms. The heat in the room rises, mingling with the scent of sex and sweat. This is my favorite way to kill time.

"Fuck, yes," the guy growls, his voice guttural and raw as he thrusts harder into the girl beneath him. Her moans rise in pitch, echoing through the small room like a siren call. I move a little bit further into the room and lean against the wall, crossing my arms tighter across my chest, eyes fixed on their bodies. Perfect position to watch both of their faces and to watch his cock slip in and out of her tight little cunt.

The girl's nails dig into his back, leaving angry red trails that catch the dim light. She arches her back, pressing her breasts against his chest, her whimpers becoming more desperate with each movement.

"That's it, don't hold back," I tell them, feeling the tension between my legs intensify. They both get off on my words.

"Please." The pretty little redhead begs, but it's not him she's talking to as her eyes drill right into mine. The guy glances at me, catching my eye with a smile before focusing back on the girl.

"You're missing out, sweetheart," he grunts, his pace quickening. "We could've made it real fun for you."

"Trust me, I'm having plenty of fun just watching," I shoot back, my tone dripping with sarcasm. But there's no denying the heat pooling in my belly, the way my breath hitches every time she gasps or he groans.

Their movements become frantic. The girl's cries turn into screams, her body shuddering violently as she comes. The guy follows soon after, his muscles tensing as he spills into her, a low, satisfied grunt escaping his lips.

I take a deep breath, feeling the weight of everything settle back onto my shoulders. The show is over, and reality starts to creep back in. The couple disentangle themselves, panting and sweaty, casting glances my way.

"Enjoyed the show?" the girl asks, her voice still breathless.

"More than you know," I reply, pushing off the wall. "But I've got places to be." I pull my hair up into a bun before slipping off my flannel and tying it around my waist. I rip my shirt off so I'm only in my black push-up bra. That should be enough of a change just in case the three musketeers are still lurking. Here's hoping they just gave up.

"Let me know if you want a repeat performance," the guy tells me with a wink.

"Count on it," I say, flashing a grin that's more wolfish

than friendly. I turn and slip out of the room and back to the bar's main area.

I push through the crowd, ignoring the leering looks from drunken patrons, and step out into the cool night air. The chill bites at my exposed skin, but it clears my head.

I walk quickly, keeping my head down, my thoughts a jumbled mess of lust and violence. By the time I reach my apartment, I'm exhausted but wired, nerves frayed. I lock the door behind me, leaning against it for a moment, letting the silence wash over me.

I really need to get a better fucking hobby, but first let me go pull my rabbit out and give myself an orgasm thinking about that deviant fucking bastard.

CONTENT LIST / SHOPPING LIST

What can you expect to see in Wicked Scorn?

College Football, Friends to Enemies to Lovers, Ex-Best Friends Little Sister, Jealous Possessive Hero, Romantic Suspense

Touch her x die, Mine!, Breeding kink (no pregnancy), Size difference, SA (heroine, past, off page), Murder/Violence (not between the main characters), Bad boy x good girl, Teach me x please me (sex lessons), Dirty talk, Jealous/Possessive, Orgasm denial/Forced orgasms, Abandonment (familial), Forced proximity, Light mask kink play, Virgin FMC, Praise, Light cam play

Acknowledgments

Thank you to my sister for pushing me to follow my dreams and write this story after getting tired of me always talking about it in one way or another.

Thank you to my parents for being amazing and I hope they never read this and question my sanity.

Thank you to my designer, Shay who took me on and doesn't scoff when I ramble a ton of things in her inbox that I want to order from her.

Thank you to my editor and proofreader because I was a mess and you helped wrangle this book into what it is now.

Thank you to The Author Agency and The Bookish Girls Services for the all the lovely PR you've done!

Thank you to the Beta/ARC readers that took a chance on a new author and read this book and gave me invaluable feedback.

And last but not least if you are reading this then thank you! You picked up this book and read it and whether you loved it or not, I am forever grateful you took a chance on Wicked Scorn.

ABOUT THE AUTHOR

Havoc Wilde is not just an author; she's a whirlwind of creativity and passion. With a penchant for exploring the darker side of love and obsession, her novels often blur the lines between passion and madness.

Unapologetically bold, Havoc's writing is a mirror to her pseudonym - wild, untamed, and irresistibly captivating.

Havoc has an unhealthy obsession with all the villains of the story. Who wouldn't want to be tied to Damon Salvatore, Klaus Mikaelson, or Spike?

You can find Havoc on all socials and she has as Facebook reader group called Havoc Girls!

Also by Havoc Wilde

<u>Wicked Brothers of SCU</u>

Wicked Fury - Lincoln Blackwood's Book

Wicked Scorn - Jeremiah Blackwood's Book

Wicked Spite - Penn Blackwood's Book

Wicked Wrath - Graham Blackwood's Book

Made in the USA
Middletown, DE
27 July 2024

58045814R10239